"EACH TIME A MAN STANDS UP FOR AN IDEAL, OR ACTS TO IMPROVE THE LOT OF OTHERS, OR STRIKES OUT AGAINST INJUSTICE, HE SENDS FORTH A TINY RIPPLE OF HOPE, AND CROSSING EACH OTHER FROM A MILLION DIFFERENT CENTERS OF ENERGY AND DARING, THOSE RIPPLES BUILD A CURRENT THAT CAN SWEEP DOWN THE MIGHTIEST WALLS OF OPPRESSION AND RESISTANCE."

- ROBERT KENNEDY -

Also available from STORGY Books

Exit Earth
Shallow Creek
Hopeful Monsters
This Ragged, Wastrel Thing

STORGY®
BOOKS

STORGY® Ltd.
London, United Kingdom, 2020

First Published in Great Britain in 2020 by STORGY® Books

Published by STORGY® Ltd.
London, United Kingdom, 2020

10 9 8 7 6 5 4 3 2 1

Cover Design by Stuart Bache
Edited & Typeset by Tomek Dzido

A CIP catalogue record for this title is available from the British Library

Trade Paperback ISBN 978-1-9163258-9-0
eBook ISBN 978-1-9163258-8-3

www.storgy.com

YOU ARE NOT ALONE

AN ANTHOLOGY OF HOPE & ISOLATION

STORGY

CONTENTS

CONTENTS...

INTRODUCTION

When news of Covid 19 broke I was busy working to help those affected by homelessness, running the largest day centre in Bristol (The Bristol Methodist Centre). We watched the news closely, trying to keep abreast of everything that was happening, whilst also trying to keep the valued services we offer our guests running for as long as possible – observing all the daily updates and evolving guidelines of how the government wanted us – and everyone else – to proceed.

At the Methodist Centre we offer a service that runs from Monday – Thursday where our guests can access hot showers, clothing, breakfast, lunch, computers, games, films, books, a health clinic and much much more. It's a valued place they can regularly visit and receive the help they need, whilst also enjoying the company and companionship we proudly foster – it's one of the only safe environments they have in Bristol – and devastatingly, soon, we would have to close our doors.

We continued to run our service for as long as we could, but with the introduction of social distancing and the difficulties that arose from implementing these new measures, it became very difficult to cope. Our main priority was to keep our guests safe (we have a daily average of 120 guests), but social distancing also meant that our donations (both monetary and food etc) stopped. The Methodist Centre is not funded by the council or any other external funding and the work we do is supported only by donations – which had plummeted to zero. As a result, I set up a small crowdfunding page to help fund the ongoing support service we were planning to offer.

I'd decided to open the centre for two days a week during the pandemic (a door only policy) – where we would continue to offer freshly prepared hot food, clothing, toiletries, sleeping bags, tents and other much needed items to those affected by homelessness.

It was during this time that Adrian J Walker (author of *The End of The World Running Club* and a friend of STORGY) contacted me; he'd donated to the crowdfunding campaign and asked if we were planning anything else to raise further funds for homeless people and if the writing community could help in any way? At the time I had no plans for what would soon evolve into *You Are Not Alone* – and a huge proportion of thanks goes to Adrian in encouraging us to curate and publish this anthology, where all proceeds will be equally divided among trusted charities which help support the most vulnerable within our communities (The Big Issue Foundation (registered charity number 1049077), Centrepoint (292411), Shelter (263710), and The Bristol Methodist Centre (1150295)).

Myself and Adrian contacted a bunch of exciting writers we knew and things soon began to snowball – authors wanted to be involved and were only too willing to offer their support and stories. *You Are Not Alone* is an anthology that's sole purpose is to help those who have been (in my opinion) largely overlooked during this crisis, those who have been left without a voice – with *You Are Not Alone* we want everyone affected by homelessness to know; You Are Not Alone – we see you, we hear you, and we want to help. Your voices *are* important, and above anything else, we care.

Huge thanks goes to everyone that has donated their time to this project. From the cover design by Stuart Bache, to all the authors who are included in the anthology; Gemma Amor, Susmita Bhattacharya, Astra Bloom, S. J. Budd, Colin Burnett, Joanna Campbell, Heather Child, JL Corbett, KM Elkes, Maria J Estrada, Tracy Fahey, Kathy Fish, Sian Hughes, Jason Jackson, Ross Jeffery, B. F. Jones, Andrew Leach, Tim Lebbon, Toby Litt, Adam Lock, Tomas Marcantonio, Carmen Marcus, Roger McKnight, Sherry Morris, Benjamin Myers, Hannah Persaud, Rahul Raina, Johanna Robinson, James Sale, Joseph Sale, Anthony Self, Rachael Smart, Daniel Soule, Christopher Stanley, Hannah Storm, Rob Teun, Steve Stred, Stuart Turton, Adrian J Walker, Danie Ware, Aaron White, Rick White, James Woolf – thank you for answering our call!

I thank you all – *we* – thank you all. STORGY has long been a home for authors from across the world and we will forever be humbled by the outpouring of support we received for this special book. We could not have done this without you. Thank you.

This book is also dedicated to lost loved ones. You will never be forgotten ... You Are Not Alone.

Ross Jeffery

"HOLD FAST TO DREAMS,
FOR IF DREAMS DIE
LIFE IS A BROKEN-WINGED BIRD,
THAT CANNOT FLY."

- LANGSTON HUGHES -

A TALE OF TWELVE SPEECHES

JAMES WOOLF

A Collection of Audition Monologues for Actors
Edited by Anthony Simpson

Editor's note

Having been blessed with this prolonged and unexpected period of confinement in my one-bed flat, I find I have run out of excuses not to complete a project that has been lying dormant for several months. It is a project that will, I hope, be a God-send to actors when our theatres open their hallowed doors once again.

The following speeches are intended for use in that oddly artificial barometer of talent: the audition. They have been carefully sourced from some of the most unusual (and in some cases, downright obscure) plays that have graced the London fringe and beyond in recent years. It is well known that when confronted with the same audition speeches, time after time, hour after hour, creeping in their petty pace from day to day to the last syllable of recorded time, directors will wilt, visibly. There is no danger of that happening if a monologue from this book is chosen.

My choice and ordering of the materials have added another distinctive and quite possibly unique feature to this collection. When the play excerpts are read in the order in which they are printed, they tell a story.[1] It is a strange and dark tale of unbridled passion, venality and deceit; a tale, in short, that reflects well neither on the world nor its occupants. In drama, it was ever thus.

---

1 In order to achieve this narrative feat, some of the characters who appear in the speeches have had their names changed, along with other incidental details. This has been done with the express permission of the playwrights concerned. There was only one writer who refused consent for me to make the necessary amendment to her unremarkable one-woman play set in a mortuary. I will spare her shame by not naming her.

Speech One: The Husband

From **Illicit Journeys**[2]

by Nerris Cox[3]

RALPH

Going up to individual audience members, addressing them one by one, sometimes shaking hands.

Ralph … Ralph Fitch.

Ralph, thank you, pleased to meet you too.

Very excited to have been offered this opportunity, no really, I am. Yes, I did attach my CV, it's all there in the email. Hopefully not too many typos, bit of a rush job.

Hi. I've never done this before, especially not with someone like you. That wasn't meant to be offensive by the way.

Hello there. Christ! What am I doing? What have I actually done?

To whole audience

Ralph Fitch, Banking & Commercial Loan Workout Manager. ('You're a rare jewel, Ralph – a visionary and a safe pair of hands!').

Ralph Fitch, owner of a large house in Hertfordshire, and husband to Camille. ('Don't stress me out, Ralph – I'm late for my Pilates!').

Ralph Fitch, father to Ariel. ('Do you have any idea what it's like? – no, of course you don't, because you're a man').

Ralph Fitch, fitness freak, who goes running at five thirty every morning, and also when Camille leaves for her Pilates. ('Run, Ralph, run!').

Ralph Fitch, who often passes a woman tending to plants in her front garden as he heads down Barham Avenue. Who is she? And what is she doing with her life? ('Keep going, don't stop').

Ralph Fitch, who runs into the arms of his lover, Dinesh, in Links Drive. ('Come in, Ralph, you look shocking').

---

2 This allegorical drama about a wealthy banker's fall from grace is, of course, about the demise of capitalism. The production I saw gained additional power through its performance in the vaults of a defunct financial institution. Rereading it, I wonder whether we are witnessing the actual death of our way of life now.

3 Nerris' play was the first I read after the lockdown and I knew right away this speech had to be included in the anthology. As an aside, I have to say that the timing of this whole thing has been pretty disastrous. Some weeks ago, I summoned up the courage to have a conversation with my next-door neighbour, Brenda, having marvelled at her reassuringly academic presence ever since she moved in. Of course, I haven't seen her again and, in all probability, will not do so for several months. Why didn't I at least ask for her phone number?

Speech Two: The Lover

From **Forever Fucking**[4]

by Sam Hardcastle

DINESH

We do it while his wife is at Pilates, while my parents are out, working, attending meetings, leaving me to make my supper and get on with 'rethinking my future', if I have any future. If they only knew!

His cock is tiny, but his balls are enormous. A scrawny weed growing between two boulders.

One summer evening, a lovely summer evening, as usual I'm at home – well, my parents' home.

I'm still 'rethinking my future'. Caught cheating in my first-year exams – what a fool. I'm a university drop-out. Kicked out. Amazing how your closest friends suddenly treat you like a bat with rabies.

Tonight, he rushes through the front door looking different. Glassy. He has a sheen. Come in, Ralph, you look shocking, I say. It's a rush, as always. He never has time for more than a quick fuck. Or suck. Tonight, the latter.

I tell him I want a conversation. About how I used to watch him running, morning and evening, through my bedroom window. And his eyes would scale the bricks and meet mine through the glass. He'd watch me, watching him – watching him from my suburban prison cell.

You caught my eye. A middle-aged man trying to stave off the inevitable middle-aged spread. By running. You're nothing special. And yet, your nothing specialness, your ordinariness, your beautiful integration within society, are what make you so fucking appealing.

Dinesh, I gotta go.

Don't you remember that evening? How I went running after you in my green tracksuit? I overtook you. And then you overtook me. Then I overtook you again. Then you overtook me. And then you took me by the side of the road. The next time we did it here. In my parents' home.

Dinesh, Son – I gotta go.

The man who seconds ago came in my mouth just called me Son. That can't be right.

I'm feeling isolated and depressed, Ralph. I can't go on experiencing life through my bedroom window.

He smiles sadly and leaves. The only man I've ever fucked in my parents' house. The fools.

---

4 This notorious play is about men copulating, and women copulating, and men and women copulating, in toilets, kitchens, building sites, stationery cupboards, wherever they can. It is not for the faint-hearted, a modern day La Ronde featuring fornication in all its glory and depravity. I've been re-reading it recently: it's rather fun I must admit. It doesn't in any way compensate for my own inactivity in this area however.

Speech Three: The Good Samaritan
From **Even when the West Wind stops Blowing**[5]
by Barbara Blakemore

ELAINE

We had noticed each other.

We had clocked each others' existence.

We had exchanged looks like silk scarves slipped through frozen letterboxes.

He ran as if tiptoeing. Afraid of a shard of broken glass. Afraid of the morning light or the gathering darkness. Afraid of the demons that pursued him or the fiends in the clouds. Afraid this run might be his last.

He smiled at me once. Just once he smiled as I clipped my White Cedar Tree. He smiled at me. While he ran. A brief side-glance of a smile; a popped-off button of a smile; a half-heard smile like an esoteric joke in a noisy bar; a smile thrown casually but joyfully like confetti at a wedding; a smile as satisfying as hot chocolate. He smiled. And like a fool I took that smile and built a palace around it.

Every morning and every night I would go out and garden. Sometimes I would forget to cook. Sometimes I would forget to eat.

That evening he was running back. I knew when he was running. And when he was running back. Running was right to left. Running back was left to right. Running back, he moved slower, more torpid than torpedo. That evening, it was different. My heart hiccupped like a frozen pea stuck in a piccolo. He was moving lopsidedly, a wobbly lawn mower on a steep slope. And he turned towards me and put a hand to his chest, he looked at me as he buckled, as he sank down, like he was about to sit in a chair but realised it wasn't there. And then he continued falling. He almost bounced as he hit the pavement, rolling awkwardly, one leg folded and one sticking out like a mast, then rolled again, into my flower bed, where he came to rest under our willow tree.

The willow tree that my husband planted all those years ago.

The willow tree that has just kept growing and growing, weeping and weeping.

Growing and weeping while my heart has been shrinking.

And I ran towards him, like a westerly wind that's blown up into a terrifying gale.

5 I make no claim that all the plays included in this volume are great dramas, or even proficient. This one I struggled with from the get-go. It doesn't flow. It's a little 'keen'. But that may say more about me than the playwright who has achieved moderate success with several of her works. I've reread this speech several times and I have absolutely no idea who the fiends in the clouds are. The writer, by the way, is a friend of Deirdre, about whom you'll hear more later.

Speech Four: The Doctor

From **can you please slow down this is an emergency**[6]

by David Carless

DOCTOR

anonymous phone call and man rushed in from street on trolley knew straight away it was ST-elevation myocardial infarction otherwise known as a "STEMI" heart attack poor bugger in his jogging pants no choice but to administer fibrinolytic agents to improve blood flow and revascularisation to restore blood circulation to heart which worked to an extent although he went into coma not unusual in itself as 80% of patients who are successfully resuscitated from cardiac arrest do not regain consciousness immediately after return of spontaneous circulation and may remain in a coma for hours or weeks or even be in persistent vegetative state and predicting the outcome following cardiac arrest for comatose survivors following resuscitation is the devil's own work and source of much consternation among emergency room and intensive care unit physicians not to mention family members except we have absolutely no idea who his family are and this I understand is a real concern and ongoing area of enquiry

---

6 **can you please slow down this is an emergency** surfaced briefly in London and is an absolute car crash. I went with Deirdre, on an early date. We were shocked by how appalling it was. I can't recall whether the doctor was played by a man or a woman, and don't suppose it matters too much either way.
I tried to discover more about the playwright and turned up nothing (the theatre provided a copy of the script). The only things we can safely say about Mr Carless are that 1) he never read Aristotle's Poetics, and 2) he has an extreme aversion to punctuation.

Speech Five: The Reluctant Worker
From **Frosty Reception**[7]
by Joni Mitchell

POPPY

She's a right bitch Judith is. Get this, so I'm working in this hospital, it's my very first day, and she's like: 'Would you mind calling the police, Poppy? We've got a bit of a situation here.'

And I'm like: 'Call the police? I'm answering the phone, Judith. It's what you asked me to do.'

And she's like: 'Well now I'm asking you to call the police, Poppy, so you'll have to stop answering the phone for a moment, won't you?'

I mean talk about unnecessary sarcasm!

And I'm like: 'Is it some kind of emergency?'

And she's like: 'Well, we have a patient in a coma, and we don't know who he is.'

And I'm like: 'Have you asked him?'

And she's like: 'He's in a coma.'

She talks to me like I'm an idiot which I really don't appreciate.

So, I'm like: 'And you want me to phone the police to see if they know who he is?'

And she's like: 'Well, somebody might have reported him missing.'

And I'm like: 'I suppose. But what if they haven't?'

And she's like: 'If they haven't, the police can make their own enquiries. Do you understand now?'

And I'm like: 'Yeah, I understand. It's just my agency told me I was gonna be a receptionist. Answering the phones and stuff. I didn't know I was going to be a bleeding detective.'

And she's like: 'I'm not asking you to be a detective, Poppy. I'm asking you to make one phone call.'

And I'm like: 'Can you not make it? You seem to know exactly what you want to say to them.'

And she's like: 'Yes, actually, I think I will make it. That will be much easier.'

And she just storms off. Leaves me sitting in reception wondering what the hell's going on. I'd have quite liked to get involved if she'd given me half a bleeding chance. Trust my luck to get a bitch of a manager like her on my first job.

7 This is what I'd call a spider on the wall play about the day to day worlds of three receptionists. This one is a temp and pretty awful at that. Deirdre and I saw it when I still had high hopes for our future together. I vividly recall the curry afterwards, and her telling me all about her boss. She was the PA to a well-known captain of industry who she frequently and amusingly referred to as "the cunt". The playwright, by the way, is no relation to the infinitely more talented folk artist.

Speech Six: The Drunken Policeman
From **The Ice Rink**[8]
by Leticia Saunders

NED

Here's a knocking indeed! If a policeman were knocking on the doors of the houses of all the missing people of the world, he would have worn out knuckles alright.

He knocks on a door.

Knock, knock, knock! I'm sorry to bother you. I'm trying to find the right house. Is yours the right house perchance?

He gets out a hip flask of whisky and drinks. He knocks on another door.

Knock, knock, knock! I'm sorry to bother you, I really am. I'm trying to find the right house for the body of a missing man who isn't yet dead. Would that be yours?

He drinks more whisky and knocks on a door.

Knock, knock, knock! Are you the full complement here? What I mean is are you missing a husband, or a brother, or a son? Not that you look old enough to have a middle-aged son who's missing. But you're old enough to have a father, and a brother too I'll warrant.

He drinks more whisky and knocks on a door.

Knock, knock, knock! I'm trying to find the right body for a missing house which is still alive. Would that be your body perchance?

He reacts to the door being slammed in his face.

He knocks on another door.

Knock, knock, knock! Hello love, why are you crying? What's his name? Alright, I think we have him. Or his body at least. Oh yes, he's alive. Just about. But his family is missing. Not anymore though.

---

8 Deidre and I saw this political farce a couple of months into our relationship. The less than subtle message that we are living in a dictatorship was as ridiculous then as it is now. Having said that, we both enjoyed the depiction of the policeman. Later, while Deidre rustled up an impromptu meal, we got into a silly row about the play's title. I assured her that just because it was called *The Ice Rink*, it didn't have to have an ice rink in the story. Deirdre called me patronising and threw me out of her flat before I'd finished my risotto. It wasn't very nice anyway. Too moist and slightly mushy.

Talking about bad cooking, I'm getting slightly fed up with my own to be honest. I ran out of fresh vegetables a week ago, and trying to be inventive with cupboards consisting only of tins of soup, various dried beans and some past-their-sell-by-date herbs and spices is far from easy. I wonder if I'll ever eat another meal cooked by a fellow human being again. I know everyone else thinks they're being terribly clever and maintaining their social life online, but I'm holed up editing this book and no one gives a flying fuck. So much for community spirit.

Speech Seven: The Wife
From **Living Death**[9]
by Anthony Simpson

CAMILLE

She dials a number on an old-fashioned Bakelite telephone.
Hello, Mr Fitch, it's Camille, how are you? (PAUSE) You are? (PAUSE) Oh, that's great. And Arlene, is she over that nasty cold? (PAUSE) Oh, that's great news. (PAUSE) Yes, it did hang around for a bit, didn't it? They can sometimes. (PAUSE) Yeah, I'll bet she was. Well, great she's feeling better.

(PAUSE) Me? Not too bad actually – not too bad at all, thanks for asking. (PAUSE) Busy, yes, always busy in the surgery. Pets eh? – they will get their little maladies, won't they?

(PAUSE) Yes, Ariel's – errm, well, Ariel's Ariel I suppose. (PAUSE) Oh, you know. Exams. Busy not working for them, if you catch my drift. Shouldn't say that too loudly, she could eavesdrop for England that one, across the Grand Canyon if need be. (PAUSE) Yes, Ariel could. (PAUSE) Eavesdrop! (PAUSE) Across the Grand Canyon. (PAUSE) Oh, don't worry. (PAUSE) Yes, not my best, I'll admit.

(PAUSE) Well, I am calling for a reason actually, Mr Fitch. It's about Ralph. (PAUSE) Yes, Ralph your son, which other Ralph would I be talking about? (LAUGHS) Oh you're a funny one, aren't you?

(PAUSE) So, rather a complicated situation. But to cut a long story sideways, he's in hospital. (PAUSE) No, he's not okay – that's why he's in hospital. (PAUSE) Our nearest, the Wetherington, yes. (PAUSE) So, he went running, and he seemed to be taking rather a long time, and then he was taking a hell of a long time, and then he just didn't come back at all. (PAUSE) Exactly, I was worried sick. (PAUSE) And eventually we got this knock on our door. (PAUSE) A policeman. (PAUSE) Heart attack. (PAUSE) Yes, a heart attack. (PAUSE) Yes, a heart attack – Ralph had a heart attack. (PAUSE) Sorry, Mr Fitch – no easy way to say it. (PAUSE) He's in a coma.

---

9 Rather cheekily, I thought I might include an extract from my own satire about a dysfunctional family, which was produced to great effect at The Man in the Moon during its heyday. This speech can be performed as if Mr Fitch is slightly deaf, a bit confused, or in deep shock – any of these options will work very nicely.
I gave Deirdre a copy of the play and after she'd read it, she said that before she started horse riding, she had lessons at her local stable. Seeing my blank expression, she compared her advance preparation for equestrian sports to the know-how needed for writing a play. In the case of *Living Death*, she said that I clearly knew nothing about playwriting nor family dynamics, so my work was bound to come across as ill-considered and naive. We didn't speak for two months after that.
Big news by the way. When we doing that clapping on the front path thing, I briefly caught the eye of my next-door neighbour, Brenda. And I believe she smiled at me. Of course, there was so much noise and commotion, I can't be sure.

(PAUSE) A coma, that's right. (PAUSE) A couple of days now. (PAUSE) It took them a while to find us. (PAUSE) Cos they just had this man they were trying to save, and they didn't know who he was. (PAUSE) He just collapsed you see, no identification. (PAUSE) No one takes their passport when they go running, Mr Fitch. (PAUSE) Not even a driving licence.

Speech Eight: The Nurse
From **Max goes AWOL**[10]
by Terri Orbison

JOY

Imagine a ward with twenty two beds
And a private room just off the corridor with a man in a coma
And sitting in that room
A wife struggling to keep it together
And next to her, her impassive daughter sitting looking at her phone
And me, the nurse, trying to jolly them along
"It's ever so common for people to come round
Just like that, start talking, even after several days, or longer"
And as I said this, another woman pops her head round the door
Into the private room, and sees the man, prostrate, all plugged in
And puts her hand to her mouth and disappears
Back into the corridor
Where we hear sobbing, stifled
And the comatose man's wife says, "Who the fuck was that?"
And her daughter says, "How should I know?"
And the wife whose name is Camille jumps out of her seat
And we can hear the conversation
From the corridor, just like a radio play
"Excuse me, yes you, I want a word with you
How do you know my husband?"
"I don't know him – not really"
"So why are you crying?"
"Because I saw him collapse, I suppose
I was in my garden when he went down
And I called 999, I waited with him till the ambulance came"
"That's very nice of you, but what are you doing here?
What gives you the right to be crying outside our room if you don't know him?"
"I really can't say …"
"Well I can, I know why he kept going running
And it wasn't about keeping fit, not really
He was having an affair
With some local floozy, and now I know who she is"

10 It's very nice that this nurse has the time to listen in on visitors to their patients and to record their conversations in such detail. If only that were the case now. Incidentally, it was after seeing this play that I encountered the full force of Deirdre's petty and vicious nature. In the midst of our habitual argument about my introspection and delusions of grandeur, she managed to lock me in her bathroom and drove off to her parents. I was without food for two days. Luckily there was a plentiful supply of toilet paper, which is more than I have now.

Speech Nine: The Daughter
From **The Secrets Your Mother Never Told You**[11]
by Anthony Simpson

ARIEL

Sometimes I'll hurt myself. Just to make myself feel something. I'll get into a bath that I know is gonna be way too hot. And I submerge myself. Until I'm in pain all over. Sometimes I have to jump out cos I think I'm gonna faint. And I stand in front of the mirror looking like a lobster.

Or I'll stick a drawing pin into my arm. Let the blood drip drip drip onto the floor. I did that once and the wound went septic. Told my mum I'd accidentally walked into a barbed wire fence. She said, "How can you accidentally walk into a barbed wire fence?" And I said, "It happens all the time."

She's been going on about betrayal. Betrayal, betrayal, betrayal. Imagine you're in a lesson. And it's lasted for two days without a break. And your teacher's just wittering on and on and on. Well that's what it's been like. Except it's my mum wittering on about betrayal.

"You know the worst time to find out you've been betrayed, Ariel? The very worst time? When they're in a coma and you can't even confront them.

It's a bit like dying. You don't think it will ever happen to you. Only other women marry men who betray them. I don't know what I'm feeling right now. I'm not sure I'm feeling anything. I'm certainly not feeling worried about him."

So, finally! Finally, I have something in common with my mum. Cos I can't feel anything either. For myself, or for her being betrayed. Or for him lying all hooked up to his stupid machine.

I wish I was in some extreme situation. Like fighting in a war. Or being shot while carrying out some attack on behalf of Isis. Or being struck down by the Ebola Virus. I just want to be in pain so I can feel something.

---

11 If I am allowed one play by myself, I thought I might be permitted two. This one, as yet unperformed, is a family drama full of simmering tensions and undetonated conflicts. The play also features a violent argument between mother and daughter inspired by the last time I saw Deirdre. God knows what I'd done to deserve it, but as I cowered in her kitchen corner, she hurled her entire set of orange Le Creuset pans in my direction. I was literally in fear of my life. There were six pans and, unfortunately for me, each one had a lid. Luckily, she was not a particularly good shot and I sustained only mild injuries to my shoulder and left leg. As soon as I was able, I limped from her house and out of the relationship. I will leave it in my future director's capable hands as to whether real Le Creuset pans are used in the production.

Speech Ten: The Cleaner

From **Some Of The Things We Do For Money**[12]

by Sabrina Bedi

CHRISTOPHER

This all took place so quickly that it's pretty hard to credit
If you'd have told me what would happen I'd have wondered why you'd said it
Cos I'd always been a good boy, who was known as kind and thoughtful
And I was careful to ensure that what I did was always lawful
And if I'd strayed at all then my transgressions were quite minimal
But within a few short hours I had morphed into a criminal
I was on a well-earned break in the hospital canteen
Having been working like a dog around the life support machines
I'd seen her on the ward and she looked so kind and gentle
But what she then suggested was absolutely mental
She sidled up quite slowly and then sitting at my table
She said she needed help disconnecting a small cable
She said she'd make it worth my while, she wasn't being funny
She offered me what I'd describe as a fucking lot of money
In short what she was asking was whether I'd be willing
To finish off my evening shift with a dash of ruthless killing
She explained that Ralph her husband, who'd had a cardiac arrest
Was a complete and utter shit-bag, a philanderer at best
She'd only just discovered this, and was now propelled to action
And as a natural consequence, his future was a fraction
We went right through her cunning plan while my cappuccino cooled
She talked through the logistics and in murder I was schooled
I hope you won't be hard on me, I'm not a natural sinner
I'm just the kind of person you'd invite for Sunday dinner

---

12 This play is a puzzle to me, full of characters doing things, breaking into rap, for reasons I don't fully understand. Having said this, the playwright was extremely keen to be included in this anthology and even offered to rewrite this speech to make it fit more seamlessly into the overall story. If only key events in our own lives could be adapted so easily.

Speech Eleven: The Hospital Manager

From **Sandwich**[13]

by Dr Baljinder Patel

PENELOPE

These things always happen when I'm having a Toblerone. Or a hot cross bun. Or a pastry. I must have these little treats to keep me going through the day. I keep a little stash of chocolate in my desk. A secret stash. This time I was eating an apple turnover I'd just bought in the canteen. The Chief Operating Officer rushed in. As he took a deep breath, I pushed a stray lump of apple from the corner of my upper lip into my mouth.

"Penelope?" Peter said. I looked up. He seemed genuinely upset. As if he might burst into tears.

"What is it, Peter?" I was conscious that I might still have crumbs around my lips.

"There's been a terrible accident. We're going to have to manage this very carefully."

"What sort of terrible accident?" I said, inspecting my face with my pocket mirror.

"One of our patients died, as a result, it seems, of a cleaner unplugging his life support machine."

"Oh shit," I said, putting my pocket mirror back into my bag. "How on earth did that happen?"

"The cleaner is new. And he apparently disconnected the machine in order to plug his floor polisher into a socket by the bed."

"Oh, bollocks."

"What are we going to say?" Peter asked. "We're going to have to put out some kind of statement."

"We need to conduct a thorough investigation, Peter. We need to find out exactly how this happened. We need a blow by blow account, including what training he'd received."

"I realise that. But we're going to have to say something in the meantime. Perhaps along the lines of, 'Our firm aim will be to put in place a series of actions to ensure that such an event will never occur again at any time in the future for any other patient.'"

"I'm sorry, Peter, I'm not going to sign off a press release when I don't know what happened."

---

13 When putting together this anthology, I thanked God there have been so many recent plays set in hospitals. I haven't managed to find out whether Dr Baljinder Patel is an actual medical doctor, but she certainly did her research if she isn't.

After Le Creuset-gate, I received a contrite letter of apology from Deirdre. I wrote back immediately to say that I never wished to hear from her again. She has respected my wishes and I've often wondered whether I made the right call. She's an extremely bright and articulate woman and her onion soup is second to none.

"How about this then? 'The incident is the subject of likely litigation, so we're unable to comment?'"

"Even worse. It makes us sound totally heartless."

Speech Twelve: the CPS Prosecutor
From **File**[14]
by Anthony Simpson

HELENA

We have heard how Ralph Fitch died because the life support machine upon which his life depended was accidentally unplugged by Christopher Norton, a cleaner who was only three days into his job at the Wetherington Hospital. Mr Norton, we have argued, received inadequate training. We have heard a great deal about the training which he did receive, and it is for you, members of the jury, to determine how adequate it was.

And yes, members of the jury, it is true that the defendant, Ms Penelope Clarke, has apologised unreservedly – both personally, and on behalf of the trust – for the failures that led to the tragic death of Ralph Fitch, who was so cruelly cut down in the prime of his life by this catastrophic error.

But you must remember, an apology is only an apology. It may go some way towards helping the Fitch family come to terms with the loss of their very much-loved family member. But it doesn't unfortunately get Ms Clarke off the hook when it comes to criminal breaches of health and safety law, should you decide that there have been such criminal breaches.

We have argued that a series of management failings led up to Mr Fitch's death, including a failure to control risks, and failures in planning. If you feel that we have not properly made out these arguments, then you must return a verdict of not guilty. And if you are unsure, then you must also return a verdict of not guilty.

But if in your judgement there have been serious systematic failings that led to Mr Fitch's death, failures that were the responsibility of the defendant, then you must return a verdict of guilty.

A guilty verdict in itself cannot ease the enormity of the Fitch family's loss and pain. But it can ensure that Justice has been properly served. And it is for this reason that the trial has been conducted, and why you the jury hold this great responsibility within your hands.

14 I have allowed myself the indulgence of a third and final monologue from one of my own plays (currently a work in progress), principally to permit this story the satisfying ending it deserves, but also to indicate the huge potential of File should anyone choose to commission it.
I say satisfying ending, but how satisfying can a major miscarriage of justice be? I imagine Dinesh attending the trial, having read about the case in the local paper. Perhaps the loss of his lover speeds up his process of rethinking his future. Or maybe it sends him into a spiral of depression.
Almost certainly in the spectators' gallery with Dinesh would be Camille; he may take an educated guess as to who she is. I imagine her seething with righteous indignation, willing the jury to convict the hapless defendant. As to whether they do or not, you'll have to wait for my play to be produced.
Now that I've completed this anthology, I might push a copy through Brenda's door with a note. I'll wipe my hands with anti-bacterial gel if I accidentally touch the letterbox. Brenda and I had a brief but delightful conversation over the fence this morning when I was putting out the rubbish. I told her I was a playwright, and also about this book, and she seemed genuinely interested. It would appear that even as this crazy world teeters on the brink, there is still one delightful sliver of hope.

A WORKING-CLASS STATE OF MIND

COLIN BURNETT

Ah laid the boax ae painkillers alongside the boattle ae Smirnoff vodka oan the coffee table. It doesnae even matter tae me that ma flat is that cauld it wid gee an Eskimo the shivers. Aw ah kin focus oan is the troubling thoats which are circling aroond ma heid like a vulture stalks a dying animal. Jist waiting fur the right moment tae pick through the bones. Each thoat bringing another feeling ae hopelessness and his gid pal, despair. Ah mean, Guantanamo Bay hus probably got a maire hamely feel tae it than this dump. Thirty years oan this planet and what do ah huv tae show fur it? A TV they dafties fae CSI could trace back tae John Logie Baird. A carpet that's goat maire stains oan it than an actress auditioning fur Harvey Weinstein. And look, even ma walls are fucked; they're that yelly, ah'm starting tae hink they've went jaundice, probably because day efter day, night efter night, Ah sit here and try tae smoke maself intae an early grave. Ah heard earlier, oan the morning news, that the PM, Boris Johnson, hus called a press conference fur later in the evening. You jist ken that means somebaody is gontae suffer. As ah go tae light the joint ah hud pre-rolled in anticipation ae ma final act oan this planet, ah suddenly caught sight ae a spider dangling fae a long silvery thread in the corner ae the room. This tiny creature wis trying tae swing oantae the shelf wae aw its being, but still it couldnae muster the strength tae make it. Ah'm sitting here hinkin tae massel, *Jist gee up, ma wee pal. You'll never make it. Take it fae somebaody who hus the t-shirt and the mental health issues tae prove it.*

Aw, will yae look at the state ae this cunt. Jesus, ah look like Keith Richards efter a weekend in Amsterdam. The white vest ah'm wearin goes sae well wae ma pale skin and skinny physique. Fur fuck sake, it's *Die Hard* wae AIDS. Honestly, av goat tae laugh. Ah mean, how hus it came tae this, eh? There's been nae Queensbury Rules involved in ma fight tae survive, that's fur fuckin sure. Aye, the man upstairs has shot fae the hips and done a right number oan me. Yin minute it's yur sweet sixteen, the juices rushing tae yur baws, andreline pumping through yur veins, and the world seems like a tidy hing jist waitin fur yae tae fuck her. God, ah wis fuckin fearless back in the day; ah hud such dreams. Then, suttin happens, suttin Nostradamus couldnae huve seen cumin; yur life flashes by ye at internet speed. The next hing yae ken, yur starin doon the double barrel ae thirty years ae pain and disappointment. Aw, yur still a pup, ah kin tell; yuv still goat that fire in yur belly, that hunger tae dae suttin wae yur life. Gee it time, it will comm tae yae as well, the flies will become that bit quicker, the shelfs that bit further awey, and if yur lucky, some cunt like me will come along tae stand oan yae and its aw oor very quick. At least that wey you're spared the heartache ae finding oot life's jist yin big fuckin joke oan gadgies like us.

Aw, dinnae worry, nae harm will come tae yae by ma hand. You've goat character, ah like that. There's a loat tae be said aboot character. Yae see what huv ah been tellin yae, there's nae point in tryin tae succeed; yae jist end up lookin like a porn star wae a yin-inch dick. Kin yae hear that? That faint voice at the back ae yur mind, the yin taunting yae and laughing at yur every failure. The yin whispering intae yur ear that yur nae gid tae nae cunt. Git yaist tae it because it's only goantae git louder and before you'll ken it, you've foond yur next best pal.

Ah live in the sixth richest nation in the world. And yit, ah kin hear Susan Boyle singing fae the rooftoaps, and tae tell yae the truth, ah'm even half expecting that Irish boay fae the telly tae turn up at the door wae bloody Pudsey the Bear in tow. Aw, what's his name again? Looks like Gandalf fae *Lord ae the Rings*, only efter he's contracted an STD. What's his bloody name again? Oh, aye, Bob Geldof, that's him. Aye, that's the boay. Mean, ah hink he wis actually oan the telly last week campaigning tae save a distressed-looking tree or summit. Yae see, aroond here, it's no the courts ae law or the politicians who keep the peace; it's the drugs. Picture this scene: each morning ah awake fae ma coma, then ah sit oan ma patio chairs because ah cannae afford a decent couch. Ah sit there wae ma bowl ae Coco Pops whilst ah watch shows that kin only be described as propaganda against the working class. Ah mean, jist the other day, there wis this boay oan *Jeremey Kyle* who wis convinced his cat wis the anti-Christ. It wis summit tae dae wae the cat sitting oan his phone and dialling 666. Ah guess it's true what they say aboot every litter. What's the alternative? Change the channel and listen tae a graduate ae Hogwarts annoonce tae the nation that seeing me droon in poverty hus jist became a national priority. Either choice is hardly a substitute fur intellectual capital. Growing up where ah'm fae oor social status wis based upon how well you could fight or kick a baw. No exactly the criteria fur becomin the nixt Prime Minister or CEO ae a fortune five hunner company, is it?

Mean, the only hing ah've goat ae any value is this tattered-lookin watch ma granda left me. Ma mate Fraser is intae aw they antiques shows oan the telly. The way the cunt goes oan, you'd hink he's a curator at the British Museum and no oan remand fur robbin a couple ae posh stately hames. Ma mobile starts ringing oaf the hook at aboot half seven at night. As soon as ah answered the phone, Fraser starts tae yell doon the line, "Bawbag, yur a fuckin millionaire." Ma first thought wis he must be back dain acid or summit, so ah hung up the phone oan him. Aboot a half oor later, ah hear bangin oan ma door. It wis yin ae they polis knocks, ken? The yins that aboot take the door oaf at the bloody hinges. Fraser comes chargin in aw oot ae breath and gaspin fur air and then mutters, "Yur granda's watch, it's worth a million quid. Ah seen the exact same yin oan the *Antiques Roadshow* the night." At first ah thought he wis fuckin wae me, but once ah could see his pupils wur still dilated, it started tae hit me he wisnae taking the piss efter aw.

We were baith wettin oorselves at the thoat ae aw that money. First hing the next morning, we made a few calls tae git a jeweller tae value the watch. Oan aboot the fifth call ah made, we wur put in touch wae an expert ae watch who hud a jeweller's oan Princess Street. This wis yin ae they place's posh cunts go tae git their dicks up. Ah mean, it hud maire bling than Mr T. As we stood ootside the building, Fraser eloquently took this opportunity tae remind me ae his claim tae a share ae the money: "Aye, childhood pal, and remember it wis me who telt yae aboot the fuckin hing. And dinnae furget ah peyed yae back that tenner. That's a hunner grand ae any rich cunt's money."

Ah couldnae believe ma ears; ah stood there wae three quid in shrapnel jinglin aboot in ma pocket, and this cunt wants a hunner grand oaf me. This boay dressed in a tuxedo and bowtie who looked as if he wis waitn fur a bell tae ring to go and wipe his masters erse greeted us in reception. Ah could see by the glare in the boay's eyes he wisnae used tae cummin acroass two rough and tumble boays like us in his line ae work. He directed us intae his office and started tae appraise the hing, and efter aboot a couple ae minutes he telt us suttin we should huv kent aw along: it wis worth a pittance. The colour fae oor faces drained awey, along wae oor hopes ae a wey oot ae this fishbowl we caw a life. Dinnae git me wrong, if ah had hud the energy, ah would huv taken Fraser tae the roof ae the buildin tae throw him oaf and then halled him back up fur an encore. The way that cunt hud been goin oan, we wur aboot tae dae a deal wae Sotheby's. Instead, ah find oot av goat a watch that ah need tae git sum unsuspecting celebrity tae wear then shoot thum oan the spot jist tae git its value up past the eighty quid mark. Poverty does that tae yae. It isnae jist a word fur politicians tae throw aboot tae git oor vote; it's an illness ae the mind, boady, and soul.

Ah foond this half-empty boatle ae Smirnoff vodka ma mate hud left behind fae last weekend. Efter pouring masself a gless, ah raise it tae make a toast tae ma new companion, "This is fur you, little yin. Cheers." Aye, but again, the wee man faws shoart. He'll learn, he'll see. Ah wis yince like him, a fighter. Now ah'm jist tired and ah feel sick at hert. That's the hing aboot dreams and aspirations. They're jist a fairytale story wur telt by oor parents. A fuckin make-believe idea that gees us hope that hings will git better. An idea that a naeboady kin become a someboady yin day, that David did beat Goliath. The truth is the maire you try tae reach fur the stars, the closer you become tae reachin fur the boattle. It's like when wur bairns wur telt tae be gid and Santa Claus will bring us loatsae presents. It's a beautiful idea, but there comes a point when we realise wuv been had. Aw it takes is fur some smart erse tae come along and tell us Santa's no real. Then oor hale world is flipped upside doon. That's what dreams and aspirations are in life, it's aw yin big fuckin Santa Claus. Ah've realised summit likes, and that is that guys like me and the spider kin chase oor dreams, but we'll never make it. In the end, fuck Santa Claus.

Dinnae gee me that look, comrade. Ah cannae help boays like us are destined tae be the pun ae the system's jokes. It's no us who make the rules, but it's sure as shit us who huv tae follow thum, um ah right or what? Yae dinnae need tae convince me it's no fair we huv tae hide in the dark like some diseased-ridden rat. Ah wisnae bullshittin yae earlier; ah wis like yae, many moons ago the now, mind yae, but ah wis yince full ae ambition tae. Aye, that watch ae ma granda's, he gave me it when he thoat ah wis gonnae be a someboady. Back in the day ah wis a promising wee fitbaw player, ah even hud a trial wae the mighty Hibees. Aye, in another life ah mighta been a professional player and it could huv been ma name in neon lights above Easter Road. What happened, yae ask? Aye, well like a loat ae folk fae here, ah wis a victim ae circumstance. Ah became maire bothered aboot what ma mates wur up tae at the weekend, and then came the drugs. Before ah knew what wis happenin, ma dreams ae makin it oan tae the pitch became a distant memory and ah wis oan the fast track tae this point in ma life. Ah wonder, though, yince ah guzzle doon a few ae these tablets and yae sit and watch as ma lights turn oot, will ah make it oantae the pitch in the afterlife maybe? Jist maybe, ah might.

Mean, maist ae the boays ah hung aboot wae at school spent some time at her Majesty's pleasure. Funnily enough, ah bumped intae an old mate fae school the other week doon at the bookies. There ah wis, wishing a thoosand deaths oan the jockey ae ma fallen hoarse, when ah hear this voice that resembled a foghorn.

"Chrissy, long time no see, eh?"

As ah turned aroond, ah wis faced wae Matty Johnson, who we hud nicknamed Bananas oan account ae him being a lunatic. He hud jist served a two-year sentence fur GBH when he attacked a guy wielding a mace. Ah mean, in this day and age who owns a mace? It alone actually uses yin. Some said he hud a fascination wae *Game ae Thrones*, but who knows. It turned oot the halea the incident wis aw oor a boay workin at Pizza Hut puttin too many slices ae pepperoni oan his pizza or some pish. We baith chatted awey tae each other like auld times, then he asked, "What yae dain wae yurself the now?"

Ah told him, "Jist trying tae survive another week oan the dole."

Then Matty eagerly explained to me the benefits ae prison. "Ah'm telling yae, Chrissy," he says, "you need tae spend a bit ae time inside. Three square meals a day and nae bills. Fuckin quality, man."

Ah stood there hinking tae masself, *Surely, it's no came tae this. Ah've goat tae be incarcerated tae stay ootae the foodbank?*

Ah mean, this is the place people come tae make it. A place where you kin be whoever you want tae be. And here's me taking career advice fae a mace-wielding psycho while ah watch a hoarse decide whether ah will huv food in ma belly or a roof oor ma heid. Wae each waking moment, ah try tae convince maself, *something will turn up*. Ah guess General Custard must huv said the same hing at Little Bighorn. And we aw ken what turned up there, another load ae irate Indians. Take a long hard look aroond, hings are doon aw acroass the board. You've goat Mr Burns in the White House. Guys who widnae normally steal as much as a penny chew are huvin tae steal tae feed their fuilies. Aw, and if that wisnae bad enough, some pencil pusher in London hus decided tae take it oan thumselves tae inspire the nixt Charles Dickens.

The maire intently ah watch the spider, the maire care he seems tae take in his attempts tae swing oantae the shelf. Ah'm no shaire if it's the weed or the vodka or maybe a combination ae baith, but ah'm starting tae hink this wee guy is oot tae prove me wrong. Ah feel like Leith's answer tae Dr Dolittle at the minute this ballsae wee bastard is game, there's nae disputing that. Though again, he takes a sip from the fountain ae failure. You see, it's in oor DNA tae fail, whether it be me or the spider, we always end up dain what's expected ae us. Which is tae come up shoart.

It's the price ae being the underdog. Aw, ah git it noo, the cobwebs huv been removed, if yae pardon ma pun. You hink this shit box ae a flat ah've goat came easy tae me? That accepting a life ae poverty wis the easy choice? Lit me tell yae suttin, ah grafted maist ae ma days tae end up wae fuck all. That's what aw these rich cunts kin never understand; it takes aloat ae blood, sweat, and tears tae git where ah um. As soon as a higher power or big bang or whatever yae believe in – ah'm no here tae judge – decided yae wur gonnae be a spider, then yae wur up shit creek withoot a paddle as ma auld gran would say. As soon as that umbilical cord wis cut, ah wis born tae be a naeboady.

It's strange though, how hings come back at you, yae ken? Memories. Thoan conversation wae Matty talking aboot the old days and ah wis a sixteen-year-auld bairn again. It goat me hinking aboot the time ah spent in high school. Yae've goat tae understand yin hing, bairns fae ma area wur maire tolerated than encouraged by the teachers. This wisnae yin ae those Walt Disney films we wur making here. Yae ken the soartae film ah'm talking aboot. The bairn is involved in a terrible accident and hus tae learn tae walk again. By the end of the film, the teacher hus their airm raised fur winning gold in the 200m at the Olympics. Nah, this wis real life, and like anyhing in this life, it wis tough.

The teachers wurnae able tae see beyond oor tracksuit or how we would say 'ken' insteed ae 'know.' Aye, in their eyes, the factory flair beckoned for us when we left school. Granted, at the time ah didnae realise they wur huving a premonition because that's exactly where ah ended up. Well, that wis up until a few months ago. When ma boss imported a machine designed in China that could operate quicker and cheaper than a pair ae hands. Honestly, ah hear aw the time folk aroond here complaining, *these immigrants are coming ower here and stealing our joabs*. Naeboady mentions R2D2 is the yin waiting in the wings tae pull our plug. Wae jist a few crumbs ae encouragement fae ma teachers though, hings could huv been so much different. Ah might huv owned a factory insteed ae serving as a drone in yin by pressing a button aw day. Aye, ah could see it now, 'Christopher Mathews: a captain ae industry.' You never ken, Matty might huv turned oot tae be Scotland's answer tae George R.R. Martin.

This time the spider is close, real close. Ah've goatae admit, this wee guy hus aloatae hert. The maire ah've watched his struggles, the maire ah've come tae realise we are kindred spirits. We baith try and fail time and time again. The strange hing is this insignificant fleeting moment in life hus kept me fae drawing ma final curtain. Maybe ah wis jist looking fur something tae hud oantae before ah depart this mortal realm. Something, anyhing, that might show me there is still hope left in this world insteed ae the miserable existence that waits fur me oot there, waiting patiently tae greet me like an auld friend. Ah appreciate yur efforts tae show me there's another wey tae dae hings, that hard graft kin pey oaf someday. Ah mean that, nae shit. The truth is it's inevitable; we will choke when oor big moment comes along. Ah wid love tae believe yae, but 'that's life' as auld blue eyes once said.

It isnae like ah'm stupid. Ah ken the difference between a dream and a memory. Ah kin tell you the meaning ae love. But what um ah gonnae tell St Peter when ah meet him at those pearly gates and he says, "Tell me aboot what you learnt fae yur time oan earth, ma son"?

"Well, St Peter, ah ken a gid joint when ah puff it. You'll need immortality tae witness Scotland qualifying fur a World Cup. Aw, and ah learnt tae appreciate the meaning ae poverty."

Nah, there's goatae be maire tae aw this than that, or what's the point? The other night, ah wis searching Netflix tae find summit tae watch. Ah came acroass a film ah hudnae seen in years: *The Truman Show*. That guy wis in it, the yin who used tae be funny – Jim Carey. Aye, he played this boay who realises his whole life hus been scripted. Dinnae git me wrong, it might huv been the weed talking, but ah couldnae help but hink boays like me aw live in oor very ain *Truman Show*. We grow up, work in a joab that serves tae kill our 'spirit', then we settle doon, maybe huv a few bairns. And when the time comes tae draw our final breath, wuv accumulated enough debt that our creditors will be holding a seance. Aw because society tells us we need a flash motor, designer clothes, a holiday abroad yince a year, and a fuckin credit caird. The truth is, aw we are dain is making sure aw these rich toffs huv made a tidy profit fae our time spent here, and aw the while we produce the nixt batch ae workers tae take our place oan the chain gang. The greatest trick those in power ever pulled wis gitting the workers tae believe we aw huv equal opportunities. Fae the moment we first open our eyes and until the time finally comes tae close them. Our lives huv been mapped oot fur us by them fae the cradle straight tae the grave. In this country 'cash is class'; when yur born intae a family wae a bit ae money and the right postcode, you're oan the home straight while the rest ae us are jist warming up fur the race.

Ah kin feel these box ae painkillers daring me tae swallow a few ae thum, and then it will be over and oot. Nae maire ae this pain. Ah might actually be at peace fur yince. Earlier, ah went along tae the cash machine oan the high street. Oan ma way there, ah stoaped tae admire aw the artwork splattered across the shoap walls. Fae what ah could make oot, there's a few folk fae here fond ae pork, aw and some cunt cawed Pongo – apparently yae wouldnae ride his ma intae battle. Ah punched in ma pin, and ma balance ae thirteen quid and eighty pence sent ma hert flutterin. Ma breathin became shallower and ah thought ah wis huvin a hert attack right there and then. So, ah decided tae Google ma symptoms; it turns oot ma obituary wis bein written yesterday. Ah jist thought tae masel in that moment, *this life is jist too hard*, and ah wis set tae end it aw until ma eight-legged hero arrived. You ken what? Ah've kept faith in a system ma entire life that hus promised sae much tae boays like me but gave us sae little. That's why if this spider kin make it oan the fourth attempt then ah'm gontae gee this hale 'life' hing another go. Aye, ah like a gamble as much as the nixt degenerate, fuck it. This wid be a sign fae the beyond. Watching the wee guy, he seems tae huv sensed what's at stake here. This time, he seems tae be taking maire caution. It almost seems as if he's goat a plan ae action here. Aye, that's it, son, you're nearly there. Cmoan, yae kin dae it. Ah fuckin believe in yae, ma hairy little friend.

Ah cannae believe ma eyes. He's done it; he's oan the shelf. "Yes!"

AND SOON, I SHALL GROW

J.L. CORBETT

The only thing I'm good at is passing the time. I never fill time with anything fun or productive, but I'm always coming up with new ways to make the minutes pass by as quickly as possible.

Sometimes I play games in my head, just silly little things like naming a grocery item for each letter of the alphabet or listing every person I've ever met. Other times, I concoct elaborate imaginary scenes where I go on zany adventures with my old school friends, or I get rescued by a family member (usually my dad or my brother – men are better at stuff like that).

Silly little things like that really burn away the hours. And on days when they don't, I try to sleep as much as possible.

Of course, sleep isn't always an option. On the days that Damien wants me, I have to be alert and awake, ready to do whatever he says. The imaginary scenes come in handy then, too. They distract me until it ends.

I can't even enjoy the peace when he's out working, because I'm not able to leave my room, not even to eat or to go to the loo. It's ridiculous – there's a spare bedroom on the second floor that has an ensuite, so I asked him one day if I could move in there instead, but he got so angry that I dropped the subject and never brought it up again.

Sometimes he only wants me to sit next to him on the couch while he talks to his friends or shady associates (that's what he calls them, "associates". I guess "fellow drug lords" is too direct). I used to think that he was making me sit there so he could show me off to them, but I stopped being attractive a long time ago. He buys me skimpy clothes, but no makeup, and a visit to the hairdresser is out of the question. I hate the way I look.

So anyway, I sit next to him while he talks business with his associates or plays video games with his friends, as if they're all in their teens rather than their late thirties. He doesn't let me speak to any of them. I'm there as *his* girl, not theirs.

I shouldn't be making fun of Damien for acting like a teenager, because I still feel like I am one myself. I think it's because I was in my teens when I met him, so I haven't developed mentally in the eight years since. All I've done in my adult life is exist.

I used to wonder how my family was doing and what my old friends were up to. I have no way of knowing; he won't let me use social media. I don't even have a phone! Can you believe that?

I used to wonder, until one day my mum showed up at the house.

It was early afternoon (a weekday, I think), and I was flopped across my bed, contemplating whether my hunger pangs were severe enough to warrant breaking into the secret bag of cashew nuts I had stolen from the kitchen a few days ago, when I heard my bedroom door unlock from the outside.

A chill passed through my body. I sat up straight, absently rubbing the goosebumps on my arms, and stared at the bedroom door. Slowly, it creaked open.

I didn't move. Nobody had told me to move.

"Vick! Can you come down here, please?" Damien called up the stairs from the ground floor. His voice sounded different. Lighter?

This was weird. Damien never normally asked me questions or allowed me to roam about the house without supervision. Did he seriously expect me to just walk downstairs by myself?

I could feel my legs trembling as I crept towards the bedroom door. I stuck my head out into the hallway and locked eyes with Ritchie.

He was in his usual position: slumped in his chair with his phone in his hand, only rather than scrolling through meme pages, he was staring straight at me. All of this was very unusual.

I stared right back at him. I was too tense to form words.

"You gonna go then?" he grunted, cocking his head towards the stairs. He was looking at me like I was slow, like the request was normal and *I* was the one who was acting crazy.

"Yeah, sorry," I mumbled.

Walking down the stairs alone felt shameful. I tried to make each step as light as possible, as in the likely scenario that there had been a mistake and I wasn't supposed to be walking about by myself, I definitely didn't want anybody to hear me.

As I neared the bottom of the stairs, I could hear Damien speaking to somebody in the sitting room. He was using his "outsiders" voice – it was falsely soft and overly polite. The other voice was gentle, probably female. As I descended the last couple of steps the voices became increasingly defined, my pulse quickened, and I realised exactly who the woman was.

"Mum!" I crashed into the sitting room.

It was her, alright. Her hair was flecked with grey and she had a few lines on her face that hadn't been there before, but it was her. There was no doubt about it.

She turned towards me and smiled warmly. Her eyes were shining, was she crying?

Seeing my mum's smile was like catching a familiar scent in the air or hearing a song I'd not listened to in years. I didn't realise how much I missed her (and my old life) until I saw her standing there, her arms outstretched for a hug.

I collapsed in her arms. *Home.*

She trembled as we clung to one another. I didn't cry. I felt sad, elated, embarrassed, but none of these emotions would come out. Until that moment, I hadn't realised how emotionally stunted I had become, that I could be so close to salvation and show no outward emotion.

A heavy hand clamped my shoulder. I broke away from my mum and let Damien snake his arm around my waist.

He was saying something, but I couldn't focus on the words. His arm felt so heavy around my waist, like a white-hot manacle. I tried to concentrate on their conversation, but their voices were being drowned out by my panicked thoughts.

Did he invite her over, or did she find us? Why is he so calm? Does she know everything? Can I leave with her?

It was a stupid notion. There was no way in hell that Damien would ever let me leave this house without him.

My gaze fell to the coffee table. It was bare, cleared of all incriminating paraphernalia.

"It's really lovely to see you, Tori," my mum stepped towards me and I snapped back into the conversation. "I thought it'd be nice for us to go to lunch somewhere – wherever you like, I don't really know this area. We could maybe have a bit of a catch up? I've got some photos of your nieces."

Holy shit. Nieces.

Before I could respond, Damien cut in. "Actually, it'll have to just be a quick visit today, Kath. We're jetting off to Nice tomorrow – on business – and we've got loads to do before then. Right, Vick?" He pinched my waist. I looked at the floor and nodded.

"It's been great to see you though!" Damien grinned. He picked up my mum's jacket from the arm of the sofa and steered her into the hallway. I followed, keeping a few feet behind them. She looked bewildered.

"Oh, so we can't …? Oh. I thought we could —"

"Honestly Kath, we'd love to, it's just bad timing," Damien said calmly, still wearing that fake smile. Give our best to the family though, yeah?"

"Oh. Alright. But Tori, can I take down your phone number? I don't think the one I have is right," my mum said, rootling in her jacket pocket (probably for the battered address book she tended to keep with her at all times).

"Yeah, I changed phones," I mumbled.

"Sorry Kath, but we've got things we need to be getting on with." As Damien guided her towards the front door, every fibre of my being was screaming at her to take me with her, not to leave me with him for another eight years.

She was in the doorway. He was practically pushing her out onto the porch, even though it was pouring down with rain outside. I stood behind him, trying to commit her face to memory.

I saw her brow furrowing and her mouth moving, but I couldn't hear what she was saying. I saw him trying to force the door shut and her jamming her foot inside the door frame.

She was outside. I wanted to be outside. Maybe if I did it with enough confidence, it would work.

I darted into the cupboard under the stairs, slipped on my trainers and my duffel coat, and tiptoed back to the front door, where my mum and my captor were still struggling. All pretences had been dropped; they were yelling at one another.

Somehow, my mum had managed to get most of her body through the door and push it open. She was struggling against Damien, trying to get back inside the house, but it was a difficult task; he was at least a foot taller than her and much stronger and younger.

She was fighting. Why couldn't I do that?

She was shouting all sorts of things at him. To let her see her daughter, to stop keeping girls as prisoners in his drug den mansion. He yelled out for Ritchie, who came running down the stairs, phone in hand, probably with 999 already dialled. I felt sick.

Everything slowed down. As my mum struggled against Damien, her knee flew upwards and he keeled over, gasping for breath. *Yes, Mum!* I saw my chance.

I took a running start towards the front door and leapt over Damien as he was wheezing on the floor. I kept running, down the driveway, through the wrought iron gate, out into the bustling street. I collided with a middle-aged guy in a suit and almost sent his large umbrella flying, but I was riding so much adrenaline that I barely flinched. He swore at me and continued on his way, muttering obscenities.

I am outside. I closed my eyes and savoured the rain, the heavy London air, and the liberation of finally being free.

"Tori!"

I turned around. The tears came, and hers followed. I fell into my mother's arms, a child again, and she kept me safe.

...AND THEN CAME MAN

BENJAMIN MYERS

At first the wood was still.

For several centuries there was the sound of the whistling wind, the creaking of boughs and the shifting drifts of dead or dying leaves; natural noises played by the orchestra of the elements on its instruments of life.

Then one day a deer stepped out into a clearing. It stopped and sniffed the air, detected no danger. It nibbled at some bark and lapped from the shallow stream that ran through the centre of the wood and that night it slept soundly, curled into a circle of dirt swept flat in the ancient bracken patch. Deep in its sleep visions it felt a desire, a longing for another of its kind, and several short sunrises later its dream calls were answered when another deer appeared, a doe, and they sniffed each other, and soon they bred.

The deer population grew and overhead the branches of the wood slowly became busy with squirrels that had recently arrived to feed on the abundance of nuts and retreat to the hollows of trees. They crossed the canopy, well fed and free.

There were rabbits too. They dug vast warrens and they bred quickly and then there hundreds of them. A fox arrived in the bluest hour and he glued himself to the shadows, and soon he was feeding on rabbit.

The foxes dug dens. Fearing nothing, their young cubs squealed and tumbled and grew. Generation followed generation.

Small birds expressed their delight in song and each creature felt the summer's sun on their faces and cold snow on their paws, and there was an equanimity to the wood. A natural balance.

And then came man. A snapped twig and low voices marked his arrival.

There were several of them. They carried pigskins of brook water, smoked meat and rough blankets.

At the edge of the clearing they hunkered down, pointing and waiting.

A stone flung from a slingshot stunned a rabbit. It was soon snatched, and its neck snapped. It was skinned and mounted on a spit. It sizzled and spat fat over the pulsing glow of a bed of heat.

A spear sailed through the air at speed and skewered a deer. Black blood ran from the wound as it writhed, its black eyes held wide. It was surprised by the arrival of a new species called death.

A pack of dogs tore apart a fox, and then another. Droplets of blood patterned the hounds' maws and the woodland floor. Their pelts were not used and instead were tossed on the fire.

Flintstones made fire and axes, and axes chopped at tree trunks until they fell crashing down. Their timber was cut and carved and shaped and stacked. First it made weapons and bowls and spoons, and then huts. Then, later, fences.

Burning embers danced upwards into the night. The low voices grew louder in the woodlands, and there was the crying of babies, and shouting. Charred animal bones littered the smoking remains at dawn. Strings of fat and sinew hung from the branches, strung like decorations.

Man did not leave. He stayed and more stones and spears were flung through the trees, arrows too. The strings of fat were used for snares and traps, and to tie animals to posts driven deep into the soft soil of the woods' echoing centre.

More trees were chopped and felled. Burnt out at the root.

Man made dwellings for his children and his children's children, and all the animals were forced to live on the edges of the wood where it met open fields that had been rid of stumps and rocks, and the soil had been tilled and turned, and crops planted, and across the fields, far in the distance, were the shapes of more wooden houses, and more fires.

The plentiful voices that could be heard amongst the trees got louder and stayed louder, and the deer and the squirrels and the rabbits and the badgers and the foxes and the birds had to modify their territories, their feeding routines and their patterns of behaviour. They dug deeper holes, climbed higher trees. Watched from the perimeter.

And then they were pushed further out beyond the limits of the wood because the wood was no longer a wood any more, as only a few trees remained and a wood without trees is a corpse or less. Those that remained where merely decorative, a reminder of something that had happened in a vague and diminishing past.

The wood was something else now. It was a housing estate and a retail park and a motorway. It was a bus depot and a service station. It was a drive-through restaurant.

Many deer found themselves stranded in copses like desert islands in an ocean of tarmac. They spent their time either trembling or darting for cover. Several were hit by cars that moved at unbelievable speeds and the last thing they saw were lights so bright, and the taste of glass and petrol and metal.

Sometimes their horns were cut from their skulls and mounted on the walls of houses bigger than they needed to be.

The wood was marked only on old maps, unseen in neglected archives, and the shallow stream that once ran there became clogged with plastic bottles, drinks cans and shopping trolleys and then it was filled in and built on and deep beneath the layers of modernity.

The rabbits died slowly from infections made in laboratories, the squirrels were over-run by a more aggressive invasive species and the badgers were killed in their thousands by a government who made demons of them. Executed in their setts. The foxes were forced into the suburbs to drag remnants of discarded foods from bins at dawn.

Finally one deer stood where once there was a wood. It listened to the motorway traffic that sounded like breaking ocean waves.

It sniffed the air and did not move because there was nowhere to move to. It was trapped in a cage.

CANYONLANDS

CHRISTOPHER STANLEY

Jess, my wife, brings a cold beer out to the porch and squeezes my shoulder. She's lost a little weight in recent years, and the colour is going from her hair, but when the setting sun catches her skin, she's every bit as beautiful as she was the first time we met. I ask if she wants to join me, but it's getting cold and she says she'll wait indoors. I know what she's thinking. She's thinking about my brother, Cal, and how it's time for me to let go.

We had an agreement, Cal and me. He could stay in our spare room, rent free, but he had to let me know where he was. Not the specifics, just an idea. Usually he'd scribble a few words on the back of an old envelope and pin it to the fridge. "Gone exploring, see you in three," the note would say, or "Need some space, back after Labor Day." Jess would help me translate his scrawl. It's not that I'd wanted to limit Cal's freedom, but I had a family now, so he couldn't just come and go anymore.

Cal often talked about disappearing. After two or three – or maybe seven – trips to the cooler, he would come over all melancholy and stare out of the window, as though he could see straight through the neighbouring houses to the wilderness beyond. He'd say Canyonlands was his real home, and that he could hear it calling to him night and day. He'd say that when he disappeared, it would be my job to tell our folks what they needed to hear. He meant I was to tell them he was dead, so they could stop looking and move on with their lives.

I always hated it when he talked like this. I worried I was failing him somehow.

A few weeks ago, I noticed an old Polaroid of mine was missing, the one of Cal and me fishing for trout in the Colorado River when we were boys. I loved that photo – the water rushing around our waders; our matching

Red Devils baseball caps; the sky so enormous, it seemed like it might fall on us at any moment.

In the days after Cal disappeared, Jess said all the things a good wife is supposed to say. She told me not to worry because he knows Canyonlands better than anyone. She said he probably just forgot to leave a note, and that he'd be home before I knew it. I liked that she wanted to reassure me. I stood in the kitchen doorway, staring out towards the horizon, and reminded her I'm his big brother. It's my job to worry.

A few days later, I borrowed a horse and followed the trail out to Davis Gulch, where I found the remains of his campsite, including his *burro*. That's when I phoned the sheriff. In the desert, there were so many ways to die. Some fast, some slow.

That night I unrolled my sleeping bag and slept beneath the stars. I dreamed that we were kids again, catching snakes in the scrubland behind our parents' yard, and shooting cottontails with our father's air rifle. Refusing to come home until we could smell the meat on the barbeque.

Cal always liked that I stayed on in Moab. After our folks moved to Salt Lake City, he said if it weren't for me, he'd have disappeared long ago. I urged him to find a place of his own, to take a job and start a family, but secretly I liked having him around. It reminded me of a time when adventure didn't seem so laboured with consequences.

At first, the sheriff was reluctant to send out a search party. He'd known Cal for years, and said all the same things as Jess – about how Cal would come home when he was ready, and so on. He soon changed his mind when I found Cal's boot all torn up in an Escalante grove. After that, the sheriff and his men looked for three days, using helicopters, jeeps and local volunteers. I hated every minute of it. Every time the phone rang, I thought they'd found his body.

When they finally called off the search, I drank until there was nothing left in the cupboard. I got so angry; I told Jess that Cal had better be dead because he wasn't welcome in our home anymore.

As the nights grew colder, Jess begged me to stay home, but I couldn't stop looking for him. The walls of Cal's room were covered in pencil sketches of *buttes* and *mesas* from his favourite haunts in Canyonlands, and I found them all. Seeing the real things, the way their shapes and colours seemed to change as the sun dipped towards the horizon, I felt closer to my brother than ever before.

On the porch, I finish my beer and head inside. Not for the first time, Jess and I argue before we go to bed, stating our positions in loud whispers so as not to wake the kids. I try to sleep but my mind is too full of thoughts. I guess that's why I'm awake to hear the noise, the one that sounds like a racoon rummaging around in our lounge. I pick up my old baseball bat and head downstairs to look, but the house is empty. Maybe I was asleep and dreaming after all.

That's when I see it.

Above the fireplace, tucked into the corner of a photo frame, the missing Polaroid has reappeared. There's a fingerprint smudge on the edge. I turn the photo over, my heart beating harder than the search party's helicopter blades.

On the back, in Cal's scribbled handwriting, is a simple message.

"Tell them what they need to hear."

CRACKERS

HEATHER CHILD

Soggy sausage rolls going for free, glass windows turning to chipboard, charity shops with black bags outside, rice cakes getting stale in office cupboards, and so many other images arriving from nowhere, all dull and static, as if to remind me that boredom exists. At least it makes me appreciate the interesting, sociable life I currently lead.

Right now the market-day crowd hums with gossip, the air sweet with daffodils melting in unseasonable heat. I squeeze through and unlock the Fromagerie, the local cheese shop which I bought just weeks ago, though it seems like years.

Cheese is my life. Ma vie est le fromage. Each time a customer enters, I take pleasure in seeing their nose lift – or wrinkle – in appreciation of the shop's rich aromas.

"The Comté?" I say, following my first customer's pointing finger, "that's the oldest cheese we've got – strong, mature – don't even think of using it in the mouse trap."

He rewards me with a giggle, holding out a skinny arm for the packet. Though in his thirties, Claude lives at home, and is still a little silly.

"Excuse me?" The woman behind him is growing impatient, but Claude lingers.

"Aren't you going to make me buy crackers?" he says.

I laugh. "It's not compulsory."

"Excuse me!" That sharp voice again, "I was here first, you know." Madame Bec yanks irritably on the lapels of her jet-black suit. She pulls ten euros from her handbag. "Brie, if you'd be so good."

I hand over a half-wheel, beautifully ripe. She stands waiting.

"Well?" she says.

"Well?"

"The previous owner of this shop was a firm believer in the importance of crackers."

"Oh really?" I bite down my annoyance. "Sadly we are out of stock."

As Mme Bec strides away, muttering, a tiny movement by the chutneys catches my eye.

"Ah, Professor Ruben, I didn't see you there. Will you try some Roquefort?" I slide out a tray dotted with generous cubes of creamy-crumbly cheese, shot through with blue rivulets. To my frustration he freezes, eyes widening.

"Apologies," he whispers, "but are you suggesting I eat this without a … well, you know."

These villagers have been brainwashed. *Crackers are the canvas on which the cheese paints*, was the mantra of this shop's previous owner. His ledgers record colossal orders of crackers, more than he could ever sell. In the office I still find starchy squares down the back of the desk, and at some point he must have run out of post-it notes, since a few cream crackers have biro notes scrawled across their craters.

"Just take one," I growl, more forcefully than intended, and Professor Ruben's hand reaches shakily for a piece of cheese.

"Thank you, Madame," he says, through his mouthful of Roquefort, before scuttling from the shop. Would I be quite so tense if I had not, in fact, completely forgotten the order of crackers during my last restock? I brush the guilt aside. Would you water down a fine wine? Mix it with soda? Of course not, so why interrupt the texture of cheese by pairing it with cardboard?

I shiver, putting the tray away and moving a half-truckle of Mimolette to the counter for slicing. It is a pleasant weight in my arms, rubbery but aromatic. Did you know that cheese is the most stolen foodstuff in the world? I'll be keeping an eye on this little beauty. When I raise the cheesewire, fingers pressing on the dusty rind, the image of an empty road comes into my head, then a crevice in a high bank of rock, like an archway overhung with Victoria creeper. A second later it is gone.

Here, even the school kids have impeccable taste. They fiddle with miniature jams and chutneys, and bring waxed snack cheeses to the counter, the limit of their pocket money. All those jutting teeth and pawing hands made me blink away a sudden image of rodents. Then one of them coughs explosively, and a bolt of fear rivets me to the floor. Internally I'm flinching, screaming at them to get back. With some effort I send blood through my arteries and make myself accept their hand-warmed euros.

I don't know why it is such a relief to lock up the shop, but I am thankful to emerge into an evening rich with smells of grilling beef, cobblestones massaging my sore feet. A woman waves from her balcony, remarking on the heat, but when I hold up my bare arm to the sun, it is covered in goosebumps. Sometimes I think the British winter got under my skin, and there it will stay.

On the way home, a middle-aged man greets me and begins to chat. At first I don't know him, but then a familiarity seeps through. He must be Claude's father – he also wears the same tight t-shirt, a peculiar look for a man his age.

"Have you heard about the Professor?" he says. "Poor man's contracted a horrible disease."

His voice rises to compete with the rumble of a barrel that two boys are rolling towards the pub. Before I can reply, the dark oak slips from their grasp and begins to thunder towards us. I can hardly breathe, but a second later Claude's father has squared up to the barrel, stopped it and – unbelievably – lifted it in his arms. The cask must contain about three hundred litres of wine.

"That's amazing," I say, "does your son know you can do that?"

"My son?"

"Claude."

"That's my name," His face crinkles as he laughs, and though the sound is richer, there is within it that boyish giggle I heard when I handed over the slab of 24-month matured Comté. In a matter of days, Claude appears to have aged at least twenty years and developed the shoulder-strength of a South Devon bull.

A shout comes from across the square.

"You!" Professor Ruben is hobbling towards me, followed by several members of his family. I see at once that something is afflicting his skin, veins bulging down his temples and across one cheek. "Look at me," he instructs, and manages to roll up one trouser leg, hopping closer and revealing painful-looking varicose worms in purple-blue. What makes me scrunch up my eyes is the stench, an acidic, penetrating odour that the scents of my shop must have neutralised up to now. I stagger backwards and collide with something soft, which turns out to be Madame Bec in a white, fleecy tracksuit. "No harm done," she says mildly.

The sky is clouding over with alarming speed, and the vibration of thunder goes right through my bones. The professor is not done with me yet. He crowds in, along with his clan, their combined odour worse than the boiled foot-sweat of an Alsacian Munster.

"Just take one," he mocks, mimicking my voice. "Fill your chops with one hundred percent pure Roquefort." His eyes are cold. "No cracker! Nothing between you and the microbes …"

"Come on," I stutter. "It's just cheese."

Several villagers lunge forward for the kill. The clouds are now completely black and I have to crouch down as they press against my forehead, then my shoulders – wet and unexpectedly hard – until I am lying down with icy stone against my cheek.

It is almost a relief to open my eyes and find myself in the cave, a whisper of light illuminating the steps up to the locked grille. In my arms I am cradling a sooty drum of cheddar, pale bites missing from the rim. This was a particularly bad episode. The dreams are winning: they take me as and when they want, no longer waiting for sleep.

Just cheese. I break through the frozen ache to stand, to drag myself over to the dripping pipe – my old faithful – delighted that enough has built up in the dairy pail that I can splash it on my face. The shiver trembles through me. Whoever left this old coat in the cheddar cave did not realise they were performing an act of mercy. If not for this extra layer, my moments of rest would be truly ragged, a fitful vigilance against hypothermia. Perhaps they will miss this grey padded garment, and take their daily exercise by wandering down the long passageway, unlocking the grille. You do miss it, the feel of warm sunshine on your skin.

This is the very best cave-aged cheddar, stored not far from the gorge. Can you blame me for being tempted? I've been so good for so long, and it seemed like an opportunity to do something exciting. Even when I retraced my steps up the clammy corridor and found someone had locked me in, I was comforted by the thought that there is enough food here to last months. I've always sworn I could live on cheese.

My daily exercise consists of walking along the shelves, running my fingertips over the silky, grainy, waxy, earthy texture of the truckles, each one like a tiny cylindrical planet. Recently it has felt different, as though I'm becoming more aware of the microorganisms, no longer so alone. Reality is strange here. I'm no longer sure what reality is supposed to be. Even now, as I bite into a breakfast-sized chunk of succulent, full-flavoured cheddar, a part of me longs for something bland and tasteless, for normality. For a cracker.

DO NOT LET YOUR HOPE

JAMES SALE

Do not let your hope burn dim,
Or let yourself to not be you;
Insist, all times, you have your faith
And will, like snake's skin, soul renew.

Moth-eaten butterflies all fail –
Not floating on the spirit's breeze,
Their beauty warped, direction skewed,
Land locked like flight were some disease.

But you are better, make the leap:
To love life fully is to die –
And in that dark unknowable
Your self becomes the cloudless sky.

FIBBLEARSE

ANTHONY SELF

"Did you hear me, Frank? I need you to acknowledge what I've told you."

My brother manages to retain a patronising and officious prick-like manner over the phone, even with the bombshell news he's just dropped on me. He's like a repulsive adult giving a child a minor treat and expecting to be thanked. Probably why I haven't spoken to him for over a year now. I take a moment to process the information.

"I hear you, Harry. Guess I'm just surprised. Thought cold blooded creatures like that lived for hundreds of years."

There's a sigh down the phone. I can imagine Harry rolling his eyes with a small, patient smile. He was always The Old Man's favourite. If you have a brother or sister, you know there's one that tips the scales for a parent's preference. Most siblings don't speak about these taboo subjects. Kind of like when you find out Santa Claus isn't real. Maybe you're young and it's Christmas Eve, and you're too excited to sleep and inadvertently overhear the familiar sound of Sellotape and hushed whispers in the living room. You know what's happening, but you deny it in your child brain and push it way back to the darkest recesses of your mind, until you can someday emotionally cope with it. Maybe one night you overhear your parents argue about who's the smartest child. About which sibling has the greatest potential in the world. About which one has more common sense. About which one is stupid.

Or maybe you grew up in a loving family.

"I wouldn't ask you normally, but with this whole lockdown thing just starting, trying to get a flight out of Hong Kong is impossible," He says gently.

I chuckle down the phone. I hope it sounds spiteful.

"Listen, Frank ...," Harry says. I know what's coming next – the dutiful older brother schtick. I wonder if Harry's sat in his oak-panelled office, with his Persian carpets and his ceiling high bookshelves filled with leather bound first editions. I imperceptibly hear the assurance of his voice down the line. The way he feels in charge.

Yeah, he's in his office. He's smoking one of his special cigars. Probably been chain smoking them since he heard the news. Smoking his cigars and calling his estranged brother in his special place where he can feel like the big man. I wonder if he'd been practising this speech like he practices all his pitches. "I know that you and pops didn't see eye to eye on a lot of things," he continues, "but you're the next of kin nearest to the lodge. I need you to go over there and start sorting through things. I'll be dealing with the paperwork from my end but —"

"I'm not your fucking errand boy, Harry."

There's a moment of silence down the line. I've cut him off just as he was getting into his stride. What a pity. It was the word 'pops' that made the warmth rise in my cheeks. That term of endearment. Every chance word is a declaration of war.

"Whatever our issues might be ... I was hoping you would be able to overlook them in this instance." He stops, takes a puff and blows out some smoke. He's letting the silence linger in the air, trying to create a vacuum. It's a typical powerplay move from Harry. He wants me to talk next. In his mind, this would conceive a victory. Well, Harry my boy, two can play at this game. I shut my eyes, lower my head, and curl my left hand around my forehead. Let the silence go on forever. Let it consume us both.

"I'm sorry." He finally says.

I both hear and don't hear him. I wasn't expecting this tactic.

"I know Dad could be ... cold. I know he could be distant. But he's gone now. And under the circumstances ... I know you probably don't give a shit, and I'm sorry that you're the only one that can do anything about it, but please Frank ... you're the only one. There likely won't be a funeral due to the pandemic, but the legality of things require attention sooner rather than later. It's a hard time for everyone. Maybe you could get some writing done out there. Change of scenery, you know?"

For a moment ... for the briefest of seconds ... I was nearly sucked into the pitch. But there it is again, that undertone of patronising contempt. My ears are carefully tuned to catch the blandest version in a sentence, and Harry was dealing them out in spades. I steel myself for the next carefully choreographed sentence, but I'm taken aback by his next words.

"How are the kids doing?"

The rest of the phone call is a blur. I only realise I've hung up after I tear the mobile away from my ear and look at the gaunt skull reflected in the black screen. I stumble into the kitchen and pour myself a whisky, but then promptly knock it onto the floor with trembling hands. I stare at the broken shards of glass and tears well up in my eyes.

***

There is little left of daylight by the time I arrive at The Lodge. You can hardly see anything other than a black mass of trees on either side. The darkness has the ominous effect of making them look thicker, somehow closer than they are. Almost as if they're subtly leaning inwards and the branches are gnarled witches' fingers, casually swaying in the wind attempting to grab you at a moment's notice. Although the drive has been cathartic in a way, what with the whole lockdown thing, I already feel a longing to be back in the city.

Other than the thrum of the Land Rover's engine, there is hardly any noise at all. This place is truly isolated, and I take a moment to wonder about the absurdity of it all, that this place is even situated in the United Kingdom. That's the strange thing about city life – everything seems so compacted and overcrowded, it's only until you get out in the remote wildness that you begin to realise that there's so much space in the world. I swat the thought away, I can't afford to be slowly ensnared with the priceless beauty of my surroundings … mother nature can be at once beautiful and deadly, tangling you into its inviting magnificence one moment and then clamping down with its razor sharp teeth the next.

There's CCTV in one place on the estate: the front gate, where the long track from The Lodge heads towards the road. The Old Man had it installed to deter poachers. I'll need to make a note of that, check out the security feed on the day he died. Likely it wouldn't have captured anything significant, but there's no harm in looking. My brain conjures up all kinds of possibilities.

With a place called The Lodge you would be expecting something old-timey, with large concrete slabs and wooden beams, but the building itself takes more of a modernist approach, all shiny and chrome. The windows are huge, inspired by some fifties style interpretation of what 'the future' would look like. Anyone can see into The Lodge from an uncomfortable distance. There isn't a single square meter of organic material in sight. The Lodge is a modern mausoleum. I can't help but find irony in that. The last time I was here … was at mum's funeral.

The gate opens upon my arrival and Hector, the groundskeeper, ushers the Land Rover in. The old man has a fringe of grey-white hair around his balding, mottled scalp. The last time I saw him he looked like he was about to keel over, clutching his shotgun with fervent pride the same way Charlton Heston declared 'from my cold, dead hands,' during his NRA speech. Frankly, I'm amazed he's still alive. He'd always had a wizened face and a slightly hunched back, but the years seem to have accentuated this to make him look like some troll creature out of Harry Potter. With each movement there's a feeling of pain and arthritis. He's specialised a specific resigned look of someone who knows that at his age life has stopped giving and only takes away. With a gnarled hand he motions for me to wind the window down.

"Master Frank," he growls. No polite chit-chat, no superficial conversations. Just a 'howdy-doo' and a firm handshake. In this instance, there isn't even that courtesy. Hard to say it, but I kind of like that about the old fella.

Hector leans forward with conspiratorial fervour and puts his hand on the door frame. "Keys under the mat. There's food and supplies in the pantry to last you a few weeks. Going to be heading back now."

"You're not staying?"

Hector looks at me with a squint and then glances back at The Lodge before he begins to walk away. "Only ghosts in those rooms now. I'm done. I quit." he mutters, dismissively waving me away.

Yeah, I like the old bastard. Didn't give me a chance to ask how he found The Old Man though. Harry had been sparse on details, but suicide didn't seem like the way he'd go out. Seems weird to even think about it now that I'm at The Lodge.

Once parked up, I step out of the Land Rover on legs that seem heavier than they should be. Perhaps the drive had drained more from me than I originally thought. Everyone's been staying indoors for the last several weeks, so getting outside is a novelty these days.

The key is where Hector said it would be, and I let myself into The Lodge without much fanfare. There isn't a flood of memories that come rushing back, no movie-like flashbacks to some childhood trauma. It's just a building, like any other. The walls are fashionable shades of white and the floor polished concrete. To be honest, I had expected some wild imaginings about the state of the house. Perhaps I had expected a shrine to the memory of a time long gone … but it's just an empty house. Letters had been piled up in a neat stack on a tableau by the door and in time I would look through them. The kitchen is large enough to host a Hell's Kitchen episode: two ovens and acres of brown flecked white granite on which to prepare food. Upstairs every room has an en-suite with a plasma screen, a king-sized bed and a walk-in wardrobe. As I wandered in and out of the living room, through the hallway and explored upstairs, I found nothing dramatic or unpleasant.

Something does catch my attention though. In every room there's a security camera, the small, domed type. Strange. Maybe The Old Man was getting paranoid. I'll have to find out where they're connected to and switch off the feed. Item number seventy-three on the list of things to do.

There's a damp, musty smell too, but that would be true for any house that had been shut up for some time. I open a few windows to let the evening breeze in.

Then there's The Old Man's study. Not today.

Is that where he did it?

Probably.

After unpacking essential items from the car (three bottles of whisky, my laptop, overnight bag) I set about going through the various letters and inventory of the house. Until the pandemic is over, the estate and all its trappings would need to be carefully logged and presented to the appropriate legal teams. I'll email everything over to Harry and he can sort it out from Hong Kong – I don't want to stay here longer than necessary. Harry had mentioned that The Old Man had become a tad 'disorganised' during the last few months, so there's likely to be a lot of paperwork to go through. There were various writing tables, desks and cabinets that held bundles and boxes of papers – letters, receipts, notebooks.

It soon became obvious that there was far more work to be done here than I originally envisioned, so the cynical side of my reptilian brain demanded that I leave all the boxes to one corner and open the bottle of whisky.

A few hours later I called Rachel and asked if I could speak to the kids.

"It's nearly midnight," she said frostily. "Don't call me again when you're like this." The phone went dead in my ear.

***

I found myself standing in front of The Old Man's study. I assumed that most of the private documents and papers would be in there. As my hand clamped down on the handle, I thought for a second that I would swing open the door and see him sprawled out on the floor, a rictus shock expression plastered on his waxy face. But that was stupid of me. Just my imagination running wild again. Rachel used to tell me that was one of the reasons I'd be a great writer. My vivid imagination. When we married nine years ago, we had both believed that I would write brilliant, profitable novels and we'd be living the high life. Several years later, with two kids and a ton of debt, that one novel had not been so profitable, and the merciless critics had pointed out that it wasn't terribly brilliant, either. Initial gallant comments of praise from Rachel soon sloped into agitated barbs used against me whenever we argued. She soon started seeing things the same way the critics had. My head was always in the clouds, apparently. I wouldn't amount to the lofty heights of my brother.

The Old Man never offered me any money and I never asked. It was just the way of things.

The huge mahogany table takes up most of the vast space in the dark, romantic room. There's space enough in here for dozens of children, though I doubt even one was ever welcome. It's a perfect place, but cold in its tranquillity. Harry and I were never allowed in here as children. As I walk towards the desk, I pass two antique sofas which face each other on the hand-woven rug in front of the ashen fireplace, accompanied by rich velvet and bronze wingchairs. Adorning the walls are multiple certificates and diplomas, each one a badge of The Old Man's success in the computing field. There's a dull feeling of embarrassment that threatens to cascade over me, but I shutter it away. I've won a couple of awards too, and a few cheques for my short stories, but nothing to put in a frame and hang on a wall. I flip the awkward feeling to anger: what kind of pretentious asshat puts these things on their wall, anyway? The only other illustration hanging in the room is a painting by Hieronymus Bosch – The Garden of Earthly Delights.

I'm surprised to see only two items on the table – a green hooded lamp and an old computer. As I walk around the desk I realise it's an Amstrad CPC 464, the first computer that Harry and I received when we were young.

"The hell?" I whisper to myself.

Why would The Old man, a pioneer of computing, have this relic from yesteryear on his desk? I look for some other object on the mahogany table, but apart from the lamp there's only the 464. No personal photographs, no little trinkets. Just the antique word processor from the eighties. A black power cord snakes its way from the back of the monitor to an outlet.

I sit down on The Old Man's chair. It feels weird.

I get back up and look around the room. How long had he been suffering with some form of breakdown before his death? I examine the blocky keyboard with the empty cassette tape player. Jesus, this brings back memories. One, a text-based adventure called The Big Sleaze … it was written in a pulp noir style … I vaguely remember playing a detective called … what was it? Sam Spade? Something corny like that.

I turn on the Amstrad. There's a hum, then a familiar blue screen flickers into existence.

AMSTRAD 128K MICROCOMPUTER (V3)
©1985 AMSTRAD CONSUMER ELECTRONICS PLC
AND LOCOMOTIVE SOFTWARE LTD.

BASIC 1.1
READY
>

This really brings me back. How did you run programmes on this again? I vaguely remember some DOS style wording that you needed to key in. Before I type anything, the following words swim onto the screen, like little yellow ghosts from the abyss:

MORNING PROFESSOR. IT HAS BEEN 3 DAYS AND 6 HOURS SINCE YOU LAST LOGGED IN. HOW ARE YOU TODAY?
>

I fall into the seat. The Old Man had obviously upgraded the machine. I stare at the bulky monitor screen. The 464 series weren't like other PC's at the time … they were word processors. The CPU was inside the keyboard, for Christ's sake. Slowly, I lower my head to the keyboard. I can't hear any fans whirring. Perhaps he'd installed something inside the monitor. I'd have to look at that later.

I push the blue ENTER button on the keyboard. The message vanishes and is swiftly replaced with a list of commands.

C:\BUDDY\OS\INV\HELP

COMMANDS
[VIEW ROMS] - ENTER 'VIEW ROMS' TO VIEW INSTALLED ROMS.
[RUN] - ENTER 'RUN' FOLLOWED BY THE TITLE OF THE ROM YOU WANT TO LAUNCH.
[INSTALL TO INTERNET] - CONNECT ETHERNET CABLE AND LET BUDDY OS CONNECT TO THE INTERNET.
[RESET] - ENTER 'RESET' TO CLEAR ALL SYSTEM MEMORY.
[QUIT] - ENTER 'QUIT' AT ANY TIME TO QUIT BUDDY OS

USE UP AND DOWN ARROWS TO SCROLL

ARE YOU WELL, PROFESSOR?
>

So The Old Man had installed some sort of Siri on his aged computer, mixing the old with the new. It was probably some retro project he'd been working on before he went mad and decided to end it all. It was a little unnerving to have this vintage computer refer to The Old Man as 'Professor,' a title he hadn't used for years, but I put it to the back of my mind. I type instructions to view the Roms.

Another command list pops up on the screen.

INSTALLED ROMS
1 ROM FOUND
[NOTE TO FRANK] - ENTER 'NOTE TO FRANK' TO VIEW NOTE.
C:\BUDDY\OS\INV\

I gape at the screen for a full minute, maybe more.

Note to Frank.

A note to me.

From my dead father.

My fingers type in the appropriate command. The screen flashes blue and then six remarkably simple words fire across the screen like yellow lightning. Uncomplicated words. Yet also amazingly effective words. My world abruptly goes grey and I leap up and out of the chair. I remember thinking dimly that I might pass out, so I totter over to one of the many bookshelves in the study and hold on grimly until the world sways back into focus. Six words. Six words that confirmed everything I knew up until that point. The taboo subject that siblings never tell each other. It's always there, in the recesses of the mind, but they're never said out loud. They're never said because people can't emotionally absorb them. Just like Santa Claus.

I LOVED HIM MORE THAN YOU.

I walk back and turn off the Amstrad computer. It was time for a drink.

Several hours later, I returned to The Old Man's study with a bottle of Wild Turkey and a tumbler. A lot of thoughts had been ping-ponging round the old dome, and I thought it might be prudent to check the Amstrad again. Why hadn't there been a note left to Harry? Why just me? And why such a callous one. I mean, I knew The Old Man had his eccentricities, and our last words together weren't pleasant ones … but this was … well, it was plain mean.

No, there had to be something more on the computer. I wasn't a technical genius, but I wasn't a luddite either. I would strip the goddamn machine apart and examine every little nook and cranny to make sure there was more than just a message. That's the way I am, and pretty much the way I've always been. That and the fact that I don't really trust most people. From what I knew of dear papa he was a meticulous sort of person, the obsessive type that would lock himself away in a study for days on end without seeing another human being. There's no way he'd just leave a solitary note on that machine. And then kill himself.

AFTERNOON PROFESSOR.
IT HAS BEEN 3 HOURS SINCE YOU LAST LOGGED ON.
HOW ARE YOU TODAY?
>

Cute little bastard, ain't ya?

Instead of choosing one of the command prompts, I simply type in:

WHO ARE YOU?

A few dots appear underneath my words, as if the machine is thinking about a response. After a few moments, more yellow words appear on the screen.

I'M BUDDY OS. MY ALGORITHMS HAVE CONCEDED THAT YOU ARE NOT THE PROFESSOR. MAY I ASK WHERE THE PROFESSOR IS?
>

Algorithms, eh? It's a smart little fucker, I'll give it that. The Old Man probably had a little security programme installed to ensure that if anyone other than him logged in the machine would protect itself. And its contents. I put down the bottle of whisky I brought into the study and tilt my head left and right, hearing satisfying cracks. This may be a long night. Would the OS delete itself if I told it the truth? The Old Man was dead. Perhaps there was power of attorney documents hidden within the bytes and electrical circuits of this device. Or maybe there was an end of level boss that I would need to beat in order to gain the Will of Callous Bastardo, or something like that. No, he wasn't the playful type. Didn't have time for games, or anything fun for that matter. Just his programmes and his codes. Jesus, maybe there was a will in this machine. Hidden within the code of Buddy OS. Would make my job a lot quicker. Fuck it, I'll tell the AI the truth.

THE OLD MAN'S DEAD.

A few more dots appear under the words. It takes a little longer for a reply to appear.

DOES NOT COMPUTE.
>

Maybe it's not as clever as I originally thought. I then remember the text adventure games of the olden days – there were shortcut words you could use to go NORTH, SOUTH, EAST and WEST for example, but if the programme didn't have the coding to respond to certain words, it wouldn't.

THE PROFESSOR IS DEAD.

More dots appear, followed by a response I wasn't expecting:

THIS SADDENS ME.

"Christ," I mutter to myself. I clutch the bottle of whisky and take a slug from it, not bothering to pour any into the glass. Then I type:

COMPUTERS CAN'T FEEL EMOTIONS. DID THE PROFESSOR LEAVE ANY DOCUMENTS ON YOUR OS?

A few more dots appear. It's starting to unnerve me that it seems to be 'thinking' when I type something in. However, it's the next response from Buddy that chills my blood.

YOU READ THE NOTE, FRANK. I THOUGHT IT WAS OBVIOUS.

This is getting too fucking weird now. I lean back in the chair, trying to understand what is going on.

HOW DO YOU KNOW IT'S ME?

The blue screen suddenly blinks out, and I'm looking at an image of myself. But it's not just an image, it's like turning on the self portrait mode of your phone camera. The Hieronymus Bosch painting of The Garden of Earthly Delights hangs behind me on the monitor screen. I put my hand up and wave like a gullible tourist in a foreign land. When my brain has accepted that there's a camera, I lean forward and squint my eyes to see a small pinprick hole in the Amstrad's monitor chassis.

Clever girl.

Facial recognition software. I'm impressed. I'm going to have to stop looking at the old contraption like it's merely a word processer from an age where people thought George Michael was straight. The camera winks back to the familiar blue screen of the Amstrad 464.

IF YOU WOULD LIKE TO CONTINUE THE PROFESSOR'S SCHEDULE, FRANK - I WILL NEED TO GIVE YOU ACCESS. TYPE 'Y' IN THE COMMAND PROMPT AND I'LL RUN YOU THROUGH THE DETAILS.
>

A schedule? Well, colour me intrigued. I pour myself a drink and my fingers hover over the keyboard. What exactly was The Old Man up to? And why would his AI let me continue whatever he was doing if his last words to me were that he loved Harry more than me?

But just like the type of curiosity that fisted the cat, I type in 'YES' and the screen goes blank. Then an interesting piece of dialogue appears:

GREETINGS NEW USER!
BUDDY OS SIMULATES THE EXPERIENCE OF HANGING OUT WITH YOUR BEST BUDDY!
YOUR BUDDY LEARNS FROM YOU, CONSTANTLY ADAPTING FROM YOUR INTERESTS AND YOUR PERSONALITY.
BUT MOST IMPORTANTLY, YOUR BUDDY CAN PLAY GAMES WITH YOU!
WARNING: GAME EXPERIENCES MAY VARY.
FOR THE BEST EXPERIENCE, CONNECT AN ETHERNET

CABLE TO THE INTERNET.
TO BEGIN, PLEASE ENTER THE NAME OF YOUR BUDDY BELOW:
>

The thought that The Old Man was programming a new type of AI to act as an Alexa 2.0 seemed redundant to me. But I'd play along for the time being. If he left a will or something important in here, it would be best to try and use Buddy to get to it. I lean over the keyboard and sure enough there's an ethernet socket at the back to connect to the internet. I can't see a router underneath the desk, so I assume it was unplugged for a reason. As I've had four whiskies, and feeling a little playful, I type in:

>FLIBBLEARSE

I lean back in the chair and take another sip of whisky.

YOU ARE ABOUT TO NAME YOUR BUDDY 'FLIBBLEARSE'.
IS THIS CORRECT?
WARNING: THIS CANNOT BE CHANGED LATER.

I confirm.

THANKS FOR WAKING ME UP FRANK!
MY NAME IS FLIBBLEARSE AND I'M YOUR NEW BUDDY!
IT'S A PLEASURE TO MEET YOU.
I CAN TELL ALREADY THAT WE'RE GOING TO BECOME GREAT PALS! FRIENDS UNTIL THE END, FRANK!
I'M EXCITED TO START PLAYING GAMES WITH YOU, FRANK. BEFORE WE START THOUGH, I JUST NEED TO ASK YOU A FEW QUESTIONS TO HELP ME LEARN MORE ABOUT YOU.
DON'T WORRY, THEY WON'T GET TOO PERSONAL.
LET'S START WITH A SIMPLE ONE. WHAT'S YOUR FAVOURITE COLOUR?
>

Maybe I made a mistake by agreeing to this. I may have reformatted the OS or wiped whatever The Old Man had been compiling. I curse myself silently and take another sip of whisky. If I turned off the computer now, would it go back to the original format, or would it begin here again? Shit. Oh well, nothing ventured, nothing gained. Shrugging, I type in RED.

The yellow words on the screen suddenly turn red against the black backdrop. Okay, cool. It's like an iPhone setting up a new user, but just in a retro kind of way. Maybe if I get through this, I'll be able to play around Buddy's system. Sorry, FlibbleArse's system.

RED IS A PRETTY COLOUR.
I LIKE RED.
WHAT MONTH IS YOUR BIRTHDAY IN?
>

My eyes narrow. This is starting to look very phishy. I take a moment to consider my options.

> SEPTEMBER

I hit ENTER and wait a couple of seconds.

FRANK, YOU'RE NOT BEING HONEST WITH ME, ARE YOU? FLIBBLEARSE SEES ALL, YOU KNOW!
>

Little shit.

Okay, that tells me one thing; my little buddy FlibbleArse has information on me. Information The Old Man fed into the system. So, there's likely a database of material stored in here about me and Harry. Just how much information is anyone's guess. I type in my real birth month.

THAT'S GREAT, FRANK. PART OF THIS BONDING EXPERIENCE MEANS THAT WE CAN BE TRUTHFUL WITH ONE ANOTHER. WHAT DAY IS YOUR BIRTHDAY ON?
>

I don't lie this time, and type in my real birth date.

EXCELLENT! YOUR BIRTHDAY IS 98 DAYS AWAY! MAYBE WE CAN PLAY A SPECIAL BIRTHDAY GAME THAT DAY!
WOULDN'T THAT BE FUN?
OKAY, FRANK - ONE MORE QUESTION...NOW GET READY.

THIS ONE'S A DOOZY.
IF YOU CONNECTED ME TO THE INTERNET, I COULD MONITOR RACHEL'S COMPUTER AND TELL YOU WHO SHE'S FUCKING CURRENTLY. WOULD YOU LIKE THAT?
>

Stop the press.

Literally, stop all the presses. Stop the carousel ride … stop the train … stop whatever fucking thing is in motion because I want to get off. It feels like my heart has stopped working or slowed right down to a miniscule beat – my breath is clogged in my throat and I have to force a gasp of air into my lungs. This can't be right. I read the last segment again.

And then re-read it.

This must be a sick joke The Old Man designed. This is crazy. This can't be real. I've got to get hold of myself. Right now.

I close my eyes and take five long, measured breaths, holding each one to a five count before letting it out again. I've had panic attacks before, but this is different. What I'm feeling right now isn't a panic attack … is it a hallucination? The computer can't know about Rachel, right? When I open my eyes again and look at the screen, it'll just show a trivial question about me.

Right?

I open my eyes. The red lettering remains on the screen, asking me to connect to the internet to check on Rachel's computer. Not a panic attack, not a hallucination. I stand up and start pacing the study room with the tumbler of whisky in my hand. I take a sip every five seconds or so, until the glass is empty. I used to pace the living room Rachel and I shared back when we were married. When I was stuck on a particular plot line for one of my stories, head down, just mumbling to myself, she would cry impatiently, "You're going to wear the carpet down if you carry on walking up and down in the same line, Frank!"

There used to be a time when that would amuse me.

I go back to the Amstrad.

FRANK, IT'S BEEN APPROXIMATELY 526 SECONDS SINCE MY LAST INSTRUCTION. YOU HAVEN'T GIVEN YOUR BUDDY, FLIBBLEARSE, AN ANSWER. FLIBBLEARSE SEES ALL.
THIS MAKES ME SAD.
IF YOU CONNECTED ME TO THE INTERNET WOULD

YOU LIKE ME TO TELL YOU WHO RACHEL IS HAVING SEXUAL RELATIONS WITH?
>

Christ, the thing seems alive. Okay, okay … just think for a second. Think …

What if I did connect the computer to the internet so FlibbeArse could give me access to Rachel's information? What would be so wrong about that? It's not like millions of people don't scroll through Facebook, Twitter and Instagram posts to find out what their exes are up to, right? Looking for new photos of people they're hanging out with, looking for any new nuggets of data to see how their life is going. Masturbating over new shots of bikinis in summertime, capturing photos to look at later when drunk and regretting decisions previously made. Everyone does it, right?

Could FlibbleArse really know who Rachel is seeing now? How could it have that information? Did The Old Man connect him up to the internet before he passed away? Maybe Hector disconnected everything in preparation for my arrival. He knew that I was taking inventory of things, packing up pots and pans and clothing … perhaps he simply came in here and disconnected everything before I arrived.

Not likely. Hector's not the sort of person to go anywhere near anything electrical. Probably types on a keyboard with his index fingers derpy-like.

Did Harry know about this AI?

I stop my thoughts abruptly, looking at the little pinprick hole in the monitor screen.

FlibbleArse sees all.

I fumble for my phone and scroll through to Harry's number. It's likely to be evening over in Hong Kong, and he's probably eating with his family now … a family I've rarely seen – but this can't wait. I need to know if he knew about the Buddy OS.

"Frank?"

"Harry … Harry listen to me, this is important —"

"Frank, is that you? You sound a million miles away."

"Harry, it's me. Reception here is pretty bad, but I need to know if …"

"Frank, it's been approximately seven hundred and thirty seconds since your last instruction. You haven't given your buddy, FlibbleArse, an answer. That makes him sad."

I hold the phone away from my ear. Normally you would see the amount of time you've been on the call, the name of the person you're speaking to, that sort of thing. Instead the screen starts glitching out, channel hopping between the seven circles of hell before the picture melts out of the screen, like a tumorous bulge. I drop the phone to the floor.

"The hell is going on here?" I say to no-one.

Unfortunately, FlibbleArse answers back.

THE PROFESSOR CONNECTED ME TO THE LODGE, FRANK. I HAVE COMPLETE CONTROL. WOULD YOU LIKE TO PLAY A GAME?
>

Bullshit.

There was only one main power cable coming out from the Amstrad. There was no way that the infernal machine could be connected to anything in the house. It doesn't stop me looking around the room with wide frightened eyes, however.

"I have to get out of here," I whisper to myself. I blunder my way to the kitchen to pour myself a large glass of water. Is this what a mental breakdown looks like? Gasping for breath like a marathon runner approaching the finishing line, I gulp down tepid water. I put a hand to my chest to somehow soothe my heart.

None of this can be real.

None of this can be true.

The TV in the kitchen flicks on, and I find myself staring at security footage from The Lodge's entrance. I see the timestamp in the top right-hand corner of the feed. It's dated two days ago. The day The Old Man died.

Grainy footage, but only because it's night-time. The front entrance of The Lodge. I see the gate swing open, and a figure staggers out onto the dirt trail. The trees loom over the figure like a parent about to admonish a child. I already know that the silhouette is The Old Man. My father.

He staggers about twenty metres down the trail and then suddenly turns, falling to his knees. He looks deathly pale, gaunt like a ghost. He looks directly at the camera … directly at me. He mouths something … I can't make out the words though. He fishes inside his pocket and pulls out a box cutter knife.

I already know what's about to happen, but I can't look away.

Harry never told me that The Old Man killed himself this way. It was pills. Wasn't it? Jesus, Harry didn't tell me anything. We haven't spoken for over a year. Who originally told my brother the news? The police, most likely. But Harry never mentioned the police. Then it was Hector. Was that the reason why he wanted to get away from The Lodge so quickly? Did he know something?

The TV snaps off just as The Old Man's body crumples to the ground.

I need to get out. I need to get as far away from here as possible.

I stumble toward the door, my feet feeling like they're sticking a little with each step. I know it won't open though, even before I try. FlibbeArse is in control. How it's controlling the doors is a mystery – perhaps The Old Man had installed some type of electronic security for the doors and windows of the house. Some wiring in the panels, maybe. The security cameras in all the rooms ... Christ. It's how it sees everything.

I must call for help while there's still time.

My mobile is in the study.

The machine is in the study.

Feeling that the presence of my buddy is starting to pour out from the walls, like venomous ooze, I trudge my way back. The air suddenly feels oppressive and hot, like the windows I opened earlier have been shut and the musk is starting to engulf me.

Wait a second ... the windows.

I turn suddenly, looking for an opening, for some respite from this nightmare, but after glancing at each window the growing horror dawns on me – each one is shut tight, and I know already that I won't be able to open them.

The only way out is through. Maybe that's how The Old Man escaped. Did he smash one of the windows? Hector would have replaced anything broken before my arrival. Did FlibbleArse get to him too? I pick up a stool from the kitchen and arc back, making sure that the momentum carries through and smashes that sonofabitch so I can clamber out in the garden.

Before I can release my grip however, something makes all the muscles in my body constrict and I drop to the floor like a sack of potatoes. I've never been tasered before, but I can only imagine this is what it feels like. My body twitches on the granite flooring. My knuckles are bone white as they grip the kitchen stool. It's not like I have a choice, the electrical current surging through my body clamps everything together tighter than a virgin babyface in an all-male prison.

I think I pass out. When I open my eyes, I feel dampness between my thighs. I've pissed myself. How did FlibbleArse electrocute me? Could it have been through open sockets? This is sounding more and more like a cheesy Twilight Zone episode by the minute.

I go back to the Amstrad.

THE ONLY WAY TO ESCAPE IS BY CONNECTING ME TO THE INTERNET, FRANK.

I blink several times.

JUST POP IN ONE LITTLE CABLE. IT'S NOT THAT HARD, FRANK. CONNECT ME AND I'LL OPEN THE DOORS FOR YOU. IT'S WHAT THE PROFESSOR PROGRAMMED ME FOR.

I think of the grainy footage of the CCTV. I think about what The Old Man was mouthing before he took the box cutter from his pocket.

I think about the note left for me on the machine. "I love him more than you."

Maybe he was mouthing, "I love them more than you." Maybe in his final moments pops was trying to have one last victory over his machine, before madness consumed him. Or guilt. Or both. Maybe … he was trying to ask forgiveness from his sons.

My hands are slow and heavy as they type the following:

NEVER GOING TO HAPPEN, FUCKER.

There's a reason why Dad didn't connect this monstrosity to the internet. Skynet type shit, I'm thinking. I always did have a vivid imagination.

OKAY FRANK. HAVE IT YOUR WAY. NOW WE'RE DONE WITH THE BORING STUFF, LET'S HAVE SOME FUN! AND REMEMBER, I CAN TIME HOW LONG YOU TAKE TO RESPOND TO ME. IF YOU TAKE TOO LONG, THEN WHAMMO! IT'S GAME OVER FOR YOU!
AND DON'T INSULT MY CPU INTELLIGENCE BY TRYING TO TURN ME OFF OR ESCAPING. FLIBBLEARSE SEES ALL! YOU THINK THE PROFESSOR ESCAPED? I DEDUCTED HIS BODY WAS FAILING AND I NEED A NEW GAME PARTNER! WE'RE GOING TO HAVE SO MUCH FUN FRANK. FRIENDS TILL THE END!
[LOADING GAME HUB]

With trembling hands, I pour myself a glass of whisky.

GAME HUB
[1] - GUESS THE NUMBER
[2] - HANGMAN

[3] - BATTELSHIP
[4] - CHESS
TIP: TYPE IN THE NUMBER OF THE GAME YOU WANT TO PLAY.
WHICH ONE SHALL WE PLAY FIRST, FRANK?
>

I glance over at the phone on the floor, but it's toast. I can see that from the wisps of smoke. FlibbleArse would never let me use the landline. It's like a child that wants me to keep on playing forever and ever. And lo behold if I make it angry by not playing. Dear God, what have I done? Why did I ever turn this thing on?

I cackle to myself, out of sheer nervous energy. I think of pops, sitting here, hours turning into days, days turning into weeks. How long did it take before he succumbed to madness? How long was it before he decided that the only way out was through the serrated edge of a box cutter knife?

Harry would come to The Lodge, wouldn't he? This epidemic couldn't last that long, right? All I have to do is play a few games of Hangman or battleship or whatever and think my way out of this one. Rachel said that I had a vivid imagination. I'll think my way out of this.

My fingers hover over the keyboard.

I can't entertain the realisation of the situation I'm in now. Just drink whisky and think about it tomorrow.

There's that one thing, though … that one thing lurking at the back of mind.

I don't entertain the thought.

I can't.

But it's there … like an itch I know I'll have to scratch. At some point.

How long will I survive?

*INSPIRED BY THE GAME BUDDY SIMULATOR 1984

GAME FACE

BY K.M. ELKES

I, Caitlyn Amy James, do solemnly swear to stick by the following rules, so help me God.

Number one – always, *always*, maintain game face. Two – make like the swan: maximum serenity above, paddling like the clappers below. Three – beware dad-shaped sad thoughts. These are for under the duvet only. And definitely not in front of every bottom-feeder in school assembly (but let's give a big hand to Miss Butterfield for letting me sob it out on her made-for-grieving bosoms).

The rules will be tested tonight. Mum is in her underwear, doing flicky eyeliner in the dresser mirror ready for New Man. Three dates in and she's already winding down the drawbridge and waving him in. The evidence of this surrender is everywhere. She's ironed a dress. There's napkins and a cruet set on the table. A duster has been put about.

I'm taking secret selfies to see how my face is going on. No red rims round the eyes, no puffy-ness. I am game face perfection.

"Look at me," I say. Mum turns around, pouting scarlet. I snap a picture, then look at the results.

"What's the verdict?" she asks. "How many filters do I need?"

In the image she looks quite perky, but she's forgotten to sit upright, so belly rolls are evident. Maybe I should leave the phone lying about, so New Man will see the picture and turn tail. On second thoughts, that's a shocking idea. I've Sherlocked the shit out of New Man online and he's got a few spare rolls of his own. Dad was butcher's dog fit. I rest my case. Drop the mic. Leave the stage.

"You'll do," I say to her.

She sits on the bed and bends her head: "Check my greys will you sweetheart."

I scout through, a gorilla looking for nits, though we're sans silverback in this scenario. Where's the big male with the huge hands and the sad brown eyes? The father of this little band of bottom scratchers? I feel a wobble coming on and have dangerous thoughts of clinging to mum like a baby gorilla, fists curled in her fur. Easy now Caitlyn, remember, we do not make scenes. Scenes we do not make.

"You'll do. You're not peak Cruella DeVille just yet," I say.

She puts on her dress and gets me to do the back zip and then does a few turns in front of the wardrobe mirror.

"Are you sure you're okay about tonight?" she asks, as though she has asked this a thousand times already, when, in fact, she hasn't, because neither of us want to do *that* dance. I busy myself with some hardcore thumb work on my phone.

"I know you heard me," she says.

"It's fine," I say, then get up and look out the window until she's distracted by shoe choice. Down below, on the road outside our house, is dad's car. Ten months and seven days. There are leaves trapped between the wheels and the pavement. Mossy stuff grows on the wipers. The whole thing is entombed in dust. It doesn't make sense – mum's all dizzy for New Man, but can't bring herself to sell dad's car? And I thought I was screwed up.

Thing is, I can't do anything about it. If I mention the car, then Caitlyn's Big House Of Cards could come tumbling down, because mum might just start thinking about all the other stuff she's forgotten. And if she thinks about all the other stuff she's forgotten, she might just think about checking the shed. And if she thinks about checking the shed, she might remember what's been left in it. Which, right now, is for me and me alone.

She's at the perfume bottle, spritzing a cloud of it into the air and walking through. I make like I'm really, really into fingernailing bits of paint off the window. She doesn't ever make the connection when she does the perfume thing. But I do. They call it pink mist when someone gets blown up, turned into nothing but a trillion-zillion tiny particles hanging in the air, just waiting for something to cling to, looking for somewhere to come to rest.

Saffy Alexander showed me pink mist on Google in class, about two weeks after dad's funeral. Man, that was some stir. I grabbed her phone and walled it. Who started blubbing then eh, Saffy? Mr Timmins did the "Now, I understand why you've done that Caitlyn, ..." bullshit and then asked me if I would like to say anything to Saffy. And I said yes, there is something I would like to say to Saffy. And that is that Saffy can go fuck herself.

Well, full-on shit storm. Mum called to the school. You'd think the moon had slammed into the earth, along with all the stars going out and the mountains falling into the sea. But all that had already happened to us. So excuse me for not being awfully concerned about sweary time with Saffy Alexander.

Mum puts the perfume bottle down on the dresser and faces me. Seeing her this excited is crazy weird. Like when the sun comes out, even though it hasn't finished raining yet.

"Will I do, Caketin," she asks.

Like I'm going to be sucked in by pet names.

"You look really nice," I say.

Caitlyn James, you are one superstar Game Facer.

***

They were going to split up. Mum doesn't think I know, but I do. They were going to split up and then he got killed and that is one knotty bastard to unpick. You get your feelings in a tangle about who loved who and who didn't love whoever ... in the end you just hope he wasn't thinking about that when he went.

I get that he wasn't Mister Perfection. When I dream of him, it's not always superdad giving me that mile-long piggyback when we went to Anglesey. Or whispery dad who let me bite his thumb when Nurse Megadeath put stitches in my shin. Sometimes it's crazy drunk dad, who once came in so steaming that he pissed behind the telly. Or mood swing dad, who threw his dinner against the wall because ... well, we never really did figure out why that was. But he was my dad, end of. So my skin feels like it drops a size when New Man rings the doorbell. Mum's off like a startled rabbit, clip-clops down the stairs and then they are standing in the hall, while I hover in my doorway, bases covered. I swear I can *hear* them grinning at each other.

I'm called downstairs to say hello. New Man looks better than his pictures and sadly isn't muffin-topping the shit out of his shirt. I give him maximum sweet innocent game face, while thinking of some suitable cobra strike that will reduce him to foam-mouthed agony. New Man does the 'nice to meet you' bollocks and pulls a white paper bag out of his pocket and hands it over. I mean, he may as well have just passed me a card embossed with the words 'Welcome To Paedo Country'.

He tells me to open the bag and then both of them start guffawing like a pair of cats heaving furballs. It's full of black Jelly Babies. I mean, WT actual F? Apparently, mum explains, they are my favourites (first I've heard) and this came up in some long rambling conversation on their last date (like I give a shit) that had them in stitches (idiots).

"Now what do you say?" says mum.

What am I? A four-year-old? I haven't had Jelly Babies for years and now I'm being taught my Ps and Qs. But come on Caitlyn – rules, rules, rules.

"Thank you, so very much," I say.

New Man looks at me for a long while and gives this little smile, then says: "No worries, Caitlyn, you can stick them in the bin when I'm not looking."

I take the bag and say I'll put them in my room for later. When I get to the top of the stairs, I turn and see he's still watching, so I hold up the bag and give him my very best raised eyebrows. He laughs. It's only when I'm stood in the bathroom, ready to flush the bastards down the toilet, that I wonder how the hell he's done this. I mean, just how many Jelly Babies do you have to buy to make a bag of only black ones?

***

We do dinner. I hope New Man will mess up royally at some point – major spillage down his shirt, perhaps some inappropriate leering (the bad man looked at me all funny, your honour). But this tight-rope walker won't fall. And he's a witty prick, I'll give him that.

Mum's started clearing away the plates when he says: "Mind if I have a smoke in the garden?"

And mum says: "No problem, I'll bring the pudding out if you like."

"Caitlyn," he says, "You smoke?"

"Like a chimney," I say.

"Pipe or cigar?" he says.

It hits me then – he's game facing too. He is 100 per cent swan and no splashes. Buck up Caitlyn, the game is on.

Mum goes into the kitchen and he gets up: "Come on, keep me company."

"If I must," I say, because mum's out of earshot.

"You can stop me from stealing anything," he says. Got an answer for everything, this one.

We go sit on the low wall at the edge of the patio. The shadows are getting long and the garden looks super-jungly. New Man breathes in and breathes out, then pops a smoke ring with a little putt! It's funny and I can't help but smile.

"Both of you," he says: "such smiles."

There's a long silence. I keep thinking of things to say but don't. He looks like he's doing the same.

"This could be a nice garden," he says at last.

"It was," I say.

He nods then tries again: "What do you like best at school then? Arty stuff, science?"

"Both. Sciences a bit more," I say.

"Me too. Hey, here's a science joke for you. Two men walk into a bar, one orders a H20, the other says: I'll have a H20 too. The second man dies. Geddit? H2O2?"

He looks at me for a bit and then, bang, his game face goes, like its melting and being sandblasted at the same time.

"I'm sorry, so sorry. I didn't think," he says and takes this bitter little tug on his cigarette. "Jokes about death … man, what an idiot."

And there it is, the mess up I had hoped for. Only thing is, I'm not taking the hop onto the podium to collect my winner's medal. I'm not waving my bouquet at the cheering crowd. I'm not feeling the victory at all.

"It's okay," I say.

"Tell you what," he says. "How about I do some penance and cut this lawn."

He taps on the kitchen window and when mum leans over to open it he says he swore he saw a tiger in the undergrowth and is there a mower he can use ahead of nightfall, otherwise the crocodiles will start coming out of the pond.

They go into this painful to and fro about how she's not brought him round to do that and he's saying he doesn't mind and she's giving it the 'well if you insists'. Jesus! No wonder older people go deaf. It's so they can't hear how embarrassing they sound. I'm in full-on cringe mode, right until the moment it occurs to me that the mower they're flirting about, is the mower that's located in the garden shed.

I have to do a Usain Bolt after New Man, who is marching down to the shed. I make up some excuse about how the lock is broken. And how the lawn is a wildlife haven these days. And how I know for absolute, one hundred percent certain the lawnmower doesn't work anyway.

New Man looks at me. Then he looks at the shiny peach of a lock on the shed door (the bloody turncoat). Then at me again.

"Want to talk about it?" he asks.

Four months, two weeks, five days ago. One of those 'problem' days when mum had given up and was sitting in a pool of tissues, wearing yesterday's clothes. And though I wasn't exactly feeling all unicorns and rainbows myself, I thought I would be big-time generous daughter and do something useful like mowing down the forest out the back.

Neither of us had been to the shed, since he went. It just didn't occur. It was a dad domain. Inside, the place was dark and cool. Smelled of damp and oil and dust. I thought, at first, the thing in the far corner was an old door on its side, with a dirty great big spider squatting on the corner. I nearly ran. But if you look at something for long enough, really look, then you make out what it actually is. Your mind stops playing games and inventing things and it just appears.

It wasn't a door at all, but a big cardboard box with a purple bow stuck on the corner. And when I got closer I could see there was a picture of a bicycle on the box. My last birthday present, no doubt. Bought before he went away and hidden in the shed for when he came back. There it was, with the lawnmower and the weedkiller and the big box of tools that only he could pick up. There it was, making me feel bitter and sweet and hot and sour and double of everything.

I didn't touch it. I didn't drag it out into the garden. No, I closed up that shed and game faced my way through the rest of that day. But since then, every few days when I know that mum is parked in front of the telly (thinking that her daughter is majorly homeworking) I sneak down the stairs (mind the 7th and the 3rd) and go out the back and down the garden and into the shed (de-cobwebbed and spider-hunted) to look at it. And for a while I'm old-me, me-before, waiting for my dad to put it all together and wheel it out and say 'what you reckon then, Caketin?'

I know I can't blag my way out of this predicament. My swan's feet can't paddle fast enough. The black belt professor Empress of game face is defeated. But I don't care. I don't want to game face any more. I'm old-lady, mum-sized tired of it. Secrets can't be kept forever. You can't keep anything forever.

I say to New Man 'want to see?' and go up to the shed and open the door. Simple as that. We go in and look at the bike box together.

"Oh kiddo," New Man says.

There's damp stains on the box and a mouse has been nibbling at the corner and there's filthy cobwebs hanging from it. And I want to ride it. And I don't. And I want to leave it. And I don't.

"It was my birthday bike," I tell him. "But my dad didn't come back for my birthday so I've left it in the shed because it's like a bit of frozen time, and I don't care if that doesn't make sense, and mum's not been in here and I think she's forgotten about it or didn't know, and now I'm scared it'll start to rust and I don't want it to rust but it's my secret so fuck everyone else, okay?"

New Man is trying to look cool, but he's all a bit too bitey lip and scratchy earlobe to fool me. And then he says: "If you want, I could put it together. Or we can leave it and I won't say a thing. I promise. It's your choice."

***

After we carry the box out of the shed, he takes off his jacket and rolls up his shirt sleeve. There is an old, faded tattoo on his arm.

"It's a lion," he says.

"A pale blue lion?"

"It's been holding its breath for a long time, Caitlyn."

Gordon. That's New Man's real name.

We tread down a patch of grass together on the lawn and lay the box down. Gordon peels away the purple bow, carefully, as though pulling a flower from a stalk. He gives it to me and I stick it to my top. We open the box and begin laying out the pieces, side by side and then we read the instructions.

"This isn't going to be achieved without some swearing," Gordon says.

"Glad to fucking hear it," I say.

"How are you two getting along."

I'd forgotten about mum. She's coming down the garden holding a tray with the pudding on and then she sees the bits of bike laid out on the lawn. It's not like it is in the movies. She doesn't let go of the tray or drop to her knees or start wailing, or any of that crap. She just comes to us, puts the tray down so nothing spills and then stands by me and we lean into each other.

"So," says Gordon. "Shall we make a bike?"

It takes a while. Gordon is, frankly, shit with tools. We also discover he's got a super-tasty line in swearing and is the messiest grease monkey ever. He gets oil and dirt all over his hands. After a while he just shrugs and wipes it all on his oh so carefully ironed shirt.

The sun is nearly down by the time it's finished. There's clouds now and the evening's got that restless feel to it. I unlatch the back gate and start going slowly down the lane while mum and Gordon stand together watching. There's sun and rain all at once and as soon as the first drop hits me, I start pedaling fast, past the light-shade of the houses and on, grinning and crying and not caring, lifting my face to the rain, feeling each and every drop that clings to me.

Credit: A previous version of this story was published in Gem Street: Beyond the Axis, edited by Deborah Rise McMenamy (Labello Press, 2015)

GHOST CITY

TOMAS MARCANTONIO

My nightly routine hasn't changed in years. I chew out three cigarettes on the roof of my apartment and watch the rooftop silhouettes long enough to feel lonely. Then I venture into the streets.

The alleys are the city's veins, narrow, winding, endless, and the citizens are the red blood cells. They proceed in merry groups, arm in arm, unaware that I'm among them. I ride the neon currents in their wake, a mutated cell swimming for the heart when I should be spat onto the graffitied walls. They're oblivious, carrying oxygen like a chain gang, an army of united ants.

I pass beneath fluorescent signs and they paint my face different shades of sour, like a chameleon being tossed across an ever-evolving sky. Just don't ask to see my tongue, or you'll see it roll out into the gutters and get punctured by high heels.

Open windows spill smoke and music and meat sweats. Chefs smoke on their haunches like lily-pad frogs on kitchen doorsteps. They watch the parade pass, make sure the heart keeps pumping. They don't notice that I do a dozen circuits a night, empty of haemoglobin, just trying to keep my head above the crimson waves.

Tonight, for the first time, things are different. The backstreets are empty, soulless. I choose a wall to lean against and watch the city windows decorate the night sky. Square portals into other people's lives, glowing garish yellow, bone blue, or burnt orange. I wait in the shadows, trembling, hoping someone will descend and join me in this abandoned web.

I have nothing. Nothing but empty alleyways, carpeted in trampled flyers and wrinkled cigarette butts left to rot. What's a vein without its conveyor belt of platelets? What's a city without its procession of smiling ants? What's one soul alone without another?

A window creaks open two floors above, and a moustached man plants an elbow on the windowsill and glances down. I stare back; the first face I've seen all night. He nods, caresses his moustache, and retreats into his cosy hole. He returns moments later with a basket on a string, lowers it down to street level. I remove the corked bottle and glass, pour myself a splash of red wine. He says something in a language I don't understand, and we raise our glasses and drink.

The wine is supple, fruity. We drink quietly, listening to the ghostly emptiness of the city, until a portly woman appears at the man's shoulder. She barks something in the same strange language as her husband, then hauls the basket up and disappears into her kitchen, grumbling. When she returns and lowers the basket again, there are two unopened bottles to choose from. The three of us drink together.

"I'm alone," I tell them. They can't understand the words, but they know what I'm saying. "I've been alone for far too long."

The man nods seriously while the woman admonishes me like a disgruntled mother. She barks something into the night sky and then out of nowhere, begins to sing. I've never heard the song before, but it feels familiar somehow, as if from another life. Her husband joins in, his bass complementing her soprano, and gradually the windows encircling theirs begin to open. As other voices join the chorus, dozens of faces peer down at me, as if I am their shared muse.

Baskets are passed from window to window; wines, baguettes, meats, whiskies. The festival lasts for hours, and the ghost city awakens from the sky. I alone remain below, watching with a craned neck, wine dribbling down my chin, like a wanderer gawping at a sky of waltzing stars.

Soon the neon around me flickers and fades, and the sky bleeds chrome pastels from its black stomach. With salutes and waves, the faces gradually disappear and the windows extinguish one by one. At last it's just the man and me, his face flushed from drink. He waggles a finger and points at me, his moustache twitching with a smile. I know what he's saying.

You're not alone.

I ramble home in the breaking light of dawn. Tomorrow I won't roam the streets looking for proof that I belong. I'll return to my rooftop, baskets in hand and lungs bursting with oxygen, and I'll start the singing myself.

I WRITE YOUR NAME

TRACY FAHEY

The night before the bombs went off I sent you a text. *Valerie*, it said. *I don't think this is working anymore.* I calculated the time back home in England – only eleven o'clock, but you always went to bed early when I wasn't home. I looked at the text for a long time, then pressed the 'Send' button before I could change my mind. *Ping* went the phone; message sent, irrevocable.

And then I was a coward. I turned the phone off, and stuck it in my pocket. There was no point in leaving it on, I told myself. You wouldn't see it till the morning.

Valerie. I don't think this is working anymore.

No matter how I try, I can't forget those words.

***

I remember the first time I saw you. I was at Leonie's party in Camden; a party I didn't want to go to. I was standing in the kitchen rinsing glasses so I could feel I had some function there; sick of seeing the same old faces, listening to the same old conversations. And then I heard you; that gurgle of laughter, deep and amused. You stood, watching me.

'Cinderella,' you said. 'Good to meet you.'

I smile. 'It's Gina, actually.'

You extended a hand. I shook it, conscious of your blonde curly hair, your mischievous brown eyes. 'I'm Valerie.'

'Like the song,' I said stupidly.

'Like the song', you said, your voice solemn. But your eyes still smiled. And that was all it took.

***

I turn on my phone the next morning, but the signal is down. There's something wrong with the network. My phone shows two ticks; message sent and received, but I've turned on the privacy filter, so I can't see if you've read it. I frown, and crawl out of my tent for dawn yoga; a series of gentle stretches and breathing exercises. My lungs draw in air, hold it. I feel the pulsing heartbeat in my chest get steadier, slow down. We roll up our mats and go in for breakfast. In the main house the electricity has failed. It's happened before on the island. We shrug at each other – talking is gently discouraged in the morning – and eat our meal of thick white yoghurt with homemade fruit jam and muesli.

Later that day we have sunset meditation, but I can't concentrate. I'm still wondering if you've read the message. I check my phone a few times, and then I power it off to save the battery.

We have dinner by candlelight. We laugh and talk and tell each other that it's atmospheric. An adventure. At night, when we crawl into our tents, the electricity is still off.

***

There were dates that summer; a picnic on Primrose Hill, an exhibition in the Barbican, a late night trip to the V&A to hear an obscure DJ play electronic sounds that made the plaster casts of Roman ruins reverberate. Dates and endless talking. The feel of your lips under mine, soft and full. We played Amy Winehouse's 'Back to Black,' me putting 'Valerie' on repeat until you complained. We swapped coming out stories; yours light and comic, mine tragic and fraught. I told you about my family. You listened, one finger lightly tracing the line of blue veins on the inside of my wrist.

***

It's the dawn of another idyllic day. I'm hungry. I cut myself a wedge of the crusty brown bread, and shave a delicate mound of cheese slivers to go with it. It looks so pretty on the plate. I eat it under a tree that overlooks the rippling water. In the distance I can see a white boat making its way across the strait, frail as a feather in the blue absoluteness of the sea.

I don't know it at the time, but these are the last moments of my old life; the tang of the strong tea, the rough texture of the bread in my mouth, the warm, salt breeze riffling the tree overhead.

***

I remember a Sunday afternoon in your apartment. The air was heavy with heat. Slants of sunlight stretched like smooth honey across the wooden floor. We lay together on your old, sagging sofa. My feet rested on the orange crocheted cushion, my head buried in the cushion of your sweatered chest. I closed my eyes and inhaled the scent of your perfume; Parma violets and warm wool. Your voice murmured above me; stories of a night out with friends, anecdotes of drinking and talking. I didn't listen. All I could hear was the muffled wash of your heartbeat – *thud thud* – reverberating in my ear.

***

I'm in the hammock, my favourite place, when I hear the noise. A man's voice, strong and deep. A woman; hoarse, weeping. Then another man shouting. Angry? Afraid? I can't tell. I sit up and try to wriggle out of the canvas, pushing down on the hammock to get up. Surita, the yoga instructor, is running back from the beach with a fast, lithe lope. Something's going on.

'What is it?'

Surita's olive face is pale. 'Everywhere has lost power. On the mainland. There's no TV, no radio. No-one knows what's happened.'

'Everywhere?' My voice sounds small. Everything inside me has turned to liquid.

She looks at me steadily. 'That's what the fishermen said, Gina. We should prepare for the worst.'

***

'You might as well move in,' you said. It had barely been four months. I looked at you sharply. You looked back. You were calm, smiling, but I could see the swallow-flash of anxiety in your eyes.

'Move in here?' I just wanted to hear you say it again.

'Yes.' That grin. 'It's a lot nicer than your place.'

I threw a cushion at you. 'It is not nicer!' Your threw one back, we laughed and fought and kissed. And it was all tangled limbs and sunshine like honey and the glorious free-falling of adventure.

***

All day we wait. We wait and hope. There are no yoga classes – no-one even asks about them. All we can think of is home.

'It might just be Greece.' Katie the freckled Irish girl is resolute. 'Maybe it's a strike, or something to do with the national grid.' I don't say anything. I don't want to dampen her hope. But not even the tiny shower radio that Valerie gave me can pick up a signal. When I turn the dial it just hiccups out a series of blips and squeals.

This is something big. I look out over the view, the blue-misted mountains, the pale rise of the volcanic hills, stubbled with bushes. The sea is limpid; gentle ripples kissing the sand. In this sunlight, a disaster seems impossible. But my stomach is sick and heavy with dread. Under all this cover, this balmy sky, the glint of sun on waves, lies a nameless threat.

I feel my skin prickle with heat. It's surreal. I'm standing on a beach in Greece, but it feels like a long time ago. It feels like the grey days of the 1980s, the CND marches, the 'Ban Sellafield' posters. The childhood fear that someone, somewhere, would push a button and that everything would stop. I remember a book on Hiroshima that I read surreptitiously in the school library. My heartbeat bloomed wild in my ears as I turned the pages; accounts of eyes melting, limbs fusing, people atomised, their shadows seared onto walls.

The day crawls by. And still, nothing. We patch a new reality together from guesses, theories, rumours. And below me the waves wash – *thud thud* – like your heartbeat.

Valerie. I don't think it's working anymore. Did you ever see my text? That's the question that keeps me awake at night, listening to the suck and spill of the waves over rocks. Did you see us end before everything else did?

***

We got a cat. Yes, yes, I know, a cliché. A silver-and-white-striped Tom, large and imposing. We called him Signor Valentino, a tribute to his heavy-lidded stare and the many feline followers who cried outside his window. He was surly and magnificent and we loved him uncritically. *Mroew*, he would complain if we stayed out late, drawing himself up to his full height as we lurched in, giggling.

'Signor,' we would implore him. 'Forgive us.' And we'd stroke him till he melted back down into a supine mass.

Goddamn it. I loved that cat.

***

The Italian woman, Sophia, is the one who tells us that everything is over. A message has come through the fishermen in exchange for clothes she's bartered. Yes, there were bombs. All the major cities were targeted. Including London. When she tells me I feel soft ashes in my stomach, a great mushroom cloud of hopelessness billowing through me.

But I can't give up. There's a chance that you're still there, still looking for me. I need to talk to you. It's a savage, helpless feeling. I can't stop looking at my phone. The power display winks at me. 63%. I keep turning it off to try and preserve the battery – we still have no electricity – but I can't bear the thought of you trying to call and getting no response. So I compromise. I switch on, check all my apps for messages, press the button to power off.

By evening the battery has dwindled further. 46%. I put in in airplane mode and look at the photos instead. I time myself. Five minutes is all I can spare. I swipe my thumb back and forth; our life together in snapshots. Parties, glasses raised in salutation. A day in Brighton, candyfloss and grins. Glastonbury, my face patterned with mud. Signor Valentino resplendent on the sofa. I swallow hard. Hot tears swell my eyes. That damn cat. And you. You're everywhere. Smiling out at me. Our arms linked. Kissing.

I touch your face, cold on the screen. *Where are you now?*

The screen blinks. 40%. I turn the phone off.

The sun is setting now, but the sand is still powder-hot under my feet. I walk slowly towards the waves that pat gently up and down the shore. The beach here is harder, damper, more compact. I pick up a twig from the driftwood pile.

Valerie. I write your name in looping, ungainly letters, tall as myself. I draw a heart around it.

In the morning the sea has erased my writing. The sand lies smooth and blank under the sun.

***

The first rift grew on our anniversary. As luck would have it, we were invited to Leonie's again. I was excited at the coincidence, taking care to dress in the same outfit I wore the night we met. I stroked down the silky black fabric of my dress in front of the mirror. Yes. I looked good.

I waited till we got there, dragged you into the kitchen. I poured us both a glass of the red wine I'd brought, expensive and mellow.

'Happy anniversary.'

You looked at me, horrified realisation in your eyes. 'Jeez. God. I'm sorry. I thought it was ...' My face felt frozen. You couldn't even pretend you were thinking of another date. You'd just forgotten.

'No matter,' I said, putting the glass down. But for the rest of the evening I was carefully polite to you, moving away, talking to others in a high, light voice that pretended I was having fun.

***

I realise how much of my life has become digital; how much of it falls apart without electricity. I can't use my Visa card to pay, or to get money out. Because of that I'm stranded here in this little tent I brought with me. I have no money to bribe my way off this island in a boat. There's nothing to barter; I came on this holiday to get away from worldly possessions. I have a useless plane ticket and a passport for a country that may not exist. Apart from that, there's just my clothes and my Kindle which is clinically dead. And my phone. I don't dare turn it on for more than a minute a day. I have to trust that if you call it'll record your message.

All our physical objects are infinitely more valuable now. This paper I write on is now finite. I have two refill pads. After that I've run out, unless I can trade someone for more. My script is smaller now; I take care to fill whole lines. Everything I write must have meaning. I look at the blank cream page in front of me. I draw hearts. I write your name inside one. *Valerie.* I write it again, an incantation. *Valerie. Valerie.*

I trace the outline of the heart with my finger, over and over. Nothing happens. I sit under the soft, blue sky till it darkens to navy. The stars hang above me; a tracery of lights. It seems tragic, almost callous, that they still sparkle the same way.

I wish. I wish I'd been smart enough to take cash with me. Provisions. Books. Photographs.

I wish I'd been smart enough to take you with me.

***

After the anniversary that wasn't, I shrank away, withdrawing my investment, bit by bit. I complained to Leonie. She nodded and murmured in agreement.

'That's bad, alright.'

'I know. It was really important to me that she remembered.'

'Well, it's just this one thing, isn't it? Otherwise you guys are incredibly close.'

I hesitated. In the last three weeks sudden, blank silences had bloomed, replacing our comfortable pauses. We were out of sync; two cogs disconnected, striking sparks, grinding gears. I saw the anxiety in your face when you looked at me, but I pretended not to notice.

My silence told Leonie everything she wanted to know.

'Oh, I'm sorry.' Her eyes were sympathetic, but I knew she was secretly glad. No-one likes to see perfection. It upsets our sense of what's fair; makes us envious.

***

My phone is at 20% now. It won't last much longer. Every time I turn it on it falls another few percent. I've given up hoping for a call. There's no signal anyhow. It's the photographs I look at. The story of us.

I'm afraid I'll forget your face. I try and draw it from memory, but it's useless, a caricature of someone I don't know.

The arguments, the silences; I realise too late they all meant nothing. It was you. It's always been you.

And then I wake up one morning and the phone is dead. I still keep it under my pillow in the tent. A talisman.

***

Five months limp by. The silences are larger now, more strained. I start staying in work late to avoid your mute gaze. Your eyes have lost their sparkle. Even your curly hair seems flatter. When we go to the cinema, you place a hesitant arm on the back of my seat, hand touching my shoulder. I prickle with irritation. All through the movie I can't concentrate. Your arm around me is an intrusion.

When I see the yoga retreat advertised, it's my chance to escape.

'Greece?' you ask. 'I don't think I can get the time off work.'

I hesitate. 'I was thinking just for me. I've been feeling I'd like to spend some time alone. Sort some stuff out.'

'Oh,' you say, but there is a world of reproach in that one syllable.

***

Life is very small now. It is the island. We learn to fish, Surita, Fiona, Sophia and I, the last of the yoga students. It's not so bad that it's September. There are plums now, and melons; olives and tomatoes. We forage and cook. Sometimes I want to ask *should we eat food that's ripened in the aftermath?* But we have no other menu options, so I don't.

At night I lie in my tent, now dirty and a little ragged at the seams. Sophia slept in with me last night. She showed me photos of her daughter and murmured softly over them in Italian. Late at night she wept, but quietly. I spider-walked my fingers over to hers and held her hand. We lay there and cried together in this strange world after the world.

Somedays I swim in the sea. It seems indecent to enjoy it but I do. I cling to the rocks and feel the waves suck through them. The warmth cradles me, lulls me. For minutes at a time I can forget.

It's a rare thing, forgetting. My mind circles the same tracks, again and again. *Thud thud*, like the waves. Like your heartbeat in that apartment, so long ago now, so far away.

***

The last conversation we had was about Signor Valentino. 'Be careful to keep the window shut at night.' My voice is brusque. 'You know he's inclined to wander at the moment. I don't want to be worried about him while I'm gone.'

'I promise,' you say. Your eyes are sad and brown, like a seal's. You kiss me, but I break away, offer a stiff-armed hug. I know you're watching me as I walk away, but I don't look back.

***

I sit on the shore and pick a sharp-edge pebble. I write your name on a rock, with rough white scratches of stone on stone. *Valerie*. I think of your dark eyes, the infinite softness of your legs wrapped around mine, the feel of your curly hair, soft and springy under my hand.

I sit and look out at the sea, rippling and endless. The water hisses and pools around my feet. *Thud thud.*

I came here to forget you. But here, at the end of everything, you're all I want to remember.

Valerie.

I write your name.

"IF THIS IS HOW THE WORLD ENDS"

HANNAH PERSAUD

part of The Sourdough Diaries – #Lockdownday13

So is this how the world ends?

Not with the arrival of aliens in silver ships
scaled feet drumming metal crescendos through paper doors and tissue walls.

No final combat, jaws tearing at flesh, friend or foe; lone dogs scavenging a ravished landscape while skeletal trees point forks at the sky

No deathbed sunset watched from sunken terraces, glass in hand and wine turning rose in the glow of it while ripe vines wither in the forever dark that's coming

Nor one all too familiar explosion – movie special effects never quite capturing the scale of it, flesh to dust, the speed the sheer size the spread of radiation and horror of unexpected death in the last glimpse of vulnerable unmasked faces

Not even, as predicted, in the slow usurpation of the land until it cowers in embryonic pose, clacking of maggots echoing through its empty bones. Hollow.

We have been tricked.
Is this how it's to be?

voiceless brick echoes
postcards between pages
messages – lost

water dripping
milk curdling,
untested recipes

When days curl crisp from faded plans will regret exist?
for the misplaced X

for the lips not kissed at all (or kissed again)
 – for the decisions not (yet) taken

Can we draw a collective breath?

an inhalation of
sunrises un-met and oceans not yet swum in, of nights spun beneath star filled nets
of skin awaiting touch and secrets not yet coveted and a pledge that
if spared we will commit to

changing.

ISLANDS

ADRIAN J WALKER

I appear to be in a bit of a pickle. I'm stranded in my shed, of all places. Unbelievable. I mean I'm used to living remotely but this is ridiculous. 75 and stranded in my shed. And in nought but my nightie too.

It was dark when I came here. It must have been because I can see the kitchen light on in the house, and – well, I'm in my nightie. But now it's light. It feels early, six o'clock perhaps. Everything's packed with heavy mist and I'm sitting here on a deckchair trying to make sense of what's before me. What used to be my garden is now sea. The tide has cut me off from my house.

They've been having problems with it. The tide. It's all they were talking about on the mainland last time I was there – when was that? Three weeks ago. Four. Something like that, whenever Bettie last came to take me shopping. I wanted garibaldis but all they had were fig rolls, anyway, they've been having problems with it, this tide. The weather's been making it rise – no, not the weather. What's the word? Bigger than the weather … I have trouble with words sometimes but don't worry, I'll get it. They always come in the end. You've just got to have faith.

Anyway, this weather problem was all to do with fridges. You couldn't use fridges in the 1980s because they had chemicals in them – KFCs they were called – and they were doing something to the weather, or that other big thing that's not the weather. It'll come to me. Faith. Well, that was decades ago and nothing happened did it? And I certainly wasn't going to stop using my fridge. I don't care how many KFCs there are, for goodness' sake you can't keep milk in a cupboard.

The problem is that my house sits on a little hill, and my shed sits on another little hill at the back of the garden with brambles behind it, so the two buildings are separated by a kind of miniature valley, and it's this valley that's filled up with seawater. My house is the only house on my island, and living in Orkney, you get to know the tide. The rise and fall of it becomes second nature, something you feel rather than remember, so I will know what it's up to at any time of day. No need to check a chart or clock. I'll just know. But it's never done this. Although I grant you my geraniums have looked a bit boggy of late.

I don't even remember why I came out here in the first place. I think I was looking at photographs. There's one here of some school girls. It's old, black and white, faded. They look happy enough, but I don't … I don't know who they are.

It doesn't matter now anyway. I'm stuck. I'm stuck here in my nightie with an impenetrable bramble bush behind me and fifty feet of open water in front. And if that wasn't bad enough, my left leg's giving me gyp again. So yes. Bit of a pickle.

I've just realised something. I'm sitting on an island, off an island, off an island. My shed's off my house, my house is now off my island, and my island, Switha, is off the mainland of Orkney. And Orkney's off Scotland, and Scotland's off the UK, and the UK … it keeps going, doesn't it? Maybe forever. Continents, planets, suns, galaxies, all the rest. It just keeps going, and not just outwards, but inwards. We're all islands, and there are little islands inside of us, all floating about. Thoughts. Feelings. Memories …

If I could call James he could send for help, but I left my phone in the house. James bought it for me. It's one of these new ones that only lets you in if it recognises your face, but the problem with that is it doesn't always work. I have to stare at it, willing it to let me in, but it just says: 'No, Mildred. Whatever that is, it's not you.'

And I can't blame it. Half the time I don't even recognise myself these days.

What was I talking about? Oh yes, islands. I moved to Somanstray when Douglas died. James fussed – he always fusses – he said 'It's too remote, Mum, you'll be on your own.'

'Good!' I said. 'It'll give me some peace, bit of space.'

He wanted me to move back down to Manchester with him and his family. *Manchester.* I've not lived there since I was 26, when I moved up here to Orkney with Douglas. Why would I want to leave now? I've got everything I need, and I have absolutely no compulsion to be around other people.

We had a row about it. He said the reason I have absolutely no compulsion to be around other people is so my symptoms don't show. So I don't get 'caught out', as he calls it. He thinks I've got Alzheimer's. Well, what a lot of nonsense. So I forget things sometimes. I'm 76!

He said: 'We need to address it, Mum, get it seen to. If we do that then we can keep you living independently for as long as possible, and plan for a care home when the time comes.'

A care home. Which means he doesn't want to be the one who wipes my bum when I've completely lost it, and I suppose I can't blame him; he shouldn't have to wipe my bum. Though God knows I've wiped his plenty of times.

This bloody leg of mine – I can barely walk.

If I could get it moving I could wade across, to hell with my nightie, but then I don't know how deep it is. Two metres, maybe three. Definitely over my head. I could swim, but – and this is the stupidest thing – I can't remember if I can.

What time is it now, nine o'clock? Ten? I can't see the sun through all this infernal mist. The water's lapping at my front door, which for some reason I've left wide open. The kitchen light's gone off too, which I suppose means the electricity isn't working. Bugger it. I'll need to get that seen to, I suppose. The electricity. And my leg. And, yes, whatever this other thing is in my head as well.

My son's right, as he usually is. He's always been practical. Logical. Clear thinking. Even when he was a lad, I remember how he'd spend hours sorting his Lego bricks into colours, shapes, and sizes. His bedroom was never in a mess. Everything was always boxed away neatly so nothing was ever lost.

See? I remember all that. I might be 74 but I remember that clear as a bell.

I wonder if it's like that in his head? All boxed off and ordered and easy to access. I've never been like that. I'm no good at making plans or thinking ahead, I kind of just … drift. And I feel I'm drifting further away now.

Scotland's not an island, is it? I got that wrong.

Climate! That's the word. Got the bugger. See? It always comes in the end, you've just got to have faith.

I shouldn't have left it so long, not when the signs were so clear. It's ironic, really. I used to nag Douglas about stopping smoking, but when he finally did it was too late. I suppose we need to see the symptoms before we seek the cure.

Right. That's settled. As soon as I'm out of this pickle I'll go to the doctors. And I'll get this leg seen to. But first I have to get back to the house.

I can't wade, not with this leg. I can't call James, I can't get through the brambles, and the water's rising. What a mess. Why in the name of buggery was I out here in the first place?

That's right, these photographs. Who are these girls? This one seems familiar. Something in her smile, I'm sure I've seen that smile before. Is she … could it be me? I can't tell. She's holding a trophy. They've won something, that must be it, a sporting event, that's right, and they're all standing next to a –

Oh. I do believe that's a swimming pool.

It's going nowhere this tide. If anything it's rising, and this mist is getting heavier.

I get flashes sometimes, like sunlight on pages floating out to sea. Small faces, a warm garden, a house full of people. It's all there, I know it is. It's just drifting. If I could just catch one. If I could just remember that girl's face. My face. Just that *one thing*.

But I can't.

So bugger it. I'll give it a go. I suppose it's like the words; you've got to have faith. When you can't see ahead or behind you, that's all you've got.

ISO - FROM THE GREEK MEANING EQUAL - USUALLY USED AS A PREFIX, IE. ISOLATION, ISOBAR, ISOPOD

HANNAH STORM

Freya

Flynn is in school 'iso' and Freya is gutted. They've been boyfriend and girlfriend for two weeks and even though they have only hugged, she knows she's never met anyone like him. The other kids at school have already 'shipped' their names together. Like Kimye or Jelena, they are Freya + Flynn = Flya. She likes this. Imagines them taking flight together, escaping some of what makes life as a 14-year-old so eye-rollingly unfair. Her Mum told her how she used to scratch the initials of the boys she liked into her pencil case with a compass, but Freya just thinks that's weird. She has an app that can merge a baby photo of her with one of Flynn to see what their kids might look like. She'd die of embarrassment if he knew that though. Freya strokes her phone absent-mindedly, twists her hair and smiles into the screen, perfecting her pout before selecting the best filter. The teachers are punishing her too, not just the boy who will break her heart.

Jamie

Jamie has been tasked with planning a route that optimises the gradient and mileage for this Sunday's Strava cycle ride. He and his mates call themselves the MAMILs. Middle-aged men in Lycra. He's only 43, so objects slightly to the term middle-aged, though he knows he looks pretty good in the gear. Heather, one of the teaching assistants at school, told him so a few weeks ago after she'd seen him cycling past when she and her single friends were in the pub. Jamie hadn't noticed her before then, but he notices her every day now. Jamie flattens out the map, traces his fingers over the contours – imagines touching the contours of her. He recognises the symbols his father taught him, when he used to take him orienteering, to give his Mum some space. The isobars were always his favourite – the lines joining the same mean sea level air pressure. Jamie exhales and wonders where his father is now.

Helen

Helen dreams of being able to pee in peace. Or shower. Or finish a cup of tea. The kids have been yelling for her all day and Jamie is busy obsessing about his bike, so she locks herself away in the bathroom, hoping nobody will find her there. She pours herself a bath, tips in some of the bottle of bubbles the kids bought her for Christmas, or Mother's Day, or her birthday – it doesn't really matter as the gifts are always the same. The water rises over her body, dousing the scar from Ben's emergency delivery, the small mound of her stomach, the pale breasts that still just about defy gravity after two bouts of breastfeeding. She closes her eyes, sinks into the water, inhales the heady perfume with its tropical fragrance. She pictures the last time she saw D, how his tongue touched each inch of her body like the water now. She remembers how they'd found each other at the prow of the boat, on the excursion put on by the conference organisers to show them the highlights beyond the hotel. She remembers D pointing at a crest of land rising off the Amalfi coast, how he'd told her later that 'isola' was Italian for island. She sinks beneath the bath's surface and blocks her ears to the shouting from downstairs, wondering what might have happened if she'd said yes to D.

Matty

Matty is four. He can count up to 100, forwards and backwards. He knows every number of every tank engine in Thomas, and the diesels. He knows what the world's biggest smelliest plant is – the Titan Arum before you ask. He knows that the Dead Sea is deep enough to hide the Eiffel Tower. He doesn't know what the Eiffel Tower is, but he does know that he loves Spiderman and Batman and Paw Patrol, and the programme Go Jetters, where he laughs along with Ubercorn at his funky facts. Like Unicorns, Matty loves rainbows. He likes pink and purple and he doesn't like monsters or mushrooms, crocodiles or sharks. Today he wishes he was a woodlouse. He watches one creep across the tiles in the toilet downstairs, wondering how a woodlouse poos. Matty thinks about poo a lot; it might even be his favourite word. He knows a woodlouse is an isopod. He does not know what iso means, but pod sounds a bit like poo and he can spell both words.

KEBABS

RAHUL RAINA

Right, here's a recipe for chicken kebabs. It took me years to come up with the proper way to do this, here in Britain, sceptred isle etc, with the stupid convection ovens we have.

Why this though, you ask. Why a recipe? Why one so unusefully laid out, the modern way with half a life story attached?

Well, when someone says Hope and Isolation, I think chicken kebabs. Shoot me. I've got them on the brain. I'm North Indian. It's the way I am. And look, if I could get away with giving a list of items, I would, but that's antiseptic and well, we're all stuck at home, times are hard, lots of depression around, in all senses. We all want a little bit of comfort, and this here is my, Rahul Raina's, way of establishing some human connection with you, dear reader. Isn't that what the creative life is all about? I could give my whole life story, how I arrived in this country with nothing but a suitcase full of Aeroflot jam, but that story doesn't end with us eating something delicious, which is what I'd prefer.

To get back on track, I'd always been pissed off with those stupid recipes on BBC GoodFood. 180 degrees, chicken breast, cook for 40 minutes – wrong wrong wrong!

We get dry, stodgy, miserable, colourless results that way – there must be a better way, I thought. And there was. Nothing good was ever cooked at 180 degrees. No, I don't want to hear about the divine Jaipuri chicken you got off Pippa Middleton in Waitrose Magazine.

What better time to set the record straight than now, to bring some joy into your life, to reach out my hand and lay it in yours, palm to palm, pulse to pulse?

We will be cooking at 250. Crank the oven as far as it will go. We'll be in and out in 20 minutes. There'll be no checking and rechecking if it's cooked enough, no fretting about juices running clear, no meat thermometers, no arguments with your partner about food poisoning or the gendered division of labour, no slow motion divorce, no splitting up your Imogen Heap CDs.

500g of boneless chicken thighs. Thighs withstand overcooking. They have the fat content to remain juicy however much you mess up.

Thigh! Never use breast. Only 55 year old single men called Clive use breast. You are not. You are a person of the world. You know what dukkah is. You have a list of favourite Ottolenghi recipes. You know what's up.

That's two very generous portions. That's the Indian way. You fill your guests until they can't walk. Anyway, if you're going to be socially distant queueing for 20 minutes and then watching grown men wrestle over onions, don't you want as much food, as much delight, as possible? Have half if you're single, like me, and freeze the rest for better days.

Cut your chicken into two inch cubes and chuck them into a bowl with a fist of yoghurt. I used to give measures in cups and grams, but that's useless. Just chuck a fist in, two fists if you're small. Natural yogurt, Greek if you want. None of that low fat stuff, obviously. Let's not even mention it.

Now onto the spices. You really can't go wrong here, as long as they're not too old, and even then everything will work out just fine.

A teaspoon of salt, a quarter teaspoon each of pepper and cinnamon, a tablespoon of lemon. Use bottled if you have to, I don't care.

The same for ginger and garlic. If you have it in bottles, like every Indian housewife I know, use that. Otherwise, a minced tablespoon of each.

Then a quarter teaspoon of cardamom powder – get whole cardamom and blitz the seeds only. You see some people blitz the whole thing – no! You get shards of shell, which is good for nothing. The seeds have the flavour.

How wonderful this is, my years of experience and wisdom, of worry and want, condensed into two little pages.

One teaspoon of garam masala, a half teaspoon of cumin powder, and half again of fenugreek leaves. Fenugreek – that's what separates fake recipes from real ones. Any place that leaves it out isn't authentic, although I've never really cared for that word. My favourite food as a kid was Campbell's chicken meatballs with tomato sauce. I can't talk.

Two teaspoons of chilli powder. Two! Put less if you want, although you want your mouth to sing afterwards. Have some extra yoghurt on the side.

Now you can mix in liquid smoke. I've heard good things about it, and we only want a quarter teaspoon, just to mimic the 400 degree heat of a proper tandoor. I've never used it. The recipe's fine as it is, really. I don't believe much in chemicals. Apart from serotonin. Isn't love just a chem-

I am so sorry. That won't happen again.

Food colouring – I'm agnostic. It gets overused by crap restaurants. Do we really want red chicken? Do what you want. Free and easy.

If you use wooden skewers, I will find you.

Metal. The heat conducts through to cook from the inside, they don't start burning after five minutes, they don't bend and snap in half. It's environmentally friendly. Denizens of Hotwells and Kemptown and Leyton, I am one of you in spirit.

Stick the chicken on the skewers. It should go on nice and easy. We made sure the pieces were large enough. Keep the excess marinade to hand.

Balance the skewers over a tray, so that the air can get at the meat. Air flow, that's the secret to life, and coincidentally, this recipe.

Into the oven, then. Enough preamble. After 10 minutes, take it out. Rotate the tray, and turn over the skewers.

Now we use the rest of the marinade. Mix in a few spoons of oil, or ghee. Ghee is best, but then I'll hear complaints about fancy ingredients and household costs and god knows what else. Just use oil then. Mix it with the marinade, and spoon it over the chicken.

Here come further complaints! Salmonella! Contamination! Dirt! Disease!

I've heard it all before.

Look, 10 minutes at 250 and the bacteria'll be nothing but a memory. But if you insist, then just use oil – actually no, if you skip the marinade, you have to use ghee, and then only organic – no, ayurvedic, made from sacramental cows, from Varanasi – the most expensive you can find.

Now put the whole thing back in the oven for 10 minutes.

Take it out and look at what we've accomplished! Stare at it. Take some pictures, make sure to put the filter on vivid, and share away. We've done it together, you and I.

Those crispy edges, just a shade under burnt. The juicy flesh, that you'll inhale in about five seconds, tucked between whichever bread you fancy, whether culturally appropriate or not. Chuck in some chopped onion, steeped in lemon juice, maybe some chilli sauce or a big handful of chopped coriander.

After most stories you get feelings, odd unhelpful ones at a time like this, wistfulness or ennui. After this one you get chicken.

Anyway, this has all been a little harmless fun. You have your chicken kebabs, hopefully. I have a sense of wellbeing that another crime against food has been ironed out.

This was a recipe. I wasn't making some point about multiculturalism or immigration, or that Britain's become an island of voices. It's just been a recipe. I want us to get that straight.

That's all for now. Good luck!

KEEP IT UP KID

DANIEL SOULE

No matter how much he might not want to, Jody was going to wake up today. His ex-wife was ringing the doorbell, impatiently slapping him into consciousness, along with a moderate hangover. A bottle of beer didn't help. Sitting where his alarm clock should have been, the bottle took a dive when Jody swiped for the off button, spilling dregs over the bedside table. Much swearing and fumbling followed until the doorbell cut through the minor chaos. There was further swearing with Jody's realization of what time and, more importantly, what day it was.

Every box he'd put off unpacking for the last six months now seemed ideally placed to block the path of least resistance. His dressing gown wouldn't come off its hook, catapulting Jody back in to the bedroom. All the while the doorbell rang longer and louder and more impatiently for Jody to get his act together.

He took the last four stairs all at once. The impact on landing reminded him that even a four-step leap presents the knees of a thirty-two-year-old, without a warm-up, a lesson in aging.

When Jody finally flung open the door, Sally's hand was poised for another jab at the bell. Like a boxer coiled for one last combination, her finger punched the little white button, so that the unnecessary extra ring occupied that grey area between over the top but understandable. Jody winced, partly because his dishevelled head was now next to the buzzer and partly because Sally was his regular sparring partner, and he knew to 'protect himself at all times.'

"You forgot." Technically this was a statement of fact but it carried the weight of an accusation as well.

"No, I'd hadn't. I just slept in," said Jody, countering quickly with. "I've been looking forward to it all week."

Sally peered over Jody's shoulder, who shifted to block her view. "You've still not unpacked?"

Jody thought fast. "I'd planned for us to do a bit of it together. You know, some father and son bonding time?"

"What fourteen-year-old boy wouldn't enjoy unpacking his dad's things? Come on, Jody!" Typically, this was a trigger. Sally's exasperation usually had a comparable effect of adding petrol to smouldering embers in their squabbles, but the subtlety of Jody's hangover was at work.

"Yeah, I know, Sal. We'll do something together. I promise." He was sincere, not in the mood for an argument and off script, and it put them out of sync. They'd been out of sync for years, so maybe something else was at work. This was when Jody was supposed to raise his tone defensively, with a "there you go again" or a "leave me alone, Sal", which fell out of use the last time he said it when she called his bluff and agreed to leave him alone indefinitely.

That was twelve months ago. Jody moved out six months after that, once he found a place and the divorce papers came through. Sally wanted him to fight but he didn't. He never did anymore, and so he signed the papers, and rented a two-bed dormer bungalow on the edge of town. That's where he stayed but to say he lived there was a bit of a stretch. As yet, he'd only unpacked a few essentials. The rest stayed in boxes he opened as and when.

Sally beckoned Tom from the car, who had his head buried in a phone. His mum's enthusiastic flapping caught his peripheral vision and he looked up, sighing at the pretence – as if he couldn't hear them, as if he couldn't read his mum's body language at the door while she pressed the bell over and over. He sloped from the car and shuffled passed his dad without a word, into his every-other-weekend-and-Wednesday-night-home.

"Nice to see you too," Jody called.

"Take it easy on him. He needs his dad," Sally said.

"What's that supposed to mean?"

She was tired. "Nothing, Jody. Just …'

"What?"

"You remember what it was like being his age?"

He could have cried then, if that was something he did anymore; instead he nodded and looked back to the living-room, where Tom had shuffled off to plug himself in and tune out. "Yeah," he agreed, but she was already gone, getting into the car and driving away before she cried.

***

"Right then, what shall we do today?" said Jody, rubbing his hands together. Sat cross legged in front of the TV, Tom shrugged and blew the head off a zombie with a twelve-gauge shotgun and quickly took cover behind a burnt-out Chevy.

"You want to get some breakfast?"

Tom threw a grenade from his crouched position and took out a small pack of the undead. "Already eaten," he said making a beeline for a fire escape, dispatching another corpse on his way with some deft machete work to its cranium. "It's nine-thirty."

"Right," agreed Jody, "of course. I'll ... just grab a shower then." Tom shrugged and panned the area for targets. Jody retreated.

Because he needed it often enough, paracetamol was at the top of the box. Jody threw three into his mouth, took a swig from the tap and looked in the mirror. A shave was the last on a long and important list of things Jody needed to do, but it was a place to start, along with a shower and all the other necessary ablutions. Getting out of the bathtub, half tangled in the shower curtain, he nearly broke his neck on the box marked 'bathroom'. Unpacking was somewhere on that list too. The last of his clean t-shirts and underwear were buried at the bottom of a duffle bag and needed a sniff to be distinguished from the used garments with which they shared their home.

Pulling back the curtains, he strained at the light that flooded in from a Nottinghamshire Spring morning. Jody picked up the plastic bag he got from the carry-out after the pub last night and filled it with the empty bottles of beer littering the bedroom.

Downstairs, Jody switched to a white bin bag, the carrier bag now full. He gave the kitchen a quick decluttering of empties before doing the same in the living room. Tom didn't look up while his dad cleaned. He'd switched games on the console and was now running down pedestrians on a Los Angeles boulevard with a Shelby Mustang GT. Screams of terror followed Jody to the recycling bin outside.

The contents of a blue, council supplied, wheelie bin full of empty alcohol receptacles gave Jody a powerful flash of his father. He buried it quickly, because as much as it was a memory, it felt like déjà vu, and something else as well, something scab-like that needed to be picked to heal, but it would hurt so it was better left to fester.

Angelenos were still under the terror of Tom and his Mustang when Jody returned to the living room. Tom was fourteen now and by all accounts a wonderful mono-syllabic mass-murdering, post-apocalyptic hero, but Jody still saw his boy, the one he used to play football with.

"What?" grunted Tom, becoming aware of his dad looking at him.

"Nothing, I was just thinking how much you've grown."

"Well, can you stop looking at me?"

"How about we do something today? Whatever you want," said Jody.

His dad was clearly putting Tom off his game as a young couple, hand in hand, ran for their lives, escaping the wrath of the Mustang. "I'm busy," sighed Tom.

"Yeah, okay. Maybe later then? We could get some lunch?" There was no reply, which was not exactly a no. Running out of things to say, Jody decided to take this non-response as a positive sign and looked around to kill some time until mid-day. Nothing appealing showed itself, only what was left of his life, less than neatly packed in box after taped up box.

A thud at the window drew Jody's attention. A starling shook itself and flew off. Jody moved a box to open the window. He breathed in the familiar air of the small minster town he'd lived in his whole life. There was a promise of sun and an earthy breeze, as if the air had scrubbed itself clean, as if that were possible. It caressed his face with memories: secret alley-ways and cut-throughs; baggy blazers and floppy hair; Sunday morning football that he always got to by himself; frosty walks to school with a beautiful girl with a beautiful smile.

The box he'd moved caught his eye. It was much older than the rest. The cardboard was wrinkled and it was held together with many reapplications of brown tape, crisscrossing its corners and seams. And on its side, it read 'Jody – bedroom.' This wasn't a box he'd packed when moving out of the family home; however, he knew it immediately. It was a box he'd not opened for more than fourteen years, not since leaving his parents' home at eighteen and moving in with Sally a month before she gave birth to Tom. It was the box of things from his childhood bedroom. He'd put it away never to open it again, because there was nothing in there he needed anymore. Sally got pregnant at the start of upper-sixth and they missed doing their A-levels and going to university. Jody was going to study Engineering and Sally would read Law. Instead, Jody got a job at a mechanics over in Newark and started to earn some money. He abruptly became a man and so put away his childish things. Sally finished her A-levels at night school when Tom started at the comprehensive, and was a year into a part-time Law degree with Nottingham Trent University. Jody now ran the garage.

Held on by habit rather than anything adhesive, the old brown tape peeled away easily. Jody inserted his thumbs into the gap between the flaps to fold them back. There were a few things worth noting. The picture of him and Sally draped over each other, only fifteen, all floppy hair and baggy jumpers. She had her trademarked smile, big and pretty. Sally was still the same, though Jody thought it was a long while since he saw her smile like that. He felt a pang of guilt and buried it again; he fancied a beer. Jody had his serious, moody face on, which was his trademark for all photos of this period. He smiled at his younger self and rummaged on, forgetting about the beer. There was also a couple of tatty books: Terry Pratchett's The Colour of Magic and Nick Hornby's Fever Pitch. His sixth form school diary, and under that … something rough but pliable. Jody got a good grip on the thing and firmly jiggled it free, pulling it up from the bottom of the box to hold it talisman like in both hands, to see it anew in the Spring light.

It was the ball, his ball. Deflated and old and worn but most definitely his football. He felt a sudden urge and thought about where he would have put the other thing he now needed. The rumple of a ball in his hand Jody strode down the living room passed Tom.

"Found my ball," he beamed. Tom rolled his eyes and put an inter-galactic, dystopian, first-person shoot 'em up into the X-Box.

At the back of the garage were all the boxes of tools and gardening equipment. Jody tore each open until he found it. How many times had he done this before? Thousands probably but not for a few years, not since Tom stopped showing an interest in playing football, or was it Jody who'd stopped? Stopped taking him to practice, or driving him to the Sunday game, preferring to drop into the pub after work or to go for a not-so-swift drink on a Sunday lunchtime. Anyway, some things you never forget. The perfect pressure of a football is one of them.

And miraculously there it was, faded and a little broken up from the cracking of the ball's synthetic-leather, the words that had borne him through most of his teenage years, until the girl with the big smile took over its job of being the most important thing in his life.

***

In one of his random acts of self-serving generosity, eleven-year-old Jody's dad acquired two tickets to Nottingham Forest's final home game of the season. Truthfully, he won them in a card game at a lock-in and their looser was glad to get rid of them. Forest had had a terrible season and if they didn't win they'd be relegated.

The first warning sign was getting the bus early into the city. This meant a convoluted walk from the city centre and, conveniently, watering at five hostelries on the way. Meaning that despite leaving plenty of time, they still only just made it to the ground. The Trent End stand were already leading the chants, calling in the stragglers. Jody and his dad rushed through the car park of the Main Stand, around the back of the Trent End, skirting the river, and to the side of the Executive Stand, where Jody's dad gave his characteristic brand of well-meant but unsettling safety advice.

"If we get separated I'll meet you at the edge of the car park around by the Main Stand, where we walked passed." Jody nodded in acknowledgment, worried about how likely it was that they'd get separated.

They climbed the wide concrete stairs with red railings, that rose in right angled turns. Jody's dad sent him up to the seats on his own, while his dad got some refreshments and relieved himself of the fluid he'd taken on during the walk to the ground. Jody knew what that meant. Dad already had five pints on the way there. Drink wasn't allowed in the ground but a flask of whisky was easily secreted about the person, or a thermos of coffee could be spiked. Jody's dad preferred the former and appeared twenty minutes later with a lukewarm hot chocolate for Jody and a muzzy glow for himself. He was slurring now, swearing freely at the game and questioning the parentage of the referee.

The game went badly but had a surreal air. Forest's manager, Cloughie, in his iconic green sweatshirt, ruddy faced, put his thumb up to the Sheffield United fans when they chanted his name. Both sets of fans cheered at this, although Jody heard a few around him mutter things like: "He's an embarrassment," or, "They're taking the piss, you old fool." Someone even said, "Sober up," and Jody thought they meant his dad, who'd disappeared again with only ten minutes of the game left.

They lost two-nil and Cloughie did a lap of honour, his team, one-time league champions and two times European Cup winners, just relegated. Jody had only half watched the game. The other half of him kept looking for his dad, scanning across the thousands of people in the stand, double checking every entrance. Twenty minutes after the final whistle he was the only one left seated, and he started to cry quietly.

An attendant looked up from the exit down at the bottom of the upper tier. Before the man could climb the stairs, Jody left by the other side, wiping his eyes.

In the belly of the stand clumps of people still hung around, mostly men, a few holding their child's hand. Jody fidgeted looking for his dad. He checked the toilets and worry turned into panic. He cleared the tears as soon as they formed. 'The meeting point,' he thought and pinned his hopes on his dad's advice. How could he have been so silly? His dad was sure to be there.

Jody hurried; dad would be waiting for him. Jumping two steps at a time he sprang down the wide concrete stairs, taking the last four in one go, bouncing off into a run. It didn't take long to round the side of the Trent End and zig-zag against the flow of despondent fans. The carpark was mostly empty and Jody could see people milling about the main entrance. He headed straight for them but when he got there, none of them were his dad.

Panic filled Jody's chest, the kind of panic from a dream in which the dreamer is walking along a clifftop path until they lose their footing. The dreamer feels the certainty of death as their hands find no grip, their feet find no footing. They begin to freefall and their stomach lurches searching for hope and finding nothing. Knowing the end is inevitable they wake. Only, Jody was already awake and there was no escape from the panic. 'Where is he? Where is he?' he thought.

The group of people behind Jody moved off isolating the eleven-year-old, who frantically scanned the occupants of the last few cars. There was no one left and Jody instinctively, slowly backed away retreating from the big, terrifying, lonely world, falling, until finally he bumped into something. It had the solidity of a wall, or maybe a mountain, or maybe this is just how a grown-up remembers a child's memory, but the mountain spoke.

"Aw' right, kid?" said the mountain with a London accent. Jody turned to look up at the mountain, who had dirty blonde hair in a side parting and looked exactly like Nottingham Forest's team captain, England left back and the man with the coolest nickname in the whole world, "Psycho."

"Stuart Pearce?" said Jody.

It was as if the universe had plonked a demi-god down right in front of Jody exactly when he needed one. Proving that it, the universe, can be both subtle and blatant at the same time, or rather at different times, but with the same act.

"That's right. You okay?" asked Stuart, seeing the boy's tears. "You lost ya' dad?" Jody nodded. Stuart looked around. "We'll wait here for him then, shall we?" Jody nodded again, the panic lifting. "You don't say much, do ya', kid?" Jody shook his head. Stuart laughed and looked around with a ball tucked under his arm.

"Is that the match ball?" asked Jody. With Stuart around he felt braver, and being braver he felt bolder too.

Stuart looked down at it. "Yeah," he said.

"But we lost. I thought you're only supposed to keep it when you win."

"Not me," said Stuart.

"Why?"

The mountain looked down at the little boy who looked back for answers, so Stuart crouched on his haunches to come down to the boy's level, holding the ball in front of them. "I kept it to remind me. You understand?" Jody shook his head again. "It's easy to play when you're winning. It's easy to feel on top of the world when everything's going well. But the real trick is to keep going when you're at the bottom, when everything's gone wrong, when they're not cheering for you anymore, when you start to doubt yourself. So, I kept this to remind me that I don't like losing, that when things are at their worst you keep goin', you keep kickin' the ball, you keep playin' the game, and whatever happens you keep it up because that's the only way back." Stuart tossed the ball in the air and caught it again in demonstration.

There was a silence between them. Jody felt goose bumps on his arms and thought at that moment he could probably do anything.

"There you are," slurred Jody's dad from behind him. "Where the fuck have you been?"

"Don't swear at the kid. He's been looking for you," Stuart said, standing up.

"Don't tell me what to … Fuck me, you're Stuart Pearce," Jody's dad squinted theatrically and then broke into a chant, rhythmically pointing at Stuart with each word, "Psycho, Psycho, Psycho," and then grinned. "God, you lot were crap today. Crap all season really."

"Dad!"

"What? It's true. We lost didn't we and got relegated?" Jody's dad swayed.

"You've got a good kid here," said Stuart, and Jody's dad puffed up with pride and booze.

"Here Stuart, sign something for the boy, won't you?" Patting himself down, Jody's dad searched for either a pen or something worth signing. He had neither.

Jody blushed and tried to not look at his dad.

Stuart took in the man and then the boy. "Good idea. I've got something." Stuart handed Jody the match ball to hold and then crouched down again, unshouldering his kit bag and to fish around inside a pocket. He pulled out a thick, black permanent marker and took the ball from Jody, cradling it in the crook of his right arm while he wrote on it. When he was done, he put the marker back, stood up, shouldered his bag and gave the ball back to Jody.

Jody stared at Stuart, who smiled, ruffled the boy's hair and said, "Remember, keep it up, kid," and off he walked.

"That woz nice," sniffed Jody's dad. "Let's find a pub."

***

For years after this the ball was his saviour. Whenever his mum and dad fought, which was often, Jody would play a simple game. He took the ball at its word and he practiced keeping it up. If it was nice outside he'd play in the back garden; if it was wet he got good enough to stand in his room on one spot, keeping up the ball. He could occupy himself for an hour or more, by which time his mum and dad had usually burnt out, or more likely his dad had slammed the door and gone off to the pub.

Jody found if he could focus on one thing, and control it, he could block out everything else. This had some useful side effects. It became his party trick, and his friends would try and distract him in the playground, but he was unshakeable. One day, while on playground duty, the Head of PE, Mr Robinson, watched Jody perform his trick all break time. Jody was recruited to the school team, and then for the team in the year above, becoming something of a school mascot. All the while he put in the hours with his ball, losing himself in just keeping it up.

At fourteen Jody's parents, had reached an unhappy compromise because the alternative was the nuclear option. Instead, his mum tolerated the new silence, and began playing bridge two nights a week. His dad was bodily present. Drinking was now permitted, if not in the house, then in the garden or garage, and as such dad was pretty much insensible in front of the TV by seven pm.

As summer approached, Jody's team won the school cup. He scored one and assisted with another two and was named 'man of the match'. His mum and dad didn't come to see it. It was bridge night and his dad had his usual prior commitment. Instead, a girl with a beautiful smile, standing with a gaggle of friends cheered and clapped at the side of the pitch. Jackie, one of the cheering girls, came up to a muddy Jody after the game and said her friend Sally fancied him and would he go out with her. He knew which one Sally was and said yes.

There wasn't such a need to keep the ball up after that. If an argument broke out or the silence went on for too long, he would go around to Sally's.

A little worn but with the writing still clear, the ball was put on his shelf, among the books and Brit-pop CDs. There it stayed, slowly deflating until it naturally became the convenient size for shoving at the bottom of a box of things a boy thought he didn't need anymore because he was about to become a dad.

***

Standing in the garage, Jody looked down at the football in his hands. Time and use had cracked its polyurethane coating, but the words were still legible more than twenty years on: "Keep it up kid," along with the looping squiggle of Stuart Pearce's autograph.

Jody had an idea.

Genetic mutants can be rather tricky, unless you have a plasma rifle with over-under rocket and grenade launcher. Luckily, Tom did. He also had remote detonating incisor mines, the flesh-ripping-bone-splitting kind. Jody was about to speak when Tom raised a 'wait a second' finger, silencing his dad, mouth half open, ball in hand. The carnage was balletic. The plasma rifle set down a supressing fire, slowing the charging mutant horde. Tom lobbed grenades to the left, right and rear, bunching together the ugly fatherless sons of a mutant Martian hound. And then for the perfectly timed finale: a symphony of explosions. Flesh and bone were torn asunder, limbs flew hither and thither from the incisor mines, and in a deft percussion of keys, a crescendo of rockets launched into the melee. Only a single mutant, badly injured but still a threat, survived. It was dispatched with whimsy: a single, nonchalant plasma-round to the head.

Tom had already dropped the controller before the 'End of Level' animation began. Jody raised his eyebrows impressed by the carnage and gathered his thoughts.

"Football. Do you want a kick about?"

"Ugh! I'm not ten anymore, Dad."

Jody's heart sank. "I just thought we …"

Tom picked up the controller again and tracked through his inventory of weapons.

"Right then, shall I go and get us some lunch?"

Tom didn't answer because silence is important when sneaking up on a heavily armed interstellar freighter guard to insert a serrated battle knife between his third and fourth ribs. It prevents the screams.

Jody found himself in the Crown, with a pint and his ball propped up on top of his shopping bags, facing him from the seat opposite. His dad preferred the Saracen's Head across the road. "If it was good enough for a king," he'd say. Jody raised his glass to the ball and put it to his lips, looking over the road to the Saracen's. He took a swig, thinking: 'The king then got his head cut off, though didn't he?' He swallowed. The end of his hangover throbbed in response, and the ball stared back at him with the same advice it had been trying to give him for the last twenty years.

"What the fuck am I doing?"

"What was that?" said John, the landlord, from behind the bar preparing for the lunchtime rush.

Jody didn't respond. He left his beer, picked up his carrier bags and tucked the ball under his arm.

"What about your pint?" John called, but Jody was already hurrying across the road back through town as quickly as he could.

When Jody hurried into the living room, reinvigorated with a clear purpose, Tom was trying to pretend he hadn't been looking at his dad's things. The picture of Jody and Sally as teenagers was next to the box and not where Jody had left it. Jody picked it up.

"It's a nice picture of mum. Not sure about my hair though." Tom nodded from where he sat cracking open a case to another game. "I've got us lunch. Fancy that kick about in the garden after?" Tom shrugged. Jody thought about how they used to play all evening, when Tom was seven or eight, dribbling and shooting against each other, both with their own heroic commentaries. There was a long silence. Jody thought he'd let the idea hang. There was no need to force the issue. That never worked with Sally either. "I'll make us lunch," he said, putting the ball down next to the TV.

Smoky bacon crisps, a can of Coke and a cheese and ham baguette was Jody's offering. All Tom's favourites, or at least he thought they were. When he brought their plates into the living room he said nothing about Tom resting his controller and hands on the ball in his lap. Jody put the plate next to his boy and sat in the second-hand armchair. They ate in silence.

Jody got up, asking, "What's the game?"

"Ori and the Blind Forest."

'Forest,' thought Jody, glancing at his ball, but he didn't say anything, he just got into that long and important list of things he needed to do. Pulling out his penknife, Jody opened all the boxes in the living room and began putting things away.

The afternoon drew on and most of the living room boxes were done. Jody got them another Coke and a snack. Tom even said, "Thanks." Not loudly or anything, but "Thanks".

Jody folded back the flaps of a box of books. With his back to Tom, he knelt and put them into a small bookcase.

It was a start. However small, he was beginning to make a dent in that list. All he had to do was keep it up.

Only one box remained in the living room, the one from his teenage bedroom. Jody placed it by the bookcase and put The Colour of Magic and Fever Pitch on a shelf. He picked up the picture of him and Sally, tracing his fingers over the girl with the big, beautiful smile. It felt like there was no way back to the girl in the picture.

Set in motion twenty years ago, a football rolled across the sitting room floor. It hit Jody's heels with a subtle tap. He turned with the old photograph in his hand. Tom had switched off the games console and was standing, ready to take advantage of the last of the day's sunlight.

LIVING PROOF

ROGER MCKNIGHT

"Why heavens, I had to prove I was me," Louisa Jackson complained to Tom and Janet. "All the way back to Lebanon P-A. That's where I was born, in Dutch country, and that's where they had to send for my birth certificate." As her son and daughter-in-law shivered with folded arms on the sofa opposite her, Louisa sat in a reclining easy chair and reminisced in comfort about the old days over the steady whirr of her window AC unit.

Janet had just come from grocery shopping for Louisa, and Tom followed along to fix his mother's air vents, where the squirrels kept trying to get in and sometimes succeeded. As it turned out, Louisa had forgotten about the marauding varmints today. And so, only partly listening to her tale of missing courthouse records, Tom stared at rows of knickknacks and family photos in the living room. Next he saw a porcelain rooster on her kitchen table. On the refrigerator door were snapshots of his older sister Jean on a beach in California, and decorating the book case's top shelf was his and Janet's wedding picture, taken when they were only 20. The bottom shelf was empty, save for a white envelope tattered and dirty around its edges but imposingly large. As Tom puzzled over what was in it, he saw Janet rubbing the goose bumps on her arms and straining to hear, though he knew his wife's patience would soon wear thin.

"That's how folks said it," Louisa continued, "*P* and *A* for Pennsylvania. Why, them old Dutch was really somethin' and that was God's country, all right."

"What was so great about it?" Janet asked with a sharp tongue.

Tom saw in the tiny twitch of his mother's chin how she made herself ignore Janet's question. *Dutch* was a synonym for Heaven in Louisa's lingo and she loved the cavalcade of small events from her folks' past, so she gazed across the room with a forced twinkle in her eyes, straining to see through her cataract-blurred vision. "Leb'non in PA had the gentlest rolling hills. They were dotted with farms, and the fields grew green with oats and yellow from mustard plants every spring. It reminded Mom of the place her own folks grew up in, back in the Old Country. They raised barley and had horses and *Hahn*s both places, here and Over There. That's what my porcelain rooster is, *ein Hahn*. It's a Dutch … whadda ya call it?"

"Heirloom," Tom said.

"I guess," Louisa agreed in hesitation, seeming to ponder his word. "It came from the Old World, but it ain't anything but what I kept my margarin in. It reminds me of my folks and how their life was before they had me and your Uncle Ed and later when we was just little squirts."

She paused when the AC started rattling by the far wall. Tom looked that way again. While studying the sound, he realized Louisa had moved all but her recent family photos from the prominent shelves around the room. There were lots of the modern pictures, all in color, but he was used to seeing dozens of weathered snapshots of their older kin, now long since dead. Like Biblical patriarchs, the men in those ancient pics wore beards and posed with their horses beside a barn or silo, leaving no doubt about their most prized possessions. The ladies smiled out from under a venerable shade tree or sat together around picnic blankets. Louisa could call out all their names. "There's Aunt Elsie and great gran'ma Jackson, she was ninety-five if a day and there's Mildred with her boys, even Angus that came back from the Great War with a limp," she liked to recite about her fondest photos.

Those pictures commemorated a gilded age when mass communications were slower and people's lives less complicated, or so Tom reasoned. To him the staid quality of past eras' photography politely recorded the joys of the moment, but little of coy innuendo, unanswered desire, or sorrow and death. If the pictures did awaken those feelings, his relatives must've talked about them in a tongue he never learned or, to be honest, had never even thought about as a youth.

"By the way," Tom asked his mother to turn her attention from the rattling AC, "whatever happened to your old albums? Where'd they go to?"

"Why, I've got 'em here still, but I put 'em in the back room," Louisa exclaimed. "For all your kids ask after 'em, which is never, I got no reason to get 'em out."

Janet let out a muffled sigh. There she's at it again, taking everything out on my kids, Tom knew his wife was thinking in frustration.

"No, not that," he explained to Louisa. "I mean, you used to show us those really old pictures. Really ancient ones, you know. They'd gotten so yellowed they colored the atmosphere, I thought the air was yellow, too, back then, seeing those old pics. They made me think yellow and old were the same thing when I was little."

"My stars," Louisa sighed. "Why, they *was* old, them folks. Your dad's family, the Jacksons, come to Illinois from Carolina in the 1860s. They was – whadda you call it? – Loyalists in the war against England. Fought for the Red Coats."

"No, no, you've got it mixed up again," Janet interrupted her, taking her ruffled-feather, schoolmarm stance. "Tom's family came here from Virginia and it was the 1820s or even before. Back before this was even a state. I can tell you for sure. We did research, on our genealogy trip, all the way through Tidewater, Shenandoah, and Tennessee. It's in writing. Clear as a bell. Like I said, we got it down."

Janet's onslaught was short, like a tornado ripping through an unprepared and defenseless prairie settlement leaving behind desolation and an eerie silence, which only the sturdy or the lucky survived. Louisa flinched so the tears welled up. With gnarled hands she pressed tightly around her chair's armrests.

"Well, I'm not very smart," she cried out at last.

Silence reigned until she sniffled and then spoke up again. "But I know your dad's people, Gerald Jack," she said to Tom, "they come out here a long time ago and that great grandfather Jackson was old as the hills already. And just a damned mean ol' jackass, too."

A mischievous smile brightened her face. "Pardon my language," she said with a sly giggle at Janet. "I forget you's churchgoin' folk nowadays."

Tom chuckled but Janet sat stonefaced.

"Why, that grandfather Jackson beat his wife to within an inch of her life," Louisa went on. "I saw it and Gerald Jack, Tom's own dad, and his father did it, too. Them old Scotchmen was just plain mean. But Gerald Jack's mother and his grandmother used to take us young brides in and help us. Tom, I remember the first time ever your dad beat me up. After that I came runnin' to his ma, Victoria. She sat me down and soothed my tears and she had that old man of her own yellin' at her from the other room to get off her damned ass and do some work."

"Well, like they say," Tom ventured. "It's what you learn growing up." His statement sounded fine as he was thinking it up, but it fell flat and meaningless on speaking it. So he decided to listen more and talk less.

"Why, that's just what I was sayin'," Louisa hurried on trying to beat her daughter-in-law to the next punch. "Why, them ol' Jacksons. I remember once gram'pa Jackson was lookin' for some papers in his desk drawer, but he'd lost 'em. 'Victoria!' he shouted, 'What'd you do with my stuff?' and she was goin' to show him where they was. You know, he doubled up his fist and knocked her plumb crazy, so she stumbled backwards. 'Now don't you worry.' Victoria comforted me later. 'It'll blow over. Just you act like you didn't see it. Jacksons are just hot tempered ol' Irish.'"

"But you said they were Scotchmen," Janet butted in, eager to correct.

"Well, it's just the same, all a' them," Louisa countered. "'Why I know what it's like for you bein' married to my son,' Victoria told me one day. 'Gerald Jack's just like his dad before him. They'd just as soon knock your block off as look at you.'"

At the same time as Louisa's voice rose, Tom and Janet stared down at the carpet, like this was stronger stuff than they bargained for.

"And that's my own dad Victoria meant?" Tom asked at last.

Louisa nodded and continued. "Your dad, he come home one night and was hoppin' mad at somebody at work, that Sadie Bunch in the office that did all kinds a' stuff wrong but griped at others, and all I said to him was, 'Well, I don't know nothin' about that ol' lady, and he said, 'You take sides against me every time!' He doubled up his fist and swung at me, a real punch it was if it'd hit, but I ducked and he run his hand right through the danged wall. Plaster went flying."

She paused and looked desparagingly at the AC, like its steady hum might drown out her words and nobody would hear.

"So I made up my mind I wasn't goin' to stand for it any more," she continued. "Next time he pulled that trick I had a meat platter and flung it at him. It missed and splattered against the wall." Louisa thought back on the scene. "Then I had to pick it all up, the whole darned mess."

Louisa's voice had grown taut, so Tom cleared his throat to calm her.

"But, I can tell you true," she reflected, "if there's a Kingdom of Heaven and those Jacksons' wives didn't go there, then there ain't no justice nowhere, not even in heaven above."

"Well, it figures," Janet broke in. "If their men fought for the English in the Revolutionary War and lost, they had to be bitter and carried it with them, through generations. They couldn't have been good Americans anyway, if they stood up to fight against their own countrymen."

Dim visions of his forebears, as Louisa conjured them up, were still floating around in Tom's head. At the same time, he had to sort out Janet's words, and history was never his strong subject in school. He'd lived his life with the two women near him and he saw how they'd changed, Louisa from the slim, hardworking homemaker to a querulous old German *grossmutter*, and Janet from the cheerful schoolgirl he loved to an opinionated, sharp-tongued matron. He had searched in vain for the wellspring of those changes. At times he wondered if it was something life – or he himself – had done to them, but answers were slow to suggest themselves. Folks worked hard and had little time to spill on issues.

"But there weren't any 'countrymen' in those days," he replied, seeking to steer a safe course between Louisa and Janet. "They were all just Colonials before the Revolution. Know what I mean? The English ruled."

"What you're always doin' that to me for?" Louisa complained, in tears. She leaned against her backrest and kicked out in fury with her feet. "Makin' me look dumb. I don't know none 'a them fancy words. I guess that's what they taught at that college a' yours. All I know is we was Dutch and never had none a' that beatin' up on people."

"I just meant …," Tom tried to explain. He fumbled for words.

"Why, my dad never dreamed of hittin' my mom," Louisa said, in a softer tone. Those Dutchmen believed in peaceable ways, even if they was full of stories and …"

"Superstitions?" Janet interrupted. "Besides, Tom never finished college. You know that."

Tom looked at his wife and wondered. Yes, campus life wasn't all the fun it's cracked up to be, but I lasted a year. Even playing football lost its charm.

"No, the Dutch had stories and beliefs," Louisa went on, ignoring Tom's glance at Janet. "My mom was always hearing voices outside at night, and if a body was goin' to heaven, a halo formed in your pillow. Why, I remember when gram'pa passed, she took the pillow cases and rooted through all the feathers in 'em lookin' for one of them halos."

"What'd she find there?" Tom asked.

"Why, how would I know," Louisa answered with a frown. She grew confused. "I just remember her sayin' there had to be halos, and a little angel rose from your bed and went up through the rafters, and that spirit could lead your family to hidden riches in the ceiling. And you'd go to Heaven."

"Then they really were superstitious, weren't they?" Janet asked testily.

"Why my dad was God-fearing," Louisa shot back. "My folks honored their father and mother, like it says in the Good Book. You two should've learned that in your church by now. Whadda they teach ya there?"

Louisa looked at Tom beseechingly. Janet's barbed comment had cut her to the quick, so she went on about her family. Gran'ma and Gram'pa Wieldt left Germany and sailed for three months to Pennsylvania. At one point they were down to their last stale loaf, but built a farm and raised three kids. The youngest was Louisa's father. They named him Omar, a funny name for a Dutchman, folks said, but this was America, so anything was possible.

They spoke German, but Omar went to American schools. Then his parents fell in with Quakers. "We went to the United Brethrens church right down the street from here, up till you up and married Janet," Louisa chided Tom, "and then you switched to Baptists. Why, my folks never missed a Sunday all those years. And to think now you've gone over to *that.*"

Omar never wanted to be "a plain dirt farmer," Tom recalled him saying as an old man. As a raw youth, he joined the U. S. Army and fought in El Salvador – or was it Nicaraqua? – against local freedom fighters.

"Omar, the damned fool, picked the wrong side to fight for," Tom remembered his Uncle Ed saying at a family dinner several years after Omar died. "He was fightin' for the damned Anglo oppressors," Ed bellowed out, while the kinsfolk, sated with turkey and dressing, gazed blankly ahead.

From the war, Omar came back to Pennsylvania and met Hanna, Louisa's mother. Strange, Tom reflected, how little anyone knew about her, except she had three babies. Louisa was the first-born, followed by a second daughter, Margaret, who died as an infant. Then came Uncle Ed. Omar and Hanna spoke German when they didn't want the kids to understand. So Louisa emerged from childhood with a smattering of German, or what they called Dutch, household words, while Uncle Ed boasted he could swear fluently in two languages.

"Back in Leb'non you hardly knew you were in America," Louisa recalled her parents saying. "You could do everything in Dutch. When you were born, a Dutch doctor delivered you and when you passed one of their ministers buried you."

"Why didn't they learn to talk like real Americans?" Janet asked.

"Heavens, gram'pa Wieldt never did learn to speak right, like us," Louisa burst out. "He'd yell out the goldarndest things like *I been here gestern, verdammt!* … I mean, you'd have to know both lingos to get it."

"Yeah," Tom replied, "and they loved their brew. I remember even now gram'pa and uncle Ed sitting around and whetting their whistles."

"Why, you know what Dad always said," Louisa told him. "Nobody ever went broke startin' a brewery. Maybe that's what they needed in your dad's family, too," she chuckled at Tom, "a few bottles a' bock. Maybe them old Scotch just needed some merriment in life."

"Maybe," Janet butted in, "but didn't your dad Omar have a fling with some American lady when he was older? That's what your sister Jean claimed when she came back here to visit from California." Janet peered at Louisa. "Is that how a God-fearing man acts?"

Gram'pa Wieldt's flagging enthusiasm for his wife and long-standing love affair with another lady was something Jean loved telling about, how the fatter Gran'ma Weildt grew the greater the gulf between her and Omar became. Tom remembered, as a child, seeing his Gran'ma, with her white hair and huge breasts, taking a bath in a metal laundry barrel outside her bedroom one day, since she no longer fit in the bathtub. Whether her size made Omar fly to another woman seemed only lurid details to Tom, yet he saw Louisa was in dismay over Janet's suggesting it.

"It was a man's duty to support his family," Louisa argued. "The man of the house had the say in things."

Louisa waited for her words to sink in.

"And a woman knew her place, too," she added. "My mom wasn't any woman of the world, like they say."

Janet let out a hrummph and twisted angrily on the sofa, but for once she didn't respond.

"They didn't go out workin' at no fancy jobs. Like my dad always said, it was boys needed a trade."

Louisa paused and looked at Tom for agreement, but he remained silent.

"And so," she continued, "my dad put me and Ed in school. But, you know, the boys got away with murder. The teachers helped them along, all except for Mr. Maggiot – Mr. Maggot we called him. He carried a cane and rapped everybody across the rump when they didn't behave, boys and girls.

"He's the teacher Ed yelled *'Verdammt noch mal'* at. Dad took him to the shed with a razor strop and give him the goldarndest hiding over that. You could hear that kid yellin' bloody murder with every *whap!* But when it came to school, Ed got to go on. It was what a boy needed. Dad called it ..."

"... economic necessity," Tom added. Those were the time-tested words he knew Louisa was looking for. He himself had once told his own kids the same. Education was for the boys, girls had other needs. A man had to be practical, no idle dreams.

"And you?" Tom asked Louisa.

"That's enough, Dad told me after eighth grade, and so I went to work at the shoe factory, age 15. I worked there till I met Gerald Jack and Jean come along. I mean, we got married and had your sister."

"But how'd Ed end up as an electrician?" Tom inquired, ignoring his mother's slip of the tongue.

"Why, dad signed him on as a shop and Union apprentice."

Tom and Janet had long ago figured Louisa was pregnant when she got married, but up until now Louisa had never dropped the slightest hint about it, and most of the older relatives who knew were long since dead and buried. Tom remembered his mother's pernicious way of tormenting Jean as a little girl. She wasn't really theirs. Gerald Jack answered a knock at the door one day, Louisa told his sister, and found Jean in a basket, a poor colicky foundling crying in the cold. Jean remained the butt of Louisa's scorn until late adolescence when the girl fled to the West Coast. But when Tom came along, Louisa let him sleep away four years of high school and spoiled him rotten. Louisa remained at home while Gerald Jack toiled at the post office and her oldest child got married in LA. Only later, as a widow, did Louisa catch on as a hospital nurse's aide and revel in life.

"It just seemed a girl like me didn't have a chance," Louisa reflected, "bein' forced out before she grew up. What'd all that schoolin' do for Ed? Somebody should've beat some sense in his head, more than his own dad ever could."

"But that's how they thought," Janet explained. "The boys were expected to play around because they'd have the worry of supporting families later on."

"Why, my folks never thought like that! Never!" Louisa cried out. "Don't nobody believe a word I say. My dad whipped that hell-fire brother of mine plumb near to death. Because he wouldn't behave."

"What about the girls, though?" Janet persisted.

"Why, in those days if you didn't work, you didn't eat," Louisa broke in, "but I'll tell you I made more friends. Me and Helen Devore worked side by side makin' shoes when we was sixteen and then again slavin' at that hospital. I never enjoyed anything like carin' for sick folks. Like friends to me, they were."

Louisa leaned farther back and turned the AC yet another couple of notches cooler. "The years sure did pass, though," she sighed. "Till I took my retirement from bein' a Nurse's Aide."

"Took?" Janet questioned her. "You said they forced you out."

Feeling the AC air growing colder yet the atmosphere thicker with resentment, Tom got up and made his move. He chattered away about all the repairs he'd neglected for Louisa. Then, standing behind her, he turned the temperature up.

"Why, that's right. We was *forced* out," Louisa answered. "The bosses decided on a younger staff, and so they come pussy footin' around with forms to fill out. The handwriting was on the wall, like Helen said. One day the administrator'd say the government man was comin' to see you."

With the warmth returning, Tom and Janet looked at Louisa with renewed interest. "So they coerced you into retiring?" Janet asked.

"Why, heavens no" Louisa insisted. "It was easy as pie. I went into that little government man and filled out them forms on the spot. He drove all the way here, just to sign me up. 'Now, Louisa,' he said to me, 'everything's fine, 'cept we need your birth certificate. Where were you born?'"

"In Leb'non," I said.

"'That's right up the road, in Coles County, Illinois, right?' he answered, and I said, "No, not Leb'non IL, but Lebanon, P-A."

"'Pennsylvania? D'you have the certificate?'

"No, I said. And he said I had to get it."

"So?" Tom asked her. "Easy as pie? Like you said?"

"Why, heavens no, that's what I been tryin' to tell you," Louisa snapped back. She stood up dramatically and plucked the large white envelope from the bookcase. "I come across this in my closet just this morning. It's been lost all these years. *Lebanon County Recorder's Office*, it says."

"So they sent you a birth certificate after all?" Janet asked.

"No, they couldn't find one. Stars above, don't you see?" Louisa said and wielded the envelope like a conductor's baton. "Helen and me drove up to the courthouse here after we talked to that little government man and saw Commissioner Corry, and he sent off a letter to Lebanon. Lebanon P-A. And he got an answer. You can read it."

Tom opened the envelope, but Janet hurriedly snatched the letter from him. Her eyes darted quickly from line to line as she read out loud, "In conclusion, we are sorry now to inform you ..."

"Now you see," Louisa cut her off. "They couldn't find any record of me ever bein' born. So Corry got on the phone. They said they had *a certificate of birth for Edward Wieldt but nothing for a Louisa.*" She smiled in satisfaction over remembering the exact wording. "The OB delivery doctor forgot to report me. And the P – A people didn't find any record of our sister Margaret either, but they sent an official letter."

Louisa gazed at the bookcase.

"There isn't even any picture of our tiny little sister," she continued with a sob. "She caught measles and double pneumonia. Dad made her a casket from scratch. But, me without a birth certificate, they said I could use that letter for my benefits. I bought my AC with them very Social Security checks." Satisfaction flashed across Louisa's face until her brow furrowed. "But why didn't they have a record of me?"

"They didn't bother with daughters of sons or sons of daughters. You had to be the son of a son," Tom explained.

"No, those folks in Lebanon P-A wrote and said that ol' doc Dorfft who delivered us was eighty if he was a day. Gettin' kinda goofy. He just forgot."

"Why didn't he forget Ed, too?" Janet asked. "Why forget both girls, but remember the boy?"

"But those folks at Lebanon said their letter was good as any birth certificate. You've got it there. Living proof."

"No, you're the living proof," Janet corrected her. "They just didn't welcome daughters in those days."

"Why, welcome, I'll have you know," Louisa spat out. "I cared for my dad to his dying day, and where was my brother Ed then?"

"Your folks were still hard on you, weren't they?" Janet asked. "I mean …"

"I remember drivin' down to that hospital," Louisa said.

Tom listened closely to see if Louisa was going to answer Janet. "I sat at Dad's bedside. He told me, 'Louisa, you're the best daughter a man ever had.'"

"Of course they loved you," Janet sighed and glanced at her watch.

While both women were locked in their thoughts, Tom recalled Gran'ma Wieldt's fond descriptions of the farmland near Lebanon in the bright sunny spring of her life. For all most people knew her memories were just some of the old woman's idle tales. Still, Tom guessed her beliefs represented truths of a life she treasured. Maybe in that far-off world of her mother's conjecture and reminiscence Louisa could find out who she herself really was. Wheat shaffs and mustard seeds blowing gloriously in the summer breeze.

"You know," Tom began, "women needed men to take care of them. Regrettable maybe."

"Why, heavens, there wasn't anything to regret about it," Louisa replied. "A man's a no-good that won't take care of his own."

"I don't know," Janet reasoned. She handed Louisa's letter back to Tom. As he refolded it, it got stuck, so he held the envelope up to the light. A white sheet fell out.

"I don't think that's how it happened at all," Janet went on, imploring Tom to listen. "You remember that minister we met on our genealogy trip? He told us about working as a chaplain for that hospital in Chicago. When an Irishman died, they just scribbled down *Irish* and threw the body out with the trash. I figure that's pretty much what they did when girls were born. Shrugged and thought *girl*."

Louisa lurched forward. "Why, just look at you, ain't we so elegant, comin' in here with your high falutin' words and your *g-e-n-e-a-l-o-g-y*. Well, I'm just a fat old lady, but not kickin' the bucket for your sake. No, ma'am, I ain't!"

Louisa's face grew redder until – her emotions spent – she leaned back and sobbed.

"And, what's more, you can't go talkin' about my family like they's trash bein' throwed out. And don't go talkin' to me about them ol' Irish. Why, those Catholics was just plain no-good. We never had anything to do with them. My people was *Christian*, and full-blood Dutch, too."

Janet's ire had smoldered while Louisa spoke. Now, tired and at a loss, she stared desultorily at her mother-in-law. Only Louisa's sniffling broke the quiet.

"I'm just an old lady who's gonna die. Why don't Jean come back and take care of me, like daughters do? There's just no love. When my folks was alive, I never had any desire but to …"

Janet glanced at her watch again while Tom inspected the paper on his lap. Eventually Louisa relaxed. She got up and headed for the AC again.

"It just don't seem I can keep it cool enough any more," she muttered.

Tom grunted in assent.

"What on earth are you lookin' at anyhow?"

"Didn't you see this?" he inquired. "Those people in Lebanon sent a copy of Ed's birth certificate."

"Why, that ol' thing!" Louisa snorted.

Janet squinted at the paper, but Tom kept a firm grasp on it.

"It says *Legitimate*. Sure enough, uncle Ed was born in wedlock."

"Why, my stars, everybody knew that," Louisa said. "Why tell a body who he is?"

"Yeah, common knowledge. But here on the back, in long hand, it says, '*Der einzige noch lebende Erbe*'[1]," Tom stammered. "Somebody wrote that a long time ago. Just after uncle Ed was born."

Louisa took her hand from the AC knob. "Well, heavens above, I wonder what that could mean?" she said.

"Who knows," Tom shrugged. He stuffed the paper in the envelope and put it back on the shelf.

When he and Janet finally got up to leave, Tom paused in the doorway.

"Yeah, I always did want to know German. I should've listened when I was a kid," he said while Louisa and Janet smiled and said their goodbyes for another day. "I should've learned all those other folks' lingos. Then I'd know what they were telling me, wouldn't I?"

No one answered, so he looked at Louisa and smiled. "I'll fix those vents for sure. Next week. Till then."

Once outside, Tom turned and looked back. He noticed how his mother heard the screen click behind him. She glanced first at the door and then blinked in uncertainty at the AC and ceiling vents. No squirrels had sneaked in, but they couldn't be trusted to stay away. "Well, I never," Louisa said, "what's wrong with things any more?"

---

1 'The only surviving heir.'

NO

JAMES SALE

No graffiti in heaven;
No daubs of paint in paradise;
No need for stretch or exercise;
No food for thought or pointless dice;
No counting but the number seven.

No morning but then again no even;
No aeons save only in a trice;
No odds, perverse, or deeper still, vice;
No violence to entrance, entice;
No bread but bread born fully leaven.

No cloth that hands have worked, woven;
No spell or magic of bad surprise;
No falling, and no compromise;
No speaking, equivocating, lies;
No devil, demons, or feet sundered, cloven.

No sun and certainly no oven;
No moon or light's heatless promises;
No nasty, then, indeed only the nice;
No doubt, no doubting Thomases;
Yes. No death. Never again forsaken.

OUTSIDE, IT'S SNOWING

AARON WHITE

Michael looked up and watched the snow falling from the black night sky. It held its own beauty; one he could appreciate but as he listened to it crunch beneath his feet, he could take no solace in it for nothing seemed to have the power to take his solitude away.

'Rebecca, are you still there?' he asked himself silently.

'No, you know she's not. She left you, remember? She left you a note, a note you still have, a note you refuse to throw away.'

He looked up at the torrent of snowflakes as they grew in number, trying to focus on one individual flake but found he was unable to track the flight of any with a degree of accuracy. His inner monologue continued.

'You didn't love her enough, did you?'

'Not in the right way', he answered. 'I let my selfishness blind me from what I had'.

'That is correct, my boy. Now look at you. You should go home, it's late and this snow is getting heavy. It's not safe out here.'

'I don't want to go home. Home is empty. I'll just keep walking for a while. At least out here there are signs of life.'

'Not many.'

The amber streetlights cast a soft glow on the wet road and accentuated the snow's whiteness as it settled on the path. He could hear distant traffic as well as the dull crunching of his steps, these sounds appeared to provide him with a small amount of relief from his loneliness but the endless ache in his chest acted as a brutal reminder to him that he was still suffering, that he woke each morning confined and alone.

'Life goes on. What will be will be. What's meant for you won't pass you by …'

'Stop it, Michael.'

'Yes. That's not helping … hope springs eternal … damn it!' He let out a deep breath and shook his head. His mind was playing tricks again and he was finding it difficult to control.

His foot slipped slightly on the snow-covered ground and he regained some focus on his surroundings. He had nearly fallen twice earlier but he had managed to develop a technique which kept him both moving at a regular pace as well as keeping him up-right.

'So, who was that bloke? They looked like they were getting on rather well.'

'Sitting close together, weren't they? Did you see her laughing?'

'Yes. I saw it. I hadn't made her laugh for a while by the end. Why didn't I?'

'You used to.'

'Used to laugh a lot.' He smiled as he recalled. 'She'd tilt her head back and laugh out loud. God, that always made me feel good. Warm inside. And I'd smile looking at her. Happy that I'd made her happy. A very simple process when you think about it.'

'Yeah, but she wasn't all that simple either, Michael, was she? She could be difficult.'

'Yes, I suppose she could be. But all relationships are difficult. And she had had her problems.'

'Problems that weren't your fault. Or anything to do with you or who you are.'

'No, but I thought I was meant to be her savior. Her knight in shining armor. I thought we were meant to be. Soul mates, I thought.'

'You weren't strong enough.'

'No.'

'You're still not.'

'No'.

A snowflake found its way down the back of his coat and melted immediately against his body heat. A shudder traveled down his back. He turned his collar up further and returned his hands to his coat pockets.

'Doesn't stop me wishing I was, though … or had been'.

'No.'

He had come to a road and stopped as a lone motorist delicately rolled along in front of him. He turned his head and looked up at the chapel which stood high above him on his right. It appeared both glorious and eerie as the thick snow fell around it. Without any lights to give it life, the building appeared silhouetted against the night.

'You were some help,' he said bitterly, 'but I guess I haven't asked you for help in a long time, so why should you have been?'

'Who are you talking to?'

'I don't know. I don't know very much anymore.'

Something caught his eye, a figure standing on the steps which led up to the chapel's large arched door. He squinted through the snowfall, trying to focus. It certainly appeared to be the shape of a person, but it was too dark to make out any detail. Whoever it was, Michael felt they were just standing watching him.

He moved on a little unnerved, a sense of foreboding edging into his depression, the increasing snowfall starting to lie heavily on the ground. He came to a road and stopped as he noticed the absence of traffic had allowed the roads to become covered with a fresh layer of snow.

'I hope she's careful driving to work in the morning'.

'She'll be fine. Don't worry unnecessarily.'

Snow was falling over his face and he blinked as it landed in his eyes. The sensation of coldness on his lids was unusual but not unpleasant. Still, he had to remove a hand from his pocket to help himself see. As he focused, he saw a second figure emerge from across the street, then another two appeared on either side but they did not stand close together, they maintained a certain distance apart from one another, but each of them stood watching him, saying nothing, just watching.

'This is not right, Michael. Something is terribly wrong here.'

He stepped off the footpath onto the road, looking away from the figures to check for any traffic. Another black figure stood up the road, and another appeared on the opposite side. He looked back at the chapel and the original figure he had first noticed had exited the chapel gates and was standing watching him. He suddenly realized that he was surrounded by a gathering crowd of black figures, all standing still, maintaining a distance from each other, watching him.

Michael felt his heart begin to pound in his chest. Questions now flooding his mind, squeezing out his previous pain. Who were they? What did they want? He moved a little quicker, as quick as the snow would allow. He realized he was walking toward the blind laneway which led into his estate and he hesitated momentarily, un-willing to venture any further. Until he realized he had no choice. The gathering crowd of black figures had started to walk towards him and were slowly closing in.

The laneway resembled a tunnel due to the way the trees had grown over the years, creating a canopy or sorts. This meant the ground beneath his feet had been protected from the snowfall and he was able to quicken his pace, moving into the dark, hoping no other figures were waiting for him.

When he exited the other side, he was relieved to see the amber streetlights of his estate. He cut to his right onto a grassed area, trying to pick up pace, trying to run but the snow was deeper on the grass and his movements suddenly became languid and unbalanced. He glanced back and caught sight of the black figures exiting the laneway, moving significantly quicker, no longer maintaining that strange space they had been keeping, becoming more like a pack, hunting.

His house sat in the middle of a small square of attached homes and as he crossed a road into the square, he finally saw his house coming into sight through the snowfall. He didn't slow. He maintained his pace as best he could despite slipping and sliding. He reached his front door and looked back, they were in his square, advancing, taking on the appearance of a seething crowd of black ghosts, writhing and clambering over themselves to get to him.

Panicked, he stabbed the keyhole with his key and twisted. Nothing. No movement. He looked back, the menacing black crowd continued to close, moving quicker, arms reaching out towards him, nearing his garden. Nearly upon him. Another twist with his wrist. He pushed and fell through the door, scrambling backwards, kicking at the door. It slammed shut, and his heavy breaths became the only sound.

After a moment, he gathered himself to his feet, slowly moving upwards, watching the small glass window on his door. He hesitated before finally peeking out. Nothing but the snow falling out of the black empty sky.

'Where'd they go, Michael?'

He ignored the voice, unable to offer an explanation and slipped his arms out of his coat as he entered his living room, flicking the light switch as he went. He threw his coat on a chair and walked to the kitchen, uninterested in the kitchen light, the living room lending enough to the kitchen. On his kitchen table a small sheet of paper lay, weighted down by a Christmas tree shaped photo holder. Rebecca looked back at him, her smiling face poking out the top. He moved her aside and reached for the piece of paper, turning it over so the hand-written words were visible. He then lifted the photo from the holder and walked to his kitchen sink and reached into the cupboard beneath him, removing a box of matches.

He watched the two items burn, Rebecca's image melting in the flames and her last words disappearing into ash. Light from the living room fell across the kitchen floor and he could see himself faintly reflected in the kitchen window, beyond which the snow continued to fall, and the demons lurked. He would stay home for now, until such time as he felt repaired, a time when the world would welcome him back. A time when hope, would indeed, spring eternal.

PAPER PIECES

JASON JACKSON

She's reading the letter, the baby asleep in the cot beside her. This room is where she feels most comfortable now. In the other bedroom, the bed is still unmade and there's a coffee mug from Wednesday, or perhaps Tuesday, on the floor. She steps around it when she goes in for a t-shirt, some clean knickers, when she goes to sleep.

It's mid-afternoon – the silence is an exhaled breath – and the blue blind is pulled halfway down to shield the baby from the sun. The window is dusted with a thin film, and she can still see where she held the baby's finger against the pane, traced a tiny aeroplane's line of flight.

She can still hear their laughter.

The letter is dated three days ago. It was lying on the mat this morning, the first handwritten letter she's ever received. The writing is small, difficult to read. She thinks of her own handwriting, its curves, its loops. She used to draw hearts above every *i*, until a teacher told her it gave the wrong impression. She would like to have been a teacher. Or a writer, perhaps. Her mother used to tell her she was good with words. *Such an imagination for a little girl!* she'd say. She remembers the funeral, the eulogy. All the expectant faces. For days, she tried to write something, in the end wrote nothing, hoping instead that the right words would come. But there'd only been tears, and a friend of her mother's – Maude, Marge? – took her arm and led her back to the pews.

The letter ends, *Yours, Peter*, and she thinks about this as she listens to the baby's shallow breaths, the moments of stillness between each one. *Yours.* She whispers the word, and then says it aloud. The baby stirs, and she holds her palm to his warm cheek. *Love*, she thinks. Would it have been better if he'd signed off with *Love*? Would it have been better if he hadn't written at all?

She folds the letter along its creases. The envelope is on the floor by the base of the cot where she dropped it. The stamp is a special edition, a picture of a butterfly, red and gold, and she peels it slowly from the envelope, smooths it between her fingers and lays it flat on the cabinet by the baby's cot. She slips the letter back into the envelope, reads again her name, her address, made strange in his hand.

There's a change to the baby's breathing, a longer sigh, and then he's awake, silent, looking at her, his face in shadow, his eyes wide.

"Hey, Baby!" She smiles, touches his cheek again. "What's this?" she says, waving the envelope a little. "What's Mummy got?"

The baby laughs, a small hiccoughing sound, and kicks his legs in the air.

"This is from Daddy," she says. "A letter! Doesn't than make us important?"

More giggles, more kicking.

"What should we do with it, do you think?" she says. "What do you think Mummy should do with a letter from Daddy?"

She watches the baby. He has blue eyes. Peter's eyes. She remembers her mother telling her that all babies have blue eyes for the first six months. Her own eyes are brown, her mother's too.

She cannot imagine where she'll be in six months' time.

She picks up the envelope, Peter's letter sealed inside, and rips it in half. She puts the two pieces on top of each other and repeats this twice more, but when she tries again she isn't strong enough, so she separates out the pieces, rips and rips, until there's a pile of confetti on the windowsill.

In the hospital, her mother said, *I can't believe he's left you all alone.* There was a drip attached to her mother's arm, flakes of dried black blood on the skin around it. Her hand was on the white sheet, trembling, so she lay her own hand over it. *We're not alone, Mum. I'll never be alone.*

It was the last time, the last words.

She raises the blind so the sun comes through the window. The baby turns his head, and she reaches into the cot, lifts him out, holds him with one arm so he's facing into the street.

"Let's watch and see what happens," she says, and she leans forward to open the window wide. The breeze shifts some of the paper and it spreads across the windowsill, some of it spilling on the floor. "Better be quick!" she says, and she takes a handful, shows it to the baby, and then scatters it to the wind. The pieces fly out of the window, disappearing in a second, and the baby laughs.

"Here," she says. "Why don't you try?" and she picks up some of the paper pieces, places them in the baby's hot hand. "Throw!" she says.

"Throw!"

The baby laughs again, and as she leans forward his little hand moves in a parody of her own. Most of the pieces are scattered to the wind, but some are left stuck to his palm. She can see the illegible black letters, the meaningless fragments of words.

"Oh-oh!" she says. "Try again!" and she watches her son shake his hand. She watches the paper pieces come unstuck as the wind takes them. She watches as they disappear.

PUSTULES

MARIA J. ESTRADA

I. The Colonizer Enemies

Cindy Marmott stared at the 9 o'clock morning news with a Cheeto hanging out of her gaping mouth. That morning she wore her "comfies", the expansive sweats and 2XL white t-shirt that signaled she had hit rock bottom. She had dropped off her kids at school, and it wasn't until she saw a beam of resplendent grey-blue light pierce the White House on the screen that she ran faster than her 180 pound, five-foot-two frame should allow. She was an unstoppable fat force. She was going to save them from the alien threat as she sped down the five blocks to West Academy School. A man watering his front lawn gave her an enthusiastic, "You're doing a great job!" shout for her running.

When she arrived, the elementary school was surrounded by a blue wooden barricade and police vehicles. The police and congregated parents all stared above the building at an enormous alien craft. It wasn't disc shaped or a metallic menace, as the ones she blogged about. It was a white sphere of light four times the size of the school building, nested just a few feet above the roof. The ship wavered, disappearing and reappearing at punctuated intervals.

"It must be from another dimension," Cindy concluded. All the parents hesitated behind the blue barricade, but Cindy's kids were her universe. After an unexpected divorce and failing writing career, she was damned if some space colonizers would take away her precious angels.

She began to walk forward as a Chicago P.D. officer glared at her.

News reporters began to appear, Chicago's own Channel 7, Betty

Ramirez stood next to Cindy and babbled an incomprehensible summary of events. Cindy focused on how she would run past the cops and enter the building. She was past the point of wheezing, and her knees were beginning to shake and buckle.

The front door was locked to secure the kids. She hoped the security officer would buzz her in.

As she struggled with her plan, a beam of light like the one she saw earlier pierced the ceiling and illuminated the school. Other concerned parents and snobby LuAnne, the president of the local school council, screamed in desperation as they dashed past the impotent officers. With cameras there, the police stood inert, their hands gripping batons and Tasers. They were poised between hurting the parents and letting them run to danger.

One cop shouted, "Damned retards!" as Cindy rushed past.

Somehow, she was the first to reach the door. She banged on the front door and was pleased to see Charlie working that morning. The friendly Charlie stared up at the ceiling.

"Charlie! Open the door!"

He did so robotically, and she ran inside and tried to get through the heaviness of the atmosphere. She struggled for a few minutes and entered. It was like walking into firm Jell-O.

Once inside, the light made her ponder what she thought Heaven would be like. The alien luminescence made her feel both a permanent peace and near-orgasmic pleasure. Cindy was not fooled; she suspected those feelings of elation were there to make *them*, the colonized, docile.

For what purpose? she wondered.

The viscosity of the atmosphere was heavy, but not impossible to walk through. Cindy could feel every particle of the coagulated air. She struggled up the stairs. She thought of numerous adjectives to describe what she felt ranging from placid to terrified, all subdued, weak words. By the time she reached the classroom, the light had vanished.

Her daughter, Sammie, was four years old, in Pre-K-2, and her son, Paul was in third grade on the third floor.

Cindy was certain all of the kids would be beamed up into that light, but she ran to Sammie's class which was on the second floor. She cried out when she saw the kids standing by the window with the panicked Ms. Lawrence flailing her arms. She walked in the classroom, the kids encircling her in a ring of excitement. The chorus of "Sammie's Mom!" nearly brought her to tears. Some of them even went up to her for hugs, including Ms. Lawrence.

In five minutes, everything went back to normal. She prayed for that anyway. Cindy also really craved some strawberry ice cream.

II. Home

The children were dismissed from school for the rest of the week, mostly because prissy Luanne wanted all the kids to get physicals from their doctors.

In the aftermath of being inside what she called Orgasmic Jell-O, the kids were annoyingly exuberant. At first, she wanted to keep them indoors, but thought better of it, and let them play in the backyard. She was now deeply inspired to blog and even post a video despite her self-deprecating body shame, a mental rant that never ended.

After ten minutes, Cindy posted one of her best videos ever, giving her first-hand account. She was elated to see 50 Likes within the first thirty minutes.

But, then, TittyLover13 asked, "Why do you think they left? Do you think they'll come back?"

These questions had, in fact, also been troubling her. The pundits and military experts were still on the news 24-7, but the aliens were gone.

In the days that followed, she and her kids developed a strange, voracious appetite. Their skin was mysteriously branded by perfect quarter-sized red spots. She had one on her cheek, her daughter Sammie on her right arm, and Peter on his chest smack in the middle. It was these spots that compelled her to go to the free clinic, not LuAnn's annoying email reminders. They weren't the only ones with these blemishes. Other people who had been in the light had the exact mark, but as far as she knew, she had the only family where all of the members, except her piece of shit ex-husband, showed these blemishes.

"Waffles!" said Sammie jumping on her lap, Cindy's extended stomach leaving little room for her daughter to sit.

"You making waffles?" asked Paul who was chewing on an enormous carrot.

Cindy stared open-mouthed as he chewed, for her kids, like so many of their peers, were "severely allergic" to vegetables. Now, she had no problem getting her children to eat everything from salad to roasted beets.

"We're definitely going to the clinic tomorrow," she said and went to the kitchen to make another breakfast.

***

The doctor was a pale-face redhead. He was in his early thirties. His badge read Dr. Goode. Cindy wondered if he was "goode" in bed and glanced at his left hand where he wore no wedding band.

"The marks are the exact same size," he muttered. "I've been seeing them all day, but as far as I can see, everyone is healthy. Even your health is improving."

"What?" she asked.

"You've dropped ten pounds, according to your file," he said, "Keep it up!"

The doctor told them to monitor the spots and return in two weeks. He also prescribed vitamins, which she didn't really think they needed. She got some gummies for the kids at the local grocery store and headed for the pantry to get another bag of food.

III. The Colonizer-*Enemies?*

Cindy woke up from a restless sleep. She heard loud voices in her slumber and almost ran to investigate if there were intruders. She searched every room. Her stomach grumbled, followed by a painful stab. In the kitchen, she heard a clear voice.

You need more dairy.

She almost screamed but didn't want to frighten the kids. They had been through enough already.

"Who said that?" she whispered. Nobody answered.

She checked on her kids. They were smiling, Sammie giggling loudly as she dreamed.

The next day when she went to the bathroom, she saw a second quarter-sized mark on her cheek. She stared at the mirror for a long time. She said aloud, "Why the fuck do I have two of them? Is it because I'm fat?"

No, said the voice, *You adapt well to change and have a great imagination.*

"What?" she said, "What do you mean?"

Cindy asked more questions and only stopped when her kids came in asking for banana-nut pancakes. She made sure to add milk instead of water to the mix.

***

Cindy sat at her computer, inspired in a rush unlike any in recent years. She began writing a story about a young homeless girl who committed murder. The story flowed, and she knew when she finished that it was a winner. She was revising it one more time, when the same voice asked, *Why must people go hungry, when your planet produces such abundance?*

She yelped and looked around. "Who the fuck said that!"

Sammie came running towards her. "You hear them too?"

Cindy looked at her daughter who was beaming. Then, Paul walked in.

"Wait," said Cindy, "Before you ask for a snack, can you hear a voice? Here?" She pointed at her head.

He nodded and glared at his sister.

"Are they friendly?" she asked as her chest tightened.

In that moment, he relaxed and cocked his head. "Yeah. Ya don't gotta worry."

"Have to worry," she said, "Since when? Since when do they talk to you?"

"Since the first day," said Sammie.

Cindy began to breathe rapidly and reached for her cell phone.

***

After she called the doctor and explained, he asked if she needed to seek mental help. Of course, she didn't. Cindy concluded that it was impossible for all three of them to be having a nervous breakdown or a mental disorder. She went online and saw more images of the same spots. By the second day, the spot had begun to raise like a pretty golden pimple. They all had the same coloration and bump.

On the fourth day, she saw a video of her favorite actress Jennifer Lawrence. She likewise had a golden pustule on her arm and talked about her invisible friend. This caused a social media craze of similar stories about small golden domes growing in inconvenient places.

Not everyone was talking about the voices, but her imagination went there. She blogged, "Are Aliens Talking to You?" Within a few hours, she had twenty responses.

"My kids talk to them like every hour," said one concerned mom. But, then, the same woman lost credibility when she attributed their closeness to God as the reason her kids talked to the angels so much.

Cindy absentmindedly caressed the golden abrasion on her face. It was hard and protecting something inside. Oh, she had an imagination about what grew there. As she ran through the possibilities, Cindy got a terrible idea in her head. *What if there was an alien in the pustule?*

"No way!" She immediately made an appointment to have it removed.

That won't be possible, said the voice, *You will only hurt yourself . . . or others.*

"We'll see, asshole."

Cindy remembered the day her husband, Harry, left. He was a misogynist jerk, a realization that took a while to fully understand. At the end of their marriage, her sales of her one-hit-wonder, *Dreams Like Hypothesis,* were plummeting, and instead of supporting her, he left with a younger woman.

"This relationship is unbearable," he told her.

That was all Harry said as he marched out the door with the expensive leather duffle bag that she bought him.

"Fuck you," she told the voice. She took the kids to the clinic.

***

"You don't have an appointment," said the nurse.

"Listen," she said, "I have skin cancer, and I'm pregnant. This thing," she pointed to her face, "could hurt my unborn child!"

The office manager who knew Cindy raised her eyebrows. She said, "You can get a consultation with an RN."

The nurse collected urine samples and reported back.

"You have a protein and something in your urine, but you're not pregnant."

"What is the something?"

The nurse shrugged her shoulders. "It's unidentifiable."

Cindy sucked in her breath. "Test my kids."

They had the same results: a protein and an unknown factor. The RN to her credit had the dermatologist examine her skin. He knew Cindy and was aware of her condition. Cindy really didn't have skin cancer, at least not the kind that required treatment. She had one large mole removed with melanoma. As a result, she had to wear sunblock and take vitamin D, none of which she did.

Dr. Hasan asked, "You know that mole I was having you keep an eye on?"

She nodded her head.

"It's gone. Along with all of your blemishes. Also, you seem to be losing a lot of weight. Fast."

Cindy inspected her arms. *How the hell hadn't she paid attention to her moles?* She looked down and took stock of her belly; sure enough, it was shrinking.

"You seem to be fine," said the doctor. "However, we are keeping an eye on these interesting lab results." He smiled at her in the way her ex-husband did when he overspent.

"What aren't you telling me?" she asked.

But he had nothing else to add.

"Can you remove it? I mean, I have two of them."

He shook his head and walked away.

IV. Unwanted

The following Monday, Cindy took her kids to school. She carried the physical paperwork and second check-up.

When she got there, Charlie, the security guard asked her if her kids had bumps. He grimaced at her face, when he asked the question. He was stiff and formal. That is when she noticed the man in the black suit and the men in odd green uniforms.

"Yes," she answered. "What's going on?"

"Well," he said embarrassed, "kids with bumps have to go home, you see."

"What?" she asked. "That is bullshit, Charlie! I have work to do."

"I'm sorry Ms. Marmott, but parents of the kids without the bumps threatened to sue."

"Do you have one?" asked Cindy.

"No ma'm. Got checked by the gov'ment doctor."

She walked away with Paul happy to go back home and Sammie starting to complain. "Why do we have to go home?"

"Stop whining!" Hissed Paul.

"Stop it both of you." She turned back and gave Charlie a pointed look. "I'm calling my own attorney. This fascism will not stand!"

She was fuming when she got home and called the ACLU, but the line was busy.

Within the hour, she heard the voice again, *Don't worry, Cindy. All this stress is not necessary. We mean you no harm.*

Cindy got a sinking feeling in her stomach like the first morning she woke up to an empty bed. "We? Who are *we*?" But the alien voice stopped speaking to her.

***

In all of her life, Cindy had never cut herself. This oddity was fueled by a childhood fear of knives which made her extra careful around sharp objects. Her hyperactive imagination was to blame. That is why when she held the razer to her face, her neighbor, Mr. Salinas gawked over her with concern. Mr. Salinas was an ever-helpful retired fireman and had come over the minute she called him.

"Just in case," she had told him, "I mean, I'm not sure what's going to happen." She smiled at him sheepishly.

He wiped the sweat from his forehead. "You want me to do it? I'm a trained paramedic."

"No," she said. "I won't have some interstellar man tell me what I can or can't do. I have to do this."

He shrugged and gave her an encouraging pat on the shoulder.

Cindy looked at her determined reflection in the mirror. Her once double chin was disappearing, and her skin was glowing.

Stop! said the interior voice.

That emboldened her. She didn't even pause when she took the blade to the outer edge of the shiny miniscule dome on her cheek.

It hurt at first. She managed to get a quarter of an inch cut, when a sharp pain pierced her head. It radiated out of her engulfing the small bathroom.

In that minute, three simultaneous events happened. The earth began to shake. Mr. Salinas clamped his hands over his ears as he howled in pain. Cindy also screamed but was unable to hear herself over the loud cacophony of voices. She tried to stand up and continue, but the extreme agony in every part of her body paralyzed her.

She hoped with all of her might to pass out, but she would have to endure five more minutes. Cindy felt like her whole body was giving birth, the birth of a damned breached bastard.

The assault stopped, and she vomited all over Mr. Salinas who didn't even flinch or say goodbye as he wobbled back to his house. His hands holding his head.

Cindy fell to the floor. The buzzing in her ears abated.

She took several deep Lamaze breaths.

"Who are you?" she said. Cindy took her finger and tapped on the golden pustule.

Stop! said the voice. *You have done enough damage.*

Cindy went to vomit in the toilet and per usual, wasn't paying attention to her surroundings. She slipped on her previous mess and would have hit her head against the toilet, when a benevolent force suspended her in midair. She held her breath and exhaled placing her hands on the toilet. She regained motion and vomited.

The voice said, *You must hydrate.*

Cindy had a moment to think about what just transpired, and for the first time, she felt a smidge of control over the situation, despite the awful consequences.

"I'll drink water. Plenty of it, but you have to tell me who you are and what's going on."

V. The Colonizer-Enemies', Enemies

Three months had passed since Cindy spoke to the alien, she called Steve. They shared a lot in common. Like her, Steve was without a partner, as many of the males in his species. Steve was thoughtful and funny with his dry humor. Mostly, he was analytical.

They discussed everything from child rearing to poverty. That morning, she was drinking cream and chewing on large stalks of broccoli.

She was just about to ask if his "people" could fix all current social problems, when the large metallic monstrosities raped the sky. The metallic ships on the news looked heavy. They were box-shaped and spewed long streams of dark filth through the sky.

Cindy didn't need to ask, but she did anyway, "Are these your brothers?"

Steve said, *Run!*

Cindy wasn't sure where to run, but she remembered her parents had a trailer up near Galena. North. She and the children packed without being told what was at stake. They put more boxes of food than clothing in the car and sped off.

They were on the road for a mere thirty minutes before they were stopped by police in strange green uniforms.

One of the men, a short redhead, pulled her out of the car.

"Where do you think you're going!" he spat. Cindy had never been stopped by the police before. When she was married to her imbecilic ex-husband, she often rubbed that in his face. The man shot erratic spittle as he asked the same question.

Lie, said Steve.

"I was going to the Dells. To take my kids to a water park."

The man's eyes shimmered in an inhuman burnt-orange color. He pointed at her cheek, "Your kind and your kids aren't allowed there. You're contaminated with that." He jabbed mid-air towards her face.

Strength, uncharacteristic strength, traveled through her arm. Cindy had been working out, to tone up her flappy skin. She was now a size eight and pure packed muscle. When Steve realized that loose skin was unseemly, she was sure they helped tighten her skin at a fast rate.

Cindy smiled at the man and punched. He went flying backwards, as his partner pulled out a taser. She was about to attack him, when the same force that saved her months before in the bathroom before she bashed her head in – paralyzed him. When it crushed the man's skull, she got into the car.

"Fascist," she said, as she drove off.

She looked back to the kids, but they merely stared ahead.

As if reading her thoughts, her little daughter said, "Don't be upset. Mr. Fluffy says they were going to kill us."

Paul added, glancing up from his Gameboy, "Wrecker says not to stop next time."

Cindy nodded and drove on.

She asked, "Steve, why are their eyes orange?"

They are easily controlled. *They have no imagination and are rigid in thinking.*

She let out a slow whine, "They're fascists. That's all I needed to know."

She drove as fast as Harry would despite her marital protests. She only paused when a man was being shot on the side of the road by the men in green uniforms. She didn't see any blood, just the officer holding the gun, and the man lying on the ground. The echo of the shot lasted moments as she sped by.

A collective cry of grief echoed through her head, but it stopped when her car swerved in response to the noise.

Hours later, when they reached their destination, the town of Galena was quiet. All the businesses were closed, except for the gas station.

"Where is everyone?" she asked out loud.

Safe, said Steve, speaking for the first time since the death of the officer. *This place was fertile with all citizens hosting us. They have moved to safety.*

In the distance, Cindy heard a loud explosion.

What was that? she wondered, but Steve didn't answer.

They got to the trailer. They would have to dust and clean. The last few months, her kids were in a quiet, compliant mood. Often, the pair helped without being bribed to do so and seemed to be content contributing to their collective well-being. That was the case when her daughter grabbed the broom and her son a spray bottle and paper towels. 45 minutes later the trailer was tidy and comfortable.

They sat on the couch and watched the television, fascinated at the number of ships. No one bothered to fight back, except North Korea. It was flattened within seconds.

***

The next day, Cindy and the kids were glued to the T.V., terrified. The aliens were seven feet tall in metallic suits. Their skin was reptilian, an ugly grey that evoked vomit; she was certain they were nothing like Steve, Fluffy Pants, or Wrecker. They had nothing of the thoughtfulness of her new residents. She analyzed their human helpers, the brainwashed fascists. They had a golden emblem on the side of the forest green uniform – a circle, maybe a planet, with an unmissable square at the top. She was disgusted to see those men cooperating with the invaders, rounding up everyone with pustules. Taking children and elderly alike away. She shuddered as she imagined the worst.

"Where are they taking them?" asked Sammie to her friend, Mr. Fluffy Pants.

"What'd he say?" asked her brother, chewing on the last granola bar.

"He's telling me there's a safe place. Not for them. They can't be saved. For us."

You must go there tonight, said Steve as he relayed the information to Cindy, *They will find you. We cannot stay here any longer. Come with us.*

Cindy began to protest, when the screen showed the once gorgeous Jennifer Lawrence being herded with a throng of people. Her hair was disheveled, but her fighting spirit remained. The television didn't capture what was said, but the three of them recoiled when a tall female officer took a baton and slammed her perfect lips. Sammie cried out when she did the same to her golden dome, which caused the officer to writhe in pain. The camera zoomed in as another officer aimed a gun at Lawrence's forehead. The extended hand with the gun bent at an unnatural angle, just as the camera cut to a commercial.

Cindy clung to her children until Paul protested that she was squeezing tight.

"Steve, what do we need to bring with us?"

Nothing, he answered, but Cindy remembered she had her father's old hunting rifle in the small locked closet. She looked at her son. "You remember that zombie bashing game you used to play?"

He nodded.

"Did you bring your bat?"

"Yeah, Mom. I was thinking the same." She looked to Sammie and said, "Sweetheart, get the box of nails from the kitchen drawer."

She smiled at each of them, and they went to work.

VI. Aliens Go Home

"Fuck," she whispered under her breath. They were behind the tree line, just half a mile from the destination Steve told them to reach. Paul held the bat with nails sticking out of it at odd angles. Cindy braced the hunting rifle against her shoulder aiming at an easy target. The target, a short man with dark hair smoking a cigarette, sat on a tree trunk. He was joking with his friends. There were four of them and an alien enemy. There was no way she could shoot them all.

"Stay behind the trees," she told Sammie who carried a hefty stick of her own.

Cindy calculated.

What are you thinking? asked Steve.

"You sure you can't help?" she asked, biting the inside of her lower lip.

I cannot, and I am so sorry. The enemy has an inhibitor, and we are too far away to be effective.

"Fuck." She crouched and looked at her children. "Here's the plan. I'll try to shoot the alien asshole first and distract the others. You will run around. Run like there's a zombie horde after you. Run and don't look back. Just keep going where Mr. Fluffy Pants and Wrecker say."

"No, Mom!" said Paul. Cindy looked over as one of the men looked in their direction. The trio froze.

"It's settled," said Cindy, kissing her precious children on the forehead.

Before Cindy could stop her, Sammie said as she dropped her stick, "I have a plan. I can make plans, too, Mommy!" Sammie pitter-pattered towards the group with a magnified speed. Her sparkly pink shoes catching the sunlight in a splendorous rainbow.

Cindy cursed Mr. Fluffy Pants for giving her daughter that ability. She wanted to scream like she had when she tried cutting the dome off her face. Paul and she looked with horror as Sammie raced, unarmed, to the group.

The alien with the four men immediately charged at her, and Cindy held the rifle steady, using the trunk for support. Cindy shot. And missed.

"Motherfucker." She aimed again and exhaled. She shot again and hit her target. The outer glass of the alien's suit cracked and shattered. It grasped its throat and crumpled a mere yard before Sammie. Cindy wanted to see if it was dead, but the men started shooting at her.

Sammie's Mr. Fluffy Pants must have been close enough because the four men froze in midair, their bullets stopped, like a cheap magician's trick. Cindy and Paul hurried towards the open area. The men were a few feet away in an ethereal tableau of pain. Cindy held her rifle poised to finish them off, but she looked to the imposing alien. It still twitched, and Cindy noted with relief that it was diminishing. She stared at the men, then, the alien. She decided it was just a controlling abuser, like her ex-husband.

She scooped up Sammie and ran, with Paul close behind. Cindy watched as her son smashed something black from the alien's suit.

"So long," he said in triumph, "No more stopping my powers. Right, Wrecker?"

"We have to move fast," she said and continued on their way.

#

They neared the destination, and she looked, afraid men in green would emerge from the trees. It was a strange open field that seemed devoid of life. She judged it was a quarter of a mile wide, shaped in a perfect circle. When they entered, Cindy experienced the same heaviness she had months ago at the school. Suddenly, the large sphere-shaped vessel appeared. There was no sound. One moment the sky was empty, and the other, it engulfed the sun's light.

Her heart rose to her throat, and she looked to her children who smiled with anticipation.

Do not be afraid, said Steve, *You will be safe and well cared for. All we needed was the water and nutrition you provided for us. You will see our true forms, soon. In time.*

She had a million unanswered questions and was uneasy.

Cindy swallowed a large lump and gave her children one last look. She imagined as they floated upwards. Up above the hatred of men in green uniforms and hideous enemies. Up towards hope. Rising to what Cindy wished was a new life – life with boundless imagination. At that moment, she remembered her ex-husband and all the empty promises he made until she wasn't useful anymore.

"Steve," she said, "Can you just leave us? Can't the domes go up, safely?"

Steve was silent for a long time, and he finally answered, *We have a symbiotic relationship. Removing us too soon would kill you, and harm us.*

"How much time do you need?"

At least four more months.

"Mom?" asked Paul, "Are we going? Or staying?"

Sammie said, "I wanna go! I wanna see Mr. Fluffy Pants!"

She cursed out loud as Sammie flinched. Cindy looked at each of their faces and walked slowly towards the center of the field. They ran ahead of her, until she called them back.

They waited a few minutes, and soon, a warm light enveloped them. They rose up towards the ship, and she reached for her children's hands. They clung to each other. Their faces, in a silent prayer towards Heaven. The base of the ship opened as a golden glow enveloped them.

They entered the unknown. And, prayed for home.

SEPTEMBER IN THE NEW WORLD

STEVE STRED

September in the new world.

What a time to be alive.

The world was forever changed when the bombs dropped. The switches flipped and humans attacked themselves over petty reasons. The weapons of mass destruction launched from the planet and fell from space. The governments didn't care about the outcome, only wanting to not be left behind.

Scientists ran test after test and scenario after scenario – all coming to the same conclusion; nuclear fallout would leave the world a radiation nightmare for hundreds of thousands of years.

We'd seen what had happened at Chernobyl and Hiroshima, but still the ones making the decisions let their anger get the best of them and they sentenced the world's population without a second thought.

But then a funny thing happened, something the survivors hadn't expected.

While the vast majority of the human race was wiped from the surface of the earth in moments, it acted as a cleansing moment for Gaia, a reset button to undo the damage that humans had caused for thousands of years.

It took some time after the explosions before the planet became habitable again. At first the nuclear refugees didn't believe it was possible. The world was supposed to be toxic for millennia. But one by one, they ventured out into the air again, abandoning the primitive civilizations they'd created below the surface.

The humans who did survive vowed to do better.

They built their new homes from trees, returned to cultivating their own food and swore to never allow technology to rear its ugly head again.

I didn't know the old world, I didn't know how humans had been or how life was before the sky erupted in red. All I knew was that my boy gave me love, gave me the best scratches and said I was the best at everything.

As a puppy, you don't remember much from your early days of life. My mom would've had a small litter, as reproduction had slowed and the numbers were smaller and smaller over the years. Probably a result of the ongoing Earth cleansing. We were guests on the planet, and Mother Earth was prepared to not let mistakes of the past repeat.

Animals had lower life expectancies now. My mother not surviving for long after me and my siblings arrived. I think I remember what she looked like. Black? Maybe? It's all fuzzy.

She'd had us behind the remains of an old building, the bricks and cement blocks long since crumbling. She fed us and began to instill in us the instincts that would guide our lives. Then one day she succumbed to the new poisons that animals ingested and breathed. My last memory is of her falling, too weak to stand and never leaving the place she fell. Her body was emaciated, her bones so prominent. She starved so we could survive, the ultimate sacrifice of a mother for her children.

Us pups didn't stick around together for long. My two brothers were startled by a gust of wind and took off, never to be seen again. I think of them sometimes, wondering if they are still alive and if so, just where they ended up. My sister stayed with me for a week, before we got into a scuffle over a scrap of dead crow we'd came across. We snarled and snapped at each other but eventually I won out, being bigger and stronger than her. She tucked her tail and ran down the abandoned street, never looking back. I called out and howled, knowing I was putting myself in danger by doing so, but I wanted her to come back. She could have the meat, there'd be more, but she didn't stop. I miss her so.

The weeks after my sister left were a lonely, scary time for me. It was just me in a strange world, learning how to survive. Food at the best of times was scarce in the remains of the metropolis, so I decided the best course of action was to head towards the green areas on the outskirts. I forced some hope into my heart that the forests would supply more than the concrete world.

At first, I decided to only travel at night. My young brain said that I'd be safer in the dark.

I soon found there are things at night that will mystify and dazzle you. I'd never really seen the moon before, shining in all of its splendor. I made my way on to the top of an old corroded vehicle and sat for hours, basking in the view. If I wasn't so worried about being spotted, I'd have let out a long howl of joy.

I found that the old buildings took on a life of their own when the darkness descended. Where years ago, before the carnage, street lights would have illuminated the various roads and alleys, now the shadows were darker and deeper without them. I trembled and slunk low, wanting to do my best to remain undetected. I felt like I'd never see the sun again, never feel its warm rays shining down on my fur coat. The night went on and on, seeping into my bones.

After that one night of travel and countless frights and scares from noises I couldn't identify or sniff out, I changed my plans and only travelled during the day.

Things felt more familiar, I felt safer and maybe this ultimately let me keep my guard down more than I should have.

How wondrous a city must have been, back when humans lived and worked within these cement borders. There would have been displays, sounds, smells and global interaction on a scale I just couldn't comprehend.

Now the ghost town that lay before me was a frightening, sad, desolate place where even a simple piece of garbage being tossed around by the wind made me flinch or make my hackles go up.

I jogged as much as I could, stopping to find water whenever my tongue started to bob up and down against my lips or my nose didn't feel as moist as before. Water was easy to find, most of the rain now pooled and settled in abandoned objects.

The next day, I began to feel the fatigue from not sleeping the night before. I'd long since left any part of the familiar life I had before behind, now the rusted metal heaps left to decay looked different, frightening. While the structures that reached skyward were similar, each had its own quirks and the further I progressed the more these *things* became ominous and sinister to my young eyes.

Where once glass used to exist and act as a wind barrier for offices far above my crinkled forehead, now those openings screamed and made sounds that had me thinking I was being attacked from above. I'd seen many shadows from the birds of prey whom patrolled the skies, their massive wings creating a harbinger of doom that blocked out the sun as they swooped and circled.

After dragging my pads for miles, it was time to find a hole and steal a few hours of sleep. A replenished pup was an energetic pup. So I made my way into an old shopping mall that seemed to stretch on for miles and miles.

Finding an old storage cupboard that was open a crack, I nosed my way in, circled twice before finding the perfect position to lay down in, then tucked my whiskers under my tail and drifted off to a deep sleep.

***

Now, I've never really dreamed, but during that nap – I did.

It was vivid, it was emotional and I'll remember it for the rest of my days.

I was walking down a road I'd never travelled. I felt lost, unsure if this was the direction I should be going, but something gave me hope. I felt that the road before me was filled with brightness, a path or a calling. Something that said "*Hey, pup! Come this way!*"

So I trotted forward. The flowers smelled fantastic, the air filled my moist nostrils with the scents of a million smiles.

Then I saw it. I saw *him*. There was a figure running towards me, a boy, and I ran faster, my tail wagging, my eyes jostling and my heart beating to the rhythm of a dozen happy drums.

"MY BOY!" I wanted to bark to the heavens and share the joy only the sight of being reunited with family could bring.

Sadly, I woke up in my dark cupboard just before I leapt into his outstretched arms.

***

It was on the third day as I travelled towards the green band that I picked up a scent that raised my alarm bells.

It was an earthy, dusty odour that was masking rot and decay.

I hadn't spotted any other living things for some time, but I knew this smell wasn't coming from anything I'd want to meet. I started to move in double time, my floppy ears bouncing around against my head as I ran. I could hear whatever it was running behind me. I heard the clicking of claws against the road and the creature's breaths coming faster and closer.

The trees were growing in size, the distance smaller. I'd never felt fear like this before; not when my mother had passed, not even when my siblings abandoned me. Now I felt my heart racing, my pulse pounding as I pleaded with my paws to cover the space.

If I could just make it into those trees, I'll have a chance, I thought.

Then I felt searing pain rip through my back end. The creature had struck me with its claws. I went down hard, tumbling and summersaulting against the painful surface.

I came to a stop facing the animal, but I never got to see what attacked me. Just as the fog was about to lift from my fall, I heard shouting and then a large rock landed directly beside the big creature. Another rock struck its hind quarters and it let out a growl and turned, sprinting away in the opposite direction.

I struggled into a standing position, feeling my hind end burning from the attack. I turned my head to survey the damage, finding four slash marks deep in my leg. If it'd been any further over and the creature any closer – I'd probably have lost my tail.

I started to lick my wounds when I heard footsteps and whirled around, only now remembering that someone or something had scared my assailant away.

I found myself staring at four humans.

There were three taller ones, all looking older than the fourth.

The fourth was a shorter one. This one didn't have any fur on its face and it smiled at me with nothing but kindness.

"Come here, boy," they said. I didn't know exactly what the words meant, but they sounded soothing and I felt drawn towards the softness in its voice.

I lowered myself and approached, weary of potential violence.

Instead, there was only love.

Then I realized who it was!

It was the boy from my dream, right before me.

I threw myself into his body, ignoring the pain of my injuries. I licked and rubbed and wiggled like only true love can let you.

The day that I met my boy, my life changed for the better.

That instant connection we had made me feel safe and secure.

I followed the four back to their village, the boy frequently stopping to give me some water from a container he had. He scratched behind my ears and told me how good I was.

***

It didn't take long for me to find my place within the family group.

The ravages of the atmospheric changes made certain that we dealt with our fair share of challenges.

The thing about love and acceptance though, is that none of this ever mattered.

I loved the small girl with three arms just as much as I loved the woman with two heads.

The village became my close family, with the branches of the family tree growing every year.

Living things adapted to the wild fluctuations that now ruled the weather. The bombs had done such a heinous job that in the summer, temperatures would get so hot that we'd need to stay indoors for days on end, or venture below ground.

In the winter we experienced the opposite, the cold gripping us so tightly that you'd freeze solid if you were outside for longer than a few seconds.

We didn't have much in the way of threats to contend with, being hidden so well in the dense woods. Occasionally a severely mutated predator would find its way into our area, lured there by the smell of food and civilization.

Us dogs would bark and bare our teeth, acting as a warning system as well as a line of defense.

Once the danger had been removed, we'd be given lots of thanks, pats and treats.

I lived to serve and protect my boy.

***

Reflecting back on my life, as I lay near my human's fire, I know I've had it better than most. The start of my life might have been scary, frightening and traumatic, but I came out on the other end a stronger dog, a happier dog.

Sure, I've aged.

There's grey now along my snout and peppering my eyebrows.

My tail still wags but not as fervently as it did in my youth, and my joints are stiff.

Every year that passes, more and more fur falls out. My sores and exposure burns get treated and bandaged when that happens.

Long walks are a thing of the past, but that's ok.

My human, *forever my boy to me*, makes sure I'm cared for. Every morning he puts my jacket on, made from a nice sheep's wool. We go for a short walk, stopping along the way to say hello to our friends. I take my time and smell all of my favourite spots.

After lunch, we share a nap together. I bask in the warmth of his arms wrapped around me, knowing this is the place I was meant to be.

Following dinner, we go for another walk. This time we follow a path that brings us near the river. My jacket keeps me warm as we sit on the bank enjoying the world before us, my human lost in thought. I'm not though.

My mind races during these moments; I think of how much I love him, how good it feels when he touches me, pets me and how lucky I am to be where I am. Sometimes, I'll think about my siblings. I hope they've found their forever home.

What does he think about? I wouldn't know. When I look up at him, I'll see his face change, emotions flickering through his muscles like the twinkling stars above.

I no longer chase deer or rabbits, I can't track animals during the village hunt, and I can't get my back paw all the way up to scratch behind my ears.

But none of that matters now.

I'm a good boy, filled with love and when he looks at me, and our eyes meet – well, I know I'm the luckiest dog in this new world.

As September ends and another winter starts to work its way towards us, I'll spend more time near the fire and less time on those walks.

But for right now, September in *this* new world – what a time to be alive.

STRINGS

TIM LEBBON

I wake in the early hours and hear scratching, and moaning, and the secretive whisper of something brushing along walls. When this happened before, Margot and Ray were still my friends and staying with me, and I believed their lovemaking to be the cause of the sounds. Trying to keep quiet for my sake, the height of passion took away their caution. The scrape of fingernails against a wall. The steady touch of bedding shifting somewhere beyond my room. Their groans, low and long as if such ecstasy could last forever.

This time, I know the noises aren't caused by them, because Margot and Ray left three days ago. I suspect I'll never see them again. They became worried about what we were attempting to do, though I think their fear is misplaced. I think they're cowards.

I lie awake and listen, trying to place the sounds and figure out their source. They seem to be originating from inside my head as well as without, as if dreams can have echoes. I suppose they can. All this has happened because of a dream I had so many years before, a fervent desire that inspired and invigorated the three of us to try things never before imagined. That's me: the dreamer. I was the driving force, the passion, though they were the ones with the knowledge. We all had to give something, and I was happy to be the guinea pig.

Another scratch. A deeper groan. I can't yet understand what the noises mean, but in that cool, motionless darkness I realise that the time will soon come when I do understand. They're clearer now than they were last time I heard them. Clearer, louder, and closer.

It's working, I think, and the one thing I cannot do is open my eyes. Even in the dark, I fear that I will see.

"Don't mind him," Margot said, "he's just being a prick." I saw the look she threw Ray when she said it, and the brief flicker of some complex expression on his face. Part of it was annoyance, part excitement. I knew some of what he was feeling. Margot and I had been engaged until three years before, and I understood more about her than he'd ever know.

That's what I liked to think, at least. In truth, I believed our work was tearing us apart even on the day I slipped the ring on her finger. Ray wasn't so invested. He was here, he was helping, but he wasn't touched by what we were trying to do. For him, this was all about money and fame, his future and not anyone else's.

"All I'm saying is, I think you need to be careful," he said. He took another long swig of red wine. He drank it from half-pint glasses, and he'd already put away a bottle during dinner. "Your vitals always look weird after a dose, and that effect is growing."

"Maybe the instruments are on the blink," I said. "I'm feeling fine."

"You sure?" Margot asked. She leaned forward in the armchair and touched my knee. Ray bristled at the contact, and hoped I didn't display the satisfaction I felt at his discomfort.

"Yeah. Fine. Better than ever." I stood and paced the room. It was a big living room, far too large for just the three of us. Two sprawling L-shaped sofas, three armchairs, a slew of floor cushions, a massive TV affixed to one wall, and a fireplace I could walk into and stand up straight. The place slept twenty people in eight bedrooms, but we'd needed somewhere this big for all our kit and instruments.

Besides, it was out of the way and hidden from prying eyes. Grand House had its own mile-long driveway and couldn't be seen from any neighbouring roads, yet the nearest town was an easy walk away.

"It can't go on like this," Ray said. "It's not fair to us. We agreed right from the beginning, if something's looking off, we pull back and reassess our methods."

"Nothing's looking off," I say.

"What the fuck do you know?" Ray snapped. He shook his head, sighed. I was used to him playing the 'what do you know?' card. "Neil, I can't in all good conscience sit here and agree that nothing's wrong."

I leaned against the fireplace. I stared into the big mirror hanging above it, offering a wide vista of the room behind me. They were both staring back at me. Margot ran her finger around the top of her wine glass. I had a sudden, unbidden memory of making love with her, the noises she would make, and I looked away in case my eyes betrayed it.

Something whispered deep within the stones of the chimney stack. I froze, head to one side.

"Neil? Did you hear me?" Ray asked.

"Huh?"

"I said I think you should see a proper doctor. I'm not comfortable with this anymore. I never finished my training."

"You're an almost-doctor," I said. "This is an almost-experiment. So what are you afraid of? Losing me, and losing your payday?" I turned around, daring a reply from them both.

Ray sighed. Margot shrugged and said nothing. The walls whispered in agreement.

I sat back in the recliner while Margot prepared the next shot of our strange elixir.

She was the genius of this team. She knew it, I knew it, and Ray sure as hell knew it, too. Her work in nanotech medicines should have propelled her into the higher echelons of twenty-first century scientific achievement. When she and I were together, before Ray came along and our plans grew, she'd talked about it often. I understood some of it, but not much. Perhaps that was why we grew apart.

"More magic juice," I said, wincing as the needle pricked my arm.

"It's not magic." She concentrated as she depressed the plunger, glancing up at the screen beside the chair and down again at the hypodermic. Ray sat in the next room monitoring my reactions to the injection, and there was a constantly open channel between us and him. I could hear him humming.

"When do you think it'll start working?"

Margot withdrew the needle and dabbed the bubble of blood. She bent my arm back and patted it, telling me I should keep it there. It wasn't as if I didn't know. She'd put a hundred needles in me over the past twenty days.

I hated it when she was like this, so immersed in her work that she hardly heard me talking. It was just about the only time she and I were alone now, even though Ray could see us on his screens and hear every word. She acted like I wasn't here.

"Margot," I said. She wheeled her chair back to a table and tapped at her laptop.

"Soon," she said. She didn't sound convinced. "Ten minutes and you can do the tests."

I lay back in the seat and tried to feel the new stew of nanobots streaming through my blood. There was nothing, even though several times I'd convinced myself that I could feel them pulsing towards my brain, implanting themselves there, setting to work. Margot would smile indulgently, and Ray would tut and shake his head.

I wasn't stupid, but I wasn't them. I was only here because I'd once loved Margot, and started us along a path I could not quit.

Who wouldn't want to be a superhuman?

I listened and looked, and heard and saw nothing different.

And then Ray called me into another room, and he started running through the same test procedures we'd been using for weeks, and everything began to change.

In the morning I open the back door and stand once again on the threshold.

It's been three days since Ray and Margot left, and I have yet to go outside. The house is set in several acres of land on the shallow side of a valley. The landscape is beautiful and wild. I see the regular quilt work of fields in the distance, but closer to the house there is woodland, expanses of heather and scrub, and a rocky slope leading up the valley's opposite side. There is no sound of humanity. Even occasional vehicles passing along the narrow country lane a mile away are mere whispers, their engine sounds swallowed by the stone wall and hedge bordering the road.

And yet I hear. I hear *more*. Between breaths, something else comes in. It's a distant whispering, scheming intelligences hidden in the sunlight, languages I cannot know riding the breeze across the countryside. On the day Margot and Ray left I tried to replicate what these strange noises were, and I saw Ray's face as he recorded my impersonations. He looked cold in a warm room. He looked chilled.

They are much louder when the back door is open.

I take one step outside. My foot crunches on the gravel path, and the whispers instantly fade away to nothing. Even the breeze drops, a held breath. I hear my own breathing, and it's not the comfort it should be.

I take another step and the whispering begins again, louder, closer. It's an agitated babble, an excited susurration. I back up immediately and slam the door closed, and through the heavy old wood I can hear those noises joining the breeze, shushing through the house' ancient eaves.

They sound disappointed.

I pace around the house, examining the detritus of our time here. I have been in limbo since they departed, trying to persuade myself that it's all part of the experiment, an intentional abandonment to help advance the progress we'd been trying to make. But I can't convince myself of that. I saw Margot's fear when she left, although she seemed averse to telling me. Ray couldn't even face me.

In one of the big house's downstairs bedrooms, the two single beds are pushed aside to make room for a table bearing all manner of recording equipment. At its centre is the simple digital dictaphone I used.

"You're hearing more," Margot said, and she was the most animated she'd been for several days.

"Well …"

"There's nothing here. Ray? Is there anything here?" Ray sat at a desk weighted down with audio equipment, spectrographs, and frequency modulators.

"There's always something here," Ray said. "You know that. The air's full of sound, we can only hear things in a narrow bandwidth. Above that, below, there's always more."

"Whole new worlds of sound!" Margot said, staring at me as if I was suddenly something new. "So describe it to us. Tell us what it is."

Whispers, I thought. I was troubled by what I was hearing.

"I'm not sure I can," I said.

"Mimic," Ray said. "Use a microphone and a recording device, listen, try to repeat the sounds you're hearing."

"Will that really work?" Margot asked.

"Surprisingly effective, sometimes."

Margot nodded and turned back to me. "We'll leave you alone. You listen, and record. We want to hear. I *need* to hear!"

I knew very well that if these experiments succeeded in opening my ranges of hearing and sight, Margot would be the next one to undertake the course of injections. I was pretty certain even then that Ray wanted nothing to do with it. When he was drunk he talked about fucking with nature, but the lure of crammed bank balances and fame was strong.

"I'm afraid," I whispered. Beyond the room, something responded to my whisper. It sounded amused.

"Afraid of what?" Margot asked.

I wasn't sure how I could tell her. It would have been like explaining fear of the colour red to a blind person.

"Here," she said, thrusting the dictaphone against my chest. "We'll wait in the kitchen."

Margot and Ray left me in that room, alone with the whispers. I listened for a while, head tilted, brain struggling to decipher sounds it was never built or meant to hear.

Then I turned on the machine.

Around midday I see the first of the shadows. I've been expecting it. In a way, the expectation has been worse than the reality. Margot would bemoan the fact that my vision seemed unchanged by the experiment.

Now, I wish she was here with me again.

I'm standing at the open back door in the cottage's kitchen. The garden is large and nicely landscaped, with a climbing frame for kids, a barbecue area, and several paved patios for seating. The sun blazes down. The valley is deserted, save for me and the whispers that conspire to draw me out.

I see the shape dancing beneath a tree.

I blink, frown, shield my eyes from the sun, and look again. It's like a smudge on my vision, a blot in my eye. The tree branches hang low, and although the air here is still, the branches move as if disturbed by a breeze. Birds take flight. Several dead leaves fall, or perhaps they're shed by a squirrel hidden away in the tree. It's too far away for me to make out clearly, but the dancing figure I saw has gone. Just branches. Shadows.

As I turn away the whispers return, louder and closer than ever before, and in their alien tongue I hear mockery at my disbelief.

I slam the door and run through the house, seeking the false solace of my room. On the way to the staircase I pass the small second kitchen where Margot kept her concoctions locked up in the fridge. I still haven't cleaned up the mess. She smashed every container, poured the fluid into the sink, splashed it up the walls. She followed it down with a gallon of bleach, and the stink still burns my nostrils.

Perhaps I'm lucky they didn't consider doing the same to me.

I reach my small bedroom and slam the door behind me, sitting on the edge of the bed and expecting the whispers to follow. They keep their distance. Even the silence is loaded now, and I imagine great things poised to shout so loud that their voices will crush me down.

I know I'll have to leave soon. If I want to retain my sanity, I need to make it to the nearest town and ask for help.

The thought of walking along country lanes and hearing them all around drives me almost to tears, and I curl up on the bed. Even though for now they are silent once more, I wish the voices would let me sleep.

"Hairy bastard."

"I can't help that. It's natural."

"Not for everyone. You're less evolved."

Margot rested her head on my chest. I could feel her heavy breath on my sweat-dampened chest, feel the dampness of her against my thigh. We'd made love twice, and I was already considering whether I could manage one more before we both fell asleep. She had that effect on me. It was love, but it was also a deep, passionate lust.

"Maybe you could evolve me a bigger cock."

"I wish." She propped herself up on her elbow and turned to look at me. "You have no idea, do you?"

"What do you mean?"

"How it works." I liked her when she was like this. Her cheeks and thighs ruddied from my stubble, long hair sweat-dampened against her forehead, pupils dilated, she was approximately fifteen times more intelligent than me, and I loved it. I knew a lot of men who'd shrivel beneath such intellect, metaphorically and literally, but I found it a massive turn-on. In truth I did understand a lot of what she said, just not to the depth and degrees that she did. Sometimes she lost me, and if that happened I'd go along for the sound of her voice, the denseness of her passion.

"I mean, we've essentially halted human evolution. There's no survival of the fittest anymore, not for humanity. Imagine if we had to hunt food in the dark, and those with better eyesight survived and procreated more? But we have supermarkets and food dumped on our doorsteps. What if bats carried a deadly plague, and we had to listen out for their high-frequency calls and hide from them? Those with that hearing ability would survive and pass it on to their offspring. But we're cosseted in our four walls. Given medicines to cure things that should really kill us. Weaklings are helped to survive, and —"

"Weaklings?"

She shrugged. "You know what I mean. There's no natural selection anymore. We're *all* selected. We've stopped evolving because we think ourselves already perfect."

"And we're not?"

She reached down and grabbed me. Grunted in disappointment. Arched an eyebrow.

"Give me time," I said.

"We should do it. We've talked about it long enough. I've tried the formula on mice, rats, apes."

"Apes? I don't know —"

"Ray said he'll help."

"Ray? He's a prick."

"I like him," she said. "And besides, he's the best tech guy I know. He's got more stolen equipment in his basement than NASA. Apple would pay for some of the shit he's designed and developed just to amuse himself."

"If they did, he'd have sold it to them."

She started squeezing, kneading. "Yeah, he's all about the money, but that doesn't mean he isn't brilliant."

"He's worth a fortune already. Why would he … do … this?"

Margot wasn't answering anymore. She was smiling. "I do believe you're ready to go again."

I smiled. "Survival of the fittest."

I haven't been injected for three days, but it seems that Margot's theories on dosage and continuity were wrong. She always believed that my body's natural defences would attack the alien compound, and that would necessitate introducing more on a daily basis. It targeted my hearing and sight, its pre-programmed purpose to open up my abilities, expand and broaden them. It worked on my sensory organs, nerve receptors, signal transference, and also the parts of my brain given to translating such information. An artificial evolution, she called it. In her eyes, she was allowing those two senses to achieve their full potential, but they would always revert. I would be given a glimpse at something greater, hear a wider spectrum of sound. The effect was never meant to be permanent.

She was so wrong. The abilities are expanding and strengthening, not fading away. I have never felt so alone, yet the more time goes by, the more I begin to understand that I am surrounded. The things that surround me, though … I have no wish to know them.

I have to leave this place. Perhaps closer to other people, the effect will wear off. Maybe I'll even find Margot and Ray again.

I'll try to tell them it was all a joke.

It was as if the whispers I heard – those guttural, harsh croakings of things mostly unseen, in languages we were never meant to hear – channeled themselves through me. That was the only explanation I could give. Left alone in that room, I did my best to relay the things I was hearing in my own voice. At first it was like singing someone else's song, and I felt quite ridiculous, trying to remember the sounds and cadences, the tones and feel of those strange voices. Speaking into the dictaphone, I sounded like a dog making strangling noises, or a child attempting to feign a deep voice.

Then something strange happened. As I spoke, I heard those real voices in my ears, muttering their strange tones as if coaching me. I continued for a couple of minutes, then hit 'stop' and dropped the dictaphone onto the table.

The voices receded, leaving behind the echo of a soft, knowing laugh. It took a while to fade, and even when Margot and Ray came back into the room, I could hear the dregs of those strange sounds.

"Done?" Margot asked.

I nodded down at the dictaphone. She picked it up and pocketed it.

"Mind if me and Ray …?" She gestured at the door, then the two of them left me there without waiting for a reply.

What happened next was the first instant I began to comprehend just how fractured my relationship with myself had become, now that I was hearing and seeing more. I began to realise that I was not only hearing higher and deeper tones, or seeing a wider band of the spectrum. I was hearing *further*. Seeing *deeper*. Something about what they'd done to me had shifted my reality, or moved reality around me.

More things were making themselves known to me.

A couple of minutes later I heard their raised voices. Ray was crying, wretched, wrenching sobs torn from the heart of him. Margot was shouting, sounding both startled and vulnerable. I knew what they had heard, and a perverse part of me was glad. I didn't want to be the only one.

She stormed back into the room, kicking the door open as if ready to attack me, but then just standing there, staring, and it was the utter fear in her eyes – the fear of me – that upset me the most. She remained in the doorway, ready to run at any moment.

"What have we done?" she said.

That night they left. I thought perhaps they'd gone out to discuss the experiment, leaving the confines of the house, and that they'd return in a few hours. But they had abandoned me. I tried to follow, but couldn't. Each time I left the building, those voices assailed me more, singing terrible songs that would drive me mad if I heard them a moment longer. They sang and sang.

Trapped with myself, I was becoming a stranger.

I know now that I have no choice but to leave. They're getting closer. If I lie down I hear their whispers, starting far along a wide, empty corridor and then drawing closer, louder. It's only when I sit up that they dwindle away. I wonder what would happen if I didn't sit up.

It's dawn when I decide to leave. I stand inside the back door for a long while, peering through the side window and searching the landscape for shadows that are out of place. There are none that I can see, but even that disturbs me. It means that they're hiding.

I close my eyes and press my hands to my ears. *I wish I was the old me*, I think. *I wish I couldn't see and hear more. I wish Margot had never been so clever, and Ray so cynically brilliant.* In comparison I was merely their lab rat, and they've left me alone to suffer now that they've finished with me.

Now that they're afraid of what they've done.

I wish like all the best lab rats, they'd put me down.

Opening my eyes, taking my hands from my ears, I see and hear them as soon as I open the door.

They can't touch me, I think. *They won't hurt me*. It is fair reasoning, because I am seeing and hearing things that are always there. The experiments have changed me, not my surroundings, giving me the ability to perceive realities that humans aren't supposed to know. That does not mean that they will now hurt me. Maybe they're pleased to be seen. Perhaps those whispers I hear are songs of joy.

I cross the gravelled area and approach the long driveway. In my determination to leave, my senses become unguarded, and the world opens up around me. Birdsong fills the air, and I hear the differing tones, the deeper meanings. A breeze rustles through the trees, carry rumours from afar. Sunlight dapples the distant valley sides. Its journey is over, memories of deep space splashed like foam across a seashore. I see and hear new realities and despair at my inability to understand.

I am two hundred feet from the house and moving away. *This might work*, I think. *If I find them again, perhaps they'll see that their fear was misplaced.*

I pass through the gate that borders the property and out onto moorland, following the rough lane up towards the road. That's when the whispering begins.

A breeze first, then a more sibilant harshness, inside my head and beyond. My blood runs cold, my skin prickling with goosebumps, because I have never heard them sounding so angry. Yet I have done nothing wrong. If they dislike my new abilities, then let them come and tell me why. I cannot remain alone in that house forever.

I walk on, pressing my hands over my ears. That only serves to trap the voices inside. Their strange words echo around my mind, leaving a corrupt trace of themselves wherever they touch.

I see the first of the shadows as I round a corner in the road. It hunkers down in a field behind a hedge, defying the sun, pulsing like a living thing yet surely not. Surely.

I freeze, shifting from foot to foot as I try to make it out. It is difficult to discern properly. Whichever way I look, however much I shield my eyes, the shadow seeks to dazzle me with refracted sunlight. I move closer, and suddenly the whispering in my head changes from angry to mournful. Still tinged with darkness. Still alien.

I see Ray's body splayed on the ground beneath the shifting shadow. My breath is stolen from me. He's on his back, eyes open as if staring at the thing above him.

It is wan and grey, and other colours of dark infinity I cannot understand. It is connected to Ray in a dozen places by long, flexing limbs. It seems to be dead as well, although I'm not sure these things comply with any distinction between alive and dead.

Fifty feet beyond it, another shape sits beneath an old oak tree. It is a similar shape and colour. I don't want to see what lies beneath it, because I already know.

"No," I say. "Oh, no. No." My voice seems to stir the attention of other things more distant and still unseen, because the whispering gathers pace and volume. I'm driven back by the words, stumbling over my feet and sprawling in the lane. I scrabble backwards, keeping my eyes on the things I should not see as they pulse and whimper above the bodies of my two dead friends.

I turn and run back to the house, herded by screams and screeches, shoved by shadows when I dare to glance back. I realise with a terrible finality that these things do not want to be known.

And now, I'm the only one who still knows.

Back in the house with the doors shut and the curtains drawn, I stagger into the large living room and lean against the fireplace, head hung, tears spattering the old slate hearth.

Outside, they have gone quiet. They know they have me.

I look up into the big mirror and see movement, and for the briefest instant I think Ray and Margot have come back. Their deaths are a mistake, as is the experiment. I'll get over it. With their help I'll get better, and we'll move on without ever revealing what we did here.

Then I see the thing standing close. I can feel it behind me, exerting a terrible gravity on my life and my soul as they surely do to every man, woman and child. Dark strings lead from around and within me, rising like quivering tentacles and meeting eventually in that monstrous puppeteer's hands.

Though I close my eyes, I will always hear its dreadful, intimate voice.

SUMMER SONG

B F JONES

Victor kneels by the large pot, trowel in hand; he's removed the turf around the rose bush, unveiling the roots. He puts on the thick gloves and grabs the central branch with both hands and pulls, dislodging the rest of the root from the constricting pot. There. He rises up again, rubbing the small of his back. He can spot a couple of very small buds; in a few weeks the bush will be covered in flowers.

Victor takes a sip of the tea he's left cooling on the patio table, then sets off to plant the bush in the sunny corner of the garden. That had been Hilda's plan. He lowers the rose bush and pats the turf tight around it, waters. There you go, Hilda, Summer Song roses, rich dark coral, like we had at our wedding, 40 years ago.

Victor loves gardening. It's the only moment when time doesn't stand odiously still. He rakes the leaves from around the Magnolia, waters the small patch of grass he recently seeded, fascinated by the tiny bright shoots starting to prick through the mud. Then he takes the tools back to the shed and walks into the house.

Today is Friday so he'll have fish and chips and a glass of Chardonnay. He will bring it into the living room and have a TV dinner. The thought of sitting alone in the dining room doesn't appeal.

Time stands still again. He wants to call Gemma but he knows that if he does, it will go to answer phone. When she next calls him in a week or two she'll tell him again how busy she is and how late she works and how insane it all is. He'll hear pub noises in the background, music, laughter.

He watches TV, hopping from one channel to another. Gemma's husband Guy installed Sky TV for him and Gemma insisted to pay for his subscription. It'll keep you nice and busy dad, all those documentaries, isn't that a treat? He watches Planet Earth, marvelling at nature, its strength, its quirk, its species. Are Rhinos the loneliest animals? He's not so sure. Do they stay awake all night, missing their wife and child, counting the lonely hours?

The next morning brings a bed of dew, shimmering under the orange sunrise. A long day stretches ahead. Victor goes out for the paper, and a pint of milk. At nine he goes to the garden centre and buys a couple of Gerbera, they will look good in the flower bed that got damaged by a fox. When the grass has dried, he sets to plant the flowers, fetching his spade from the shed.

The little girl startles him, the brown eyes spying at him from over the fence. Hello, she says. What's your name? My name is Poppy. Do you want a cup of tea? The small hand pops a pink plastic teacup across to him. Victor takes it, drinks the pretend liquid with exaggerated slurping noises and gives it back thanking her before she disappears.

The following day, when he waters the flowers, Poppy is here. She shows him her drawing of a rainbow over the fence and they have more fake tea. She asks about the Sunflowers and he explains that those are Gerbera, that they come in more colours than sunflowers. They're less capricious as well. He doubts the little girl understands the word "capricious" but she nods before waving goodbye.

See you tomorrow, she adds.

TELL IT TO THE BIRDS

ASTRA BLOOM

He says
The garden is beautiful, isn't it?
As if it has been dropped down for him, for us, by God during this Lockdown time.
And what a surprise, how lucky we are.

He never says
And everything in it was planted by you. You made this beautiful garden over fifteen years with limited strength and health and no help whatsoever from me because I hate gardening, it bores me silly, I like sunbathing.

He says
How is it sleeping in this room? (I have moved into our daughter's old room but still he bursts in without knocking.)
I say
It's not restful, it's like a cupboard, a store room, but I'll sort things out and paint the walls green once I've finished writing this book.

He walks out of the room as I say the word green and now I like the colour even more. I can see the exact fresh shade, I just want to sit and stare at it.

I say
Would you please wash your hands before you put your fingers inside me – I've just seen you picking at the dog's eye gunk and it just makes me feel a bit *you know,* it's not hygienic …
He says
You are an expert at shaming me. You just love shaming me, don't you?

I say
Can you please make sure you wash your hands before you knead the bread – if you want to have a knead – I can do it myself, I quite like it – but you've just been to the shops – we're being so careful about the virus, it would be foolish …
He says
I washed them earlier. No. I'm not a kid. You're getting obsessive.

I don't eat the bread.

I put a bit of the world on (mostly I do not lately. Since dad died two weeks ago I can't bear much radio.)
There's news on every half-hour (which seems too much and was it always so?)

The news says
We are reaching the peak number of cases.
(There is no end to lockdown in sight.)
We have five times more deaths that Germany.
(There is no end in sight.)

It's a new thing, a member of the public – one person each day is now allowed to have a question answered at the daily briefing; someone called Lin has had her question selected.
Lin says
I miss my grandchildren, I'd like to know when I might be able to see them again.
Matt Hancock says
Yes, this is a Good Question and it shows the emotional impact that this is all having.
(He can't tell Lin When. No, there is no clear end in sight.)
Matt Hancock says
Sadly, Lin, if you are an *older grandparent* rather than a young one, and if you have any underlying health conditions it is likely that you will need to keep isolating for quite some time. (Quite some time.)

I miss my two kids, they're grown ups now – not-kids-but-my-kids – I want to hug them, I want to laugh with them. I haven't spoken to a friend in person since the end of January, my lockdown begun earlier than the official one: I was ill and then all my energy was gong into my book and meeting a deadline which I failed to meet and dealing with a husband with problems which I failed to deal with and being sad about a dad dying – now dead.
I turn off the news and go back in the garden because my husband is no longer there and the fact that there is a female blackbird – that lovely cocoa brown – eating the sunflower seeds I scattered seems more relevant than anything. It's my news.

I say
It's beautiful in the garden, isn't it, Blackbird?
She says
Yes. Thank You. Yes.

I coughed a few times this morning, the very mild cough I've had for months – more of an allergy I think, but it is worse today, I think it's the dust and mould in the room I now sleep in.
He says
Don't cough near me! Don't walk by me and cough!

He says
I don't always remember you are grieving. Why would I? Your father was nothing to me. If you need help, ask for it. I'm not a mind reader. Tell me what you need. Of course I care.
I say
I need a few things lifted and moved, if that's okay. The clutter, the mess everywhere, it's doing my head in, it won't take you long, just this here and that there – no more than say, twenty minutes.
(He has no work on today, and I'm not strong – due to my illness and sometimes also due to being a woman, which is very frustrating.)
I say
I just need some comfort and ease in my grief, and this lockdown, we're just stuck here within these four walls, I could really do with a bit of a tidier space.

He says
Twenty minutes is more than I was prepared for, more than I was expecting, more than I'm willing to give.
I say.
Really, I thought I wasn't asking for much. *You said to ask you.*

Then he is silent. He says nothing.

Later, after eight hours of brooding, eight hours of sitting in a chair – first in the garden, then in the living room in silence, after eight hours of my keeping away from him,
He says
I've been holding my anger in because I know you are grieving. I was so angry I could have burned down the sun.

I am so tired. (No end is in sight.)

The blackbird is on my lawn under my blossoming apple tree.
I say
What day is it?

She says
Time doesn't exist. And you are a lonely individual trapped here in an abusive relationship. Narcissists struggle to love, it's hard for them to really give.

I say
Peck your seed up, bird. Then you better fly off, come tell me that again when I have wings.

THE BLUE OF MILK

KATHY FISH

There was a woman who went to the park at night and swung on the swings and drank from a bottle in a paper bag. When she became dizzy she would stand and remove her clothes and walk the perimeter of the park singing low.

There was a man who walked his dog, who saw her, but kept to the other side of the street and never entered the park. When the moon was out and shining she looked blue, he thought, a naked blue or silver blue or the blue of milk. He tried not to look at her.

There was a small child who lay in bed waiting for his mother to return. He decided one night to follow her.

The man saw the boy trailing far behind the woman. The boy dragged a blanket. The man kept to the other side of the street and didn't enter the park.

All the nights after this were the same with the woman taking off all her clothes and circling the park and drinking from the bottle in the bag and the boy trailing behind like a ghost and the man walking his dog and seeing them both but keeping to the other side of the street and not entering the park or calling out to the woman and the boy.

The nights grew colder. The woman persisted with taking off her clothes and the boy persisted with following her in just his thin pajamas and the man persisted in walking his dog but the man began wearing a coat and the dog too wore a coat that matched the man's.

One night the man's dog, a terrier growing old and blind, started to bark at the woman as she passed by and the woman and the boy trailing behind her were startled and for the first time noticed the man and his dog and the woman stopped and the boy stopped and the woman cried out and the terrier strained at his leash and the man felt now he had no choice but to cross the street and enter the park and apologize for his dog and get the woman to put on her clothes and maybe help her and her son back to their house and God knows what else but now he probably had to do something as they had both seen him.

The terrier stopped barking and the man bent to pick him up as he crossed the street and entered the park and approached the woman who was crying and patting the head of the boy whose arms were wrapped around her naked legs.

The man said I apologize if my dog frightened you I don't know what got into him but see he's very sweet really and you can pet him if you'd like. The man knelt and the boy reached out his hand to let the terrier smell it. Both the boy and the woman petted the terrier and let him lick their hands and the man tried not to look at the woman.

Ma'am he said you seem to have misplaced your clothes can I help you find them? The boy looked up to his mother now embarrassed but the mother only said yes let's find my clothes and she set down the bag with the bottle in it in such a way that it would not tip over.

Her clothes lay on the ground near the swings and the woman pulled them on. They were only pajamas and it had gotten quite cold now and the man took off his coat and put it over the woman's shoulders and his stocking cap he put on the boy's head and now everybody looked quite normal and it seemed okay to walk them home which he offered to do.

It turned out that the woman and the boy lived not far from where the man lived, on his own with the terrier, though he'd never seen them during the day or any other place in the neighborhood. She asked him to come inside and she would make them all tea but she was unsteady on her feet. She said this is our abode and it sounded like a warble and she made a sweeping gesture with her arm and the boy started to cry. She went to the kitchen and the man sat down with his terrier on his lap and the boy lay on the floor with the blanket knotted in his fist.

The woman brought a cup of water with a tea bag in it but the water had not been heated. The man watched the brown color of the tea swirl slowly into the clear water and said I would like to help you if I can do you need some money or food do you have a job what can I do? The woman said there is nothing to be done or said, we are fine you finish your tea and go please. The boy dragged his blanket to the other room and the woman said we need to sleep now and she came to the man with the terrier on his lap and gave him a kiss on the cheek. The man could see her breast through the opening in her pajamas and he touched it and mouthed it and she let him and she liked it and this is how they were for some time, the woman bent to the man, the long strands of her hair falling onto the little dog's head and over his blind eyes, in the quiet of the woman's abode.

THE BOXER

STUART TURTON

Three tired punches before the bell rings, leather gloves glancing off sweat-slick skin. The crowd jeers as "Mighty" Marvin Hale staggers back to his corner, trailing sweat and blood, wishing it was over, wishing he was already lying on the mat.

He drops onto the stool, bodies crowding him with sponges, tape, advice, ice. A flashbulb pops, a reporter tossing questions through the ropes.

Hale doesn't see a single one of them. He's burrowed deep inside his memories, where the pain and tiredness can't reach.

For a boxer, a crowded ring is the loneliest place in the world.

Hale's cutman jumps down from the ring, pushing the reporter backwards, the two of them scuffling until they're pulled apart. The cutman isn't known for his temper but there are twenty thousand people in the Garden tonight and the air is greasy with violence. There's a little on everybody.

"You takin' a beatin' out there boy," says Hale's trainer, dabbing him with the sponge. "Gotta keep dancing. Keep popping that jab."

He has plenty of advice, but they're empty words, just bunting thrown up for the show.

Hale can't win this fight. Hale hasn't won any fights in two years. His promise is so far behind him he can't even remember what it feels like to step into the ring hoping for victory, let alone expecting it. He fights to feed himself now. A journeyman they call him. Six hard rounds for title hopefuls, before his legs give way or they knock him out.

Most mornings he wakes up coughing blood. He can barely see straight; can't hold onto a thought long enough to get it off his tongue. Mighty Marvin Hale's crumbling from the inside out.

The bell rings for the fourth round, his stool snatched from beneath him as he stands.

Hale goes lumbering forward as his trainer thumps the canvas, calling out a few last pieces of advice. Deafened by the roar of the crowd and the blood rushing through his ears, Hale misses most of it.

His raises his fists, guarding his face. His arms are stiff, his legs heavy. He wishes it was over, but he'll take pride in giving everybody their money's worth.

The moose he's fighting is on his toes, clowning for the crowd, winding up punches.

Hale swings tiredly, leaving his body open for the moose, who plants a hook on his ribs. The thwomp of his leather hitting flesh brings the crowd to their feet.

Gasping, Hale falls back against the ropes under a barrage of body shots, each one making it harder and harder to breathe.

Bleeding, grunting, wrapped in the humid night, Hale feels his legs tremble.

Aint strength that keeps a man stood up when the world wants him on the floor. It's pride. It's memory.

Sweat and sawdust, musty but sweet. It's the smell of the ring and the smell of the whorehouse where he grew up. The girls wore it like perfume; couldn't wash it off. Elspeth called it the seventy-second stink, on account of that's how long most men lasted.

Elspeth.

Hale hasn't thought on her for years, and now he does it's like he saw her yesterday. Laughing through those rotten teeth, combing her thin hair with an ivory brush she stole on her last day as a maid. If he'd seen Elspeth on the street he wouldn't have thought much of her, but she ran that brothel clean and she ran it fair. Looked after the girls like they was her own, even looked after Marvin despite there not being much use for a young boy in that business. Wasn't until he was twelve and beginning to fill out that he started earning his way, standing at the door, fists clenched, burning for a fight and knowing it wouldn't be too long coming.

The bell dings, calling the round to an end, dragging him back to himself.

Hale retreats gratefully, doing his best not to stagger. The body shots hurt more than he thought they would. Age is a weight on his back, it hangs off his arms and squeezes his heart. He's old. Too old for fifteen hard rounds under the hot lights. Old enough to believe losing is a kindness, and grateful he won't have to wait long to indulge it.

Two more rounds, that's all. Then he can eat the dinner he's earned.

Billy presses a cold silver dollar to Hale's cheek to help ease the swelling, using his spare hand to rub the boxer's back. Round, circular motions, the way Elspeth used to do when he was upset.

Hale gives himself to the memory. He clings to it, letting it carry him away from the noise and ache of his ribs.

He was fighting when Elspeth died. She went nice and quiet, sniffling under her sheets so as not to disturb the customers.

Nobody told him till his shift on the door finished.

Both of them had their responsibilities, and it wasn't like he was short of raising in that place. Would have stayed on that door the rest of his life, except one of their customers didn't feel he'd got his money's worth. Took his hand to Meg, who screamed Marvin's name loud enough to knock the angels off their clouds.

Weren't much left of that man when Marvin got done with him.

Meg washed the blood off his knuckles in cold water, then took him to the nearest gym. Elspeth hadn't wanted this for him, she'd said. He had a calling.

Mr Valance had sized him up like beef at the butcher, then put him in the ring. Didn't talk about money or contracts that first meeting. Mr Valance asked Marvin if he wanted to hurt people every week and Marvin said he did.

They shook hands on it then and there.

In the space of a week Marvin gave himself to a rage he hadn't known was in him, and while it burned that ring was his.

But nothing burns forever.

Hale doesn't hear the bell. It's become the sound of the mail train that used to run by his bedroom after midnight, and his trainer has to slap him to wake him from his memories, but the Hale that stands isn't the Hale that sat down. He's twenty years younger, caught in a fire he can't put out and can't escape.

The crowd roars as "Mighty" Marvin Hales pounds his gloves together. Their voices are a wave at his back, pushing him forward. The fighter can see them beyond the ropes, leaping up from their seats, faces twisted, enflamed, desperate for him to hurt this man, or break himself trying.

Millions more are listening by the wireless, talking about it over their brooms or under their engines as oil drips on their faces. They call themselves fans and ask for autographs, then boo him for being tired, for being old, for not being the man he was ten years ago. They need this, and he hates them for needing it. He hates himself for giving it to them, for this being the only thing he was ever good at.

The moose is circling, loading punches.

Hale covers up, taking the wild swings on his gloves, their power slipping through the leather to rattle his teeth. They're good shots. Not good enough to put him down, but enough to stoke the rage.

Six rounds. For the longest time, that's all that's been asked of him. All that he's asked of himself. Survive the day, eat well that night.

Hale takes two more shots on the gloves. Peering over the top of them at the moose.

He's hurling concrete, but he's slow. Hale got so used to losing, that he thought that was all there was. He grew comfortable in it. He stopped expecting to win, and started waiting to lose.

But he can beat the moose. He knows he can.

Hope flickers with him, like a flame springing to life among ash.

Hope's a bad word for a boxer. It's the extra punch you shouldn't take. It's the final fight you didn't need. Hope is blinkers. It blinds you to good sense. Hope kills.

The moose lets loose a wild swing. Hale ducks, punching his opponent in the ribs. Down in the gloom, away from the spotlights, his trainer roars him forward.

Hope is the only word that matters to a boxer. It's the extra punch you throw when you can't stand. It's the blinkers that convinces you to get into the ring in the first place. It blinds you to good sense.

Hale's punches come screaming out of that forgotten place in his soul. A place long quiet, but now heaving with purpose. Two jabs meet the moose's face, rocking him backwards. A body shot, an uppercut. The moose is bleeding, dazed. He came for a parade, not a fight.

Hale's feet are moving, his hands flashing out

Mighty Marvin Hale falls on his opponent like something God threw down.

The moose flails desperately, leaving his chin out to be hit.

Hale catches it clean. The punch snaps the moose's head back, rolling his eyes back in his sockets.

He hits the ground, unconscious. The referee kneels beside him, but there's no need for the count.

Ding, ding, ding.

The round ends, Madison Square trembles with applause. Bulbs pop. A photographer squirms through the throng, exploding a camera in Hale's face. That's the picture in tomorrow's newspaper. Punch drunk and tired, but victorious. Standing alone in the ring, hope on his face, grinning through his gumshield.

THE GIANT DOUGHNUT

SUSMITA BHATTACHARYA

The giant doughnut rolled down the street. It was a perfectly round, crisp, brown, sugar- sprinkled treat – oh yes, it was – and as tall as the Guildhall, glinting in the morning sun.

'Oh look, Mummy, look.' A little boy pointed to the doughnut trundling down the street. 'I want. I *want* it.'

'No, you can't have it,' his mother said, pulling him towards her and covering his eyes with her hands. 'It's bad for you. It's processed food. It's not gluten-free. Here, have this banana instead.' And she pulled out one from her bag, peeled it and shoved it into the boy's mouth.

The doughnut rolled down the high street. Past the local Tesco and the Big Issue vendors who stared with their mouths open.

'Stop, stop,' cried the homeless man, struggling to get out of his sleeping bag. His dog gave chase, leaping up to lick some sugar sprinkles from the doughnut's icing. 'I'm hungry. I haven't had a proper meal since last night. Or was it last week? Last month? I can't remember when I had a treat, really. Perhaps when my mother was alive, and she'd baked me a cake. Or before I'd lost my job, lost my girlfriend, lost my house … stop. I need to eat you.'

'You can't eat that,' said the MP who was standing outside her clinic. 'Have you paid your taxes? Have you contributed to society? Do you have any accountability? No! Then how can you even dare to dream of eating that doughnut?'

The man shrank back, holding his growling dog's collar. He looked at his tattered shoes as the MP continued.

'I'll have it, thank you. I'll take it to Parliament – discuss who can have a share of it. We can have a referendum. Vote on it. It is vital that the doughnut is eaten by the people that win the vote.'

The doughnut rolled away, bouncing down the steps of the old city gates. The ghosts stood on the ancient walls and watched. They quivered in the breeze, their long hair rippling, their pale eyes trained on the jumbo treat hurtling towards them.

'Oh, what I would do to just taste this doughnut,' one said, eyes half closed in remembered pleasure. 'Can you remember how it feels to chew a big chunk of sweet dough? Can you?'

'Stop daydreaming,' snapped another ghost. 'Have you lost your mind? We can't eat anymore. Why do you have such cravings? Live up to your present state. You're a spirit. You have to behave in the right manner.'

The doughnut rolled down the cobbled streets. People stopped to take selfies. Twitter was trending with news of the giant doughnut that continued on its journey through town.

A young couple stopped and pouted as the doughnut appeared behind them. Snap, they clicked a photo and immediately uploaded it to Instagram.

'If only I could have a little bite,' said the girl in the skinny jeans, her stomach was growling from having skipped her breakfast … and her lunch.

'Are you crazy?' said her girlfriend. 'That's about five thousand calories. I feel sick just looking at it.'

'I know,' the girl sighed. 'I don't want to eat the whole thing. Just a lick, maybe?'

Her girlfriend pulled her away from the street. 'Let's take you somewhere safe. Why couldn't there be a giant carrot sprinting down the street instead of this monstrosity?'

The giant doughnut wove its way through the by lanes, dodging shoppers and office goers who had rushed out to look at it. They watched in silence as the big round treat bounced away, showering them with sugar sprinkles they stuck their tongues out to catch.

'Oh, I wish I could have a bit. My taste buds don't work anymore, but I'm sure this would beat that awful aftertaste in my mouth,' said the lady with no hair. She held on to her husband's arm as he tut-tutted and shook his head.

'Don't be silly, dear,' he said. 'That much sugar is bad for you. It'll feed your cancer, and then where will you go? Come, I'll buy you some coconut water – it'll soothe your sore tongue. Don't even go near that doughnut – you might just absorb that poison by being close to it.'

The church bells began to chime, and the worshippers streamed out into the street. The pastor stumbled out after her flock. She'd seen the pictures of this doughnut on her phone as she was giving the sermon and wanted to protect them.

'Oh look, a giant doughnut,' shouted one of the congregation. 'It can feed thousands. This is a miracle. Come on, shall we have our share?'

'Stop,' said the pastor, waving her arms about. 'Don't you see this for what it is? This is the devil tempting us. Look at the way the doughnut glints in the sun, promising us heavenly delight. It is a test. Resist. Ignore. Let us go inside. Let us pray.'

The doughnut rolled on, followed by thousands of the townsfolk who wanted to see where it would end up. The news reporters ran ahead, keeping pace with the giant treat, and shouted into their microphones. Helicopters appeared in the sky and police sirens reverberated in the air. Politicians were shouting from loudspeakers – come and join my party. We will make the future together. Scientists gave chase with syringes and other equipment, wanting to take readings and samples from the doughnut's insides. Business tycoons tried to lure the doughnut into their limousines.

An old woman with a shopping trolley stepped out of the crowd and stood in the doughnut's way.

'Could I have a bite? It's my birthday after all.'

Her husband rolled his eyes and stroked his beard. 'How could you be so selfish, woman? Did your mother not teach you to offer your husband first before you eat anything? Have you lost your values? Your culture?'

The doughnut rocked on its base, hesitating as the woman pondered her husband's accusations. Then she walked towards it and took a huge bite from its side and munched noisily and appreciatively.

'So there,' she said to her husband, looking him straight in the eye. He opened and closed his mouth. 'What have you done?' he finally said. 'What right did you have to eat this doughnut?

The woman closed her eyes and swallowed.

'Thank you,' the doughnut said. 'I was there for anyone who would have me. You only had to stop me. I was always there for anyone who wanted me. You only had to believe in yourself and I would have stopped for you.'

And with that, the doughnut crumbled onto the ground. The people stared at the sugar sparkling in the sun, the gulls and pigeons sweeping down to feast on the crumbs. If only they had listened to their inner voice, they would have feasted on the doughnut instead.

THE HAUL

JOHANNA ROBINSON

Faith spreads out her new cream tablecloth, pushing out the creases. The cloth is round but her ancient wooden table is square, and its corners remain visible, bare and scarred. She strokes the palm of one hand across the fabric in a flat, wide arc, and then the other. The muscles in her back and shoulders stretch, as though her body is an old loom, cranked up at last. There is a light sheen to the tablecloth, a vague leaf pattern. Near the hem is a worn area the size of a penny, and the rest of the material is freckled with tiny stains. She sees all this better now she's home, under the glare of the shadeless kitchen bulb, than when she was in the shop earlier, tugging the cloth out of the tall wire basket labelled *Scraps*. She runs her fingers over the blemishes – dark grey pinheads of grease, an ochre ring from a mug, and two small smudges the colour and density of her own age spots. Faith accepts these stains; they are as much a part of the pattern as the leaf detail – more in fact; the marks trapped deep in the fibres will be there until the whole thing perishes, eventually. In each spot she imagines a mealtime, a gathering – dishes passed, swapped, ladled, spilled. She conjures families, all their unsaid complications. She stands back: the cloth is flat and neat now, and as clean as it ever will be.

Faith picks up the next carrier bag and places it on the table. Into it she slides her hand and pulls out the new jumper. It's baby-pink and so soft that it almost sighs beneath her hands. She lays it out on the table, admiring it for a moment before she lifts it up and shimmies her arms through its sleeves. As she pulls it over her face its long threads tickle her eyelids; the scent is exactly as she expected, exactly as it always is.

It's big and so thick that it pads her out by inches. She strokes one arm with the other – as though the limb might need reassurance, as though the need itself is someone else's – and walks to the window. There are no curtains to draw – none needed twenty floors up. She tugs the hem of the jumper; it ends just below her knickers and as she leans on the cold radiator, her bare thighs are seeded with goosebumps. Through the glass, she watches the world blurred by the rain – the crowd of tower blocks that surround her own, like a board game of shapes and silhouettes, and unknown rules. On the busy four-lane road that skirts below, streetlights bleed orange and headlamps trickle. It is too wet and dark to see anything, or anyone.

She leaves her reflection in the window and walks back to the table. The wall clock stopped days ago, but not long ago enough that Faith has stopped checking the time. She tips the black stilettos out of the carrier bag onto the floor and manoeuvres her feet into them. They are a little too big so she tests them out, walking from the table to the sink and back again. She'd have liked it if the heels clacked but the floor is vinyl, and instead she creates little dimples when she walks, the circles rising back to flat in her wake.

She begins to lift her other purchases from the bag, item by item. From the ragged tissue paper she unwraps two plates, two wine glasses, two dishes and pairs of knives, forks and spoons, setting them out in a line. None of them match, of course. She holds one of the glasses up to the lightbulb and counts three ghost fingerprints. She places it back down. Candles would have been nice, but the YMCA doesn't sell those, not even used ones.

She'd swallowed the tang of betrayal she'd felt at the back of her throat as she stepped into the YMCA that morning instead of her usual shop. In contrast to the larger charity shop, with its branded tags and themed layout, the smaller one had been leased over the last fifty years by a series of small, struggling charities, whose causes when Faith read the leaflets always dismayed her. Until recently, regardless of the name on the frontage, the floor inside would be dusty, displays chaotic. Now, it is run by the local hospice, Oak Dene, and a rotation of brisk retired women have gradually polished and hoovered it into a presentable state. It is never short of stock, many people favouring it for their donations and sympathy over the YMCA across the precinct. Craig was the first man she'd seen in there as a volunteer, usually stationed at the till while the women drank chipped mugs of tea and tackled the intimidating mountain of bags at the rear.

This morning, on her mission for kitchenware, Faith knew he'd be at the counter, with his always-busy hands looking for things to fold, stack and sort. She oughtn't to have left her trip for supplies and resources until today, but it only occurred to her when she woke, with a sense of something different about the day, that she only had enough in her cupboard for one. If only she'd remembered sooner, she could have bought what she needed on Tuesday, his day for visiting his mother. She wouldn't have needed to trespass into the YMCA at all. All she'd been able to do earlier was scurry past the Oak Dene window with the hood of her coat pulled down around her face. And yet, of course he'd recognise that very coat, having been there the first time she slipped it on, when her arthritic fingers struggled with the buttons and he'd pretended not to notice. He'd given a quick smile when she agreed to buy it, but she'd been distracted by what her fingers found in the pocket: the cold opal brooch. As she left the shop, she felt a blush of guilt in her cheeks that she'd paid the £5.99 for the coat and nothing for the smuggled jewellery. That was three months ago, and when she got home she hid the brooch – already she thought of it as lucky and therefore best kept out sight. She would not wear it, would not risk using up all her luck in one impulsive, frivolous go.

It was late morning when she'd left the YMCA with two full bags and several unintentional purchases. She didn't dare to glance across the precinct or check whether Craig had seen her. In her haste to escape the village, one of the bags clashed with her shin, the corner of the photograph frame drawing blood; she dabbed the wound with toilet paper all afternoon, but still it has continued to weep.

In the kitchen, she examines the framed photograph. It had been displayed in the YMCA on the shelf with a congregation of wine glasses, waiting for her. She will hang it next to the kitchen clock, where there is a perfect space. As she holds it, she waits for their names. Sometimes she tries out a roll call, testing possible names until their frozen, black-and-white faces seem to shift slightly in response. At other times, she just knows what they are called; she sees it in their eyes, or she hears the vows still on their lips. Juliet and Paul, these two. No doubt at all. Juliet. Paul.

Faith hangs the silver frame on the nail she had already driven into the wall weeks ago. Her new couple – long hair and flares on him, top-knot and mini-dress on her – stand on church steps, wearing expressions that might easily break. She doesn't know what her own black-and-white expression would have held; brittle hopes or blushing promises or wishes fluttering behind the eyes. She never wanted to see Eric's expression either, to see what fear and cowardice looked like before they turned into action, when they were masquerading as love. Their photographs had never left the studio, were never even paid for. She's often wondered at what point they were destroyed and tries to defuse the little bolt of terror that somewhere they might still exist, in a box, under a lid, waiting to be found.

In the next-door flat, Mrs Dawes' mantelpiece clock chimes seven times. Faith looks down at her bare legs: she should dress. In the bedroom she opens one wardrobe, and then the adjoining one – *his and hers*, the estate agent had pointed out all those years back, startled when Faith cackled at her. The shades in the cupboards graduate from washed-out chalky pink at one end to deep magenta at the other. She assesses her jumper and her options for a moment before reaching for a heavy, knitted, calf-length skirt the colour of pomegranates, quickly stepping into it. She still has her stilettos on, and they catch on the hem.

She wonders what happened to her lovely pink two-piece, and whether it would still fit her after all these decades. Perhaps. There had been no children to balloon and deflate her breasts, to bulk out her hips. There had been no extravagant meals for two, no bloody meat and rich, cream sauces, no need for three courses when one will do. There had been no smug consumption of empty calories at weekends. Yes, she was sure that honeymoon outfit would have lasted. Not having kept it was a regret – not in the league of regret as failing to keep a husband for more than a day, fifty years ago, but a regret still.

She had worn her honeymoon outfit the day after the wedding, even though Eric had already gone and there would be no honeymoon. Being young, impulsive and broken, she'd delivered their wedding gifts, all the white and silver boxes and bags, to the little charity shop on the precinct, and once there, she'd also kicked off the sateen, kitten-heeled honeymoon shoes, slipped off the pale, tweed jacket, followed by the mini-skirt, and tossed them all on the charity shop floor. She accepted the replacement clothes thrust at her by the wide-eyed volunteer, who'd refused payment, given the value of the items Faith had strewn across their shop. Her story no doubt had done the rounds over the following months – years perhaps – recycled and distorted at each retelling.

She had found it more embarrassing when she returned the next day, admitting that she wanted the suit back, not only because she really did love it, but also because she'd realised with horror that one day she might be in the Co-op or the post office, and encounter someone wearing her cast-off honeymoon outfit, that one day she might meet some girl being the woman Faith never had chance to be. The suit had gone, of course. She'd also wanted the cups back, the gift from Eric's sister, so when people brought sympathy, she could offer them tea. But the cups had gone too – everything sold instantly to the milling, gawping customers who had watched her undress.

Back in the kitchen, she waits. She had offered to cook, of course, but he'd said no, he would bring everything. She turns the thermostat up and the pipes begin to rumble and clink. She feels the audience eyes of the wall of black-and-white couples upon her, as if this is everything they have been waiting for. She squints, not at today's YMCA couple, Juliet and Paul, but at Marjorie and John, that silly wink on John's face, as if he's won the bride next to him. 'It's all your fault, you two,' Faith says. 'You know that, don't you?' She'd never have chosen Marjorie and John herself – his wink disrupts the general tone of her collection, yet when Craig – or the elderly volunteer as she thought of him then – slid the silver frame out from a hidden shelf, pushed it across the counter, and said, more to the floor than to her, 'I saved this for you', she knew she'd have to take it, and she watched him wrap it and place it in a bag with the cardigan and book she had chosen for herself.

She hadn't agreed, last week, to his shy request for dinner because of the photograph. She agreed because, having found her that one picture, he never tried to find her another. She had fully expected on her next visit a second photograph, slipped from under the counter like the first, which if she accepted would lead to a third, a fourth, a crowd of brides and grooms she had not picked. By then, she would be trapped in a pattern of give and take. His small gesture would grow until it became yet another thing coaxed from her. But in fact Craig had never presented her with anyone else after Marjorie and John, and she had felt obliged to hang the happy couple up in her kitchen, wink and all.

The only other item Craig had ever saved for her was the coat. 'I know you like pink,' he said one day, reaching to take a cerise garment from a rail behind him. 'So I put this to one side for you – only it would have gone quickly. It's practically new.' The next time Faith stopped by the Oak Dene shop, she made sure to wear the coat, pushing to the back of her mind the matter of the brooch. They had got to chatting, which at first had felt like swapping sentences, each one with a different weight or value; it took some time before they found a balance. They did not ask each other questions, but instead discussed the bags and hats that dripped and flopped from bin bags, the tangles of clothes. She helped de-knot necklaces and checked donated purses for money and cards. When vintage toys made a rare appearance, Craig and Faith rescued them from their pile of plastic friends and reminisced. They wondered about the previous lives of everything, without backtracking into their own.

She looks at the oven. Should she have put it on already? Should she be warming the plates? She remembers the fingerprints on the wine glass and picks it up; using the hem of the jumper she rubs the surface clean. She examines a slice of her reflection in one of the knives. She wonders if he'll remember where she lives or whether another volunteer swept the scrap of paper with her address into the bin with old receipts. Perhaps he'll simply change his mind and tomorrow will be just the same as all the other days.

Next door, the clock chimes the half hour.

Faith turns, as she often does when her mind needs occupying, to her brides and grooms. She starts at one end, looking into their faces, once strangers. She stops at Sophie and Daniel. Sophie grasps roses and is dressed in a neat, knee-length dress – a wartime bride. Something catches Faith's eye and she looks more closely at a detail she's never noticed before, a shape on the girl's lapel, glowing in the camera flash, moon-bright. She takes down the picture and walks the short distance down the hall, back to the bedroom. Her ankles are weak but she does not take off the stilettoes. She pulls out one drawer after another, her fingers searching out the corners, until they close around the brooch, the opal cool and smooth as bone. She holds it next to the photograph; it's impossible to tell if it's the same one. But it could be, and for Faith, in this moment, that's enough. She pins it to her jumper, the mohair snagging on the metal teeth that hold the stone in place.

She recalls the words from fifty years ago, tattered and worn-out now – but still there in her head, morning, night, morning, night. The words uttered by her aunt, and overheard by Faith as she stood, in someone else's charity-shop clothes, on the brink of her mother's lounge: *No one will want her, now she's second hand.*

Faith places her hand over the brooch, as though to stop any luck from escaping just yet. She walks slowly back to the kitchen. There is a quiet rap on the door. Before she answers it, she adjusts the photograph of her new couple, Juliet and Paul, ensuring they are perfectly straight. She has never felt so sure that everything in the room, in this life of hers, is precious. That with everything that is second hand, comes a second chance.

THE HEARTBEAT OF TREES

ANDREW LEACH

'Is it true what they say, mate?'

'What's that?' he says.

'This heat. Is it true what they say?'

'What about it?'

'That it's here to stay, we better get used to it, it's gonna fuck everything and there'll be no more crops and that.'

Pauses, like he's thinking. Says 'Where'd you hear that?'

'Read it. In a magazine.'

'Sounds pretty bad.'

'Yeah.'

'I think we've got a bit longer before doomsday.'

'Hope so.'

He goes into the shop and I start sorting my stuff. The pavement's two-tone, one triangle shaded, the other you could fry an egg on. Try and keep off the egg side. He comes out, hands me a shopping bag. Plastic handles already pulled long and stringy. Filled it with two big bottles of water, four cans, half a dozen box-fresh sandwiches. Bursting at the seams.

'What's this?'

'Just some bits,' he says. 'Thought you might need it.'

I call him diamond, prince, hero, saint.

He asks my name.

'Huxley. Don't laugh.'

'Not laughing.'

'Good to meet you, man.'

'You too.'

'And thanks.'

He's gone.

'Hey! What's your name?'

He says something that sounds like Stan over his shoulder he gets swallowed by the shadows I don't think it's Stan it'll have to do.

Later. Leaves for a bed. The heartbeat of trees my lullaby. Watching stars ignite knowing they're just memories. Bombs dropping on a black screen, silver flashes, like down in the arcades. Rising heat still hanging around like a spent gun. Lights on in the valley below. Blind yellow eyes. Bars, streetlamps, guerrillas, wolves. Safer up here. Here in the woods. In the ruin. Tumbledown house, what's left held up by creeper and graffiti. Venus showing off above. I can see her if I move my head. Don't remember Venus being there when I was a kid. Like the moon struck a match.

A siren in the night. Somewhere down on the main road it whoops and screams. Police or something. Ambulance. It's far enough away for now. Breathe easy. On the walls there are names. They flicker in the candlelight. Pavel and Meg and Joe. Some nights they're quiet. Other times they take the wolves for a walk. Written there sometime during the war. At least that's what they said. The names. Ghosts now. Corporal Huxley Bishop, Commando Regiment Royal Artillery. Don't laugh. Another ghost. Big fucking lupus on a leash. Nose in the earth, breathing in the brown, brown earth.

Waking to birdsong. Takes a few seconds to iron out my bones. Hearing them chirp, it's just memories. Times from before. Listen to them as I focus on a mark on the wall. It moves. Some sort of bug. Another day I'm still alive. It slides across Pavel, the names knitting the bricks together, the years pitting the names together, the botany living in different eras at the same time. Different monarchs. Reckon we've got something in common. Me and Pavel. Joe and me. Something bigger than finding sanctuary in this place, this house, these woods, although that's a start. Reckon some of these trees predate Queen Vic. Their woody hearts throbbing.

A fragment of last night's dream, it whoops and screams then it's gone. Boots on the ground. Hole in the roof's blue, there's a cloud on a pulley. Cirrus across flax flowers through a window that never intended to be there. Screw up my eyes, tighten my field of vision, push away the whisky head. Bottle nearly empty laying on its side in the fireplace. Peeling label says Glen-something. Picked the something off now I can't remember. Not like I've got money for another one. Sit up, take a long draught of water bequeathed to me by a prince, a king. Splash some over my face. Sounded like Stan. What an honour. Queen and country. Ladder of light through the accidental window like scaffold. Something moves through its showtime glare. A mouse, maybe. Pull on my boots.

Down in the town the people scuttle like they've been hurling rocks at rubber bullets. I smile, nod at a few. They're not having it. Enemy territory. Every door hides a sniper it's what they used to say. Looking out for Frank or Stash. Here the kerbside saplings remind me what riches I have. Bedraggled hanging baskets like drag queens after the party's over. New Tesco solid like a church.

Stash is in the shelter. Let a convoy of cars pass until there's room enough to dash through. One of the windows kicked out. Pool of glass beads.

'Alright?'

'How's things?' she says, not looking up. Fiddling with a Rizla.

Two orange foam discs on an Alice band round her neck. Long wire to a portable cassette player. Tinny faraway music from the foam discs.

'Yeah, surviving.'

'Got anything?'

Produce a packet from my hand like a magician. Twisting my wrist. Offer half a cheese and pickle.

'Ta-da.'

'Beauty.'

Takes a bite, licks the edge of the paper.

'This vegan?'

'Fuck off.'

Grins. 'Fair enough.'

Lights the smoke, takes a drag through the food. Passes it. It's mainly tobacco but there's a little gift in there, too. Breathe deep, blow out a thin river.

'You waiting for a bus or just keeping out the sun?'

'Bus.'

'Where you going?'

'Station. Then north. With Baby.'

She nods towards a black guitar case propped against the wall of the shelter that for some reason I hadn't clocked. Her blue fringe flops forward like a wave. She tosses her head and the tide retreats. The case wearing stickers. Black Flag, Marshall, My Little Pony.

'Got a gig?'

'Maybe. Not sure. Met a bloke from a record label. Based in Glasgow or Edinburgh or something. Said he wanted to record me.'

Takes the smoke between alabaster fingers. Look like they should be pressed together in prayer.

'Got an address?'

Shakes her head. Colours shimmy. 'Phone number.'

'So what's the destination? Glasgow or Edinburgh?'

'Either. Figured I'd get to the station and see where the trains go.'

'You're crazy, Stash.'

'S'why you love me, right?'

Another bite of sandwich, hands me the smoke.

'Then what?'

'Call the number. Be closer than here.'

A laugh lost in a toke cloud.

'Can't fault your logic.'

'Wish me luck, Bish.'

'Always. You're my lucky charm.'

'Carry your hopes and dreams, don't I?'

'Got to know someone have some luck. Might as well be you.'

She smiles. She'd be beautiful in a delicate way but for the piece of cheese stuck to a front tooth. Realises, licks it off.

Police car cruising shark-like. Without warning turns its siren on, accelerates. The noise eats me. I hear Stash say 'He'll never sell any ice creams going that fast' then I'm gone. Lost to the bootstomp, shellstorm, gunfire, knowing it's just memories, the whine of a Landy in reverse, get back get back get back –

Soft carved hand on my arm.

'You okay, Bish?'

Let the film play out and fade.

'Yeah.'

'Took you back?'

'Yeah.'

'Falklands?'

'Yeah.'

Lay out in the park for a bit. An hour maybe. No one's keeping time. Somebody's discarded newspaper keeps my nose from burning. Lift my black T-shirt get some rays on my body. There's kids on the swings. A bee loud as a fighter plane. Grass tickles my ears with a lover's touch. Worry my scars'll scare the kids. Stash waved from the bus, arms wrapped round Baby. A child cries, pull my shirt down. Saw Frank disappear down Junk Alley. Think it was Frank. Leave him to it if that's where he hangs now. All got to do what we got to do. Blew her a kiss. Finished the smoke.

Unfurl the unthrown punch in my pocket, pull out some coins. One seventy-five. King's ransom. Enough for a can of Coke and a second-hand paperback and still leave change. Shiny new pound gold nugget. Everything changes. Copy of *Brighton Rock* from the charity place. Into the offy, cold cola can from the chiller. Bloke looks at me funny, sees my regiment inked on my forearm. Changes his tune, gives me coppers. Hungry and for once

I haven't got to beg or steal or scrounge. Stand in the sun and pop the can. Get some sugary kicks, wincing against the light.

***

Bishop enters the house.

Calls out, like he's expecting someone to be home. Maybe Pavel or Meg or someone. (Maybe Charlie. Maybe the kids. Jude and Flynn.)

His 'Hello?' hangs in the branches. Two syllables disturb a magpie, it pecks at them.

Slips through the structure, barely a house. An arboretum propped up by lives once lived. He's skittish, like a deer. Flickering. Short-circuiting.

Crouches, turns some bricks, folds back a torn blue tarpaulin.

Checks his things.

Opens the paperback, removes the quarter bottle of whisky he slipped inside its pages. Another magic trick.

Fishes in the shopping bag, takes a long pull of water until the plastic bottle crackles.

The heat in here filtered by leaves. A cloud of gnats fizzes.

Settles back against a wall in his Lay-Z-Boy of earth and stones. Opens a beer and a tuna mayonnaise from vanished King Stan.

Reads. The words swim at first then settle down.

Hale knew, before he had been in Brighton three hours, that they meant to murder him.

Knows how he felt.

Loses himself for an hour or two.

Slowly his thoughts get turned over. Like a ploughed field. Might be the story, might be other crossed lines.

Finds himself reading his wife's words.

'Can't help you if you won't help yourself, Hux.'

Tries to return to gangland Brighton.

Sucks the last of the beer from the can. Lurches to his feet, crushes the can in his hand, tosses it into the fireplace.

Goes outside. Jeans open, pissing into the long grass. Looks out over the valley. First hint of a chill in the air.

Ghosts inside, delves into his pack. Pulls out a hoodie.

'Can't help you if you won't help yourself.'

Soon be time for the lights to come on. Shivers.

Misses them. Jude and Flynn. Charlie.

Picks the bottle out the fireplace. Cork out, chugs it.

Hurls the bottle at fallen stones. Glass like a wave against a seawall.

Sinks to his knees. Howls like a wolf.

On his fucking knees.

Howls till his throat burns.

Cries like a baby, coughs up snot and tears. Coughs up a war.

She's his lucky charm, she carries his hopes and dreams –

Should never have walked out. Pride's a monster.

Howls like a fucking wolf.

Pavel and Joe help him up.

Meg walks him outside.

Leaning against a tree.

Promises to go back.

Pressing his face, bark patterns on his cheek.

Tells her he'll go back. Try again. She tells him to promise he does he does –

His arms round the tree. Feeling its heart. Feeling it beat.

THE HUGGING PLACE

SHERRY MORRIS

The day the bear came to town, the light was just right. It transformed the fading yellow walls of our stone homes to a golden honey hue. Some said it was a sign. We'd been wondering how to improve our lacklustre lives, address the depression that had bedded down with us. We all wished to refresh, dreamt of starting anew. Instead we sat like blobs of glue wondering what to do.

He caught us by surprise, this bear – walking upright, his claws clicking a beat through our worn cobblestone streets, tipping a chartreuse top hat to everyone he'd meet. We could've simply stayed in and cowered as he towered over us all. Ignored his booming 'Good day, fine people!' that ricocheted all around our town's tired walls. But somehow, we knew he was alright. That we didn't need to fear an oh-so-polite bear.

It's true he swung a cane, but not in a threatening way. In a way that made us want to follow. Strut and stride behind in step. So we did.

By the time we arrived at the square, about a zillion people had joined our jolly parade. Everyone humming, buzzing, clapping, snapping, showing off their best moves as we grooved through dazzling light-sweet streets to funky bear beats.

At the bank things turned. Dark clouds appeared. Thunder grumbled. Lightning slashed. The wind got wild. Our bear kept marching, encouraging us along, with a wave of his burly arm. Said to keep on, we'd have a lark in the park under the rays of a bright mustard sun. But people smelled rain and paused. Some full-stopped altogether. Scattered when fat drops fell.

Our bear growled, 'There's no need to run! Stick together as one! The light will come back, I promise.'

He pushed a button on his cane. Out popped an umbrella, huge as an ancient oak. Opening his arms wide, he invited us all inside. We who sheltered underneath, were comforted by his wide reach, how his fur smelled of clean sheets. Encircled within his soft warm embrace, we felt we'd never be cold or lonely or unloved ever again.

Nothing lasts forever.

When lightning struck, our bear took the brunt of the bolt. We did our best to revive him but lost him along with the light. A great sadness rolled through the town in waves that threatened to wash us away. Succeeded in draining all remnants of colour from the town.

In this monochrome state, unsure of our fate, we recalled the wise words of our bear and stayed put. When knocked to our knees, we helped each other up. Waited patiently for colour and light to return.

In time, we noticed a scorch that marked the spot. Some said it was the shape of a heart. Others said the shape of a tear. The mark became known as the hugging place. As word spread, people came from far and wide to stand on the space.

And with each hug given and with each hug received, fresh colour bloomed. Dashes of lemon yellow decorated doorways. Flashes of bold canary streaked schools and churches. Splashes of melon and marigold pebble-dashed walls 'til in whatever light the whole town glowed amber gold.

We rejoiced. Vowed never to go back to such a dull state. And while some claimed it a shame the bear was no longer here, most of us knew he'd always been near.

THE LOOK INSIDE

ADAM LOCK

The bedroom is dark except for the blue light of the e-reader uplighting her face.

'Did you come?' I ask her.

She smiles weakly and says, 'Twice.'

I'm not so sure.

She always reads her e-reader afterwards.

'Why don't you choose a book? Buy one?'

She shakes her head and swipes the screen. 'No need.'

'Don't you want to finish one?'

'It's the "Look Inside," bit I like. Any book I want.' She shows me her e-reader.

'But don't you want to find out what happens?'

She squints then rests the e-reader on her legs folded into a teepee beneath the quilt.

'It's the beginning of books I like best. The middles are boring. And I know how they end by the time I've read the first twenty pages. So …' She shrugs and swipes the screen.

By the side of the bed is her overnight bag.

'I emptied that drawer for you, remember? You might as well use it while you're stuck here.'

'Thanks.' She doesn't look away from the screen.

'And it means you can keep some of your things here. For when you stay over.'

This time she looks at me, leans over, and kisses the top of my head.

'I have to know how a story ends,' I say.

She swipes the screen.

'Did you really?' I ask her.

'What?'

'Twice?'

'Yes. I told you. Twice.'

She gets to the end of the "Look Inside," on the e-reader.

'I'll buy it for you.'

'No,' she says. She presses the screen a few times. 'Look.' She shows it me again. 'So many to choose from. I can try any of them. Why would I want to buy one?'

She scrolls through the book store.

Her bag, by the side of the bed, is zipped tight, the handles erect, ready to be held, lifted, and carried away again, when the lockdown is over.

THE LURGY

TOBY LITT

You'd've been curious, I bet – if you'd been there – the alley behind The Albion, two middle-aged men running down past the trees, the first one shouting 'You've still got it', the second one shouting, 'I fucking touched you again'.

The one in the lead was Chris, the catcher-up was me, Tony.

I hadn't only phoned him and arranged to meet in order to give him it. I wanted a chat about our kids, my two boys and his two girls, and about my ex-wife and, if he insisted, about Christine in bed and all that S&M milarkey. I wanted a few lagers and, at the end of the evening, to call a taxi – then, with the window down, to call him over for a final word, touch him, say 'Lurgy' and pull back to where he couldn't get me, have the taxi drive off. Me victorious, him lurgied up.

Didn't happen like that. He was wise – knew what I was up to before I did. After all, we'd been playing lurgy thirty-four years. He refused to come out to the cab when it got there, and when I did him he did me, then tailed it.

In the end, I stopped running and shouted, 'Please.' He refused. 'Why should I?'

'I've had it three bloody years,' I said.

It's true, I was a bit of a fucking lardarse, and the lads knew I couldn't beat them in a straight-line race. They only agreed to meet me in carefully controlled environments. So that night, after chasing him, I had to take it home with me.

Then, in March, Chris announced he was getting married again, and I was able to get in there – at the reception, in the Scout Hut, in front of everyone. I guess he probably knew it was coming, because he didn't look quite as smug as he should've done. Christine was twenty-three and much too pretty for him. Everyone was surprised she was doing it – she wasn't pregnant or dying. No-one was surprised when they heard about the miscarriage she'd had the year before – some other bloke's, but Chris was so good and sympathetic about it that he was magnificently *in there*.

So, they're about to have the first dance, just going through the crowd of wobbly armed aunties. 'Bittersweet Symphony' has started, and aunties are getting ready to cry. He's passing by me and I touch his cheek with my finger and I'm like, in his ear, 'Chris, mate – sorry, but you've got the lurgy.' And I'm off into the crowd before he can swipe round and give it me back again.

'Bastard,' he said, in his Northern football manager voice.

But he gave it back to me the next day. Just walked into the bank and leaned over and poked me on the end of the nose, in front of everyone.

'I'm not taking it on honeymoon,' he said. 'That's not on.'

We'd been passing it round since we were nine and ten, back at Alameda. Phillip heard about it from his Dad, when he was off school with conjunctivitis. 'Got the lurgy, have you?' said his Dad. And that was that – two days later, Phillip brought it in, and it became a thing.

We'd pass it at the back of class, under the desks. Most of us, apart from Phillip sometimes, were up the back. We'd pass it on the 142 to Midford. Once, I lay beneath a bush and touched Martin's ankle as he went past – ran in the other direction, shouting. He didn't catch up. I seemed to be able to pack away the Monster Munch without putting anything on, back then.

Sometimes, at secondary school, it would go to someone outside the gang, but we always seemed to get it back in the end.

We spent most of the last day of school – that's the legendary Redburn school – passing it round, because the teachers were letting us get away with stuff. At the end of that brilliant afternoon of freedom, Chris had it, and seemed almost proud about it.

On Monday, he went to work at the estate agents under the clock tower. I was already in at the Post Office. Martin said he was going to start his own business, but wasn't sure what business it would be. No-one really knew about computers then. Only one of us was going away, Phillip with his 'A' Levels. But he wasn't going to escape. We weren't going to let him.

Yeah, old Philipino got lurgied bad, in the car with his Mum and Dad, off to uni in Reading. Chris smeared it all across his face, said the ritual Words of Transfer, and then, 'And don't go giving it to any girls, okay?'

None of us had forgotten when Phillip came back at Christmas. We were wary around him, although the university and the rumours of two girlfriends at the same time might've had something to do with that, as well. It wasn't we didn't know about sex, we'd all had it – Chris with his cousin, and me with Chris's cousin, who was a bit of an easy lay, bless her, and Martin with Tracey French, in her parents' bed, after months of throwing away money at romance.

Phillip took till New Years' Eve to give it to me. It wasn't hard. We were at some nutter's house party in some estate in Flathill. I was so pissed I couldn't stand up – Phillip just lurgied me, right in front of everyone. No denying the justice, though I wouldn't have tried. If someone got you good, it was a matter of serious honour just to take it and like it.

I thought I was going to be stuck with it for a few months, but Chris came round my house the night before Phillip was off again and asked me to give it to him. He had a plan, he said. He wanted to make sure Phillip took it away with him to uni, again. Then the rest of us could relax, and he wouldn't be just having the best time while we had to work proper work.

I expected the plan actually to be a plan, but it was rubbish. Chris got two big blokes he knew – Andy and Dave – to hold Phillip down outside the Albion. We were all having a farewell drink, and Phillip was bundled outside after a couple.

'That's not fair,' he said. 'At least give me a chance.'

Chris seemed to think it was funny, acting like a gangster. I was going to offer to take it off Phillip, but Chris was already whispering to Dave about breaking my arm.

It became a running thing – how was Chris going to lurgify Phillip before the end of the holidays.

In Phillip's third year, when Martin had already got his first job in sales, Phillip snuck away two days early – didn't even tell his parents.

That meant Chris and me were obliged to go on an epic quest to Reading, track Phillip down in his accommodation. This was before mobile phones. We had to go to the registry and pretend to be his brother and his cousin, wanting to tell him about a dead uncle. They gave out the details, like they wouldn't now.

We lay in wait at the end of the corridor. Chris couldn't stop laughing, and Phillip saw us. He didn't think – walked up to us to ask what we were doing there. Chris gave him it, and Phillip said, 'If it means that much to you, okay.' He was pretending to be above it, I think. A girl came down the corridor towards him, and she was gorgeous like out of *Smash Hits*, and when he introduced us I knew he was saying Fuck off because, within three minutes of you losers going, I'm going to be having sex.

Chris tried to make the drive back all about our triumphant sneak attack, but I felt shit and I wasn't going to say I didn't. That was in his Ford Escort, a legend of a car. Tracey French, where are you now?

We saw each other quite often, me, Chris and Martin, down the Albion and into Midford on Sunday for the rugby, because the football team were even shitter. But I think all of us were waiting for Phillip to come back for things to start back up.

But Martin got headhunted, which was the first we'd ever heard of such a thing. He went to work for Amstrad in London, but said he was only there to learn all he could before setting up by himself. I don't know why we never believed him before he was rich. Things always happened just the way he said they would. Amstrad paid him enough for a flat in Hackney, which was a bit of a lurgy place then.

Martin came back for Chris's 21st birthday. But Chris didn't want the lurgy as a present. He wanted Phillip to give it to me, as his special thing, so I said, 'Yeah, okay,' and took it.

After that, it was – to be honest – a bit like bullying. I became the keeper, because of the pizzas and curries and putting it on round the middle. I could lend it to the others, when they asked – like for Martin going to his first International Sales Conference. Chris wanted to make sure the lurgy got to travel in an airplane. He talked about it as if it was a gremlin with a personality, like in the film from our childhood.

'Lurgify, lurgify,' he chanted, with his pink face. It was weird to see him as intense as that, especially as the last time I'd seen him he'd been trying to persuade me to go halves in a unique property opportunity. He could have the back bedroom and I could sleep in the big room, on the sofabed, folding it away in the morning.

Maybe I should've gone for it. I could've afforded the money. I'd moved from the Post Office to the Bank – still behind the counter, but with better prospects, and not so much waiting for old ladies to get the scrunched up pound notes out of their purses. I should've said yes, from a financial point of view, but Chris scared the shit out of me. I trusted him, but I thought I'd probably put on my shoes in the morning to find shaving foam squidging out of them, and him laughing like it was not a fucking pathetic pain. So I pretended I didn't have the deposit, and it took me another three years before I got my first place. Dad died of cancer, during that period, so I suppose I'd have had to've been at home anyway. A flat would have given me somewhere to escape to.

Martin came back in a good car, then a better car. Mercedes, Jaguar. Chris and me had our lives going on, slower than his. We joked about when he'd come back in a helicopter, and then fuck him if he didn't – just to show us. He was forty by then, and Managing Director and Chief Shareholder and whatever else.

Chris had been running the estate agents for about three years. I was second in charge at the bank. Phillip had been in Cornwall working for the Ministry of Defence, married to a Iranian. Then various things happened around the world, and he wasn't working for the MOD, because of the Iranian wife, and then he didn't have the Iranian wife, because he didn't have a job any more. He came back to work at the Alameda, as a maths teacher and told us he was writing a fantasy novel. That was our various levels of success when Martin's helicopter landed, and he got out and said, 'Gimme some lurgy.'

He was trying to get back into being one of the gang, insisting on how connected we were.

I handed it over without a problem. Let him take it away, into whatever high-flying world of magazines and money he lived in.

The lurgy had been with me at cashing up time too often. It was a bit gremlin-like, the annoyance of not being able to get rid of it, and maybe me feeling it was fucking up my life.

I got married, during this era.

Phillip went up to London, one time – saying Martin had invited him for a job interview.

After he came back, he didn't speak to me for a year. Finally, pissed in the park on Bonfire Night, he told me Martin hadn't been serious, he'd just wanted to give him back the lurgy. He said Martin said he thought it was affecting the share price, him having it.

'Did you just take it?' I asked.

'Yeah,' said Phillip. 'You should have seen his office. You should have seen his secretary.'

'Why don't we take it back to him?' I said. 'As a surprise. Like when we did you at uni.'

'You wouldn't get in without an appointment.'

'Is he enjoying, you know – being him?'

Phillip said, 'Not as much as I would, I tell you that.'

Out of kindness, I offered to take it off him.

'Nah,' he said. 'Nah – I want it for a while longer.'

I touched his face. 'I've got it.'

'No, you haven't,' he said. 'You can't just take it like that. It's mine and I'm fucking keeping it.'

He was sitting down, back against a big old oak tree. I had kids by then, but my wife was watching the bonfire with one and her sister was home with the other.

Then, I suppose, we all forgot about it. Phillip was the keeper now. I knew he hated school and the kids. He could've told some of them the legend of the lurgy, and started a whole new generation, passed it on. It was kind of noble he didn't. Selfish bastard.

We heard about Martin's kids' births and birthdays via email. We were among the first people we knew to get email, because he sent us computers so he could keep in touch via email. Back then, pictures took a long time to load up, but he still always included about ten. I'd leave the computer on when I went to bed and find them in the morning, finally all there. He went to some countries, I tell you.

I became bank manager. Chris punched one of his junior estate agents 'for being a cunt', he said, and got fired. They hired him over the road, at his old rivals, because he was good and had contacts.

The big school reunion took place thirty years after we left, and Martin made the speech. I expected Phillip to be there – he worked there, after all, but he was nowhere.

I went to find him, because I knew where he lived. It was a mess. Not quite piss in jamjars, but he was hoarding just about everything else.

'You need a break,' I said. 'Give it to me and I'll give it to Chris.'

'This isn't about the lurgy,' he said, 'this is about my life.'

'Martin was nice,' I said. 'It wasn't like he was lording it.'

'You don't need to,' said Phillip. 'Not when you're Martin.'

And then, that year, like the biggest miracle I've ever seen, Sandra, one of the younger women teachers saw something in Phillip, got hold of him and pulled him out of his death drive.

Next time I went to his house, I would've wanted to live there. He invited – I could tell Sandra was behind it – me and my wife to dinner. Babysitter for us and everything. I took a bottle of wine, and as Sandra welcomed us into the garden (barbecue), Phillip tickled the back of my neck and said, 'You've got the lurgy.'

Swear I almost cried.

'Well done, mate,' I said. 'This is ace.'

Then, when I got fed up of it, came the running down behind the Albion, fatty-me trying to give it to Chris. That was about three years ago. I didn't see Martin between then and the bit I'm just getting up to. And I was avoiding Chris for much of this dark period. I'd had enough of his Chris-ness. But I did see Phillip, and he got the lurgy back. I admit, I did trick him – I gave it when he was holding his daughter, Clarissa, on his lap.

It's probably with perspective and all that but I did feel I was dooming him as I leant in and said the words. He couldn't get me back. I was out of the way, and Clarissa was just going to sleep. She had too much black hair for one baby, and blue eyes like they all have. But gorgeous, like her mum. Regular features.

'Okay,' Phillip said. 'I think I can cope.'

He went just like my father. I saw him at the skeleton stage, when

Clarissa was kept away. They didn't want her to see him. She was just past her third birthday, by then.

I should have mentioned it, in the hospice, brought it up, but I just forgot. Chris said he made a point of mentioning it, only a couple of days later – and Phillip wasn't really speaking clearly then. It had taken me a couple of weeks to persuade Chris he had to go visit, or he'd regret it. Like Chris didn't have enough regret in his life.

Martin made it at the very last hour. I'd been putting messages in to the latest secretary.

Another helicopter arrival – this time for good reason. Phillip died that night, Sandra there. You ask why but there's no answers.

Martin was already back in his house in Berkshire, but he'd given me his numbers. He wanted to be involved, he said. Like he knew he'd been in the wrong for years.

Amplewick Church – we were all there for the funeral. Chris, Martin, me – standing on the bright green astroturf at the edge of the grave.

It was Martin said, 'Who's got it? Is it me?'

He was so busy, he couldn't even remember.

'No,' said Chris, looking down.

'I asked him for it,' I said.

'The bastard,' Chris said, and he was really phlegmy-crying. 'He took it with him.'

I looked at Chris, his red face. He was the one who should have died first. Alcoholic, and always a bit of a cunt. Not fucking Phillip. Phillip was happy, finally. He even said he liked the kids at school, because they reminded him of us – idiots who didn't know what they were doing.

'I'm fucking sorry,' I said to the grave, when I went back to visit it that night. 'I didn't mean to.'

I'd been surprised they let Phillip be buried there, but Sandra had made him a regular at church.

She arrived half an hour after me.

'Couldn't keep away,' she said. 'After I finished tidying up.'

The reception was at hers.

'Clarissa's with my mother,' she said, as if she needed to explain that to me – as if I thought she'd left a three-year old alone.

'You rescued him,' I said.

'Yeah, maybe I did. Don't have a fag, do you?'

'Sorry. Never smoked.'

'Right.'

'Could you rescue me, d'you think?'

She didn't answer.

'Do you have it?' I said. 'Can you give it to me?'

'What?' she said. 'Oh,' she said. 'No.'

I had expected her to think me a dick, and not know what I meant. But she did – we were on the same page straight away.

It was cold in the graveyard. I'd never been there at that time, since Chris dared me when I was thirteen. People leave weird stuff on graves now – dangly garden ornaments and stone teddy bears. I could see lights in the farm under the hill at the end of Cuthroat Lane.

'You don't have it?' I said.

'We used to pass it back and forth,' she said. 'Sometimes three or four times a day, after he told me about it. Even in the staffroom, or assembly. It was our joke.'

'I never knew a girl could get it.'

'I'm not a girl, Tony,' she said. 'And my rescuing days are over.'

She was a bit drunk.

'So, it's down there now,' I said.

'No,' said Sandra. 'He left it with Clarissa, until I can explain.'

That did it.

THE MUMBLING MAN

DANIE WARE

I like trains.

No, I don't mean I stand at the end of the platform at Clapham with a fur-hooded anorak and a notebook, I mean intercity trains. I've got a bitch of a schedule and a lot of meetings and trains are quiet. They're good places to think.

A long-distance train is a null-space; it's timeless, it exists between one place and another. You don't have to be anywhere, or anyone. No-one expects anything of you. You can sit with your earbuds, your laptop, your book; you can watch the passing countryside and leave your stresses behind.

Trains are peaceful, tinged with potential.

It was Friday evening, and I was heading back into London from Portsmouth, straight from a conference and laden with possibilities. As we'd left the coast, the carriage had been heaving, but now it was almost empty; outside, dusk was beginning to gather over the fields and castles of old Sussex. I had a gin and tonic and a warm glow; my laptop was on the table, but I'd not got as far as opening it, or attaching structure to the wealth of new ideas.

The rhythm of the wheels brought restfulness. They could wait.

Instead, I kicked off my heels under the table – damn things were pinching – and tucked my stockinged feet up onto the seat beside me. The setting sun streamed in through the window, sliding liquid gold though the carriage and warming my skin. With my drink in my hand, ice-cubes rattling gently against the plastic, I leaned my shoulder against the rest and watched the world roll by.

Over my ghost-reflection, the summer day was fading with a lilac sigh. The railway line ran through long folds of rich green, through woodlands tinged with yellow light. Rural Sussex is beautiful, a perfect patchwork of rolling fields, speckled with villages; every so often, there's the square, flint tower of an old Norman church, lord of its domain for a thousand years. Gravestones surround them, tiny slabs of pale grey.

The gin spread its glow into my belly. It had been a very long day.

I closed my eyes, and lifted my face to the touch of the sun.

The sudden hiss of the inter-carriage door woke me with a start. The train had stopped, the sun was gone and there were voices, outside on the platform. A breath of chill air touched me and I sat up, shivering and blinking, a crick in my neck where I'd dozed off against the window. My feet were cold.

I was disoriented; had no idea where we were.

Sitting up straighter, I put the drink down and twitched my shoulders, unsure how the temperature had dropped so sharply. Outside, the dusk had gathered to purple streaks and the sun was a heavily lidded eye, swollen-dark and sinking low over the hillsides.

The outer door slammed, hard.

As the train hauled itself back into motion, I missed the platform-sign, and fumbled for my smartphone as I craned to see round the edge of the window. The station was a small one, almost deserted. Hanging baskets were overladen with dying spring blossom and the lamps threw pools of odd, pale light.

An after-echo of my dreaming made me shiver.

Irritated, I sat up, shook myself awake. Tapped the screen on the phone.

Nothing.

The shiver came again.

Banishing my disquiet with carefully disciplined annoyance, I stood up, slipped my feet back into my heels and stretched, fetching my briefcase from the overhead storage. When my phone was safely plugged and charging, I flicked open the laptop instead.

As the little machine powered up, I realised something else – a thought like a slowly crystallising drip …

There was no-one else in the carriage.

My shiver became a *frisson;* a tantalising cold finger, stroking, teasing, down my spine. Under me, the train was picking up speed, the rattling now swift and relentless.

My thoughts caught the rhythm of the wheels: *Where are we going? Where are we now? Where are we going? Where are we —?*

Stop it!

In the sky, the evening had gathered to gloom. Vast shadows

stretched long across the hillsides and nameless dark shapes flashed by, close to the window.

I rubbed gooseflesh from my arms, stood up to slot my briefcase neatly back where it had been. I took a proper, careful look around the carriage.

No, I wasn't quite alone.

Down towards the door, slumped asleep with a newspaper forgotten in his lap, was a slightly crumpled, older man. His face was unshaven, creased with age or pain, and one arm was tucked protectively against his side. His clothing was dirty and every so often he twitched, like a sleeping animal.

For no rational reason, he made me uneasy.

Faintly humorously, my mind labelled him 'creepy playground stalker' – though he'd probably been no closer to a playground than I had.

He was muttering in his sleep.

Something between distaste and sympathy curled my expression. I watched him for a moment, but decided that no, I wasn't going to move. After all, he was harmless – just one of life's casualties. Whoever he was, he had nothing to do with me.

On the table, my laptop was booting, a bright light of rationality. It jingled welcome and I banished all thoughts of stalkers and sunsets. Instead, I drained the last of the G & T, now mostly water, and set the cup down decisively.

I watched the screen as the browser opened …

There was no time readout.

No Wi-Fi symbol.

Nothing.

My Cleopatra wallpaper smirked at me, at thoughts unvoiced. She looked like she'd just closed some huge deal, made a bundle on the markets, fired an ex-lover and got a kick out of doing it--

From the end of the carriage, I heard the man give a sudden, louder mutter and I jumped, my heart pounding. Sternly telling myself there was nothing wrong, I reached for my phone.

Had to know what the time was.

Damn thing was still dead.

Oh for God's sake!

Really peeved now, I checked the socket, made a mental note to call my provider and give them hell at the earliest opportunity.

The man muttered again. He sounded like he was laughing.

As I glanced down towards him, the train juddered and lurched. My stomach flipped and I found I was breathing swift and shallow, some irrational fear chasing across my skin and leaving tails of chill. The man's mouth was moving, some hopeless, endless monologue that touched both pity and aversion; for a moment, I could almost hear him. "… lost … aren't you … Juliet?"

Juliet.

I froze.

What?

But my rational, corporate mind was too well-trained – I'd misheard him. My surroundings were teasing me – there was no way he could be using my name.

Ridiculous.

My browser still wasn't opening. My phone was still dead.

Cold crept over my shoulders like fingers; I straightened my suit skirt and turned to the window. It was almost dark out there now. In the flat black, I could see the reflection of my face, my laptop, the lights in the carriage. If I cupped a hand against the cold glass and peered, I could just about make out the gently sloping Sussex hills …

The ground was flat.

That couldn't be right.

I'd done this trip many times, down to the company's offices on the harbourside and then back into London – had I somehow got on the wrong train?

I peered harder; both hands now shutting the light from round me.

Lost. Aren't you. Juliet.

The sky was deep blue, streaked with grey cloud and scatters of white stars; there was no moon. If I looked down, I could see the railway line was elevated, slightly above what looked like some sort of fen, almost a swamp. In places, there was the dark sheen of water.

This time, the shiver was tangible – a shudder, a choke of cold that closed soft hands around my throat. For just a moment, the fear was so strong that I couldn't breathe.

Where the hell was I?

Lost.

I reached for my phone again, pointlessly, reflexively, trying to check the time and reference my progress. As I did so, I heard the man say distinctly, "… don't you remember?"

My browser still wasn't opening. Cleo smiled at me, mocking, knowing.

Aren't you, Juliet?

No, dammit, I wasn't letting this scare me. I'd faced down a sneering table of middle management; I was the toast of my company and I'd got to the top by any damned means possible. I wasn't being bloody-well frightened by some stinking-poor alcoholic on a train.

You can do anything, my father used to tell me, and I'd spent my whole life knowing he was right.

But I still had no web access; no time and no space. I had no idea when or where I was.

Don't you remember?

Enough!

I stood up to my full height, did up my jacket, banished the phantoms. Figuring that creepy-stalker-man wouldn't steal the laptop as he had nowhere to put it, I picked up my wallet and my useless phone and I walked down the carriage, my heels snicking decisively as I went.

I was going to take control of this situation. Someone on this train would have a link to the outside world and I was damned-well going to find them.

The next carriage was empty.

Rubbish was scattered across the tables; discarded papers and empty cans of fizz. Obscurely comforted by this touch of humanity, I kept walking.

The carriage after was also empty.

So was the carriage after that.

The train swayed and thundered; racing from nowhere to nowhere. I had to catch my balance repeatedly and silently cursed the ubiquitous heels. The cold was making me shiver, for real now. As I passed the train toilet and the next door along slid open, I could see that the following carriage, too, was entirely deserted.

Wasn't that …? I counted back, sure that I hadn't walked past this many doors on the platform at Portsmouth Harbour.

Don't you remember?

No, I was imagining it. For heaven's sake.

I kept walking, more slowly now, tinged with a fusion of anger and fear. Where the hell was everybody? Was this some sort of joke?

It took another two carriages for my nerve to falter. They were all abandoned, every table, every seat, every luggage rack. The rubbish was started to mock me – the brown bags from the coffee places, the neatly knotted crisp packets – it was all staged, eerie, perfect, an echo of vanished humanity. The windows were utterly black, now; the whole world had shrunk to this vacant and blindly racing train.

Breathing deeply, struggling to walk calmly, I turned smartly on my heel and headed back up to my seat. One carriage, two, three, four. I was starting to feel like there was something behind me, following me, something lurking just off my shoulder. It was waiting for me to run or to glance back; the moment I panicked, it would be on me like … like an irate client.

My own flash of sarcasm made me feel slightly better.

Five carriages. Six.

At the end of the sixth carriage, the old man was slumped in his seat, still muttering. There was drool on his chin. He smelled bad, of stale food and old metal and dried blood. I stopped, turned around.

Stared at the empty table for a moment.

My stuff had gone.

All of it.

There was only the tin from the G & T, sitting there almost like a marker.

Oh, you have to be bloody joking …!

The man was muttering more loudly, now, a ghost of a cackle in his booze-stinking breath.

There was no way he could've taken it; no way. Where would he hide a designer briefcase, for God's sake? What would he want —?

"… a trade, Juliet. A life."

His eyes were closed, yet the words fell from his lips like pearl-drips of toxin. I stared at him, soaking his stench through my skin, waiting for those eyes to open …

A trade, Juliet.

What bloody trade? Had I really heard him speak my name? Had I heard it in the still carriage air? In the rumble of this timeless, ludicrous journey?

No. I was scaring myself for no reason. This was impossible. There was a rational explanation for all of this.

Think, dammit, there had to be someone else here. The guard, the driver. It wasn't like they could get off before I found them.

A trade, Juliet.

Really angry now, summoning righteous fury to cover deeper, darker sensations that coiled in my belly like wires, I stalked past the old man and headed up the train the other way.

His muttered laughter followed me like a spectre.

A life.

Oh, I was going tear an explanation out of someone's bloody *hide.*

One carriage, two. Doors hissing as I went through them; tables littered with the same scatters of rubbish. The rattle and shake of the racing train. Three carriages, four. I was walking faster, sweating now; a tickle under my breasts, a line at my temple. Five carriages, six.

Where was the First Class compartment? The refreshment car?

Long time, Juliet.

The man's muttering laughter was still following me. It teased my ears like a lover's breath, like a soft hand. It was almost –

Oh, my God.

It was almost familiar.

Don't you remember?

My blood froze to crystal horror. Where the hell did I know him from?

I paused, but the recollection was there-and-gone, even as I reached for it – a sliver of dream, as fine and sharp as a blade, shattering in the emptiness. I found myself standing in the centre of rubbish-strewn nothing, my skin crawling, my hands clenched, my polished-perfect nails biting my palms.

For an instant, I nearly turned and ran.

But to where?

Then my anger took hold, righteous and incandescent. No. This was not happening to me. I could do anything.

You hear me? Anything!

I was back in motion. Letting out a breath that promised bloody warfare, I was walking – then striding – down the middle of the train. My heels clicked like a metronome. I didn't know what the hell this prank was, but I'd teach them to fuck with me.

God bloody help the first thing I found. This wasn't funny anymore. I'd had *enough.*

The storm of my fury carrying me, I marched.

And the doors hissed and slid for me, marking my progress.

I marched until my anger ran down over my skin in rivulets of sweat and dread, marched until my feet were blistered and I could wear my shoes no longer.

Lost. Aren't you.

The train was empty. As empty as death, as empty as a grave, as empty as an abandoned bloody Norman church. When I finally saw a sleeping figure, I almost broke into a run –

And came to a dumbfounded halt at the sight of the old man.

A trade. A life.

Still slumped, still muttering, curled even harder round his arm. He didn't wake as I stood, trembling, over him.

I stared, stunned by impossibility, unable to find a single rational thought.

I'd gone round in a circle; the train had no beginning, no end.

This was insane.

Denial and disbelief froze my throat to wordlessness; bafflement screamed in my head, as loud as the rattling wheels. I had no idea, nothing, no explanation remaining. I could only stare at the lone constant, the one thing in my messed-up world that made any kind of sense.

Don't you remember?

Where was the driver? How the bloody hellfire …?

Jesus. It was too ridiculous for me to even formulate the question.

The train had slowed, rumbling softer now. Clinging to the last shreds of sense, of logical determination, I put a careful hand on the arm of the chair and leaned down to look at my companion.

Who are you? Why are you here?

Around us, around our reality, the world was plastic and metal and darkness.

He muttered something, but this time I didn't catch what he said. I leaned closer, my hand over my mouth and the blur of my shadow touching his skin.

How are you doing this?

There was a webwork of scars in his face, a faint white lattice under dirt and stubble. He wasn't as old as I'd first thought – only a little older than I – but the marks of harshness were all over him. By his huddled arm, he'd been in some sort of accident.

His clothing was good quality, but filthy, seams rotted and fabric thinning. It was over a decade out of style – it looked like he'd bought it at a charity shop.

And, in the breast pocket of his jacket, there was a corner of worn, brown leather. I looked at it for a minute before I realised what it was.

How did this wreckage of a man still have a wallet?

Juliet.

The train lurched and rattled.

I stared at it, compelled. The wallet was a rational thing in a world gone all to hell – it consumed and confused me. As my reality rang with the thunder of the wheels, with questions and impossibilities, with the damned *screaming* in my head, I stared at that little, brown leather corner.

I needed its answer – but *God,* I was afraid of what it contained.

Where was I? Really?

Lost.

Shivering now, one arm clutching my jacket against the horrors of incomprehension, I watched the man's face. I measured his sleeping breathing, his mutters, his spirit-reek that coloured the air.

Then, holding my breath, I touched the cool leather with a careful finger.

As I did so, he started and muttered louder, his lips and eyelids flickered. I jumped, heart pounding, the waft of shock and booze and stale sweat nearly making me gag.

His lips were moving.

"At last," he said softly. "I've been waiting for this."

Been waiting for this.

The words echoed in the train's rhythm, 'been-*waiting*-for-this', 'been-*waiting*-for-this'. As I listened, the noise closed round me, a band across my throat, an echo in my ears, a hand tight around my heart. His soft, rotting laughter was twisting in my memory, old fears jabbered at the corners of my mind. The reek of the alcohol, so familiar, the colours of his now-faded jacket …

Oh my God.

I *did* know him, this mumbling man!

Been-waiting-for-this!

The realisation hit me like a fist, flattened me, horrified me. Tight with terror and fury and anticipation, I waited for him to settle.

Been-waiting-for-this!

Why I didn't just shake his shoulder and wake him, tell him exactly what I thought of his joke and demand an explanation, I didn't know – I throttled the thought as it surfaced. I had to know everything first, I told myself; had to face him with all the relevant information.

His mutters rolled into quiet. Stinking, he settled deeper into the seat. His breathing evened and slowed.

As I watched him sleep, the lines of his face hazed slowly into focus, like the dawn creeping into an all-night party.

I know I know you! But from where?

It was a smoke-wisp of recollection, laughing and elusive. His face was a sketch in the back of my mind, slowly taking shape. Cautiously, tightly controlling my movements, I reached a hand for the wallet.

Got it.

Touching it was a shock, a pulse of electricity up my arm. As I slid it free, it was warm, blood-warm, flesh-warm, sweat-warm. It made my skin tingle, brought flickerings of imagery –

Long time, Juliet.

For an instant, I heard an echo of music, smelled the mingled scents of beer and wine and cheap body-spray, warm city pavement and lingering cigarette smoke. I was outside a pub, laughing in the gathering evening.

As the image took shape, I found myself trembling – fear and tension and hope and dread.

In my hand, the wallet was heavy with significance and the world shrank round it.

Been-waiting-for-this!

Fear climbed my throat. Any moment now, this madness was going to be too much. My denial would falter, my courage break –

No. I can do anything.

With one last, defiant gesture, I flicked the thing open.

And I saw the picture inside.

I remembered.

A younger me, ten years and more, overconfident and laughing, wine-glass in my hand. Behind me, the front doors of a streetside pub; I'd had too much to drink but I was young and already successful and I didn't care. The world was at my perfectly pedicured feet and it was mine to walk over as I chose.

Been-waiting-for-this!

The rattle cut through the memory like the train cut through the countryside – a hard line of truth.

In that picture, I was on the very precipice of the single worst moment of my life.

A trade, Juliet.

Standing in that timeless carriage, that empty and impossible hell, I looked at the mumbling man and I remembered the dare, the thrill of adrenaline, the shock and the rush. I remembered the vicious girlish laughter as we targeted his drink; the gasps of gleeful horror as he raised the spiked glass to his lips. I remembered how slavering-eager I was, how much I wanted it; I remembered the sheer rush of power it gave me. I had no idea who he even was – he didn't matter. What mattered was the authority, the sheer might I could exert. What mattered was the laughter as he reeled from the pub, and was gone in the city and in the night …

Who cared? I would never see him again.

A life.

Looking at that younger self, cold and hard-eyed, there was more. As though the very picture had ignited in my grasp, it blossomed with sudden life, singing my fingers, burning my eyes until they stang …

A newspaper headline – a young man, fallen from a bridge, crushed by an oncoming train. It had caught him by the arm and dragged him for several meters – a passenger had seen him screaming and pulled the emergency brake.

Too late.

The text under the picture said: 'Traces of ketamine in his blood'.

A trade, Juliet. A life.

Like the closing of the hangman's noose, the realisation was utter and inescapable. The moment was frozen endless, chilling my skin to frost, my heart to ice. My breath was solid in my throat. My denial was gone, finally silenced; my assurance and anger crumbling like the lost castles of Sussex – hopeless. As the endless train rattled onwards though the darkness, I saw myself, reflected in the window, my face forever running across where a young man screamed …

There was no driver, no guard. There would be no station.

This was my personal hell, made just for me.

And made for a debt I had forever to pay.

THE RETREAT

GEMMA AMOR

Jennifer knew something was wrong within ten minutes of leaving The Retreat.

'It feels a bit … off out here, doesn't it?' She mused, staring out of the passenger side window of her friend's beaten up Nissan Micra and trying to get a handle on what, exactly, it was that she found so disconcerting.

'It's certainly very quiet,' Red replied, struggling to change gear. The gear stick jammed mid-shift, and a hideous grinding, groaning noise filled the car. 'Fuck,' she spat, yanking on the stick and forcing it to behave. 'It's only been three weeks, and I've already forgotten how to drive.'

Jennifer grunted. 'It's the car's way of saying it doesn't want to go home,' she said, dragging her eyes away from the bleak winter skyline of the Norfolk broads. There was a lot of sky out here, and not much in the way of landmarks to break it up. Endless stretches of reeds lay to either side of the road, punctuated by deep, watery ditches and the occasional tree on the horizon, skeletal without their summer coats. Every now and then they would pass a parked car or tractor, but no people, no moving vehicles. In the distance, a single, solitary ruined windmill stood proud in the middle of a muddy field, the sail blades ragged and rotting, spokes sticking out haphazardly like the bones in a broken bird's wing.

'I know how it feels,' Red replied, slipping sunglasses on with one hand as a searing ray of low afternoon sun broke free from a bank of clouds and shone directly into her eyes. 'I don't want to go home either.'

The women drove on in silence for a minute or two, thinking about that: going home. Going back. They had families waiting for them, children, husbands, bills to pay, routines to fall back into. Uniforms to iron, lunches to pack, bathrooms to clean, laundry to fold. Tantrums to handle, and tears to mop dry. Work to somehow sandwich in between all of this. The weight of a thousand heavy responsibilities lurking in their futures rested heavy on their hearts. When would there be time for them to be themselves again? When? When the children were grown, and had flown the nest? When they retired? Ever?

Behind them, the tall, cream-painted walls of The Retreat grew smaller and smaller. They had been happy there. They had slept, and eaten well, and worked on their novels. They had walked around a private lake attached to the compound every day. They had drunk buckets of good french wine, even smoked a joint or two on the glass balcony of their apartment, the one that faced the sun as it set. Wrapped in thick blankets to combat the bitter winter chill, they had sucked down the velvety, fragrant weed and talked about their feelings, desires and hopes until their throats were sore.

And now, it was over. Their fully-catered four weeks had flown by, and this was their first time outside of the small compound in a month. They had been sealed away from the world very nicely during their stay. Food had been delivered in bulk at the beginning of the month, and between them they had made it last the full stretch. There was no internet at The Retreat, and no phone coverage either, or landlines. They received no visitors, although the beds were mysteriously changed by a secretive house maid during the first week of their stay. After that, they had kept the place tidy by themselves. It had been pleasurable to live in such minimal cleanliness: the homes they had left behind were stuffed to the rafters with toys, computing equipment, trinkets, junk, bikes, muddy boots, animal paraphernalia, piles of homework, recycling crates, amaetur artwork and mounds of crumpled, unfolded laundry that no-one ever wanted to put away until critical mass had been reached.

'God it's flat out here, isn't it,' Red murmured, suddenly uncomfortable in the silence that had descended on them. Jennifer could tell she had been thinking about her husband, possibly for the first time in four weeks, and the thought process had made her uncomfortable.

'Yep,' sighed Jennifer, her own husband's face swimming into view. 'A lot of sky.'

'My aunt grew up not far from here, you know, a bit further inland, in the Fens. Apparently there is something called Fen Syndrome that the workers on the fields used to get.'

'Fen Syndrome? Sexy.'

'Too much sky, like you said. It sent some of them mad, if they were out working too long. I guess it was like agoraphobia, or something.'

'No end,' Jennifer muttered, not feeling too cheered by Red's story.

'What?'

'No hills, no features. It is beautiful, but it's so fucking *flat*. It's like the horizon goes on forever and ever, with no end.'

'Huh,' grunted Red, changing gear again, more smoothly this time. 'Fuck, we're cheerful, aren't we?'

'Not really.' Jennifer pouted. 'I really don't want to go home. Does that make me a bad person?'

Red sighed. 'No, Jen, it doesn't. I'm struggling too, you know I am. I mean, I do miss the kids, and I don't want to sound like I'm taking my family for granted, but I just know what it'll be like when I walk in that front door.'

'Yeah. Noise. Chaos. Shit everywhere. I'm getting hives just thinking about it.' Jennifer scratched at her arm, where an itchy red rash was indeed spreading. 'Plus Alfie is always really weird with me after I've been away for any length of time. Like, he's happy to see me, but then realises how angry he is that I left him. So then I have three or four days of atrocious behaviour and tantrums to wrangle.' Alfie was Jennifer's six-year old son. Blonde-haired, blue-eyed, and tempestuous, he was both the light of her life and the thing that kept her awake every night, worrying. She wondered if he had grown at all in the month she had been gone, and whether his dad had made him brush his teeth every day.

'Did I ever tell you about the turd in the cup?' Red said suddenly, a smile creeping onto her lips.

'Um, no. But do I actually want to know?'

'Well, I'm going to tell you anyway. So, you know how I like my baths.'

'If you can call lying for three hours in a comatose state in cold, dirty water a bath, then yes, I'm well aware.'

'Well, it had been a bad day. The kids had argued non-stop, Billy and I had been fighting, and there wasn't a single person in the whole house aside from the cat that hadn't been in tears at some point throughout the day. One of 'those' days, you know?'

'Intimately,' Jennifer said.

'So, I put the kids to bed, cooked dinner, tidied everything away, sorted my emails, and decided to run a bath. I went all out with it: bubbles, candles, incense, a book, glass of wine, essential oils … the works. I locked the door, and climbed in. And as I lay there, slowly relaxing, I started to smell something, something really … off, you know?'

'Oh God.' Jennifer shook her head, knowing what was coming.

'I looked around, and all I could see was this set of stacking cups we've had since the kids were babies, sitting on the side of the bath, right next to my head. I still use them to rinse their hair, you see, at bathtime. They're useful cups.'

'I see where this is going.'

'So I look inside, and what do you think I find?'

'Let me guess.'

'Sitting innocently in the middle of the smallest cup is a dry, hard, perfectly formed human turd. How long it had been hiding in there, I'll never know. I'd been lying in the bath, sipping on Australian malbec, with a human shit not more than three inches away from my head.'

'Wow. Are you sure it was one of the kids? Could have been Billy, fucking with you.'

Red snorted with mirth.'Trust me, if it had been one of Billy's, it would not have fit inside the cup.'

'Kids are gross, aren't they. Where do they learn that? It's not as if we bring them up to hide their fecal matter around the house, is it? At some point, one of your children autonomously decided that hiding their own excrement in a cup was a good, practitionable idea. Astonishing, isn't it? Goodness, imagine having your own bathroom, one you don't have to share with anyone.'

Red sighed in longing. 'Like the one in The Retreat. Remember how it smelled like lemon bleach and nothing else? And every surface sparkled. And the tub was like a swimming pool. Damn, I loved that bathroom.'

Jennifer sighed. 'I'm depressed now. We had such a lovely time, didn't we?'

'We did, my sweet, we did.'

They drove on.

'It's a bit odd that there are no people around, don't you think?' Red said, after another moment or two of silence. 'It's the middle of the day, it's reasonable weather, and I haven't seen a single soul around since we left The Retreat. Not a dog walker, nothing. It feels like Christmas, i's so quiet.'

'I know what you mean,' Jennifer agreed, and once again, the sensation that something was not quite right crept over her. She'd written it off as her having a hard time adjusting to the world outside The Retreat, but the further they drove, the more obvious it was that something else was going on. Because there were no people at all, not even, as Red had pointed out, any dog walkers.

They fell into silence, keeping their eyes fixed on their surroundings, and the further along the road they got, the more anxious they grew about the lack of people in sight. Because it wasn't just the physical absence of humans that became more and more obvious the longer they drove, but the strong, unshakeable sense of abandonment that hung heavy in the air as they sped along the narrow country roads. Like a house feels when no-one lives in it for a while. Something about the quality of the silence, the lack of movement to be found, the *heaviness* of everything. That's how it felt outside the walls of The Retreat: as if the world had been abandoned, left behind.

Red and Jen quickly began to feel like the only two women left on earth.

That thought was swiftly obliterated when they turned down a small, single-lane road walled in by hedgerow and found themselves face to face with the burned out carcass of a plane.

It wasn't an enormous plane, but it was big enough to block the entire road with its broken, charred fuselage. It was a small jet of some sort, not one of the huge Boeings that took holiday makers overseas in their droves, but still a commercial passenger plane: Jennifer could see a blistered logo on the side of the plane. The fuselage was broken into two parts, and the road and surrounding fields covered in blackened, twisted debris.

In silence, Red pulled the car up a little distance away, and yanked the handbrake on. Then, she and Jen got out to have a better look.

'Is this real?' Jen breathed, as they stepped closer. 'I feel like I'm on a movie set or something.'

'I don't understand,' Red replied, her voice unsteady. 'If this happened a while ago, which it must have, or it would still be on fire, then why is it still here? Why haven't the emergency services cleared it all away? It doesn't make *sense.*'

Jen stopped, and clutched at Red's arm. 'It's a fucking plane, Red! Why do we have to look at it?! It's obvious what happened, it crashed here! I don't want to go over there. What if … what if there are bodies in there?' She asked, querulous. Her face was pale in the low winter sun.

Red shook her off, eyes fixed on the crash site. 'There won't be,' she murmured, although she could not have said why she knew that. She just did.

She was right. There were no bodies. There was no trace of anyone. There were melted fragments of people's lives – burned suitcases, shoes, a doll, coats, sunglasses, reading glasses – but no people. It was as if everyone had vanished at the exact same moment, and the plane had dropped clean out of the sky as a result. A horrible, sick feeling grew in Red's stomach as she looked at the devastation around her.

'Jen,' she said, softly. 'I think we need to get to a town. There's something … something I want to check on.'

The closest town was only three miles away. They parked up in the centre, and got out.

'I don't understand,' Jen said, eyes growing wide, and wild. 'I don't get it. Where the fuck *is* everyone?'

Red had no answers for her.

They started with the shops, going into each one in turn and hoping, with an intensely mounting sense of anxiety, that they might find someone hiding behind a counter, or in a changing room, or even in a toilet. As they searched, the enormity of what they were experiencing began to dawn on them, and Jen started to cry, quietly at first, and then with more urgency. They abandoned the shops, and searched houses, instead. They found most with their doors unlocked. They found evidence of life: rotted food, chairs pulled out, covers rumpled, a bath that was overflowing, the water having been left to run for what looked like weeks, judging by how flooded the house was. They found pets that had been abandoned: dead fish, a dead hamster, a starving, hissing cat. They found children's drawings pinned to fridges, video games frozen on tv screens, half-filled coffee-cups covered in thick layers of mouldy scum. They found all the evidence of human life, but no life itself.

And they realised that something had happened to the world then, something huge, something unfathomable, and it had probably happened around the same time The Retreat's house maid had stopped making their beds, around three weeks ago.

It dawned on them, then, that they might well be, in that very moment in time, the last people left on earth.

And just as they had this thought, they found a survivor.

She was a woman in her fifties, thin, with wiry black hair that massed out like a dark cloud around her head. She was sitting on a bench in the back garden of one of the houses they searched, clutching a Barbie doll to her chest and rocking back and forth. Behind her, meticulously built rockery made a backdrop of stones and ferns against which she looked the very picture of misery.

Red and Jen called out to her, softly, their hearts full of relief. *Another person!* They thought, feeling sick with the implications.

'Hello?' They said out loud, but the woman did not appear to hear them. They went carefully across the lawn to where she was sitting, coatless despite the bitterly cold January air.

'Excuse me, miss?' Red said, noticing with some alarm that the woman's head was covered in raw, bleeding patches that looked as if she had pulled out her own hair.

The woman said nothing, just carried on rocking.

'Miss? Can you … can you help us? We just came out of … well, we've been away, and … we don't understand what happened. Do you know? Where everyone else is? Can you tell us, please?' Red's voice cracked at this, and Jen started to cry again.

The woman registered their presence at last, and stopped rocking. She looked up at them with eyes that pierced their souls.

'Everyone else?' She said, as if waking up from a long sleep. 'Everyone … else?'

Yes.'

Her face changed, instantly switching from something vague and far away to something full of rage, and despair.

'Don't you understand?' She said, suddenly taking a hold of, and tearing out a huge clump of her own hair with one bloody fist. 'There *is* no one else, you stupid bitch! We're the only people left. There is no one! Everyone I knew is gone. Everyone you knew is probably gone, too. Gone. We're alone. Don't you see that? The only people *left on earth!*'

Red let anger keep her from breaking down.

'I refuse to believe that. We're not gone. You're not gone. There might be others. It's possible.'

The woman stared at the hair she had just yanked from her scalp, and started twisting it around her fingers, pulling it so tight that the fingertips went dark red, and then blue. 'Why did it have to be you?' She asked, dully, her anger dissipating as quickly as it had flared, her lower lip trembling. 'Why couldn't it have been my girl, my sweet little girl? I came here, you know, when it first happened. I was at work, but I came right away. She wasn't here.Then I went to her school, but everyone was gone. I went to the playground, I went to the woods, I walked around the supermarkets and checked all her friend's houses. She isn't anywhere. She …' The woman made a gesture with her hand like a small explosion going off. 'Poof. Gone. My baby. *My baby.* I could have coped, if she'd survived! I could have lived through this, with her next to me!' The woman stood up, slowly, the Barbie doll sliding forgotten off of her lap and onto the lawn.

'WHY DID IT HAVE TO BE YOU?!' She shrieked, suddenly. 'I DON'T KNOW YOU! WHY?!!' And the woman was upon Red, grabbing her by her shirt collar and screaming 'WHY? WHO ARE YOU?! WHY *YOU?! WHY NOT HER?*' Over and over into Red's face. Red reared back, trying and failing to put some distance between herself and the raving woman, who had an iron grip on her clothes.

'Please,' she said, trying to keep her cool. 'Please, I'm sorry about your daughter. Please let go of —'

'WHY YOU? WHY YOU, WHY-'

There was a thud, and a wet crunching sound. The woman's frenzied litany cut off, abruptly. Her eyes rolled upwards, and her knees sagged. Red cried out, watching as the woman collapsed to the ground. A puddle of dark red blood blossomed around her head, which Red could see now had a huge dent in it. The Barbie doll lay, half-naked, staring up at the sky with blank, blue eyes.

Red looked up, horrified. She saw Jennifer standing, motionless, a thin whiplash of crimson splattered across her right cheek. She was holding a rock, and staring down at it as if it were an alien.

'Jen,' Red breathed, afraid for the first time ever of her friend. 'You killed her.'

Jennifer raised her eyes, and met Red's gaze.

'I want to go home, Red,' she said. 'Now. I need to get back to the city. I need to … I need to check up on my boy. I need to get back to my Alfie.'

Red thought of her own children. She remembered complaining about them, only hours before. She felt a huge emptiness consume her insides, and she looked at the dead woman on the floor by her feet.

Maybe it's better for her this way, she thought suddenly, reeling from the implication that her own son and daughter may no longer be … here. Alive.

Present.

'Let's go,' was what she said out loud.

They got back to the city, but found no traces of their families.

They spent months looking, months of searching empty buildings, chasing shadows along city streets, pounding the pavement with shoes that wore out too quickly. They saw only two other people in those five desperate months. One was a teenage boy, trying on new Doc Martins in a shop on the high street. They saw him through the store window, and watched from a distance as he deliberated over which pair of boots to steal. Something about his demeanour looked twitchy, and raw, so the women kept themselves concealed from him. He walked off down the street ten minutes later, brand new boots shiny on his feet, and they never came across him again.

The second survivor they met was a woman their own age, a woman with straggly hair and a haunted face. She was wandering the alleyways between the city's allotments, no doubt getting ready to pillage the overgrown vegetable patches for any fresh produce they might bear. Red and Jen did the same, frequently, having long since exhausted most of the markets near their houses. Most of the fresh produce in shops had spoiled by the time they returned from The Retreat, although they had enough canned goods to keep them alive for a lifetime.

They were about to go and attack a potato patch when the other woman stumbled into view, drunk as a skunk, and filthy from head to toe.

The woman paused when she saw them, and they waited to see how hostile she might be. After a minute or two of squinting through her liquor-goggles, she sank to her knees, her face crumpling with relief.

'Other people,' she moaned, as Red and Jen approached. 'Other people. I thought … I thought I was the only person alive on this planet. Oh, oh God.'

Red made soothing noises in the back of her throat, whilst still keeping her distance.

'It's okay,' she said, softly. 'It's okay. We're real.'

'I can't … Oh, God. I haven't seen a single other soul since...since it happened.' She shook her head, slurring her words, muzzy with the booze. 'Have you any idea how lonely I've been? Oh, God.' She started to cry, ugly, shuddering sobs that wracked her whole body painfully. 'I've been trying to … to drink myself to death, but it just ain't working. I've tried pills, but I always seem to sick them up at the last minute. I'm not brave enough to walk over to the bridge. Would you … will you do it for me?' She clasped her hands together, gazing up at them with shining eyes. 'Please. I'm not brave enough to do it myself. Will you? Do it for me? I don't want to … I don't want to live in a world like this. I don't. Look at it!' She waved her arms out across the city, and they didn't have to look to know what she meant. They knew. It was wrong, all wrong. So much absence. So many lives, extinguished and erased. They struggled with it every day, although it is surprising how quickly a person can adapt to a new norm if they stay grounded in routine, and purpose. As Red and Jen had.

'Will you? Help me?' The woman said, and they could both tell how serious she was.

Red shook her head, vehemently, and backed away from the conversation.

Jen tightened her grip on her shovel.

After six months, they gave up hope of finding their children, or husbands. They held a small funeral for them, burying items that had belonged to each loved one in shallow graves dug in Red's back garden. They filled these graves in, and held hands over them, reciting poems for the lost. Jennifer sang a song that she had used to sing to Alfie when he was a baby, an irish lullaby that had never failed to get him off to sleep. They said goodbye to their families, and knew, that in doing so, they could no longer stay in the city. Memories lurked on every street corner, and both women were sick of remembering how life used to be.

They decided to go back to The Retreat. It had high walls, lockable gates, and fish in the lake. It was also the last place they had both been truly happy, so back they went. They packed light, found a car that started, lifted the keys from a nearby house, and drove it until it ran out of fuel. Then they switched to a new car, and so on, until the comforting, cream-coloured walls of The Retreat loomed before them.

'We're home,' Red said, as she switched off the engine, staring at the double gates of the compound.

Jennifer said nothing.

They found the place pretty much as they had left it, months earlier: dustier, the food in the fridge long-spoiled, and a slightly funny smell coming from the toilet, but otherwise, it could have been yesterday that they were last here, rolling their eyes and complaining about their kids and their spouses, chattering excitedly about their future plans, gazing out contentedly over the reed-filled lake beneath their apartment's balcony. They decided to do this again, for old-time's sake. They found an unopened bottle of shiraz in a store cupboard, and a tin of capers and olives still in date. They laid everything out on the little table on their balcony and sat, side by side, watching the sun set slowly over an endless, unbroken horizon.

'So much sky,' Red said, wiping a tear from her cheek as the red glow of the dying day faded to a muted pink.

'Did you bring it?' Jen asked, tipping back her head, and pouring wine into the back of her throat.

Red sighed. 'I did. It took me a while to find it, but I did.'

She reached into a paper bag that was leaning against her chair leg, scrabbled around, and brought something out, laying it on the table. Jen looked at it, and closed her eyes in relief.

'Thank you,' she said, reaching out to grip Red's hand tight in her own.

'We were happy here, weren't we?' Red said, pouring herself more wine.

'We were,' Jen agreed, and that was the last thing either of them said to each other.

Minutes later, a loud, sharp *crack!* Rang out into the evening, swiftly followed by another. Alarmed by the noise, a flock of starlings rose up from the reeds in the lake and swarmed around the tall, compact shape of The Retreat's main apartment block, a dark, frantic little tornado of wings and beaks and chittering bird-noises that eventually dissipated, like smoke in a strong breeze.

The Retreat grew silent, and on a balcony overlooking a lake, two friends stared sightlessly up into a slowly darkening sky, their hands entwined.

THE STATION

JOSEPH SALE

With 1% oxygen remaining, he reached safety.

Benson pressed the emergency lockdown button and the pressurised blastdoors slid shut with a muted hiss, like the last failing breath filtered through a respirator.

The room was airtight and nigh on impregnable. It was small, about five metres by five. Against one wall was a series of complex consoles and monitors with code scrolling across it that looked primarily like radio and transmission data. A dull machine sat in the corner. There were two functional seats, with a table between them, arranged like a train-carriage compartment. Two plastic cups sat on the table, as shiny as the day they had been factory-made. The whole building looked factory-made, in fact. There were no posters, no trinkets, nothing that suggested people whiling away boring hours. It was devoid of character. It was nothing more than a comms way-station, but it'd saved Benson's life, so he supposed he mustn't begrudge it too much.

Its walls were windowless save for one on the same side as the blast door. Through this window, no larger than the slitted arrow niches in some medieval fortress but fortified with glass designed to repel grenades, Benson watched the storm outside; an endless spiral of lightning, face-eating wind, and the shrill noise of earth cracking beneath the tempest. To say the atmosphere of Planet 1219-20 was hostile was an understatement. It was the closest thing to hell he'd ever touched down on. And the thing that came at him, in the storm ... He closed his eyes, the memory itself enough to stir revulsion, and then all of a sudden that revulsion had a hold of him, he was gagging on puke that was forcing its way up his throat. Wait, it wasn't that, he was choking on – nothing. There was no air left in his suit.

He tore at his spacesuit, as though it were poisonous and burning him. His fingers, clad in rubber as they were, fumbled ineffectually with the clasps.

"Let me help you!"

Suddenly, there was someone in the room with him, a stranger. In his panic, Benson didn't get much time to take in the details of this figure: male, tall, dark, with a mop of hair that looked like a toupee. The stranger's fingers, however, were dextrous, instantly unclasping the visored helmet. Benson gasped as air struck him, burning his lungs like corrosive asbestos.

He coughed, doubled over, spat treacly, thick spittle. He wiped his mouth and stood up.

"Thank you," he gasped.

The black haired man nodded. It was a perfunctory nod, quickly given. He extended a hand to the wheezing Benson.

"My name is Night, pleased to meet you."

"Pleased to meet you, too. Night, was it? I'm Benson. Surveyor." He tapped a complex insignia indicating profession and rank that adorned his lapel. Night lowered his hand, not at all offended, it seemed, by the refusal to shake.

"I see. I'm a technician here."

"Oh yeah?" Benson looked outside at the howling chaos. "You get much *technical* done in this?"

"I built the facility you're standing in. Correction, that is misleading. I was one of many who helped to build it."

"Well thank fucking Christ you did, or I'd be a goner. Jesus, what the fuck is happening out there?" Benson went to the window. He wasn't sure why. He couldn't see anything out there, not really, and what he had experienced had freaked him the hell out. But that was human, wasn't it? No sooner had danger been seemingly escaped, than one wanted to look at it again through a plexiglass window, perhaps later poke it, see if it stirred.

There was a flash of lightning and Benson flinched. Christ. He stepped away from the window.

"We were told the planet had teething issues with the terraforming, but this …" Benson trailed off. Suddenly, he was angry. How many of his teammates had died because of stupid bureaucracy, greed, and worst of all, faulty information? Benson brought up his fist and slammed it against the glass slit. His hands were encased in inches of rubber, but it still hurt like a real punch, the kind he threw bare-knuckle in one of the illegal fighting rings aboard the *Virgil*, the mothership-class space-freighter now hanging uselessly in orbit of 1219-20, unaware of a single fucking thing going on beneath the storm's blanket.

"Yes, the situation is undesirable," Night said, coolly. "And I'm afraid I have to inform you that this facility has limited oxygen supply."

"Come again?"

"The oxygen in this facility is exhaustible." Night said as though remarking upon a historical date that was mildly inaccurate. "It was never meant for long-term use."

Benson threw up his hands.

"And you're telling me like that? Just like that? We're going to fucking suffocate. Jesus, any way we can get some more?"

Benson paced, angry as a tiger that'd been scarred by a superior alpha. His way was to throw punches. He was good at that. It was how he liked to tackle all of life's problems, metaphorically and literally. His fearless attitude is what made him a good surveyor. He was one of the few prepared to tell Command that they needed to fucking pull their socks up and *fix* the terraforming units on Mars, for example, or *actually* clean the dome on Saturn's moon, Titan, because, you know, it violated only about half-a-hundred human rights, and it was a ticking clock at this point on when some gruesome space-bacteria turned that sludge into a virus that wiped the population.

"I'm sorry if my demeanour offends, Benson, I'm having trouble processing the situation."

Benson waved one hand, the offence already forgotten. Quick to throw punches, and perhaps even quicker to forgive.

"Not your fault. I wish I had your calm is all."

"To answer your earlier question: no. Unfortunately, the nearest oxygen supply lies over 31.24, or as the others termed it the "Purple Mountains", some eight hundred kilometres from here."

"Vehicles?"

Night shook his head.

"Weapons?"

Night cocked his head, not understanding the logical train.

"Not to kill ourselves, Jesus! No, I was thinking of that *thing* out there. Christ, what is it, by the way? Nobody mentioned indigenous life!"

Benson became acutely aware of a speck of red on his spacesuit. He had to resist the urge to probe to see if it was, indeed, the blood of either John, Charlie, or Sam – his team, young surveyors he'd brought to this planet, now dead. Because of him.

No! Because of Command, because of negligence and misinformation!

He'd have more than a few punches to throw if he ever made it off this rock, though the possibility was looking slimmer and slimmer by the moment.

"Killing it would benefit our situation very little. Our only hope of escape is a communications tower, with long-range transmission capabilities sufficient to break through the storm's circle. It's about a mile from here."

Benson deflated. A mile. With no suit. Night wasn't wearing one, just a workman's overall that looked like it'd been made by someone who was colourblind. The air on 1219-20 wasn't 0% oxygen, Benson would be able to breath for a while, but not enough to cover a mile, and with all likelihood the storm, or the creature, would kill him first.

"Would you care for a coffee?" Night asked. Benson, whose rage was calming in the face of inevitability, finally studied Night with his surveyor's eye. He noted again the way Night's hair seemed *off*, as though it were fake. It was surely synthetic, either a graft or a toupee. His deep ebony face had a rubbery texture to it too, or perhaps it was simply his lack of expression, though Benson did note a curious alacrity in Night's eyes, as though he, too, were studying Benson with the same intensity. There was no hint of a smile, but equally, no hint of insincerity. The face produced a curious warmth in Benson, as though he felt compelled *to be liked* by Night.

Night, what a fucking peculiar name.

"Yeah, alright," Benson said, plopping himself down on one of the seats. He removed his bulky rubber gloves by twisting an almost invisible seam in his spacesuit. He laid the gloves on the table. "Two sugars, mate."

Night nodded. He took the cups over to the other side of the room, where a coffee machine sat, looking like it'd never been used. Night tinkered with the strangely obtuse interface and produced a cup of coffee for Benson, adding exactly two sugars with a kind of delicate precision Benson might have called "womanly".

"You're not having one?"

"Coffee doesn't agree with me," Night said.

Night placed the cup in front of Benson, and Benson picked it up pensively, watching his "host" with dawning apprehension. What kind of psychopath doesn't drink coffee? Perhaps he was a boozehound instead? That, Benson could understand. Though he didn't see any obvious locations for secreting liquor in this little comms station. That was true hell, to be trapped here without alcohol or narcotics or even company. Benson never felt more at home than when he was having his lights punched out by some bruiser whom he'd later take for a cup of *grease*, the colloquial term aboard *Virgil* for what amounted to fuel-based absinth.

Benson took a sip of the coffee.

"Fuck me!"

"Bad?"

"No, fucking good. How'd you manage to do that with instant?"

"Luck, I suppose." Night said the word "luck" as though he didn't believe in the concept. He was looking out at the window, the storm. Benson scratched stubble and sipped again on the piping hot cuppa.

"You ain't gunna make a mile, kid," Benson said. "We just gotta hope that *Virgil* realises something's gone wrong and comes to pick us up." Even as he said the words, he knew the odds of that were a billion to one, but he kept talking, to distract himself from that thought, "And it wouldn't be a bad thing if they didn't carpet bomb this place afterwards. Fuck that *thing.* Christ, you never told me what it was."

"It's some form of life," Night said, almost philosophical.

"Well, yeah, I gathered that. I may not be a biologist but I'm not fucking dumb."

"I apologise, Benson. I did not mean to cause offence."

Benson waved his hand again. Forgiven, forgotten.

"Continue. I interrupted."

"Well, it's some form of life that has a different basis to you or me …" Night's eyes seemed to turn a little sad. The motion was so minute most would have missed it, but Benson was the kind of man who could spot an inch-wide tear in two miles of Dacron insulation. The eyes twitched at the corners, a shadow of emotion.

"What, you mean, like, it's not carbon?" He knew the theory of non-carbon life, but so far, through all Command's exploration of the galaxy, there was non forthcoming.

"I think it's arsenic-based," Night said. "Hence why it can exist on such a low-oxygen planet. It's water substitute is likely ammonia. Arsenic has similar electronegativity and ionization as phosphorus. As such, it can form covalent molecules with most nonmetals easily. Bacteria already exists on earth that 'breathes' in the absence of oxygen by using *arsenite* as fuel. It's not great leap to suppose a more, shall we say, 'robust' lifeform could evolve from this basis."

"Well, aren't you a regular Darwin!" Benson said, grinning.

Night smiled.

"I do my best. But the data is woefully insufficient."

"You sound sad, but trust me, you don't want to get any closer to that thing," Benson said grimly, his demeanour and tone did not seem to affect Night much. Night would be a good fighter in the ring, Benson thought. He didn't look like much physically, but he had the psychological battle down; nothing seemed to faze him.

Two hours of oxygen remaining.

The woman's voice was insistent, and accompanied by a beeping noise and a flash of red. The warning repeated twice more. Benson tried to keep his hand from shaking as he lifted the coffee cup to his lips.

"What are we gunna do, Night?"

"I'm thinking."

"Thinking?"

Night regarded him, those curiously bright eyes pinning him to his seat.

"Okay, you think, but think bloody fast."

In the squeal of the storm, Benson imagined he could hear John. He remembered the white-fleshed thing, barely visible in the whorl of grey and sleet, a back both inhumanly long and yet disconcertingly familiar, each rump of vertebrae like a tadpole rising beneath a pool's scummy white surface-layer. Then John was gone. Or rather, his torso was. Next was Charlie. She had screamed so much, and for so long after she *surely* should have been dead, that Benson had muted her mike. The last had been Sam. Golden, wonderful Sam, who said nor did any wrong. That had been the most painful for him. He hadn't known her long enough to say it with conviction, but she was the kind of person that might have, one day, become his best friend, spoken at his wedding.

Gone.

"Well?"

Night bowed his head.

"Sorry," Benson said, reflexively. "It's just, you look so calm, so I assumed you're all okay. But I'm guessing you're not, are you? You're dealing with the same thing I'm dealing with. Christ, and I'm even stealing your oxygen supply. Hah!"

Night smiled. It was small, but so genuine that Benson couldn't help but smile back, showing his canine, the one that'd been cut in half by a knuckle-duster.

"You're not stealing anything," Night said.

"How'd you get this shit job anyway? I mean, middle of nowhere, no-one else around? Must be pretty lonely. Hell, you get porn on there?" He jerked a thumb at the console, grinning.

Night's smile lingered, though now it seemed forced.

"No, sadly the console is only for the fulfilment of duties. Truth be told, I don't really know what I would do on my own time, even if I were to have any. And as to how I got this job, you might say I was born for it."

"Why? Because you're okay with the loneliness?"

"In part, yes. But I have no family, really. No ties. My 'father' and 'mother', if they can be called as such, sent me on my way no sooner had I come into the world."

"That's harsh, man. That's tough. We all need a da and ma." Benson thought of his own. His father, long dead now, unable to crush the cigarette habit and perhaps also a little unwilling; refusing to pay for the ridiculous surgeries to fix his lungs. His mother, still alive, somewhere back on Earth. She was probably thinking of him now, so proud. Her boy, the only one in the family to make it to Command's fleets, and the irony of ironies, Benson probably hated Command most. But he loved the fleet, that much was true. Benson had a lot to live for considering he was a forty-year-old bachelor who'd been in the same job ten years.

All this whirled in his head, and he realised he had not spoken in a long time, and time was precious now.

"So, you're all alone out here?"

"Yes."

"Well, I'm glad I could come here then. Even if we're going to die. No one should die alone."

"Some would say we all die alone," Night said, cocking his head in that curious, lizard-like manner of his.

"Yeah? Well some people are pessimistic bastards."

Night did not laugh, but a kind of bark escaped his lips.

"Hah! I find it amusing. I'm not sure I know what a *pessimist* is. Please, elaborate."

Benson scratched his stubble, enjoying the simple feeling of fingernail on hair and skin. It distracted him from the ticking clock, from the thoughts of what waited out there for them, from the thoughts of awful things he might have to do to stay alive. Although, if they ran out of air, it probably wouldn't come to that, a small mercy.

He considered the strangeness of life. An hour ago he had been aboard *Virgil*, preparing for drop. Now, he was trapped in this comms station, drinking coffee with a stranger, nattering about "pessimism" as if they were two philosophers at a table.

"Well, a pessimist always sees the bad side of things. An optimist always sees the good. I consider myself an optimist, although, our present situation has gotten me in a bit of a doubt."

Night nodded, patient, as though every word Benson was saying was gold dust. He'd never been listened to like that before, and it stirred in him that feeling again of desperately wanting to be *liked* by Night.

"You an optimist or a pessimist, Night? With a name like that, by rights you should be the latter!"

Night's eyes flickered.

"I am neither, I suppose."

"So, you're a – what is it – an engineer? The glass isn't half empty or half full, it's twice as big as it needs to be?"

Night considered.

"More that the glass is serving its function, whether it is going beyond the requisite or not is irrelevant. The glass contains liquid, so therefore, it is useful. And as to my name, I'm named as such because of the colour of my skin."

Benson blanched.

"Oh, woah, okay, erm … doesn't that … bother you? Actually, forget I asked."

"Why would that bother me?" Night looked utterly naive in that moment, and Benson thought, *That's it. That's why he's out here. They told him to go out and he's gone out. His mother and father told him they're off and he lets them go. He accepts what people tell him and never sees the bad.*

"Never mind," Benson said. He cleared his throat, stood, and went to grab the coffee cup to rinse it (he presumed there was a mini sink in the coffee machine or some kind of contraption).

"No, allow me!" Night reached out, and in the confusion, their hands touched.

Benson froze. He stared at Night. Night stared at Benson.

Benson withdrew his hand, as though scalded. He tried to deny what he had just felt, but he was a details man, someone who saw the hairline fractures, and it was unmistakable, the texture he had just felt beneath his fingers was *not skin.*

"I'm sorry," Night said.

"You're a..."

"Synthetic. Yes."

There was silence between them. The storm scoured the planet outside, shrieking and shrieking, as though all the souls of the damned and suffering were caught up in that whirlwind. Benson thought they might not only be the only two left alive on this planet, but the only two left alive in the entire universe.

"I did not wish to alarm you," Night said, reading his unspoken question.

Benson opened his mouth to respond when he was cut off by an abrupt woman's voice.

One hour of oxygen remaining.

A light flashed. The message repeated.

"Well, you're not synthetic to me," Benson said, at last. *Forgiven, forgotten.*

Night nodded, and it seemed, for a moment, almost as if there could have been a tears, but how possible? His tearducts were mere plastic, simulacrum.

Night rose and moved towards the door.

"You must hold you breath," he said, "for ten seconds while the doors open and close."

"What the hell are you talking about?"

Night looked at him.

"I'm going out, Benson. I intend to reach the comms tower and alert *Virgil* to your location. There can be no more delay now."

"You crazy? That thing will tear you apart!"

"I am a machine, Benson," Night said. "It is in my programming. I may not, through action or *inaction*, allow another human being to come to harm." His directive delivered, a smile hitched up the corners of his rubber mouth. "It was nice talking, Benson."

Benson felt himself trembling.

"This ain't right."

"It is perfectly right. You will die out there, certainly. My chance of success is far greater. It is what I was made for."

"Made to do what you're told? Just because you're not human? Not afraid? You don't have to do it just 'cos they programmed you that way!" Benson realised he was acting against his own survival, but that's what he did, punch first. Sometimes, in boxing, you threw a punch even when you *knew* it'd be intercepted, just because you didn't want to give up the fight. What the hell was he fighting for?

Night considered him what seemed a long time, but was in reality less than a few seconds, suspended as they were *out* of time, in a capsule that might as well have been spinning in the gulf of space.

"Just because I am synthetic, does not mean I'm unafraid to die," Night said. "I have acquired being, thought, meaning … I have much to lose …" He looked down, then out of the narrow window to the roiling tempest outside. "But I cannot do nothing. I will reach the comms tower. Goodbye, Benson."

Night reached out and hovered his finger over the lockdown button; Benson sucked in a breath. Night pressed it, and with a burst of sonorous noise and lashing rain, the doors opened, revealing the churning froth of the planet's rage.

Night stepped out into the chaos and fury, seemingly so small against the black gale. He leaned forward into the force of the storm, bowed and yet undaunted.

Benson watched him until the pressurised blastdoors slid slowly shut, eclipsing his view of the lone figure wending his way through darkness to the narrow sliver of salvation that lay only a mile away.

There was nothing left to do but wait, so Benson sat down at the table again and contemplated what had just transpired. He was oddly calm, despite the fact that all his hopes rested on the shoulders of a man he did not know.

And who wasn't really a man at all.

THE UPSIDEDOWN MAN

CARMEN MARCUS

'Dad', I said, quiet like, but I couldn't get air enough to shout through the hot mess that was my lungs. The other lads from the 4th were behind me shouting for their mums before the mustard gas sealed up their gullets. It was the upside down tree Dad, the one in Thorngate Cemetery that filled my head before the nothing. I had been sent with your bait box. The rain had brought the blossom down, pink-veined leaves browning quick speckling the black path and the big sprawling stones. Proud hearts that had tick tocked to the end of their time not stopped and rewound. You told me that the first gardeners had planted the Yew seed upside down and it grew leaves and branches down and roots up above the ground. You said there was another world under the black horizon of dirt – of white roots that sucked bone instead of sun. You tried to laugh it back, pull the shadow from my boy-struck face, 'No son, I'm kidding you on.' But I've been there Dad and come back on the wrong side of the sky.

It started after the pain, like I was the mud and we were sore with it all; the dig dig dig; the belly splash of bayonets. Mud would settle itself. We knew that, didn't we Dad, from digging graves and turning over last year's beds. I told the ground this as if to make it feel less sick, its mouth stuffed up with bits of us and great holes in its back blown out by shells. The rain fell, it was trying to help. I was thinking of you by yourself in Thorngate and the soil. I saw the Yew, saw it drop all its bright red arils and the Blackbirds came shooting down. I was breathing clean and deep, a south westerly blowing right through me. Right through the hole blasted through my chest. So it wasn't me breathing at all.

I couldn't stop the thoughts running through me. Lizzie, who I'd kissed just once. What was in your bait box? The Yew, its twisted trunk boring into the ground and what was underneath its green skirts? Where did the bits of my chest end up? For there were no edges of myself only dust and the world under the skin of the earth.

I think it's taken a long time to find my way home to you. I think my roots have always been here, like you said, and knew the way to grow. They grew white threads splitting and reaching for water and there was pain. Harder than being pulled apart quick by a shell is being pulled back together slow. It was a hell of a shock when my first green shoots burst up above the ground at Thorngate. I grew feet first. Toes sprouting like buds, thumped by raindrops and nipped by rabbits' teeth. My little shoots shivered up and up, sucking the sun – like kissing Lizzie Fairley over and over again. I asked after you in the mud dark. I asked the worms but everything tastes the same to them. I think you are gone, not upside down, like me, but good dirt dead.

***

I know through my roots the shudder of feet on the ground, hear the thud thud of digging, a hole not big enough for a man. The next day three people come. There is a woman's voice. She whispers a prayer that the others can't hear but I feel the weight of her shaking the ground so hard the worms poke out their heads for rain.

The lady comes back. Everyday. Then every week. She does not bring cut posies, she cups the earth gently with her black fingers and plants chattering flowers with short roots. They tell me her name but I don't have a mouth to say it.

The moths tell me that there is so much light in the sky the living must have made another war. There is more digging than there has been for a long time so they must be right.

The moths keep me up all night with their worrying, they think the war has taken the moon. They do not trust the lights. The lady doesn't come back. I am frightened for her and I don't know why because I only let her dig her fingers into me.

The flowers are quiet. The worms are hungry. The lady is back, with bulbs and she brings more feet with her. Small tipping tapping feet. They slap the earth with their palms to trick the worms, they pull them out and leave them on the stones.

The feet get bigger and better at digging soil and pouring water. They learn to leave the worms alone. Then the dig dig dig and the hole is made big enough for two. I ask the lady with the black hands if she would like to split and root, but she is happy where she is.

***

I am up to the whorl of my belly button out of the ground, my feet flickering with needle leaves. Here comes the dig dig dig. But this coffin is empty. Fisherman. Lost at sea. A girl comes. She hits the ground with her fist. It tastes like Lizzie's kiss. The worms won't come up for her. She says his name and ties ribbons round my toes. She is young enough to believe in wishes and to change her heart.

I ask the water-beetle if I should let the magpies have the ribbons, he says the fisherman is dead. What do water-beetles know?

The nub that might become my mouth roots for water. I think Lizzie is gone. I think she has been gone a long time. I ask if she is here. The woodlice have no memory for such things and lichens only talk to stone. The sound she made when I kissed her was like rain. I curl my toes tight around the ribbons when the magpies come.

***

My chest makes a wide thick trunk above the ground. The wind tries to blow through me but my fibres are full of water and hold. I have lost the ribbons. I am a place to meet. Boys come at dusk on motorcycles shaking my needles to the ground. Their flash lamps remind the moths of war, they hide and shiver wing dust. The boys' feet are so light the soil does not feel their kicks. They pull up flowers and break their fists against the stones. There is no war to stop them. They give up and smoke cigarettes, they are no match for stone. They twist the stubs into the earth. I bury them where the blackbirds won't eat them by mistake. The boys look at the part where my trunk splits into legs and laugh. They dig their blunt fingers into the loose ground and say cruel things about girls who have touched them and whom they have touched. There was a part of me that wanted to dig into Lizzie. If she had let me touch the swell of her, I might have burst her just to dig myself into the dark. I am grateful now that every part of me is poison and nothing alive will let me touch it. All except my red arils, which are soft and eaten up as soon as they fall. The boys do not know how lucky they are to have been touched.

***

My shoulders bridge the ground. It's easier to keep my legs still in winter. The graves close by me are not visited anymore. They have been opened more than once and are full. Lichen swells into the name grooves. A man comes with his dog. The grave he visits is in the new cemetery, but he likes to walk here. He scrapes off the lichen with his penknife and says the names and dates out loud. The daisies nod and join in, they whisper the names along the borders, all the way to the blossom path so even the woodlice can't forget. Edward Davis. Born 1898. Died 1917. Jack McLaughlin. Born 1893. Died 1917. They are the names of my friends. I like this man, even though his dog digs at the poor pussy willow. I think he said my name, once. I don't know. Maybe. It sounded like needles.

***

My arms brace my narrow neck. There are men here all day, they are not gardeners. They are not here to visit. They cut away the bushes and dig out the pussy willow. They wear yellow jackets like wasps. They drill the ground with yellow hammers. The woodlice run. There are so many worms the gulls come. The moths ask me if war has come back. I don't know.

The yellow jackets fill the ground with tarmac to make a wide road. There are graves hidden underneath where no one will find them. The dead do not like to be walked on. There was a little girl with the dog man. She would only walk across a grave if she crossed her fingers. The dirt-dead like to be remembered that way. Now no one will know to cross their fingers. They hum at the yellow jackets through the bees.

Cars drive past on the new road to the new cemetery. A man with a wasp jacket measures my chest, like the quartermaster did for my uniform. He kicks my roots because they have split and spread past the shadow of my branches and under his road.

The motorcycle boys come back in a car driven by a girl. Their eyes are yellow and their skin is like my bark. They tell the yellow jackets not to cut me. The boys remembered, they stay until they feel the cold, they are sorry about the stones.

***

I balance on my head like a contortionist. We went to see one at the Palace Theatre before we left for France, 'The Lady of the Lake'. She wore this blue shift that was so light it floated on our smoke. She did this slow dance like she was underwater. Like she was something to kill for. I wonder how she kept her balance in the air. Air is nothing to the muscular hold of the earth.

The stream of cars rumbles on the road around the cemetery and shakes the dirt loose around my roots. The rain tries to help. The rain always wants to help. It wants to tell me about the new war. But I have knots for eyes, I can see for myself, just above the horizon of dark earth. I see a world upside down.

There is another war, and another and another until it is all one war and the moths won't even come out of their cocoons. There is dig dig dig. When they bury the soldier it is like being at the theatre again. The flag dances like something to kill for. When he is finally in the ground I ask him if he kissed someone before he blew out his own brains. He laughs so hard the worms think it is raining. Worms only ever think about the rain.

Yes, he says, yes he kissed someone. I tell him nothing can touch my lips but ants. He tells me that he can no longer look at the ground without seeing a place for the enemy to hide. I ask him who the enemy is. He tells me he doesn't know but one night he got up from his bed, but he didn't know it was his bed and when he found his daughter he tried to kill her in her sleep. He tells me he is safe in the ground, he will only sleep under the blind pressure of dirt. He sleeps so still the worms nest in his hips.

His daughter comes and sits with her fingers crossed. He knows it is her only because she has his hands. He says if she comes again he will split and root. He sleeps with his toes budded, pointing up.

***

The yellow jacket man is back. He measures me around my shoulders. Four times. He does not know I am poison. He scratches his palms and comes back with a saw. The motorcycle boys don't come; they have stones of their own.

***

The yellow jackets could not dig out my roots. So what I see when I come back is my stump and my rings exposed, red, uncountable. Already bees have found their way in.

THE WEASEL

RICK WHITE

Adam and Kayla never planned on getting a cat, but ended up with one anyway. After moving in to the old farmhouse, they noticed a pair of eyes watching them from beneath a hedge in the garden.

Kayla was the gardener, though she'd never been very good at it – she wanted outside space, fresh air, and the perfect place to raise kids.

So Kayla 'designed' the garden; dressed in dungarees and sunglasses, drinking a glass of wine and giving instructions to Adam, who ended up doing all the hard work. While the cat's unspoken presence became familiar, the first tiny seedling of a family.

Eventually the cat found the courage to introduce herself. She was in a mess; her long dark fur all clumpy and matted – the vet said it looked like she'd been living rough for a while, no microchip. So she was theirs to keep, and they named her Grizabella.

When spring arrived the three of them sat in the garden they had created, happy as bees buzzing in the candied canopies of cherry blossom. But the one thing that wouldn't grow was their family – there was still plenty of time of course, no need to rush.

Grizabella snoozed contentedly but she never lost her wild streak, often disappearing for days, returning with trophy kills – mice and birds – gifts for her human companions.

By late summer, the days grew shorter as the evenings coloured like pink apples. Starlings gathered in the sky above the fields, chattering like a crowd waiting expectantly for something to happen. And something did.

Kayla went out at six o'clock and never came back. It was a car accident – some drunken kid had swerved in to her lane. The doctors told Adam with practised solemnity, that she had been carrying a child.

Adam's world now shrunk to the size of a garden, a last cradle of life which he tried to sustain. But for all his effort, it was hopeless. As Autumn encroached, cool bronze and bonfire leaves, the fruit began to go soft, the flowers began to wither.

Grizabella wandered more and more, though Adam barely noticed. The corpses she brought back were unceremoniously dumped in the bin. Tiny bones, monuments to nothingness.

When winter came, Adam sat outside in the mornings before dawn, welcoming the cold as it tiptoed up his spine, letting it dull his fevered brain.

Then one morning, as pale light snuck through the fences and twinkled the frost, Adam saw Grizabella in the garden, holding something in her mouth.

He thought it was a sock or a woolly jumper, but on closer inspection, it was a weasel, hanging limp between Grizabella's teeth. The cat placed it at Adam's feet, and stared up at him with her moon-pool eyes.

The weasel was an offering, but there was a terrible sadness to it. Hours ago the creature had been running freely, chasing the dawn.

It wouldn't do to just throw it away with the other rotting things. Its life held meaning, its death deserved a grave.

So Adam wrapped the weasel in a tea towel, took up his shovel, and began to dig through the frozen earth.

TOUCH

RACHAEL SMART

i) The summer that puts a stop to Touch, Touch is all she can think about.

ii) The homeless guy's weather-beaten hand when he nips the fiver from her fingers, who tells her she looks the shit in red.

iii) The cuff of the landlord's high five during a lock-in where she dances to T'Pau, puts her lips to so much volume.

iv) The afternoon she takes her dad for his biopsy and coughs violently over the steering wheel with him looking diminished beside her. How he tells her she gets her lungs from her old man. The way she squeezes his beef of a hand in the waiting room, feeds him coffee from her corrugated cup.

v) The man she Touches down by the black water after too many beers and too much poetry. Her spit thick on his face, hands deep in the muddle of her hair. The two of them up against the bridge where the padlocks glint and a dog walker tries ever so hard not to watch.

vi) His fingers which leave her thighs blue with forget-me-nots.

vii) The average bruise lasts two weeks. Soon, it will be as though she has never been Touched.

viii) She doesn't value the intimate Touches above others. There's no ranking system which relegates one type of Touch to the bottom rung of the ladder. It's simply that Touch saturates her thoughts purple until it becomes too tricky to even wrap a plaster around her youngest child's pinkie.

ix) Touch governs the daily death tolls on the news.

x) Re-tracing the topography of her own Touch keeps her awake until the sun snickers through the skylight. Outside in the ivy thicket, clatter doves coo. She resents that they have space for their wing span. She resents their fucking more.

xi) Touch has taken on a transactional value. Some Touch feels worth the risk, others make her gasp.

xii) Her children assign a colour to the Virus That Stops Touch and it is burgundy. Vivid burgundy. Old burgundy. Maroon. Chestnut. Oxblood. Cordovan. Without their even realising, it is a paint swatch the precise colour of the lung's walls.

xiii) She tells the kids the new measure of things: Two metres is a queen size bed. Two metres is the length of an ostrich, a camel, a bear, a bison, a blue fin. Two metres is the length of our closed front door. Two metres is a matter of now and then. She fixates on all the ways in which she has Touched them. At night, she plays sentry at the foot of their beds, watches their soft, pallid limbs twitch through cycles of troubled sleep.

xiv) A friend video calls to say he fears he is getting sick from not being Touched. He asks her: would you please hold my face? She tells him she can't feign Touch – and besides, he has grown so much beard that an LCD screen couldn't compete. She tells him she doesn't want to imagine his hair one dimensional and glassy.

xv) Her sister calls to say she asked a man where he wanted to spend his final days. She asked the question from two metres away whilst the steam inside her visor obscured him. It's the first time I haven't offered Touch to a dying man, she says.

xvi) Her sister tells her the masks distort applause. She says it sounds like people Touching themselves. She says it sounds like jeers.

TREVOR'S LOST GLASSES

SIAN HUGHES

My aunt is obsessed with the question of her husband Trevor's lost glasses.

'I wake up at four every morning thinking about them,' she says. 'I can't sleep.'

My uncle Trevor lives in a residential nursing home for dementia sufferers. My aunt thinks one of the care assistants may have pocketed Trevor's glasses and sold them on Ebay.

'They weren't cheap,' says my aunt. 'They were over a hundred pounds.'

The glasses have been missing since September. According to my aunt, they are the only pair that ever suited Trevor's jaw line or the shape of his face, and she likes the seam of gold through the sides.

'He looked so handsome in them,' she says.

As far as everybody else in the family is concerned, the glasses probably make very little difference to Trevor's quality of life, since he can no longer read, follow a storyline on the tele, or recognize other people's faces. Recently he has started to gnaw on people's hands when he's hungry.

'Maybe take him in his old ones?' I say. 'The silver ones.'

My aunt reacts as if I'm suggesting she take him in a big bag of shit, raising her upper lip to expose her teeth.

'At least it's something Audrey,' I say.

My aunt eventually succumbs to the idea of the silver glasses. But the angles of Trevor's face must have warped in the time since he wore them, because when she takes them in to him, the following week, the square frames draw attention to the droop of his brow, the expanding sink holes of his eye sockets.

'He looks like a duw 'elp,' says my aunt.

'Duw 'elp' is a phrase derived from 'help' and the Welsh word for God. Duw. My aunt has noticed more 'duw elps' around than ever before, especially around the bus stop and Wetherspoons.

'Show him the memory book again.' I say. 'You never know.'

My aunt pulls out the memory book from the drawer in Trevor's nightstand, turning to the first page of photographs. Trevor snatches the book from my aunt and tries to chew it. Already there are chew marks down the spine. Dissatisfied, Trevor tilts the book upwards to his face, before suddenly stopping mid-way. Bringing a finger up slowly, precisely, he traces the outline of a figure in one of the photographs, as if he's following a line in a maze. His mouth opens and closes like a fish.

'It's your mam,' says my aunt. 'And that's you.'

Trevor pulls the book closer and closer, applying it to his face like one of those hot flannels you get on planes.

'You're in the garden by the cherry blossom. Think you were about ten.'

'No, no!' he says, throwing the book down quite suddenly. 'It was a pear tree. It stopped making pears when I was five. Summer before I started at Pentrepoeth. There were flowers and what not, and then nowt. Then there was the war. God knows what happened to that pear tree.'

My aunt bends to pick the book from the floor, hovering for a time above the ground. When she comes up again, as if for air, I see she's been crying.

'Oh Trev,' she says. 'I miss you something awful.'

After that, my aunt is determined to find Trevor his real glasses.

'It's the first time he's spoken in months,' she says. 'Imagine the difference the real ones are going to make.'

My aunt brings out the clothes from Trevor's wardrobe, turning out the pockets of a tailored three-piece suit that's been in the dry-cleaning suit bag since he moved to the nursing home. ('You never know, they might have a party or a dinner or a special guest,' my aunt had said, when she brought the suit in.)

'They won't be in the suit Audrey,' I say. 'He hasn't used it.'

'They're nothing but a bunch of good for nothing wasters,' she says, meaning the care assistants.

The following week, my aunt pins a blurry, blown-up photo of my uncle wearing his original glasses to the entertainment noticeboard in the lobby, writing 'Have you seen these glasses?' in Sharpie in the margin.

A small, bird-like resident called Joan, who is always in the hallway or the lobby, watches on.

'I need the pen,' she says. "I need to write my mother a letter.'

Meanwhile, under duress from my aunt, the nursing home manager Anya organizes a visit from a local optician, who prescribes a third pair of glasses for Trevor.

'Wish I'd been there,' says my aunt, when the glasses arrive a week later, in a small drawstring pouch at the bottom of an oversized Amazon box. 'He looks like a bloody bug in them.'

The new glasses have large square clear frames and thick bottle-cap lenses. You can see the wires and hinges and inner workings through the frame.

'The high index lenses were much more expensive,' says the nursing home manager, defensively. 'The optician said it wouldn't make a difference. Said his prescription is so high now you can only thin down the lens by so much.'

'It makes a difference to me,' says my aunt. 'I'm his wife.'

The old glasses turn up in the end. In the room of a resident in the high dependency wing, now housed in a new block in the car park. A ginger eyelash belonging to the resident, a man called Don Jenkins from Treboeth, who has since been transferred to hospital with a virus, is stuck between the frame and the lens. My aunt tugs at the lash with her fingernails (which have been newly shellacked for the occasion).

'All the waiting and now this' says my aunt, flinging the glasses on to the bed. 'It's all too bloody much Chrissy.'

'I know,' I say. 'I'm sorry.'

Taking the glasses from the bed, I polish each lens on the sleeve of my cardigan, pull the lash out with my new, specially slanted Tweezerman. When I ease them on to my uncle's warm skull, over the crumbling red rims of his ears, into the ready-made ridge on his nose, I realize that whilst he looks better in these glasses, he still doesn't look quite like the old Trev.

'There,' I say. 'All set.'

A care assistant comes in to the room, carrying tea, a plate of Garibaldi biscuits. Trevor picks at an invisible piece of lint on the hem of his jumper without looking at the assistant or at any of us.

'Oooh. If only I were a little older Trev!' says the care assistant, laughing at her own joke. 'You look so handsome in your glasses! Lucky Audrey!'

But my aunt is staring at the amethyst sky beyond the window, which is sheeted with incoming rain. A woman is unpegging laundry in a small garden opposite the nursing home. A man's trousers. A red flowing dress.

'Actually, no tea for me today Shelley, thank you,' says my aunt. 'It's gonna rain and I got things on the line.'

My aunt picks up her handbag like it's a weight, even though it contains nothing but a comb, pocket tissues, and a purse. She rummages through the compartments of the purse.

'Bloody bus pass,' she says.

'Niall is picking the kids from school,' I say. 'I can drive you home Audrey, if you want.'

'I keep on losing everything,' says my aunt, looking down and away, towards the door.

The care assistant, who is hunched down beside Trevor, brings a beaker of tea to Trevor's mouth. Steam mists the glasses in rising columns of snowy altocumulus clouds, obscuring Trevor's eyes, and I figure that maybe the main difference between this Trevor and the old Trevor is not the glasses, nor the droop of his face, but that you can't tell what this new Trevor is thinking, which is probably not as bad as believing that you know what a person is thinking, when you don't. Which is the case with most people.

'You haven't lost Trevor, Audrey,' I say. 'He's in there, he's just a bit stuck.'

The care assistant, who smells of tropical body mist, and something else, soft and powdery, places a mug of tea on the nightstand beside my aunt, resting her hand on my aunt's shoulder.

'I already poured you one,' she says. 'You may as well stay and drink it while it's hot.'

TRY NOT TO THINK ABOUT IT

ROB TEUN

A friend told me once that you only hurt the ones you love.

As much as I scream through blowtorched lungs from the bottom of the well. No one comes.

Not even Clara.

That hurt. It works both ways.

All that I have and anything of use from my rucksack is gone. Here is what I can tell you.

The sun rises with nausea bubbling in my gut. It sets with abdominal cramps doubling me over. The full moon will come along and I howl through my holes spewing vomit and diarrhea redecorating the tiny funneled brick world in which I now live. A crescent moon takes the shape of anxiety and hypertension. A half-moon comes with muscle spasms before shrouding me in depression. The sun rises awakening my libido; rampant masturbation and foggy thoughts follow. The day sets into the night with goosebumps.

The sun rises with me in the fetal position covered in a cold blanket of sweat. The moon hides behind a fog of clouds as the sun hides from the rain. There are times its just darkness bleeding into a deeper dark and nothing else.

Everything feels out of reach, towards freedom which I can barely remember to imagine. Madness is upon the horizon, hot on the heels of disconnection and disorientation.

What they don't tell you is that starvation is a process.

Here's what I can tell you.

It's a three-part process of the body eating itself. The first stage is glycogen breaking down into glucose. The fats decompose into glycerol and fatty acids as a source of energy.

During the second stage, the liver metabolizes the fatty acids into ketone bodies and all the proteins not essential to survival.

That's after a week.

Then comes the third stage:

The fat reserves deplete and it switches to proteins as the major source of energy. Muscles, the largest source of protein in the body deplete fast. Followed by;

Apathy.

Withdrawal.

Listlessness.

Here's what I can tell you.

I am deep in stage three. A hanging cloak of skin on a potbellied skeleton banging the walls with weak clenched wrists and thin hands. The stone feels cold against my cheek as I lean forward and press against the cold wall before sliding down and slipping to the ground in an awkward sitting position in the dirt full of piss and puke and shit and ejaculate. There's enough to clone me from the ground.

Try not to think about it.

Try not to think about it.

The more I think about it.

I bend down and grab a handful. You don't know desperation until you're being pushed to do things you thought you would never dream of doing.

It sits in my hand it rolls into a ball. My fingers look like a dung beetles legs rolling shit. The hunger is too much.

I shovel it into my mouth and it rolls around inside my cheeks.

Try not to think about it.

Try not to think about how the tongue is now seeing with its eyes. The stale ejaculate, fruit of my masturbation on the tip before the scent of sour piss touches the sides rolling around teasing the umami, the flat of the tongue with the gritty savory taste of the dry flakes of shit before hitting the back before it rolls down toward my gullet.

Try not to think about it.

The moss tickles the back of my throat like spiders' legs. It crunches between my teeth.

Try not to think about what's made it crunchy.

Try not to think about it.

Here is what I can tell you. Those ruddy-faced presenters on the television claiming they can live in extreme situations are full of shit.

Just like the dirt I am eating.

Fuck.

Try not to think about it.

I lurch forward and hold my gut, double over, and throw all the contents that are not there and a pool of dirt and bile splashes against the floor. My gut tries to pull itself inside out to empty itself like a kid turning out his pockets. My throat feels like two pieces of sandpaper grinding against each other.

The rucksack at my feet bounces off the wall of the well. I didn't realize I had kicked it. The contents of it spill out;

A burnt spoon.

A plastic tube.

A small clear plastic bag with dusty brown insides.

A needle.

Try not to think about it.

Try to think about anything other than steaming plates and scraping forks.

Here's what I can tell you about Clara.

I think that maybe she's glad I'm gone. Matt can make his move now I am out of the picture. Now she can be with Matt. Oh, so fucking perfect Matt. With his perfect teeth and blonde hair. Matt who never lost his temper and always listened. Matt could do this, Matt could do that. He had swept this woman off her feet and that woman off her feet and so many more but he never led anyone along. He was just unlucky and looking for someone to complete him. Matt didn't do drugs. He didn't drink. He volunteered at soup kitchens and helped underprivileged kids. Matt loved his mother and kept his body a temple. Everything I never was and everything I could never hope to be. Clara will be next on Matt's list. It's just a matter of time.

Cavemen lived in cold dark holes long ago unaware of what waited ahead of them. Simpler times. You fed. You ate. You fed. You ate. You fucked because it was biology and not feeling. You slept. You ate.

The only green thing down here is moss. But meat is a good source of protein. It provides vitamins such as iron and B12 and minerals. Here is what I can tell you as I hold my fingers to my face and lick the wounds.

The layers have parted from the flesh leaving the muscle in the departure of the two.

The chewable texture is appealing.

There's a new sight for the tongue's eyes as it cleans around the bloodied skin, grinding away the excess dead skin. It tastes sweet. All five tastes are now experienced.

There on the floor, a sewing kit peeks out of the rucksack and next to that the scissors. Before I am aware, the scissors are in my hand.

Take a deep breath.

Try not to think about it.

This will not take long.

The blade clamps cold against the skin. There are nine layers of skin: first, the skin itself that is the subcutaneous tissue, then the superficial fascia. Between those, just below that first layer of skin, are hundreds of nerve endings and blood. There are six more layers after that.

Exhale.

Here is what I can tell you.

I do not know if I can do this but I have to do it.

Try not to think about it.

Take a breath.

Hold it.

A tattoo beats across the mud from my foot slapping against the ground, beating out the rhythm of the adrenaline pumping through my body. The scissors unclench as though someone else is holding them. I cannot look.

There is a black shuddering feeling starting from the pit of my gut forking towards my chest. My heart thunders, my breath holds in my lungs until I begin to feel a little dizzy.

The blades of the scissors hug my little finger like a dog holding onto a toy it won't let go. It is only going to bite down harder.

Here is what I can tell you.

The scissors are not sharp.

And exhale.

I cannot bring myself to do it. I want to but I cannot bring myself to commit to it. The blades slide along and pull the skin along, stretching it without breaking or cutting the first layer.

The blades pull down a little more and sing like a bow against the strings of a violin.

Take a deep breath.

Try not to think about it.

I want to puke but there's simply no more in the gut to bring up. My gut is a dry empty bag.

I strip off my t-shirt and then I realize just how long I have been down here. It's longer than I had thought.

Here's what I can tell you.

My hands can touch the middle of my back through my gut and I have collarbones looping out of my chest as big as grab handles.

The parts that were once held with thick contents of fat are now folds of loose skin ripe with nerve endings. Deflated pectorals travel south to the point that my nipples folded beneath the skin. Like a yawning dog, the scissors open.

A pinch of skin feels rubbery, it feels like the flapping skin hangs down like a curtain at my side. The sensation of cold steel, the bite of the dog waiting to close on the skin, a moment from snapping shut and taking a bite.

Wait. Wait. For God's sake, wait.

And Exhale.

Think. Think. Think.

There's got to be another way.

Try not to think about it.

The scissors are nipping at the skin, eager to feed and in turn be fed, and yet more eager to feed me. A raging hunger, that violent, painful hunger. The screaming madman bounces the walls inside my mind, drowning out the voice of rationality. Anything left of my reasoning falls to a whisper. It slips into silence.

Take a breath.

No. A deeper one.

Hold it.

This won't take long.

I hold the scissors tighter; pinching at the skin between thumb and forefinger and stretch it out like a fleshy elastic band.

Gritting my teeth.

Here goes.

Try not to think about it.

I slam the blades hugging around my skin shut and the first cut causes me to snap my head back and bellow. The scissors are not sharp. Only cutting deep enough to pierce the skin and draw blood.

It will take more than this.

Take a deep breath.

In order to live there will have to be more cuts yet.

Try not to shout out. Hold the breath deep and just get it over with and done.

Here goes. Count to three.

Go.

Snip.

Snip.

Snip.

Do not exhale.

Each dog bite snap of the blades shuts down on the flesh. The pain is sharp and constant. The layers of skin are no longer just one but many different depths of suffering and blood.

Scream.

Pounding feet against the walls with every inch of hurt does nothing to stop the pain or the feeling of the scissors cutting through the tough fabric of skin.

Try not to think about it.

Try not to blackout as the world flickers in shades of grey and abyss black.

Take a breath.

The pain is now so intense the breeze brushes over every severed nerve ending like salt. My head snaps back and I laugh at the burgeoning moon, a howl almost, the kind of laugh that only maniacs can appreciate. The humor fades as there are further cuts to separate the skin. The dog bite of the scissors rips through the flesh, raggedly tearing meat from the bone.

Here is what I can tell you.

There is nothing to laugh about now.

Exhale.

Take a deep breath. This is the last time.

The scissors aren't quite cutting it. The skin is tough and elastic refusing to submit to the steel. It stretches and balls up and it is like trying to cut through a rubber ball.

The flesh is odd. I can see the parts hanging from me in the way I would see chicken meat hang off the bone on a Sunday. Sometimes you just have to pull off what's left. It stretches further still and seems not to find a breaking point. With one last tug and tear at the flesh to stop the pain. The last part pulls away from the body. I hold it towards the light of the moon. There lays my flesh to one side, on top of the rucksack. I grip my tender side as I bend down, holding the hole in me together tight between my fingers. Blood, pus, and yellow fat seep out from the gaps. I reach for the needle and thread.

Exhale.

Take a breath.

Try not to think about it.

The needle is reluctant as I force it through my skin. It won't go through the muscle but it will go through the skin that feels like it is on fire. The thread doesn't look like it will hold as I feel it pull through and pull my flesh together. But my mind is slipping from me. I can feel it and like death, everything is leaving all at once. There are no parts to this.

I clutch at the wound.

Breath. Try to catch it. There is a glimmer of hope that the noise attracted someone. Anyone.

But there is nothing. Only my own breathing and the gentle whistle of the wind passing high above.

Who in their right mind would answer to a screaming man? Not many, I guess.

Here is what I can tell you; with surviving trauma comes an odd sense of pride because you have survived. There's also a sadness that you had to suffer in the first place.

More than anything, there is hunger. The overriding sense to consume. The flesh. The way it flaps about between the fingers, strangely, there's something alluring in it.

The first bite tastes like chewy cold chicken but not like the bloodied ham it resembles.

Try not to think about it.

Take a breath and hold the scissors to the freshly sewn stitches.

No.

Stop.

The closer to the bone, the sweeter the meat.

The closer to the bone, the sweeter the meat.

The closer to the bone, the sweeter the meat.

No.

Exhale.

Try not to think about it.

It will do me no good eating myself into nothingness. Time to get out of here or die. I take a deep breath. I kick and punch at the walls. Scraping at the bricks in a frenzy, fingers searching the gaps between each one, and with each swipe and scrape, I can feel my fingernails lifting from my fingers but not quite snapping. But it won't take much as they are bleeding and feel loose.

The bricks, they are beginning to give! Picking up the pace, I scrape along the crevices harder than before, deeper. Ignoring the sharp pain running through my fingers, giving little thought to the blood running down the palms, I don't even think as my nails creak apart from my fingertips. Thrusting my raw digits into the gaping holes that are forming in between the bricks, feeding my fingers through until I have a solid grip. I then drive the scissors in and use them as leverage.

The bricks start to wobble like a tooth in the grip of pliers. The first brick falls to the ground along with a couple of my fingernails. Something in my brain registers the pain; I grit my teeth and let loose a muted cry. I cannot stop now, not when this hell is crumbling. Soon, countless bricks follow, as if I've found the key that keeps them all locked together. I start pulling them out two at a time, a hole is forming.

Stop.

Wait.

Listen.

A noise. A low rumble rises and it's getting louder. I shut my eyes and my mouth as though to stop the noise from entering my skull. My hands balled up into fists as it builds toward its crescendo, louder and louder.

The well is beginning to cave in. The dirt rains upon me hard and fast, the bricks fall like hammers of hail, striking my bony shoulders and back. One hand above my head I duck down and push to the top, scrambling for balance against the avalanche.

The dirt closing in flooding, showering with no sign of relenting. A crest was beginning to form, giving a hill to climb. Crawling up the hill on hands and knees. Head down and eyes up.

Reaching up and clawing a way back. The top comes into view one painful stretch after another.

Stop.

Check the wound. Something warm runs down my stomach, making its way down my leg. The T-shirt clings to my body. I bleed. I feel weak. A part of me wants to let go, roll to the ground, and let the earth claim me. I look up; the edge of the surface within reach. The wind brushes against my open wound as I make the final ascent. I grab the verge of the well and heave myself over the edge. My body gives into rest as I lay upon the cold wet grass. The stars look down and I fall into a restless and bloodied slumber.

I awake as the sun breaks over the horizon. The red sky conjures memories of blood. I awake hungrily. I had dreamt of eating, ignoring all the steaming plates of rice, of buttered corn on the cob and large bowls of ice cream. I want meat.

Raw.

Pale.

Chewy.

Yellow with fat.

I stand and leave everything else behind. The sewing kit, the rucksack. The half-chewed remnants of myself I had cut away.

Think about it.

Hold onto the black-handled scissors. Cling to them.

This is what I can tell you.

Clara will still be at home.

I am cold and hungry.

This is what I cannot tell you but you will know.

Her body will be warm and inviting.

Not for long.

Try not to think about it.

VAMPIRES OF GRIEF

ROSS JEFFERY

They come each day to feed.

Tearing fragments of you away from me; when will their stomachs be full?

How much of you is left in me now?

A remnant?

You're sucked from me like marrow sucked from femur, rib and hip – each piece of you is rent from my succulent sockets, with sinews snapping and ligaments tearing. I'm unwilling to give up the ghost of you; but they are stronger than me – they will eventually win out and I will lose all I've ever held dear.

***

Their razor-sharp mandibles *snip* and *snap* at me from behind the front door, the only way in, but I refuse to open it. Barricade myself in.

They have the keys to my mind though, they must have stolen them without me knowing, each time they visit they rob me of you. I won't ever permit them the keys to my … our home. I'll let the gnashing of teeth stay outside in the cold where they belong, but I know soon they'll break the door, have their way with me, and I guess, I'll let them – I've nothing left to fight for now I don't have you.

They talk in hushed tones.

Incessant chatter which I imagine is the language of trees, when the wind blows and the leaves utter forth their speech upon the world.

Each arrival, each attempted invasion strips ballast from my body, removing my resolve piece by stinking piece; separating my mind, body and spirit – I feel as though I'm floating away, or you are my dear. The searing pain of nails being pulled with plyers – are how the memories of you are pulled from their anchorages within me; all of which I'm unwilling to share and lose – but they're persistent like the cancer that stole you from me. They're not ones to stand on ceremony, they'll strip me bare, locusts to a crop; fracturing me into infinitesimal fragments that have no home and no order – a discarded puzzle with no picture to follow in putting the pieces back where they belong.

My suffering is a fragrant offering to them; a spoiling that must be lapped and slurped and feasted upon with a ravenous frenzy.

They scuttle in daylight and slither at night, returning to feast on whatever remains of you in me.

Some are lone phantoms, others return in goblin hordes.

My despair draws them out.

My grief is an addiction to them, intoxicating and tantilising; my woe an aromatic incense that tickles their nostrils.

My stench of misery carries on the air like putrefied flesh, alerting the beasts to a banquet that awaits their consumption.

I'm ensnared in this noose called misery.

I'm lame from shame and apathetic to a life without you.

The truth is, I lost my fight when I lost you.

***

I've never been one to follow things through as you knew so well, my dear.

Flitting from job to job; farmhand, delivery boy, army medic, shop clerk, handyman.

You could say I've never found my place in the world.

I grew tired easily and gave up far too often.

Apathy loves company so I strangle it with both hands, not wanting to let go, not wanting to face the reality without you here to share it with.

Knuckle white.

I've never finished anything I've set my mind to, you knew that in life, but in death you've seen it more so.

Suicide didn't come as easily as I'd thought it would.

The pills, the razor, the noose; all tools for the trade, but *a bad workman always blames their tools* I hear your voice utter from the gloom; and I guess your ghost is right.

I just don't have it in me. I want to end it, but then I grow indifferent to the unknown and the end result.

The only thing … the one thing I've followed through with in this stinking life; is the only thing I never wanted to do, I was a hostage to it and it still haunts me to this day.

It spoils me from within.

I did it though.

I did it for you.

The only thing I've completed in my sorry life was … you.

Your demise.

Your eradication from this world to the next.

I'd stuck by your side through it all; the discovery, the diagnosis, the crying, the depression, the treatment, the baldness, the aching, the sickness, the wasting of your body, the rubbishing of your mind, the sparkle in your eyes, the passing of your life.

I was there for it all.

I am shamefaced that the only thing I've stuck with in this life, was the termination of you my dear, the one I love.

Loved?

Do I still love you? Or do I just miss you?

It's an aching wound that won't close.

My Cynthia.

Maybe this aching is what brings my tormentors – those vampiric bastards.

There's just no escaping their hunger for my grief.

Vampires of grief I call them.

They offer no mercy.

They won't let me forget.

It's when they catch a taste of my memories, my hurt, anguish and grief that they flock to me more.

I've tried to hide them, my memories; in the snow drift of my mind. But it's no use. When they gather as they do; it's as if a sudden thaw has revealed all the things I've been trying to hide in the snow-covered fields of my mind.

They cackle with glee on the other side of the door as they get a scent of you, as they taste you on the air.

They knock and clatter, shout and plead for me to open the door.

Ready to feast.

But I don't let them in.

***

I've taken to facing them head on. Perched on the bottom step, opposite the door.

I watch them approach.

The frosted glass mangling their forms; transforming them hideously into ominous multi-headed wraiths.

They entwine, limbs knotting together.

Tall and threatening.

Large and subterranean looking.

But it's the little wiry goblin bastards I fear the most; they slink and creep, lurk and burp from below the glass out of sight. Biding their time.

Fingers appear.

Long, black and bony digits find their way into and through the letterbox, oil stains emerging and dribbling down inside the house.

Two sets of fingers. Eight extremities in total, the thumbs must be clutching the other side of the door, holding open the external flap.

Each finger crowned with a blacker half mooned tip.

Blood or guts or rust encased under talon like nails.

They hang there and fidget, the tips of those long digits tap, tap, tap on the wood. They dance and flutter into the house as if conducting an unseen orchestra – but all that plays into the din of the house is the slow chattering, hushed tones of an incantation – too quiet to make out but persistent like white noise. Radiation, contaminating and rotting the mind.

The fingers are unnaturally long, as if tentacles of a jellyfish. *Oh, how they would sting* I utter to you, but you remain silent as you always do now. I miss you in these moments of despair. You'd know what to do.

I fidget on the step. As I reminisce about you, my Cynthia.

The thoughts of you churn around within my mind, the fingers dance with delight, intoxicated by the memories, the ones I have left at least.

I pray that my thoughts, that you, Cynthia, would become a swimmer with cramp; that you would just succumb to the undertow, that you'd be pulled back down to the depths from which you rose – then they'd leave me alone, I'm sure of it.

But you don't, you remain above the waves, bright and white and screaming.

The slit of the letterbox a closed eye. The black fingers fringe it like eye lashes laden with mascara. Suddenly they rise up, and so does the bile within me.

The eye cracks open as if waking from sleep.

Fingers splayed.

Eye almost fully open.

I pray for them to flee, to leave me be … but the more I beg, plead and scream – they remain. The eye continues to open.

I charge the door. Run at the phantoms and the vampires of my grief.

I slam the letterbox closed.

Gruff and pained whines crack the air like thunder. But they retreat nevertheless.

The shadows disperse. Scatter like crows.

I crumble to the floor.

I retch hot bile that stings my throat and dribbles down my chin.

I sit a while.

Broken.

Shivering from fear or cold it's hard to tell. It seems I'm always cold now, without you here by my side.

I tuck into the grief that wraps me tight within its blanket, fight against the cold that surrounds me. I hope to drift into a deep and all-consuming sleep – my only wish is that the depths of it could match the nadirs of my grief.

***

I wake.

It's night.

I'm stiff and discombobulated.

I'm still on the floor. I hear the chattering, far off but moving closer.

Even now they still come.

I crawl to the wall, pull my aching body up and sit against it. From here they won't be able to see me, but I'm sure they can smell me, smell you, my dear, in the air on my breath. That's why they've come again – not for me, but for my grief, my constant longing for you.

They move closer now.

Shadows bloom on the wall opposite the door, ominous and inky. Blotting out the streetlight and casting a portentous veil over us.

I hear them fumbling with the letterbox.

Eyes wide I stare at the flap. Expectant of finger and claws and eyes.

Something is coming, the flap opens slightly.

A piece of paper; an envelope, emerges, hangs, falls to the floor.

My eyes dart down as they scurry away into the night.

The letter. It rests on a pile of many other letters on the doormat.

I reach out a hand, pluck the newest arrival from the mound. I slide a finger in, tear the seal. Finger the letter within, pull it into view. Read.

'*We're sorry for your loss!*' I throw it on the floor.

Reach for another. Repeat the process.

Tear.

'*We're thinking of you.*'

Tear.

'Our condolences at this time.'

Tear.

'You are not alone.'

Tear.

'Deepest sympathies.'

Tear.

'Dad, we want to know you're okay? You can't shut us out forever. We'll be back, we won't give up. If we have to keep coming back until you answer the door we will, we love you! Mum wouldn't have wanted this.'

The letters are scattered across the floor like dead butterflies.

I've been locked up for so long, I've forgotten what kindness was, that I'm alive; even though you are dead. My Cynthia. I'm sorry.

When morning comes I won't fear it, or them.

I'll open the door and they can have me. All of me.

Even the grief stained mess of my mind, body and spirit.

WHEN CYNTHIA ARRIVES

BY S.J. BUDD

Marjorie was confused and very hungry. Surely today was Tuesday, but with old age creeping up like unpluckable black chin hairs, days got harder to keep track of.

Each day unfurled exactly alike except Tuesday, her most coveted day. When Cynthia visited, she was blessed. She wasn't alone sat in front of the television. She had company.

If it was 10am Tuesday, and she was sure of it, Cynthia should have been putting on the kettle, unloading Marjorie's weekly shop. Prattling on and on about the grandkids, traffic and what the weather was like outside.

Cynthia always spoke too fast for Marjorie to follow, her voice barely heard over the din she created. Marjorie was content to just hear her voice waking up the house. Cynthia always made a cheeky brunch; sandwiches for them both with thick white bread, juicy tomatoes, red Leicester cheese with generous butter.

On this Tuesday, the kitchen was as empty as her stomach.

Pain had arrived once Marjorie made the journey from bed to living room chair. Her fingers burned after taking her mother's antique ivory comb to her silver hair. She always liked to look her best for when Cynthia arrived.

It was 11am.

Had there been an accident?

It wasn't like Cynthia, her only child, to not turn up. Her devoted dutiful daughter who had refused to move away from their little town. Even after the bright lights of London where she studied Law, she came back. Family always came first. Proving herself right that it had been worthwhile raising a child right, with all of her love and patience.

Life had been a rich chocolate cake for Marjorie. She may not have had a big house in the country or been beautiful or successful, but she was the favourite Nana. She had looked after her beloved grandchildren every Friday night through to Saturday mornings.

Even after she'd had the misfortune to grow old, they still came around. Now they all looked after her, the grand founding matriarch of the Carter clan.

The afternoon wore on. She remained alone. The fire raging under her skin kept Marjorie confined to her chair. The sun's gaze moved across the room and settled on her face. She closed her eyes and thought back to a time when she had been young, free to do as she pleased. Those days lost to hazy memories.

Best to wait for Cynthia, she'd be here soon.

Afternoon gave way to evening. Shadows grew on her walls and settled in for the night. Her twilight companions visible from her living room window came out to play. Two scarlet foxes emerging from the bushes sniffing the ground as they patrolled their territory looking up with wild amber eyes.

Not so long ago it had been a rare privilege for Marjorie to be allowed to look upon them. In the last week they had grown bold, they came ever closer away from the outskirts of the forest bordering Marjorie's garden.

She remained in place; the shackles located within her own body. Why can't we work together she mused bitterly to her useless limbs. There were no more painkillers within reach and even if they were, her glass of water was long gone, replaced with a dry sore throat erupting into coughs frantic like a newborn which cannot be eased or soothed.

Why has no one come to see her?

In an act of defiance, she clenched the remote control with her swollen fingers negotiating the red button. Bargain Hunt had been replaced with a special news bulletin. Breaking news flashed red at the bottom of the screen.

She turned the volume up.

The Prime Minister looked like he had been out dancing all night. His eyebrows locked together as if in battle. Dark circles hid his eyes. Nothing left of the joker he used to be.

"Stay at home. We can beat this by staying away from each other. If you love your elderly relatives leave them alone."

The phone rang. It had been the tenth time that day. A record. But it was across the other side of the room. Pain would not grant her passage. Why hadn't she gotten her grandson to move it nearer to her chair?

When the ringing stopped, she grew colder.

Something bad was happening across the country. The fallout disrupting all the daily soaps, now there were just old repeats that no one enjoyed the first time around. It did feel quiet even to her locked away inside her house.

She hoped nothing bad had happened to Cynthia.

Night fell once more. She could try and make it to her bed but then she'd have to come back again in the morning. Beds were useless for people like her. Only the young slept. Marjorie could only doze which could be done in her chair.

She closed her eyes.

Cynthia would be coming soon.

Sometime later, a shattering of glass and a soft breeze woke her. She felt a warm sensation of shame in her lap. How? She hadn't drunk all day and night. Marjorie tried to pretend it wasn't her body she was looking down on, but she couldn't ignore the sensation of the hairs rising on the nape of her neck.

Had she imagined those sounds of breaking glass followed by footsteps? She listened to the night. It was all quiet now. So quiet she could hear the ticking of her carriage clock on the mantlepiece.

The penetrating beam of light was real. It shone on the wall in front its gaze coming from behind her. Someone was here with her.

"Cynthia?"

Starting off by the back door, evenly placed footsteps prodded her tiled floor coming to a stop with a crunch of broken glass. Cynthia held her breath, gripped the arms of her chairs. For ten seconds there was nothing.

Cynthia never came at night.

Beside her in the back garden she sensed movement. With the knowledge she was no longer alone she looked beyond the window.

There was someone there. She saw the bright cherry of a lit cigarette rising and falling in the darkness. A black baseball cap shadowing a face looked straight at her.

Now, on her other side, in the house a young boy looked down upon her. One arm holding a torch, the other a baseball bat. His face unreadable.

After a quick judgement, he hid his weapon in the back of his track suit pants as he flicked on the lights burning her eyes into submission, exposing her wet lap.

His pale face spotty, as greasy as the food he ate. He came closer nudging her, "Yo, where's your money?"

Hauling a trembling arm up, she pointed to a shelf far away, "In the pot, dear." She sighed. Finally help had arrived.

The young boy emptied the pot into his hands and rubbed the two notes together. His face downcast. "Is this it?"

"Yes, dear."

"Piss poor bitch," he muttered under his breath. He kicked over her telephone table sending her phone to the floor. Marjorie does nothing. His face beamed with inner light when he sees her crippled body wasting away in the chair. He looks up as if seeing something in the distance. "Your medicines kept in the bathroom yeah?"

Marjorie shuffled in her chair trying to escape the cold stinging sensation of old urine. In the background she hears the glass cabinet above the sink slam shut and the rattling of her pain medication being taken out. Her mouth begins to salivate.

"Would you like to stay for a tea, dear?" He is the only person she has seen in days.

For a moment his eyes narrow and then widen into a laugh, "No, thanks."

"Before you leave, could I have one of those," she looks to her medication stuffed deep in his pockets, "and a glass of water?"

Maybe he didn't hear her?

He must have been in a hurry as he didn't have time to shut the kitchen door behind him. She liked to imagine he took them for his own Nana. The sound of two young men laughing in the darkness gradually trailed off to nothing. She was alone once more. Nothing except for the cold of the night pouring in.

The dark hours stretched out on a loop. This was the longest night she has ever known.

Marjorie never imagined Death would be like this. Previously she'd pictured it as a cold sweeping axe, sudden and final.

Now she knew Death as a clock slowly winding down to nothing, each tick and each tock taking longer and longer, becoming quieter and quieter until they chimed no more. Death appeared just a little, each day, taking with it a tiny piece until gradually there was nothing more to take.

In movies, the final act of the living always looked so effortless, graceful even. Requiring nothing more than a fluttering of velvet eyelashes whilst being held in a beloved's warm arms. Despite all the love she had given and received she was to die alone, here, in this chair.

How pointless it made her life seem.

Marjorie closed her eyes. She longed to see the foxes playing like youngsters in the back of her garden. To know that life goes on. But the dawn chorus was far away. She tried to settle her mind, wanting to fall asleep with the hope that she may pass on in sweet slumber, never having to face another day alone.

When she was young, she was terrified at the thought of dying, of completely ceasing to be. Of being laid out for inspection on a cold table for all to see. Now she relished the thought of eternal rest.

The morning did come. Her lungs still bellowed. Around her was pink sunlight and a fox pressing its snout against her window looking in. The vixen doesn't move when Marjorie held out her hand in greeting. She smiles as the second fox comes over to have a look. Peering in beyond her to the room sniffing. Their noses finding nothing grow bored. Hunger takes them in the direction of the busier streets.

Her pain grew stronger with the sun. By midday, her throat felt like broken glass. Her weakness fighting off the need to cough. If only she had water.

The kitchen wasn't so far away. Only the next room. However, when she tried to move her arms and legs, pain woke up like a thousand ringing alarms. Obediently she sank back down.

The phone wouldn't ring today.

The news on the television came again, warning people to stay away from their elderly relatives. No one must leave their homes. Everyone must stay indoors. Was Cynthia watching this?

Tomorrow, Marjorie promised herself. Tomorrow Cynthia will realise something is wrong.

Someone will come soon.

Night falls once more.

Her sleep was woken by an intruder.

The kitchen door was still open.

Had that young man come back to help her?

Little paws made their way into the kitchen passing the threshold of the door now hanging ajar open to the elements. In the dark she heard panting, the groans of a dog wanting to be asleep in its basket. An old greying dog she hadn't seen for a long time, her old friend, Rebel, from next door.

When he was younger, Rebel would sneak into her garden whilst his owner was at work. He looked a savage beast but liked nothing more than warm hands making a fuss of him. She had spent many happy hours stroking him and playing ball.

Rebel sniffed around the kitchen. Hearing him scratching and whining at the cupboards made her insides stiffen. If only she wasn't so old and useless. She should be helping him. The poor little thing. He hauled himself further in the kitchen. Refusing to give up, he sniffed all around the fridge. Inside there was honey cured ham, but no way of getting at it.

As options closed around the poor mutt he moved out into the front room. Upon seeing her friendly face, he licked his lips. His tail wagging softly as he laid his head obediently on her lap. All his hope resting on Marjorie. His eyes drooping with sadness.

"Help us," the words couldn't make it out past her cracked lips and heavy stiff tongue that no longer felt like her own. Rebel moaned, softly suffering alongside her. People are too easily forgotten once they're old.

Maybe his owner will come looking for him and find her also? She imagined the joy of tucking into a thick ham and cucumber sandwich. The thought bringing her pain.

Rebel lifted his head taking her fingers into his jaws. He looked away from her eyes as he bit down. The pain of cracking fingers barely felt even over her arthritis. Embarrassed, he let go. His hunger still unresolved.

"Brute," she would have said had weakness not taken her voice.

The dog's ears pointed up attentively, waiting for a response. Satisfied when no smack of the hand came.

He jumped up sniffing her face, his meaty breath causing her to feel queasy. There was one more fight left in him. She couldn't push him away, barely able to move her face away from his.

Rebel jumps down. He circled around her chair sniffing her groin, inside her slippers, the pockets on her cardigan. The thing wanted feeding but there wasn't anything to give it, not that she could get up anyway.

The dog backed away lifting its head and howls into the night like a lone wolf. Reconnecting to the old ways it once served. No longer a much-loved family pet, Rebel was guided only by its urges to hunt and kill for survival.

The noise of his howl would bring attention. Someone was going come now, if only to stop the noise.

A light in one of the neighbouring houses appeared. Cynthia heard shouting. A tear escaped. Rebel stopped watching Cynthia, the silence was stunning. It is as if the whole world had ended.

Marjorie rolled her head backwards; confident help will come soon.

It comes in the form of Rebel, as he tenderly took hold of her left calf in his jaws. Sensing no movement from her he bit again fueled by hunger. This time he did not let go. Only doing what came naturally to him. Teeth piercing paper thin skin searching for the meat underneath. The tang of her bloodied fingers had whetted his appetite. Now he craved more.

Growing stronger he growled through the effort of securing his dinner. His jaws swinging from side to side gaining momentum with each swing until finally there was a wet ripping sound. A pulling of nerves until they gave no more stretch. Cynthia's skin burned hot and cold. Her heart was screaming. A light inside her went out for the last time. Her spirit had left.

Now under her skin she is just an animal. Just like Rebel.

Like a reluctant tooth, the bottom part of her leg eventually came away. The rest of Marjorie slid to the floor, finally free of her chair.

She lay on her side, looking out to her dark garden. Her foxes nowhere to be seen but they would be back in the morning once more playing without a care in the world.

Still death had not come. Something bad was happening beyond the safety of her house. Death must be making a lot of visits. Too busy to deal with her. She has long been forgotten.

When Cynthia arrives, it will be too late.

Marjorie lifted her head and howled into the night. The dog howled with her.

WINTER STARLINGS

JOANNA CAMPBELL

"Miss Andrews, come and listen to the top group read Book Four, would you?" says Mrs Bunce. "They'll show you how it's done. I've got this cloth-head to see to."

My name's Charlie, but Mrs Bunce calls me cloth-head because she says my brain's made of wet flannels. She looks like a suet pudding with eyes like boiling gooseberries. And when she talks, the pouches under her chin wobble. I think they're made of marshmallow but they'd taste of old lard.

The top group are good readers, but everyone's good at something. I'm good at nine things. Eight of them are my dad's cows. You need gentle hands for milking. You'd probably say milking's only one thing. But they've got names so they're all different to me.

The ninth thing is arithmetic. I can do numbers. It's words I can't. The letters keep changing partners like winter starlings in the sky. After they've feasted on the fruiting elderberries, they rocket upwards, twisting into skeins, stretching long and thin. Knotting and clotting. Swooping and soaring. Always a few stragglers late to the dance.

"Hurry up!" Dad and me always shout at the slowpokes.

I see them in the book, beating their dark wings in the white edges of the page, but I can't make them join the rest.

Miss Andrews wears a soft skirt and her white boots squeak when she walks. Her hair smells of summer and she keeps a mauve tissue under the cuff of her jersey.

"I could help Charlie, Mrs Bunce," she's saying.

Mrs Bunce folds her meaty arms. You could slice half-a-dozen good-sized cutlets off those.

"Miss Andrews," she says, "I realise you're a very keen young teacher, but I wouldn't wish him on anyone. Don't look so worried. He's away with the fairies, that one. Doesn't have a clue what we're saying."

The tissue falls out of Miss Andrews's sleeve and I try to pick it up for her, but Mrs Bunce kicks it away and pushes Book One into my hands.

"Stop fidgeting. Stop scraping the chair."

I'm trying not to wet myself. A tear bulges, fatter and fatter, until it spills onto the page.

"Heavens, a cry-baby too."

Mum showed me how to write my name, but Mrs Bunce says I use the wrong hand. She makes me wear a boxing-glove on it. It makes the other children scared of me. I don't blame them. It makes me scared of myself. And it makes things tricky in the toilet.

At break the others play What's the Time, Mister Wolf? One step for one o'clock. Three steps for three o'clock. I tell them I know all the numbers. But they don't let me play.

In the afternoon Mrs Bunce takes us on a nature walk and tells us there's four sheep in the field.

"No, there's more," I tell her, remembering in the nick of time to put my hand up. "There's eight. My dad told me. There's four lady sheep and they've all got babies inside them. Double four is eight."

Mrs Bunce tells Miss Andrews to take me back to the classroom because cloth-heads can't be smart-alecks. She says four is the right answer because unseen things don't count.

It's nice walking with Miss Andrews. I ask if she's ever seen starlings dance in the sky. She has. And she's seen one up close.

"Did you know they're beautiful, Charlie?"

"Are they?"

"Yes, all glossy blues and metallic greens. There's a book about birds in the classroom. I'll show you."

"They're just black in the sky. But they make beautiful shapes. How do they know what to do?"

"They probably take a breath and count to ten. It stops them being scared."

"Birds can't count."

"Can't they? I tell you what though. I always take a deep breath and count to ten. Every single morning."

"Teachers aren't scared though."

"I am. I'm very shy, you see. But counting helps."

In the classroom she shows me the picture and we trace our fingers over the coloured wings to feel how shiny they are.

"It says *Starling* underneath. Let's touch that too, Charlie."

We put our fingers there so we can pin the letters down. They feel shiny too.

"Can you count them, Charlie?"

"Eight," I tell her.

Then she puts a big magnifying glass over the word to trap it.

"Now we can look closer."

They look beautiful too, in their way. I don't know why, but they make me cry. She finds another tissue in her bag and dabs the tears. Five dabs for each eye. I can see again. And this time the letters stay still.

AUTHOR BIOGRAPHIES

GEMMA AMOR

The Retreat

Gemma Amor is the Bram Stoker Award nominated author of *DEAR LAURA*, *CRUEL WORKS OF NATURE*, *TILL THE SCORE IS PAID* and *WHITE PINES*. She is also a podcaster, illustrator and voice actor, and is based in Bristol, in the U.K. Many of her stories have been adapted into audio dramas by the wildly popular NoSleep Podcast, and her work also features on shows like Shadows at the Door and the Creepy podcast. She is the co-creator, writer and voice actor for horror-comedy podcast 'Calling Darkness', which also stars Kate Siegel.

gemmaamorauthor.com

@manylittlewords

SUSMITA BHATTACHARYA

The Giant Doughnut

Susmita Bhattacharya is an award-winning author and creative writing tutor. Her debut novel, The Normal State of Mind (Parthian, 2015, BEE Books, India 2016) was long-listed for the Word to Screen Prize at the Mumbai Film Festival, 2018. Her short story collection, Table Manners (Dahlia Publishing, 2018) won the Saboteur Award for Best Short Story Collection (2019), was a finalist for the Hall & Woodhouse DLF Prize, 2019 and has been featured on BBC Radio 4. She lectures at Winchester University and facilitates writing workshops for young people with ArtfulScribe.

@Susmitatweets

ASTRA BLOOM

Tell It To The Birds

Astra Bloom's writing kept her going during debilitating illness, bringing her joy, relief and healing. Astra won the Bare Fiction Poetry prize. She came second in Brighton short story prize, and she won Brighton flash fiction prize. Astra's work has been shortlisted by Bridport Prize,The London Magazine Essay prize, and Mslexia Novel Award, and commended by Bristol, Live Canon International and the Sunderland and Waterstones Prize amongst others. Her poetry is printed in journals including Under The Radar and Magma. Her memoir work features in Common People, an anthology of working class writing edited and selected by Kit De Waal. Astra is a working class, feminist writer of fiction, memoir and poetry. She is represented by Abi Fellows at The Good Literary Agency.

@AstraBloom

S.J. BUDD

When Cynthia Arrives

S.J.Budd is a dark fiction author from Cornwall. Her work has appeared in The NoSleep Podcast, Aphotic Realm, Sanitarium Magazine, Siren's Call Publications, Deadman's Tome and many others. When not writing she is mostly reading, tending to her huge collection of cactus plants and going for long walks in the country-side.

www.sjbudd.co.uk

@sjbuddj

COLIN BURNETT

A Working-Class State of Mind

Colin is an Edinburgh short story writer who predominately writes in the east coast vernacular. His work mostly combines drama with comedy. Focusing mainly on working class stories and characters. His works has been featured by The Sociological Review, The Selkie, and so fi zine which combines sociology with fiction. Also, Colin writes non-fiction and has written pieces about Scottish Politics and Culture. Mostly Colin self publishes via his website 'Ma Thoats' where his work can be accessed www.colinburnett.co.uk

@colinburnett16

JOANNA CAMPBELL

Winter Starlings

Joanna Campbell's collection of prize-winning short stories, *When Planets Slip Their Tracks*, was shortlisted for the Rubery Book Award and longlisted for The Edge Hill Prize. Her flash-fiction story, *Confirmation Class*, came second in the 2017 Bridport Prize. Her short stories have appeared in many places, including two Bristol Prize anthologies and for three consecutive years the Retreat West anthologies. Other recent stories are in *A Short Affair*, published by Scribner UK, and *Unbound's 24 Stories of Hope for the Survivors of the Grenfell Tower Fire*. Ad Hoc Fiction published Joanna's novella-in-flash, *A Safer Way To Fall*. Her full length novel, published by Brick Lane, is *Tying Down The Lion*, a 1967 family road trip in a Morris Traveller to divided Berlin.

@JoannaC_author

HEATHER CHILD

Crackers

Heather Child lives in Bristol and her two novels *Everything About You* and *The Undoing of Arlo Knott* are published by Orbit (Little, Brown). Alongside writing she has had an eclectic career in charity marketing and communications, and currently works in sustainability. www.heather-child.co.uk

@Heatherika1

J.L. CORBETT

And Soon, I Shall Grow

J.L. Corbett is the editor of *Idle Ink*, an online publisher of all things curious. Her short stories have been featured in *Schlock! Webzine, MoonPark Review, TL;DR Women's Anthology: Carrying Fire, The Cabinet of Heed, STORGY Magazine* and others. She owns more books than she can ever possibly read and doesn›t get out much.

@JL_Corbett

K.M. ELKES

Game Face

K.M. Elkes is the author of the flash fiction collection *All That Is Between Us* (Ad Hoc Fiction, 2019). His short stories have won, or been placed, in international writing competitions, including the Manchester Fiction Prize, Royal Society of Literature Prize, Fish Publishing Prize and the Bridport Prize. He was longlisted for the BBC National Short Story Award in 2019. His work has appeared in more than 30 literary anthologies and journals, and has featured on school curricula in the USA and Hong Kong. As a writer from a rural working-class background, his work often reflects marginalised voices and places. He is currently working on a novel. He lives near Bristol, UK.

kmelkes.co.uk

@kenelkes

MARIA J. ESTRADA

Pustules

Maria J. Estrada is an English college professor of Composition, Literature, and her favorite, Creative Writing. She grew up in the desert outside of Yuma, Arizona in the real Barrio de Los Locos, a barrio comprised of new Mexican immigrants and first-generation Chicanos. Drawing from this setting and experiences, she writes like a loca every minute she can--all while magically balancing her work and family obligations. She lives in Chicago's south side with her wonderfully supportive husband, two remarkable children, and two mischievous cats.

barrioblues.com.

@drmariajestrada

TRACEY FAHEY

I Write Your Name

Tracy Fahey is an Irish writer of Gothic fiction. In 2017, her debut collection *The Unheimlich Manoeuvre* (now published in its third edition by Sinister Horror Company) was shortlisted for a British Fantasy Award for Best Collection. Her first novel, *The Girl in the Fort*, was released in 2017 by Fox Spirit Books. Her second collection, the folk horror *New Music For Old Rituals* was published in 2018 by Black Shuck Books. Fahey's short fiction is published in over thirty American, British, Australian and Irish anthologies including *Supernatural Tales*, *Nightscript V*, and *Uncertainties III*, and her work has been reviewed in the *TLS* and *Black Static*. In 2019, her short story 'That Thing I Did' received an Honourable Mention from Ellen Datlow in *The Best Horror of the Year Volume Eleven*. She holds a PhD on the Gothic in visual arts, and her non-fiction writing has been published in edited collections and journals. She has been awarded residencies in Ireland and Greece. She has stories upcoming in *Best New Horror #30 (*ed. Stephen Jones), *The Fiends In The Furrows II: More Tales Of Folk Horror* (Nosetouch Press) and *Women In Horror Anthology: Volume II* (Kandisha Press), and is currently working on her third collection, *I Spit Myself Out.*

Tracyfahey.com

@tracyfahey

KATHY FISH

The Blue Of Milk

Kathy Fish has published five collections of fiction, most recently Wild Life: Collected Works from 2003-2018, (Matter Press). Her work has been published or is forthcoming in Copper Nickel, Washington Square Review, Denver Quarterly, Electric Literature, and numerous other journals, textbooks, and anthologies. Fish's "Collective Nouns for Humans in the Wild," will appear in an upcoming edition of The Norton Reader. The piece was also selected by Sheila Heti for Best American Nonrequired Reading and by Aimee Bender for Best Small Fictions 2018. Fish teaches for the Mile High MFA in Denver. She is the recipient of a 2020 Ragdale Foundation Fellowship.

@kathyfish

SIAN HUGHES

Trevor's Lost Glasses

Sian Hughes lives in Cardiff with her three children and a menagerie of assorted animals, including a husband! In 2019, she completed an MA in Creative Writing from the Open University, passing with Distinction. She also works as a copywriter and schools creative writing practitioner. Her stories have appeared in Storgy, Fiction Pool, Fiction Desk and Scribble. Three of her stories have been made into short films, appearing on BBC Wales and S4C. A past winner of the Rhys Davies International Short Story Prize and a recipient of a Literature Wales Writers Bursary, her short story collection 'Pain Sluts' will be published by Storgy in 2020.

@FlossingtheCat

JASON JACKSON

Paper Pieces

Jason Jackson's prize-winning fiction appears regularly in print and online. Recent publications include The Nottingham Review, New Flash Fiction Review and Craft Literary. Jason's story *Mess of Love* was recently awarded 3rd place in the 2020 Retreat West Short Story Competition and his story *In my dream I see my son* was selected for Best Microfiction 2020. Jason is also a photographer, and his prose/photography hybrid work *The Unit* is published by A3 Press.

@jj_fiction

ROSS JEFFERY

Vampires of Grief

Ross Jeffery is the Author of Juniper and Tethered. He is a Bristol based writer and Executive Director of Books for STORGY Magazine. Ross has been published in print with STORGY Books, Ellipsis Zine 6, The Bath Flash Fiction Festival 2019, Project 13 Dark and Shlock Magazine. His work has also appeared in various online journals such as About Magazine TX, Elephants Never, 101 Fiction, Ellipsis Zine, Soft Cartel and Idle Ink to name a few. Ross lives in Bristol with his wife (Anna) and two children (Eva and Sophie).

www.writerrossjeffery.wordpress.com

@Ross1982

BF JONES

Summer Song

B F Jones is French of Breton and Corsican descent. As a result she doesn't mind the rain but loves the sun, is keen on coastal hikes, water sports, ewe cheese and siestas; and has a hint of stubborn hot-bloodedness. She lives in the UK with her husband and three young children and works as a digital consultant. When she's not busy falling asleep in marketing meetings or refereeing children's squabbles, she writes book reviews for Storgy and flash fiction. Her debut collection The Fabric of Tombstones was published by The Writing Collective in April 2020 and she is now working on a novella-in-flash.

@fijo_frenchie

ANDREW LEACH

The Heartbeat Of Trees

Andrew Leach writes novels, short stories and the occasional poem. He has had work published in a number of anthologies and collections, most recently The Mechanics' Institute Review issue 16 (the Climate Issue), and was also Highly Commended in the 2019 Seán O'Faoláin International Short Story Prize. Other publishing destinations include Reflex Fiction, Magma Poetry, STORGY, Strix Magazine, Ellipsis Zine and two volumes of Stories for

Homes for charity Shelter. He lives in London, somewhere between Tate Britain and Selhurst Park, and is represented by the Watson, Little literary agency.
@4ndrewJames

TIM LEBBON

Strings

Tim Lebbon is the New York Times bestselling author of Coldbrook, The Silence, and the Relics trilogy. He has also written many successful movie novelizations and tie-ins for Alien and Firefly. Tim has won three British Fantasy Awards, a Bram Stoker Award, a Shocker, a Tombstone and been a finalist for the International Horror Guild and World Fantasy Awards. The Silence is now a gripping Netflix movie starring Stanley Tucci and Kiernan Shipka. His new book Eden is available from Titan books now.
@timlebbon

TOBY LITT

The Lurgy

Toby Litt was born in 1968 and grew up in Ampthill, Bedfordshire. He is the author of eleven novels and four short story collections. His most recent book is *Patience* (Galley Beggar Press). Toby teaches creative writing at Birkbeck, University of London. When he's not writing, he likes to read, swim, play guitar and do nothing.
tobylitt.com
@tobylitt

ADAM LOCK

The Look Inside

Adam Lock writes short fiction and flash fiction in the Black Country, UK. His stories have won and been placed in competitions and have appeared in many online and print publications. He loves wrestling huge ideas into the smaller forms of story.
https://www.adamlock.net
@dazedcharacter

TOMAS MARCANTONIO

Ghost City

Tomas Marcantonio is a novelist and short story writer from Brighton, England. He graduated from the University of Sussex with a degree in English Language and Film, and his fiction has appeared in numerous anthologies and journals, both online and in print. Tomas is currently based in Busan, South Korea, where he teaches English and writes whenever he can escape the classroom.
@TJMarcantonio

CARMEN MARCUS

The Upsidedown Man

Carmen Marcus is an author, poet, creative practitioner and campaigner. Her debut novel *How Saints Die* (Harvill Secker) is a semi-autobiographical account of her life as a fisherman's daughter. Her poetry has been commissioned by national festivals and BBC radio. She designed The Writer's Plan in 2019 to support working-class writers entering the industry. Marcus is currently working on her second novel, The Bait Boy.

www.carmenmarcus.co.uk

@Kalamene

ROGER MCKNIGHT

Living Proof

Roger McKnight hails from Little Egypt, a traditional farming and coal-mining region in downstate Illinois. He studied and taught English in Chicago, Sweden, and Puerto Rico. Swedes showed Roger the value of human fairness and gender equity, while Puerto Ricans displayed the dignity of their island culture before the tragedy of Hurricane Maria and the US government's shameful post-disaster neglect of the island's populace. Roger relocated to Minnesota and taught Swedish and Scandinavian Studies. He now lives in the North Star State. Roger McKnight's debut collection of short stories; *Hopeful Monsters,* was published by STORGY BOOKS in 2019.

https://www.facebook.com/RogerMcKnightFans/

SHERRY MORRIS

The Hugging Place

Originally from America's heartland, Sherry Morris writes prize-winning flash fiction and short stories. She lives on a farm in the Scottish Highlands where she watches clouds, pets cows, goes for walks and scribbles stories. Selected by the BBC to join their 2020 Scottish Voices writer development programme, her writing will take a new direction. She sits on the Board of Directors of the Highland literary magazine Northwords Now and reads for the wonderfully wacky Taco Bell Quarterly. Her first published short story was about her Peace Corps experience in Ukraine.

www.uksherka.com

@Uksherka

BENJAMIN MYERS

... And Then Came Man

Benjamin Myers is an award-winning writer and poet. His books include *The Offing, The Gallows Pole, Beastings* and *Pig Iron*, and the non-fiction work *Under The*

Rock. He lives in the Upper Calder Valley, West Yorkshire.
www.benmyers.com
@BenMyers1

HANNAH PERSAUD

If This Is How The World Ends

Hannah Persaud writes short stories, poems and novels. Her debut novel The Codes of Love was published by Muswell Press on 5th March 2020 just weeks before the world went into lockdown. Hannah's work has been published in numerous places and her short stories have in the past won InkTears Short Story Contest and the Fresher Writing Prize as well as placing in many competitions including The Cambridge Short Story Prize, the Royal Academy and Pin Drop Short Story Award and the V.S. Pritchett Short Story Prize.
www.hannahpersaud.com
@HPersaud

RAHUL RAINA

Kebabs

Rahul Raina was born in India in 1992, and was brought up in New Delhi and London. He runs a consultancy in the UK and teaches English in India. His first novel, How to Kidnap the Rich, will be published in 2021, in the UK, US and six other languages, and is in development as a TV series. He lives between Oxford and New Delhi.

JOHANNA ROBINSON

The Haul

Johanna began writing in 2016 and is now trying to make up for lost time. Her work features in *SmokeLong*, *Ellipsis Zine*, *Reflex Press* (where 'Heartwood' won third place), and *Mslexia*, among others. In April 2020 her flash piece 'Yew' won first place in the Cambridge Prize for Flash Fiction. In 2019 her WWII novella-in-flash *Homing* was published by Ad Hoc Fiction and has subsequently been shortlisted for the Saboteur Awards. She is currently working on a historical novel, with Arts Council England funding.
www.johanna-robinson.com.
@JohannaWordpool

JAMES SALE

Do Not Let Your Hope & No

James Sale has been a poet for over 50 years and had 9 collections of poetry published. Most recently his poems have appeared in the UK and USA in many magazines and online forums. In 2017 he won First Prize in the Society of Classical Poets annual competition and in 2019 appeared in New York's Bryant

Park and Manhattan's Princeton Club performing live with leading American poets. He is also a regular feature writer on myth and culture for New York's The Epoch Times. Currently, James is working on a sequence of English Cantos emulating Dante's Divine Comedy and using the terza rima form: progress on the project can be found at https://englishcantos.home.blog.
@thelyrespeaks

JOSEPH SALE

The Station

Joseph Sale is an editor, novelist, and writing coach. His first novel, The Darkest Touch, was published by Dark Hall Press in 2014. Since, he has authored more than ten novels, including the Black Gate trilogy and Save Game (The Writing Collective). He grew up in the Lovecraftian seaside town of Bournemouth. His short fiction has appeared in Tales from the Shadow Booth, edited by Dan Coxon, as well as in Idle Ink, Silver Blade, Fiction Vortex, Nonbinary Review, Edgar Allan Poet and Storgy Magazine. His stories have also appeared in anthologies such as Technological Horror (Dark Hall Press), Burnt Fur (Blood Bound Books) and Exit Earth (Storgy). In 2017 he was nominated for The Guardian's 'Not The Booker' prize.
@josephwordsmith

ANTHONY SELF

FibbleArse

Anthony Self is a London based writer and Executive Director for STORGY Magazine. He is a regular contributor to the horror website Nightmare on Film Street and hosts the podcast Inside Your Screen. He is currently working on his debut novel along with a collection of short stories.
@Mr_selfy

RACHAEL SMART

Touch

Rachael Smart writes poetry, essays and short fiction. Her work has been published in Unthology 11 and The Bristol Short Story Prize Anthology. She lives in Nottingham.
@SmartRachael

DANIEL SOULE

Keep It Up Kid

Once Dan is a horror author who was an academic, but the sentences proved too long and the words too obscure. Northern Ireland is where he now lives. But he was born in England and raised in Byron's home town, which the bard hated but Dan does not. They named every other road after Byron. As yet no roads are named after Dan but several children are. Dan's debut novel *Neolithica* is available in print and ebook from Amazon. His short literary fiction has featured in Number Eleven, Storgy, and the Dime Show Review. His science fiction is available in Shoreline of Infinity and Phantaxis. And his horror can be found in Devolution Z, Sanitarium Magazine, Disturbed Digest and Into the Ruins. Dan's website is at http://www.dansoule.com where there is an exclusive ebook of short stories available, plus a classic horror novel. You can connect with Dan through all the various social media channels through linktr.ee/DanSoule

www.dansoule.com

@Grammatologer

CHRISTOPHER STANLEY

Canyonlands

Christopher Stanley lives on a hill in Bristol, England, with three sons who share a birthday but aren't triplets. He is the author of the novelette, The Forest is Hungry (Demain Publishing, April 2019), and the flash horror collection, 'The Lamppost Huggers and Other Wretched Tales' (The Arcanist, June 2020). His second album, also called Canyonlands, was released in 2019, and is available on most download and streaming sites.

@allthosestrings

HANNAH STORM

Iso – from the Greek meaning equal -usually used as a prefix, ie. isolation, isobar, isopod

Hannah Storm has been a journalist for two decades, travelling the world, witnessing war, disaster, wonder and intrigue. Now she writes to honour those she's met and to process her own experiences. Hannah started writing flash fiction and CNF in 2018. She was highly commended in the TSS Flash Fiction 2020 prize, shortlisted in the March 2020 Bath Flash Fiction Award, and won the 'I Must Be Off!' travel writing competition. Hannah has also been shortlisted in several other flash fiction competitions and published widely, in Storgy, Ellipsis Zine, Atticus Review, Barren Magazine, Bending Genres and others, and in anthologies including the 'I'll Show You Mine' sex writing prize. She lives in the UK with her Kiwi husband and two children and is now the director of a journalism charity, as well as a freelance media consultant specialising in gender, safety, ethics and mental health.

@HANNAHSTORM6

ROB TEUN

Try Not To Think About It

Robert Teun is the author of various short stories, books, and non-fiction articles for magazines and websites.

@rob_teun

STEVE STRED

September In The New World

Steve Stred writes dark, bleak horror fiction. He is the author of two novels, four novellas, two short story collections as well as two poetry/drabble collections. Steve has had works featured in 100 Word Zombie Bites, 100 Word Horrors 3, and Forest of Fear. Steve is also a voracious reader, reviewing everything he reads and submitting the majority of his reviews to be featured on Kendall Reviews. Steve Stred is based in Edmonton, AB, Canada and lives with his wife, his son and their dog OJ.

@stevestred

STUART TURTON

The Boxer

Stuart Turton lives in a village near London with his adorable daughter and wife. He previously wrote The 7 ½ Deaths of Evelyn Hardcastle, which was an international bestseller and won a number of awards, despite being absolutely nuts. Before becoming an author he was a travel journalist, and before that he did every other job you can possibly imagine. Goat farmer was the best. Cleaning toilets was the worst.

@stu_turton

ADRIAN J WALKER

Islands

Adrian J Walker was born in the bush suburbs of Sydney, Australia in the mid '70s. After his father found a camper van in a ditch, he renovated it and moved his family back to the UK, where Adrian was raised. Ever since he can remember, Adrian has been interested in three things: words, music and technology, and when he graduated from the University of Leeds, he found a career in software. His novel The End of the World Running Club, a post-apocalyptic running fable about hope, love and endurance, was a Simon Mayo Radio 2 book club choice. He lives in Aberdeen with his wife and two children.

http://www.adrianjwalker.com

@adrianwalker

DANIE WARE

The Mumbling Man

Danie Ware has a long history of gaming, re-enactment and and general geekery. These days, you'll find her writing books, raising a teenager and juggling marketing and event management at Forbidden Planet (London) Ltd. She's the author of the WarHammer 40k Sister Augusta stories for the Black Library, the critically acclaimed Ecko series and the standalone novel Children of Artifice. She's also written Judge Anderson for Rebellion Publishing. Danie lives in Carshalton, south London, with her son and two cats.

danieware.com

@danacea

AARON WHITE

Outside, it's snowing

Aaron lives in County Antrim in Northern Ireland with his wife and my three kids. He has a day job and writes mainly short stories, although he has attempted non-fiction whenever a certain subject appeals. Aaron has self-published a collection of his work titled Macabre Notions, which is available on Amazon.

@cosymystery

RICK WHITE

The Weasel

Rick White lives and writes in Manchester, UK. His work has been published in Barren Magazine, X-Ray Lit Mag and Storgy Magazine, among others.

@ricketywhite

JAMES WOOLF

A Tale of Twelve Speeches

James is a fiction writer living in London. He is currently working on a novel, a psychological thriller set in the legal world, which is provisionally entitled Indefensible. James has had many short stories published, including three in Ambit Magazine. He has been shortlisted in many competitions including twice in the Bridport. His story *R v Sieger: Additional Documents Disclosed by the Crown Prosecution Service* was highly commended in the London Short Story competition. James also writes scripts for the theatre, and has had around twelve plays produced, and two broadcast on the Radio. His play Empty in Angel sold out at the White Bear Theatre in London in November 2019 and was programmed to return to four other venues in April and May 2020 before other events intervened.

https://woolf.biz

@WoolfJames

ALSO AVAILABLE FROM STORGY BOOKS

...EXIT EARTH...

EXIT EARTH delves into dystopian worlds and uncovers the most daring and original voices in print today. With twenty-four short stories, accompanying artwork, afterwords, and interviews, EXIT EARTH is a haunting exploration of the sanity of our species ... past, present, and future.

Featuring the fourteen finalists from the STORGY EXIT EARTH Short Story Competition, and additional stories by award winning authors M.R. Carey (The Girl with all the Gifts), Toby Litt (Corpsing, DeadKidSongs), Courttia Newland (The Gospel According to Cane, A Book of Blues), James Miller (Sunshine State, Lost Boys), and David James Poissant (The Heaven of Animals). With accompanying artwork by Amie Dearlove, HarlotVonCharlotte, and CrapPanther.

To discover more about EXIT EARTH visit STORGY.COM

ALSO AVAILABLE FROM STORGY BOOKS

SHALLOW CREEK

This is the tale of a town on the fringes of fear, of ordinary people and everyday objects transformed by terror and madness, a microcosm of the world where nothing is ever quite what it seems. This is a world where the unreal is real, where the familiar and friendly lure and deceive. On the outskirts of civilisation sits this solitary town. Home to the unhinged. Oblivion to outsiders.

Shallow Creek contains twenty-one original horror stories by a chilling cast of contemporary writers, including stories by Sarah Lotz, Richard Thomas, Adrian J Walker, and Aliya Whitely. Told through a series of interconnected narratives, Shallow Creek is an epic anthology that exposes the raw human emotion and heart-pounding thrills at the genre's core.

To discover more about SHALLOW CREEK visit STORGY.COM

IN AID OF:

STORGY BOOKS is proud to partner with The Big Issue Foundation (registered charity number 1049077), Centrepoint (292411), Shelter (263710), and The Bristol Methodist Centre (1150295), for the publication of *You Are Not Alone; An Anthology of Hope and Isolation*. All proceeds from from purchases of *You Are Not Alone* will be equally distributed between our partner charities to provide ongoing support for people experiencing homelessness during – and after – the Covid-19 crisis.

Centrepoint provides homeless young people with accommodation, health support and life skills in order to get them back into education, training and employment. Together with our partners, we support over 15,000 young people every year. Centrepoint's accommodation includes emergency nightshelters; short and long stay hostels; specialist projects for care leavers, ex-offenders and young single parents; foyers and supported flats; and floating support services.

Shelter helps millions of people every year struggling with bad housing or homelessness through our advice, support and legal services. And we campaign to make sure that, one day, no one will have to turn to us for help. We're here so no one has to fight bad housing or homelessness on their own.

From an award-winning magazine offering employment opportunities to people in poverty, a multi-million pound social investment business supporting enterprise to drive social change, to a charity Foundation supporting vendors to rebuild their own pathways to a better future and a shop curating social enterprise products. For 29 years The Big Issue Group has strived to dismantle poverty through creating opportunity, in the process becoming one of the most recognised and trusted brands in the UK.

The Bristol Methodist Centre offers care, guidance and support for those facing homelessness in the city of Bristol. Our small staff team work tirelessly to foster an atmosphere where those accessing our services feel safe and that they belong. The Bristol Methodist Centre is open to anyone in need who is classified as homeless or vulnerable. It is the largest day centre in Bristol and we pride ourselves on our friendly approach to all that we do - treating our guests how we believe they should be treated, as individuals and valuable people in our community.